Date: 10/20/20

J GRA 741.5 BIR
Burks, James
Bird & Squirrel on the edge!

James Burks

BiRD & SQUiRReL

ON THE EDGE!

graphix

An Imprint of

SCHOLASTIC

For Bodhi -- Life is an adventure. Have fun!

All rights reserved. Published by Graphix, an imprint of Scholastic Inc., *Publishers since 1920.* SCHOLASTIC, GRAPHIX, and associated logos are trademarks and/or registered trademarks of Scholastic Inc.

The publisher does not have any control over and does not assume any responsibility for author or third-party websites or their content.

Library of Congress Control Number: 2014956158

ISBN 978-0-545-80425-7 (hardcover)
ISBN 978-0-545-80426-4 (paperback)

17 16 15 14 13   19 20 21 22/0
Printed in China   62

First edition, November 2015

Edited by Adam Rau
Book design by Phil Falco
Creative Director: David Saylor

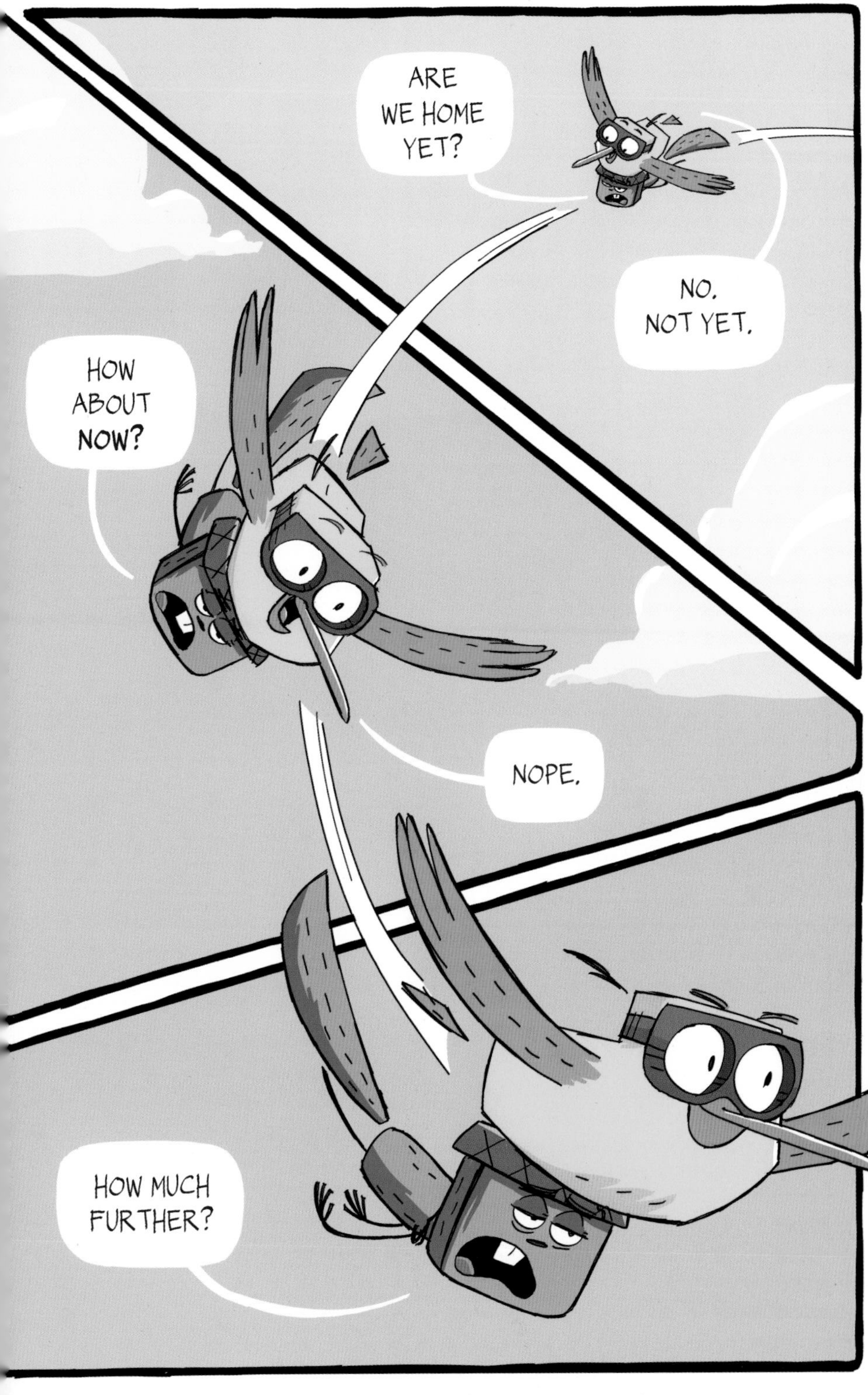
ARE WE HOME YET?
NO. NOT YET.
HOW ABOUT NOW?
NOPE.
HOW MUCH FURTHER?

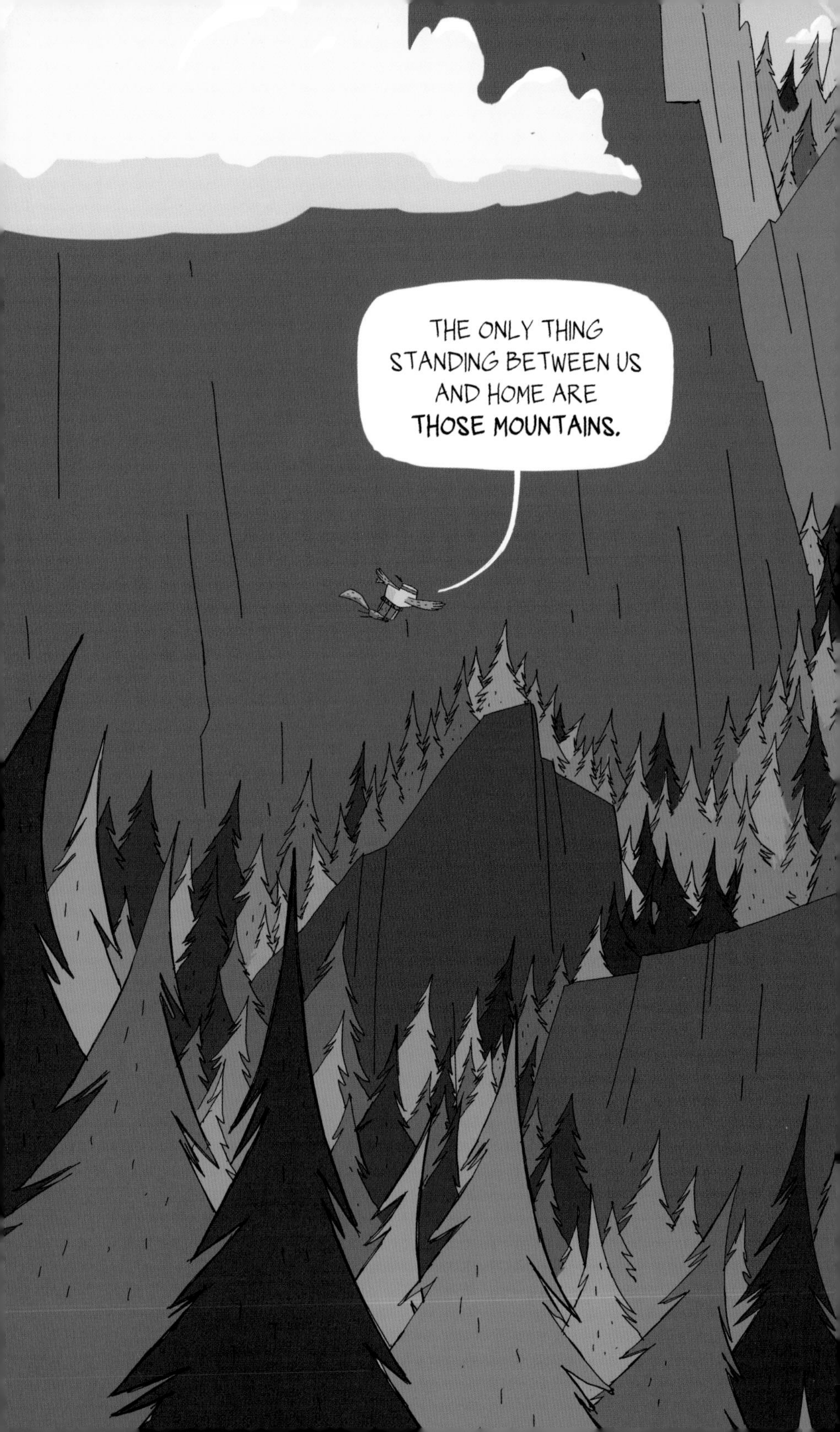
THE ONLY THING STANDING BETWEEN US AND HOME ARE THOSE MOUNTAINS.

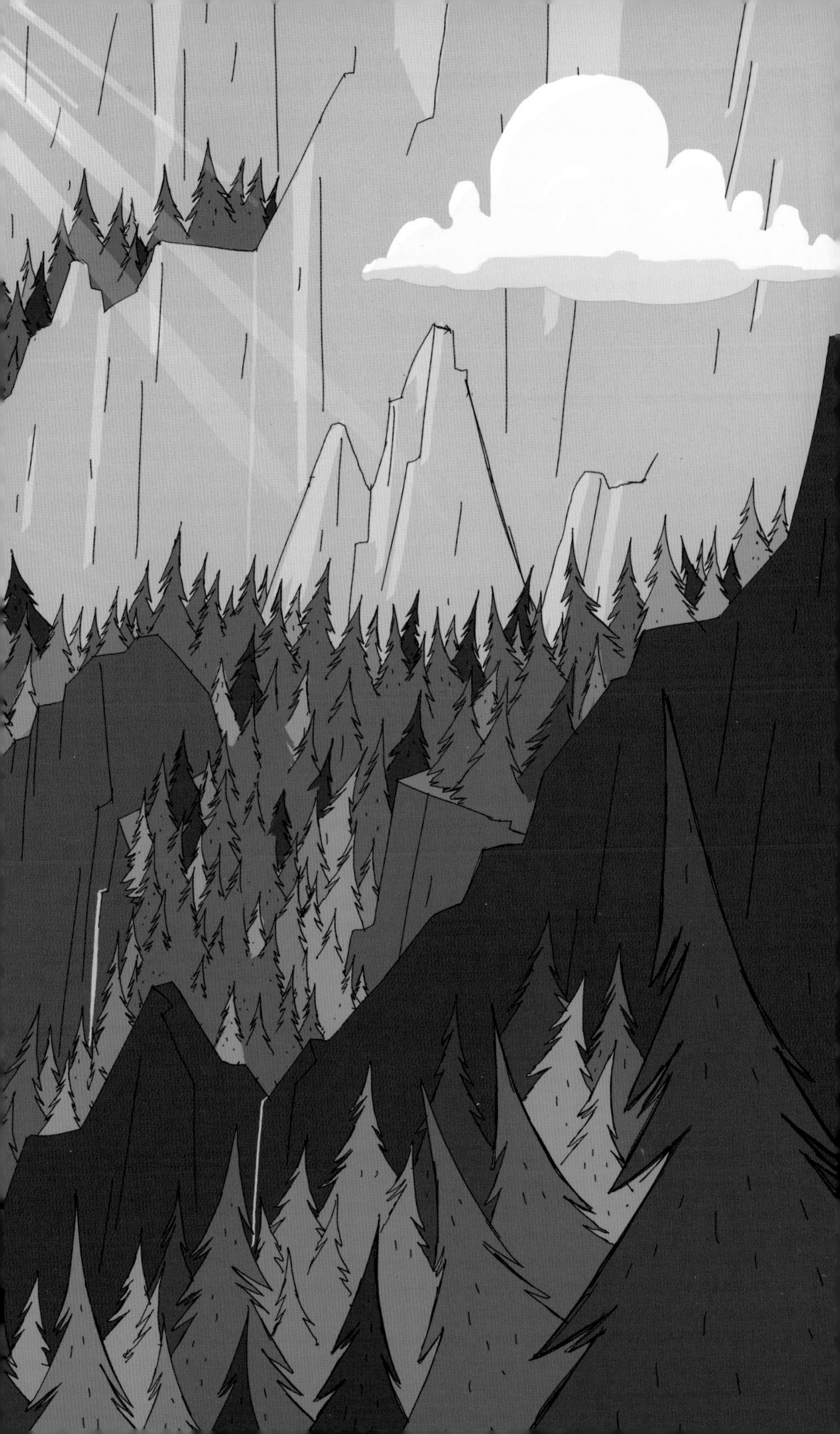

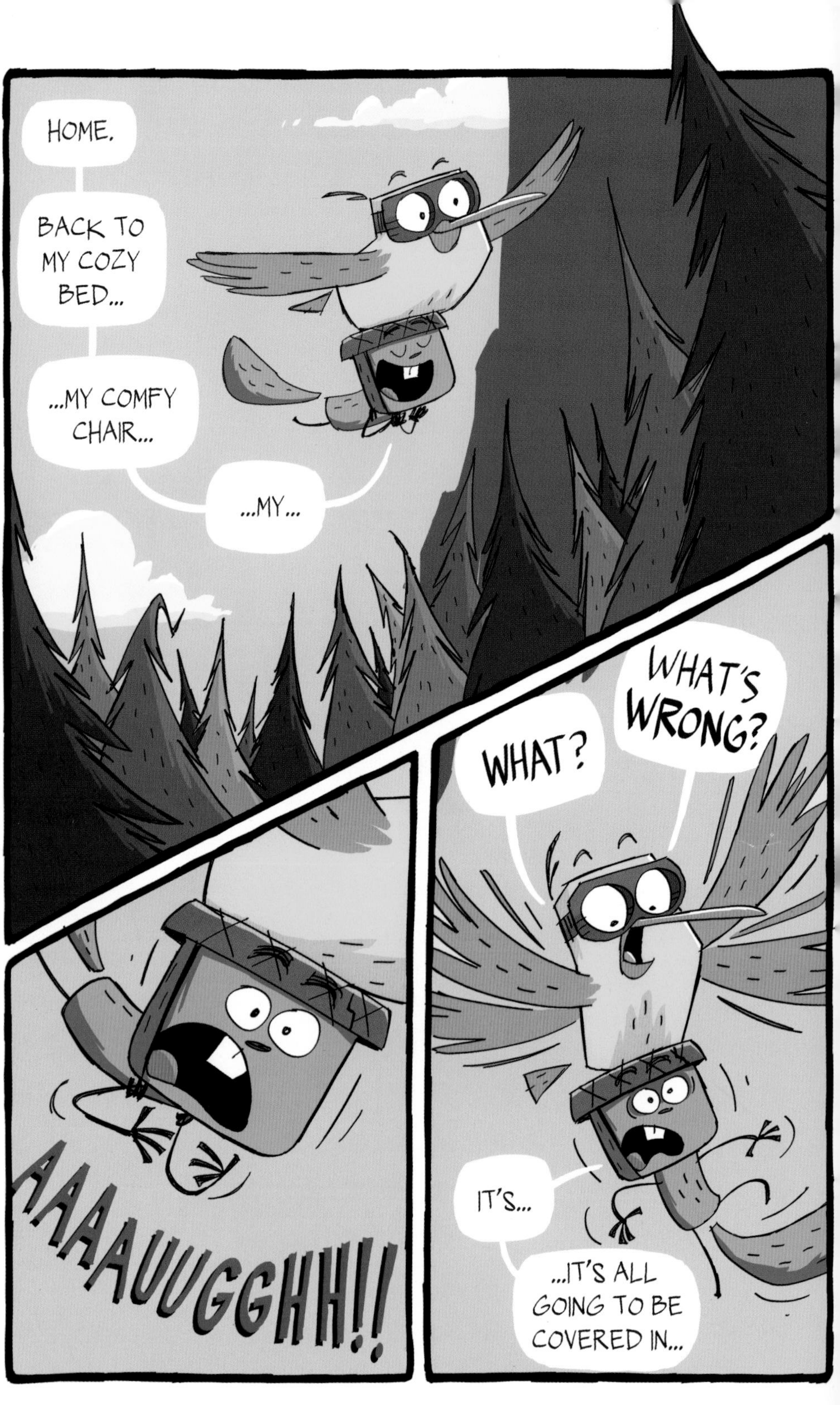
HOME.
BACK TO MY COZY BED...
...MY COMFY CHAIR...
...MY...
AAAAUUGGHH!!
WHAT?
WHAT'S WRONG?
IT'S...
...IT'S ALL GOING TO BE COVERED IN...

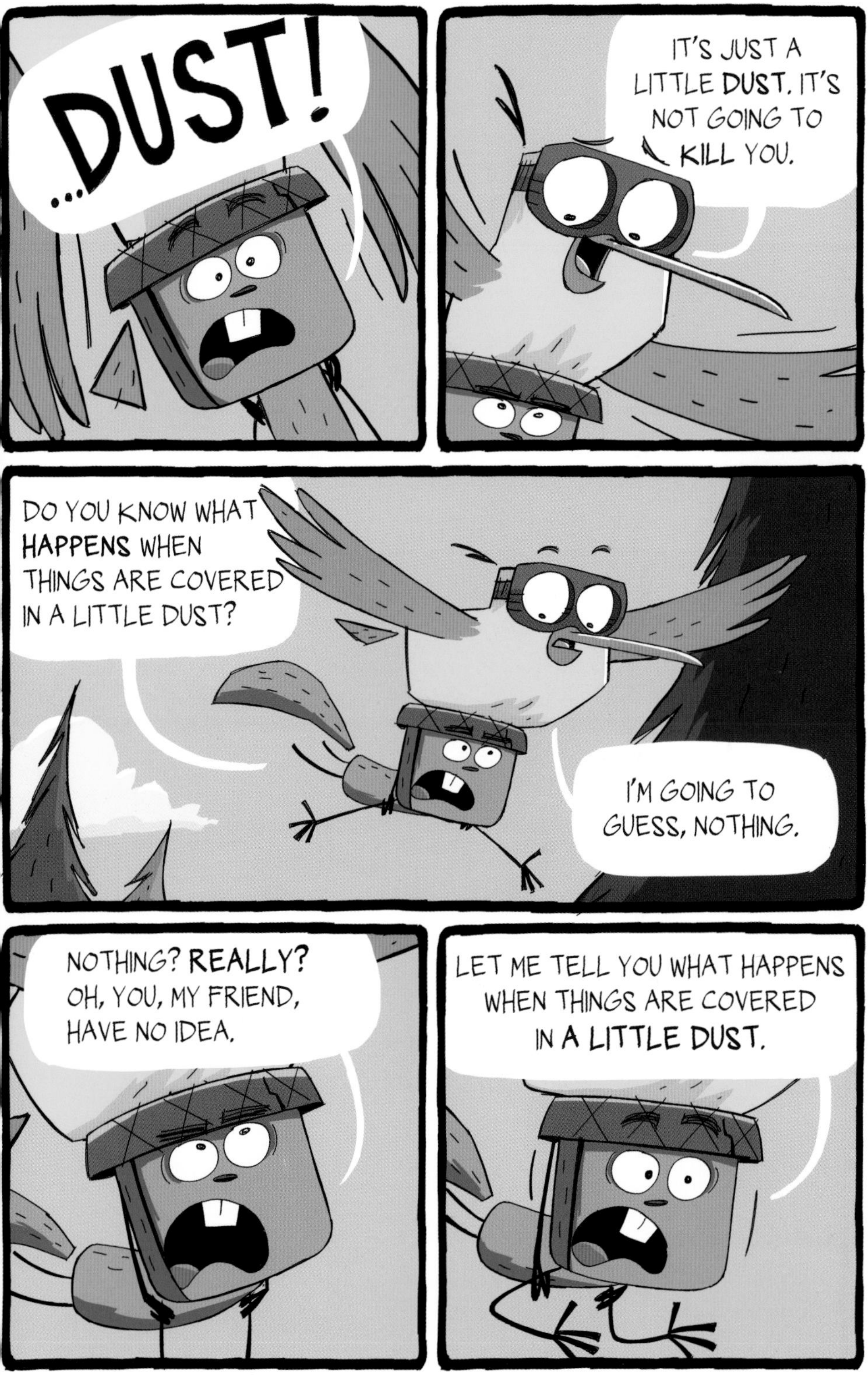
...DUST!
IT'S JUST A LITTLE DUST. IT'S NOT GOING TO KILL YOU.
DO YOU KNOW WHAT HAPPENS WHEN THINGS ARE COVERED IN A LITTLE DUST?
I'M GOING TO GUESS, NOTHING.
NOTHING? REALLY? OH, YOU, MY FRIEND, HAVE NO IDEA.
LET ME TELL YOU WHAT HAPPENS WHEN THINGS ARE COVERED IN A LITTLE DUST.

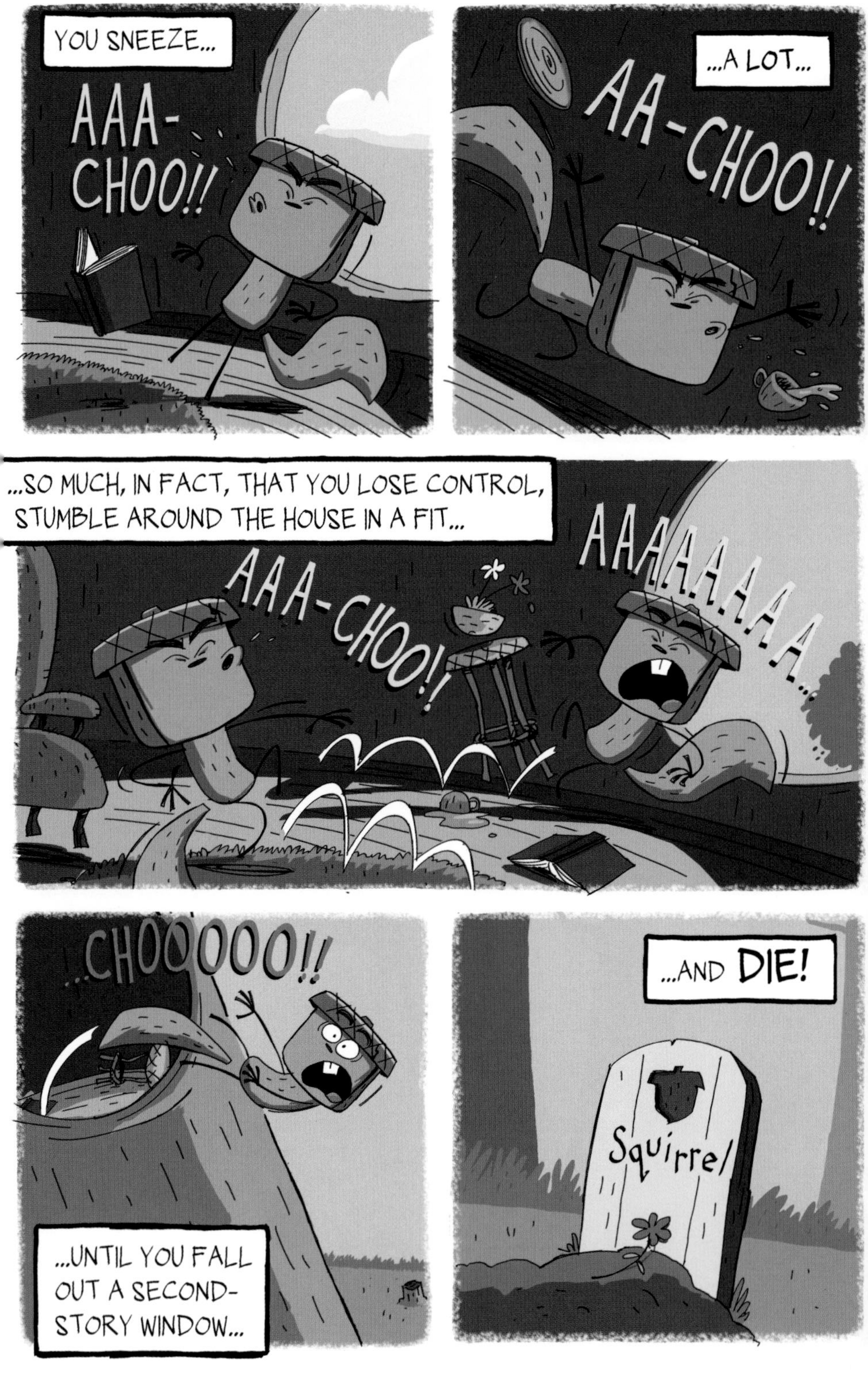
YOU SNEEZE...
AAA-CHOO!!
...A LOT...
AA-CHOO!!
...SO MUCH, IN FACT, THAT YOU LOSE CONTROL, STUMBLE AROUND THE HOUSE IN A FIT...
AAA-CHOO!!
AAAAAAAAA...
...CHOOOOOO!!
...UNTIL YOU FALL OUT A SECOND-STORY WINDOW...
...AND DIE!
Squirrel

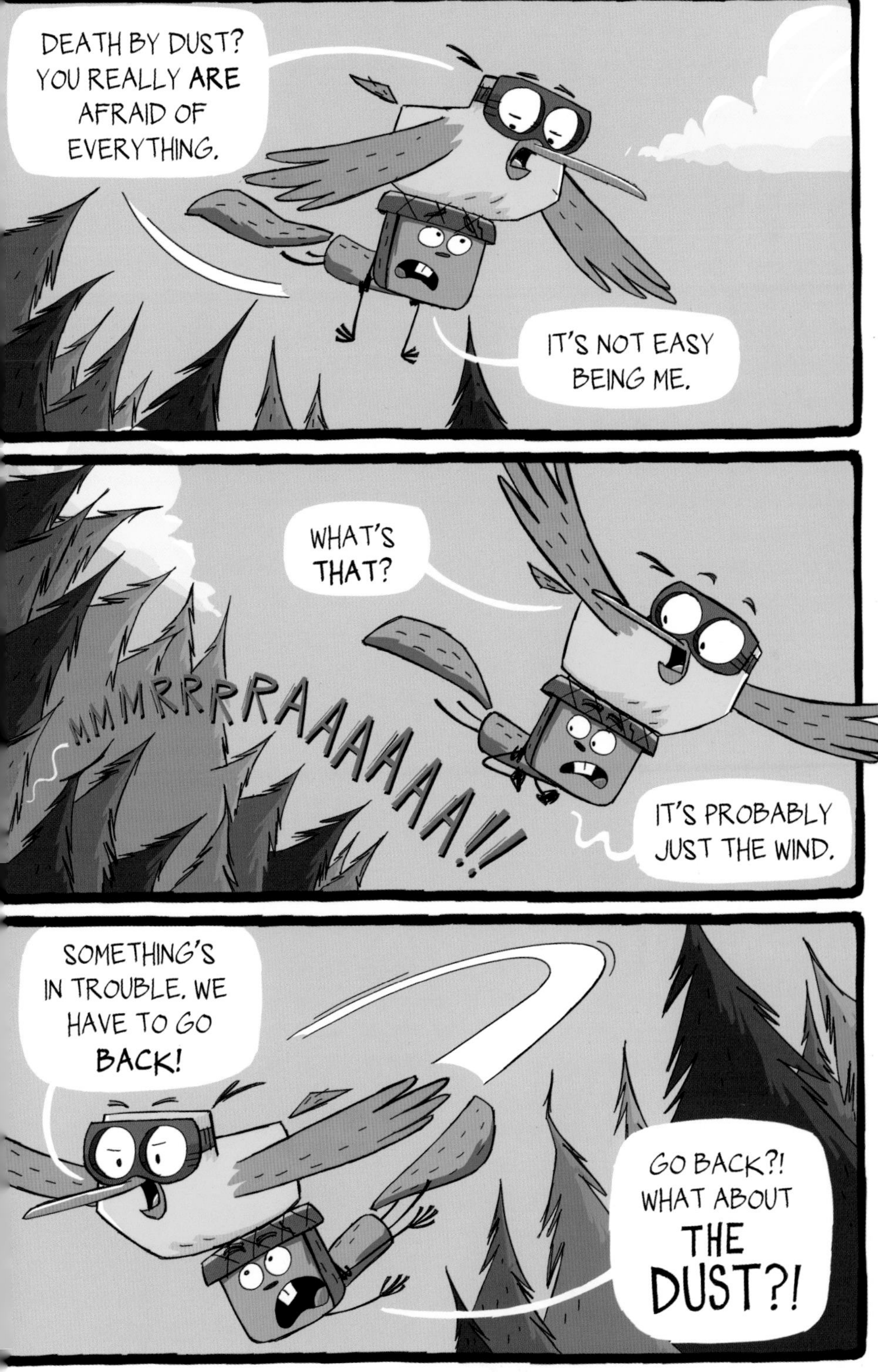
DEATH BY DUST? YOU REALLY ARE AFRAID OF EVERYTHING.
IT'S NOT EASY BEING ME.
WHAT'S THAT?
MMMRRRRAAAAAAAA!!
IT'S PROBABLY JUST THE WIND.
SOMETHING'S IN TROUBLE. WE HAVE TO GO BACK!
GO BACK?! WHAT ABOUT THE DUST?!

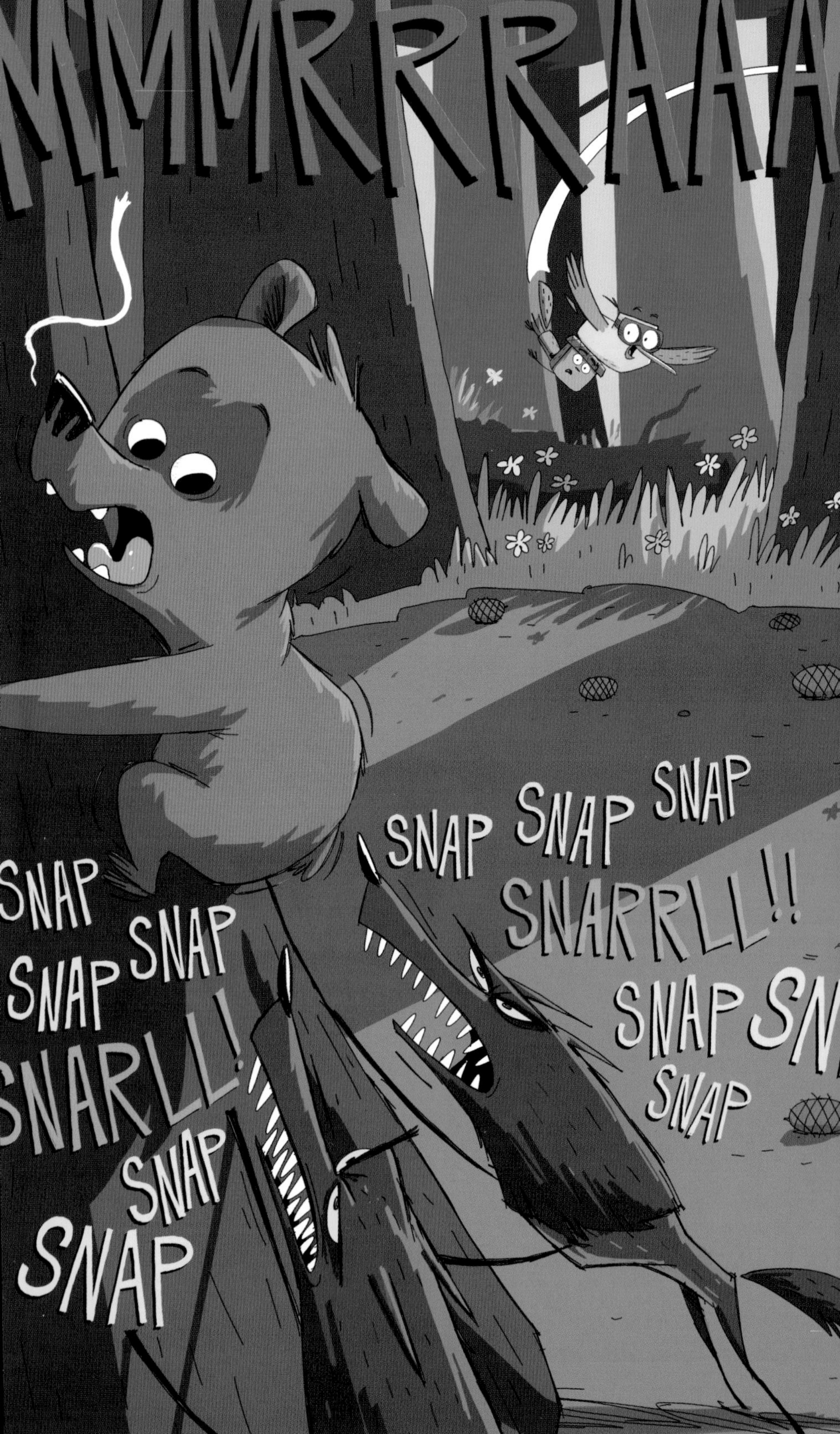
MMMRRRAAA
SNAP SNAP SNAP
SNARRLL!!
SNAP SNAP
SNAP
SNAP
SNAP SNAP
SNARLL!
SNAP
SNAP

THAT BEAR CUB IS IN TROUBLE.

MAYBE...AAAH... THEY'RE JUST PLAYING.

WE SHOULD PROBABLY JUST HEAD ON HOME AND TAKE CARE OF THE DUST.

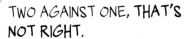

TWO AGAINST ONE, **THAT'S NOT RIGHT.**

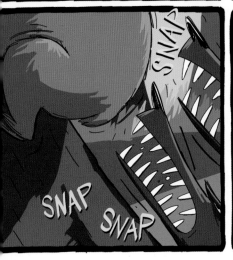

SNAP

SNAP SNAP

I DON'T THINK WE SHOULD INTERFERE. I'M SURE ITS MOTHER WILL BE ALONG ANY MINUTE.

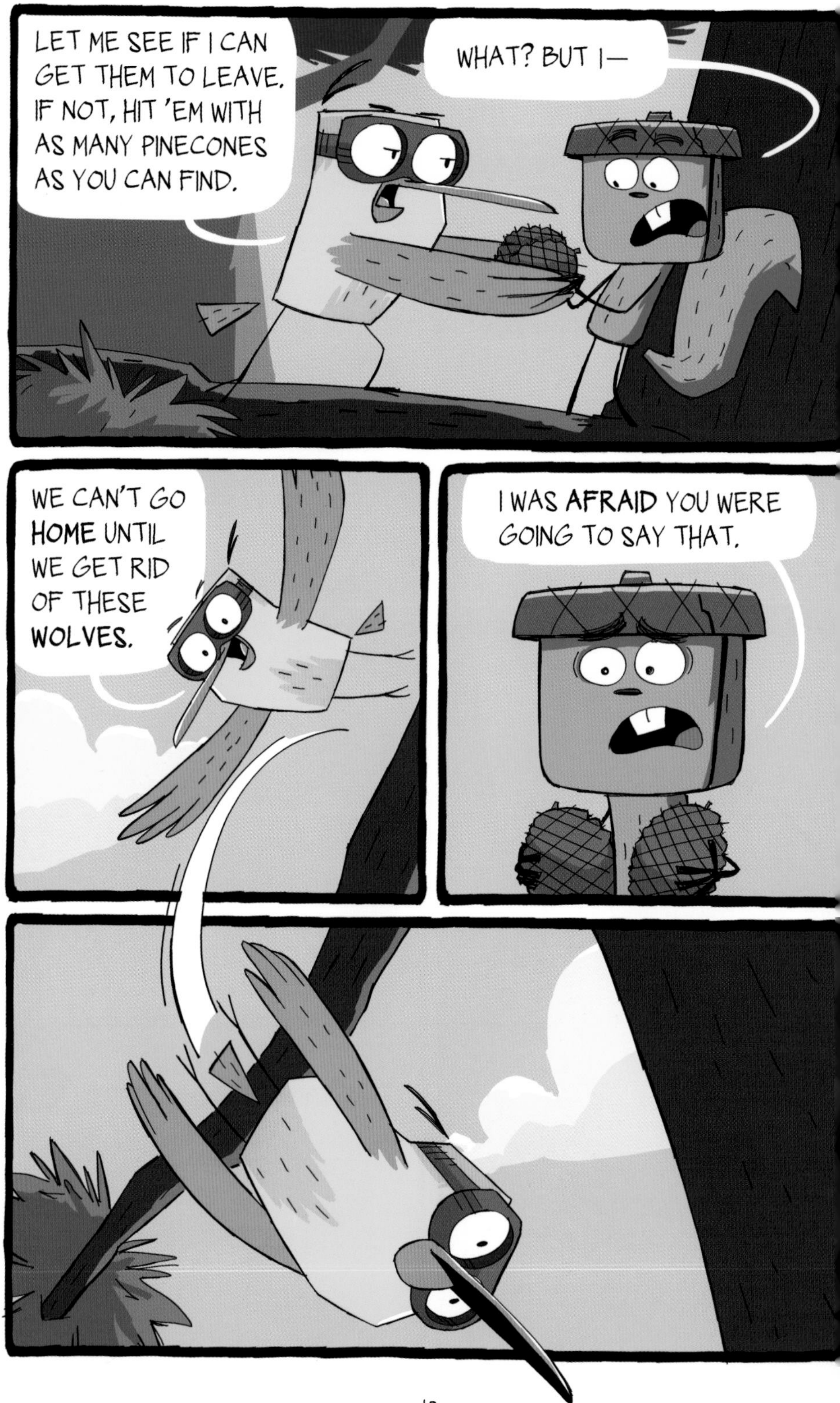
LET ME SEE IF I CAN GET THEM TO LEAVE. IF NOT, HIT 'EM WITH AS MANY PINECONES AS YOU CAN FIND.
WHAT? BUT I—
WE CAN'T GO HOME UNTIL WE GET RID OF THESE WOLVES.
I WAS AFRAID YOU WERE GOING TO SAY THAT.

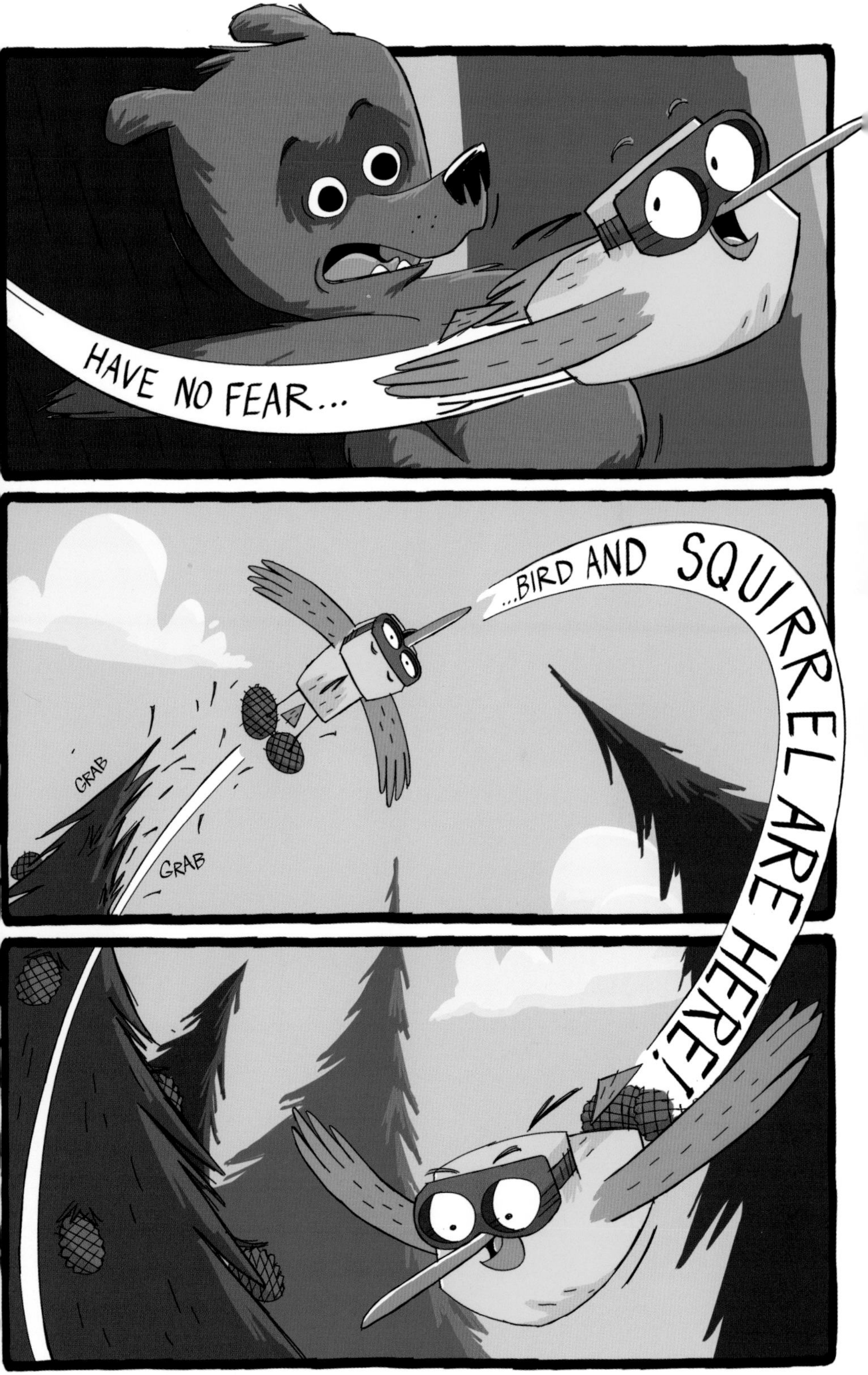
HAVE NO FEAR...
...BIRD AND SQUIRREL ARE HERE!
GRAB
GRAB

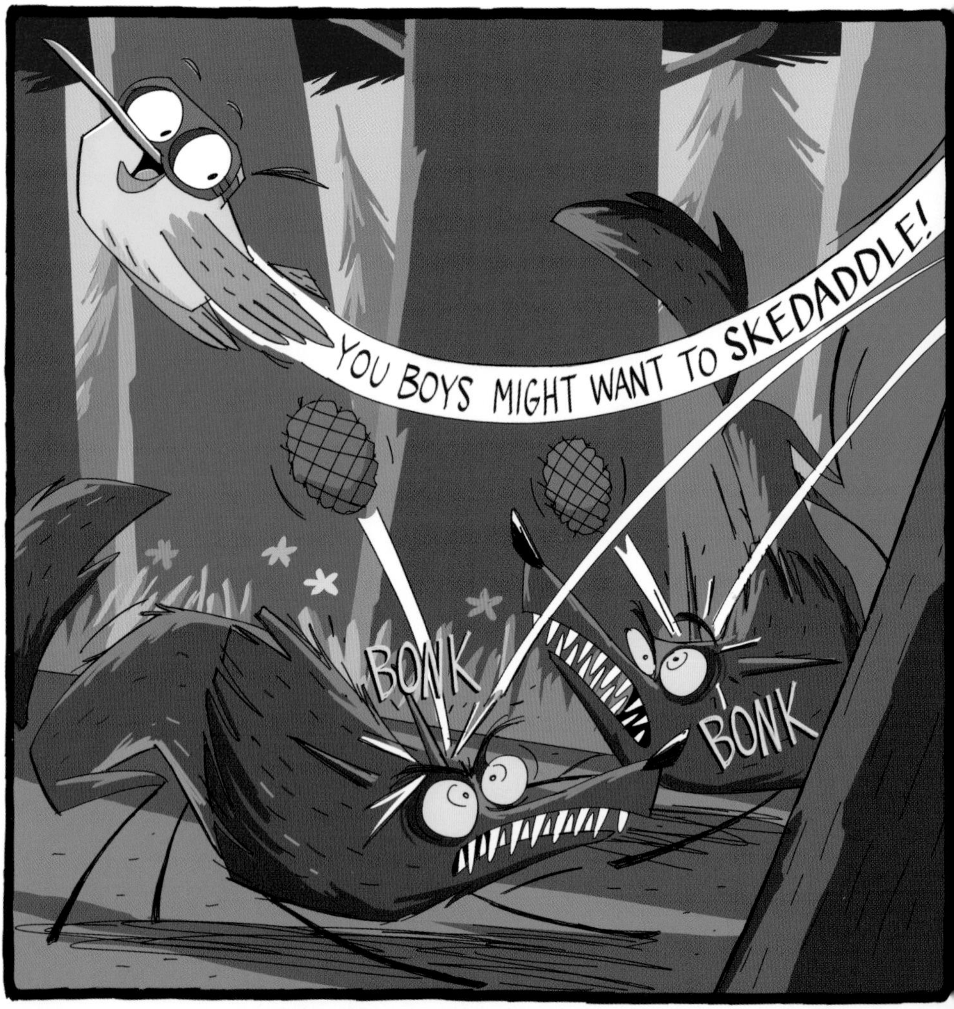
YOU BOYS MIGHT WANT TO SKEDADDLE!
BONK
BONK

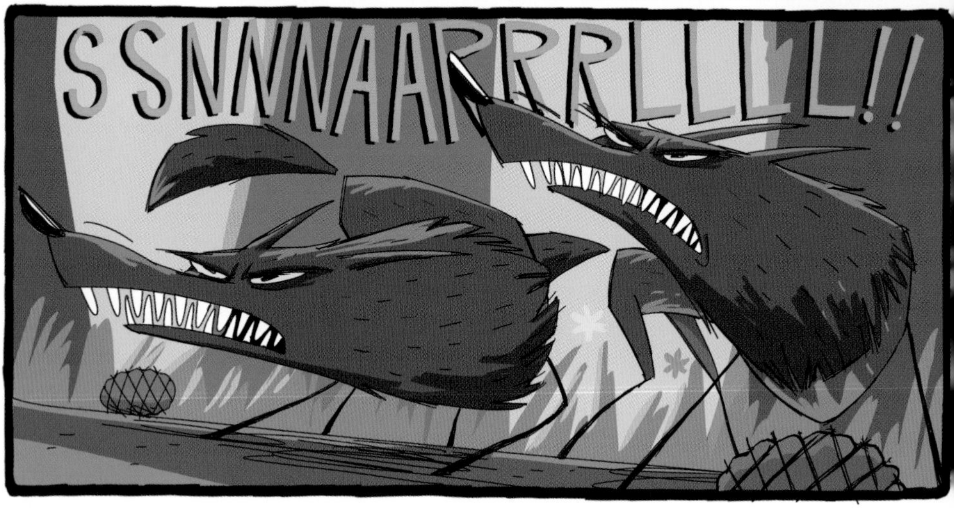
SSNNNAARRRLLLL!!

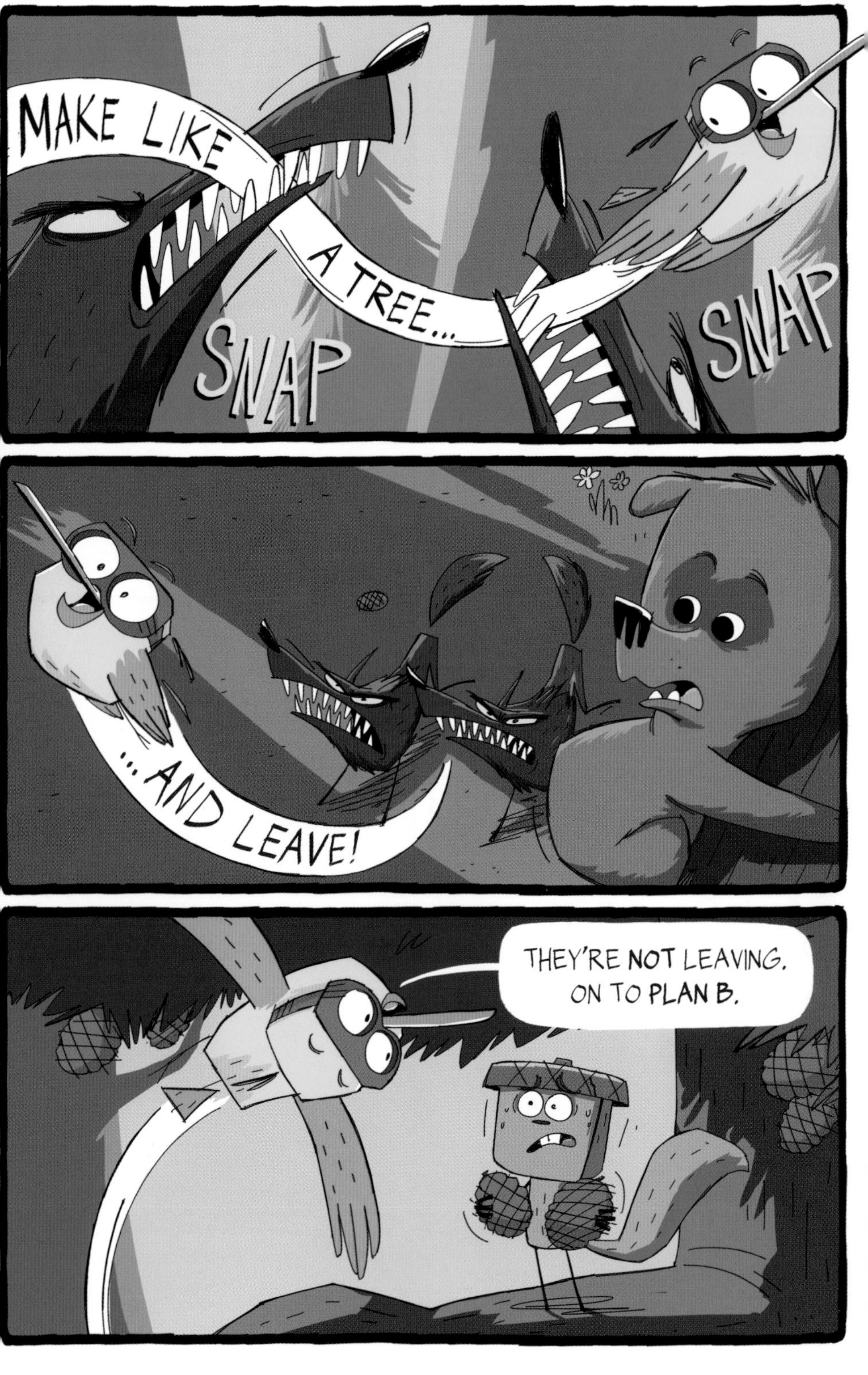
MAKE LIKE A TREE...
SNAP
SNAP
...AND LEAVE!
THEY'RE NOT LEAVING. ON TO PLAN B.

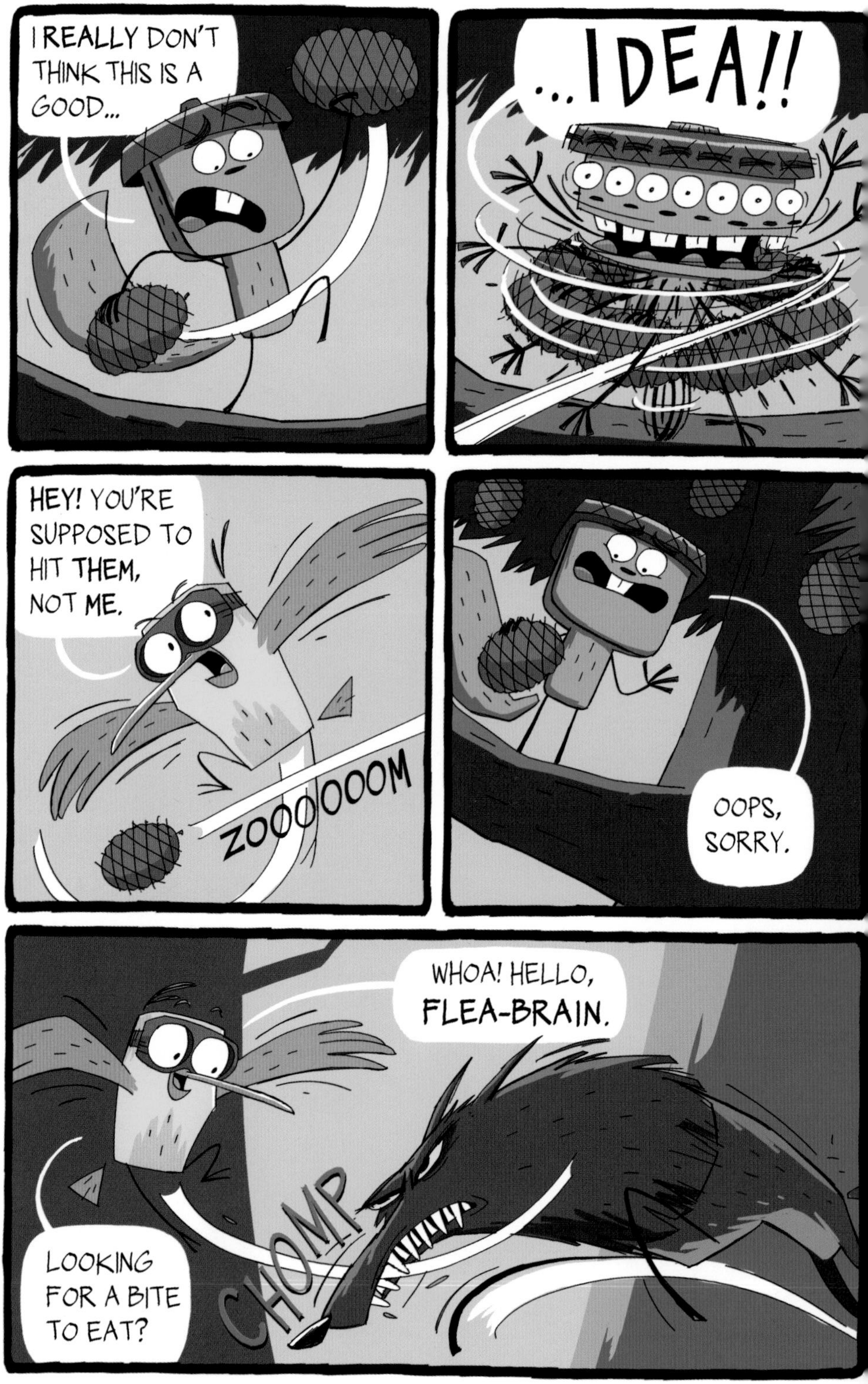
I REALLY DON'T THINK THIS IS A GOOD...
...IDEA!!
HEY! YOU'RE SUPPOSED TO HIT THEM, NOT ME.
ZOOOOOOM
OOPS, SORRY.
WHOA! HELLO, FLEA-BRAIN.
LOOKING FOR A BITE TO EAT?
CHOMP

CHOMP
I KNOW JUST THE THING.
CHOMP
CHOMP
CHOMP
CHOMP
SNARLLLL!
BON APPÉTIT!
YIPE!
CHOMP

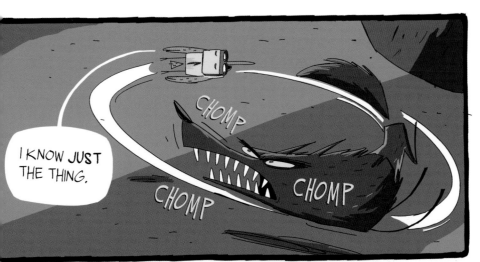

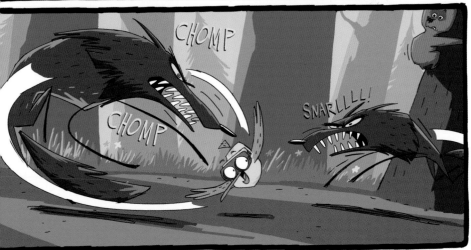

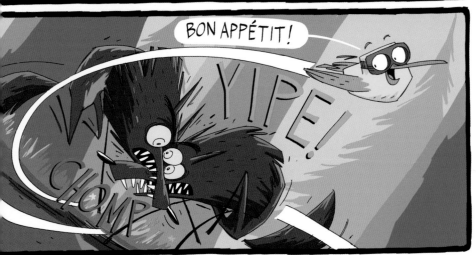

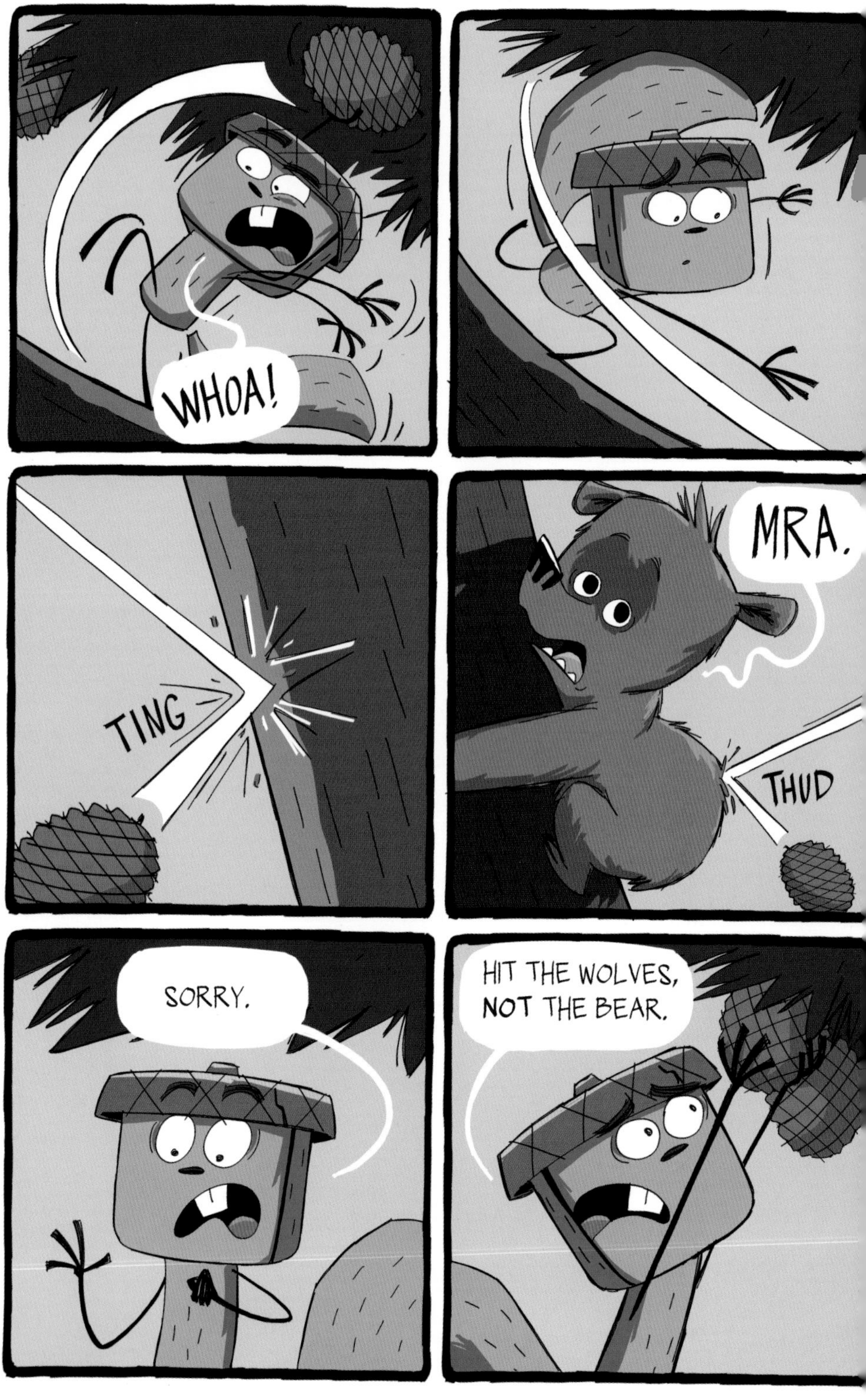
WHOA!
TING
MRA.
THUD
SORRY.
HIT THE WOLVES, NOT THE BEAR.

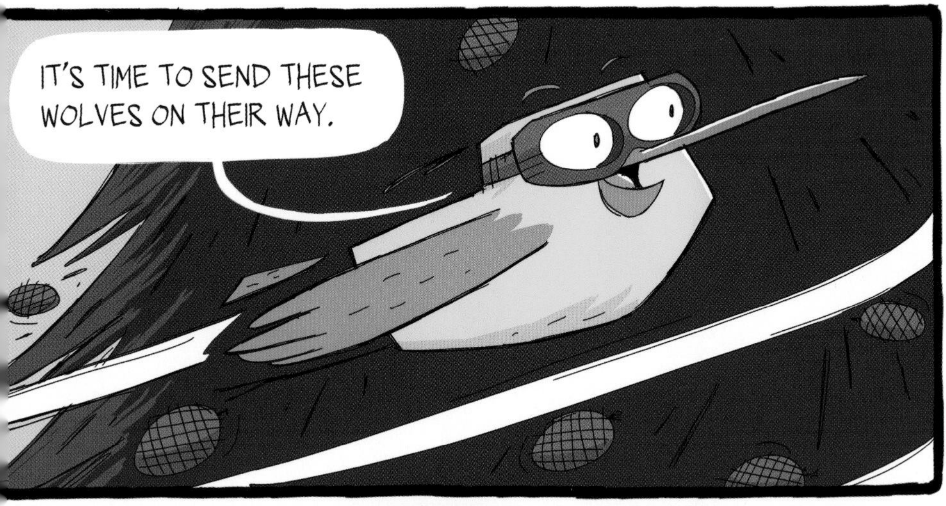
IT'S TIME TO SEND THESE WOLVES ON THEIR WAY.

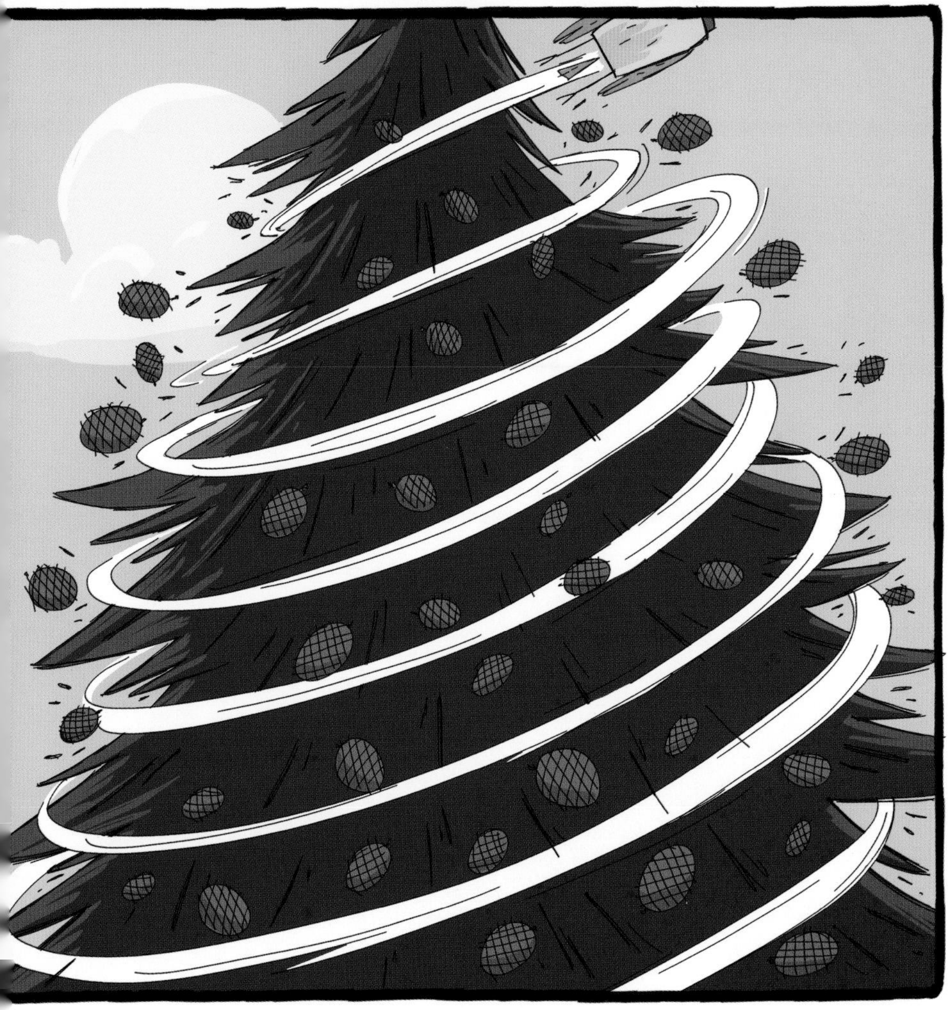

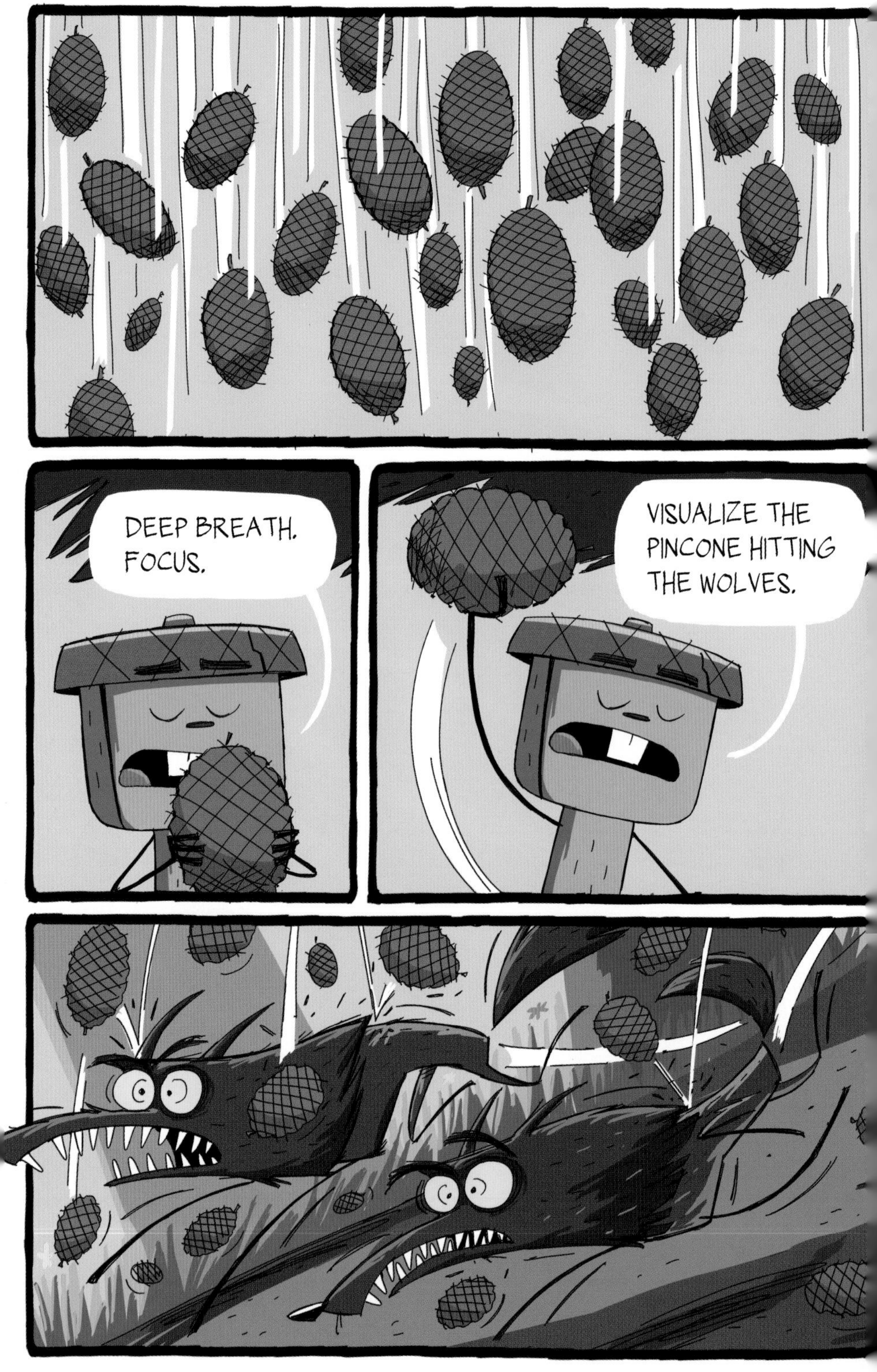
DEEP BREATH. FOCUS.
VISUALIZE THE PINCONE HITTING THE WOLVES.

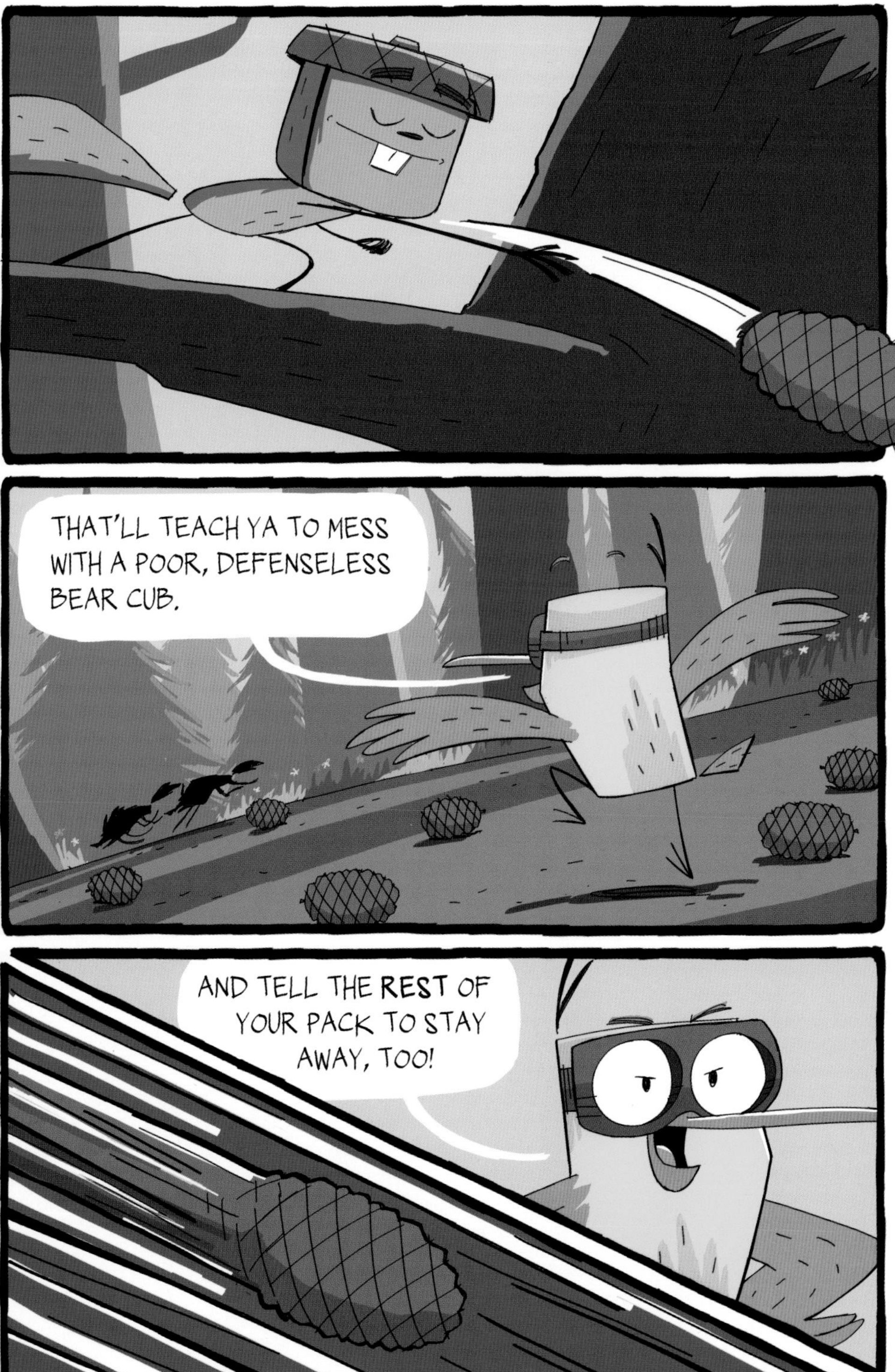
THAT'LL TEACH YA TO MESS WITH A POOR, DEFENSELESS BEAR CUB.
AND TELL THE **REST** OF YOUR PACK TO STAY AWAY, TOO!

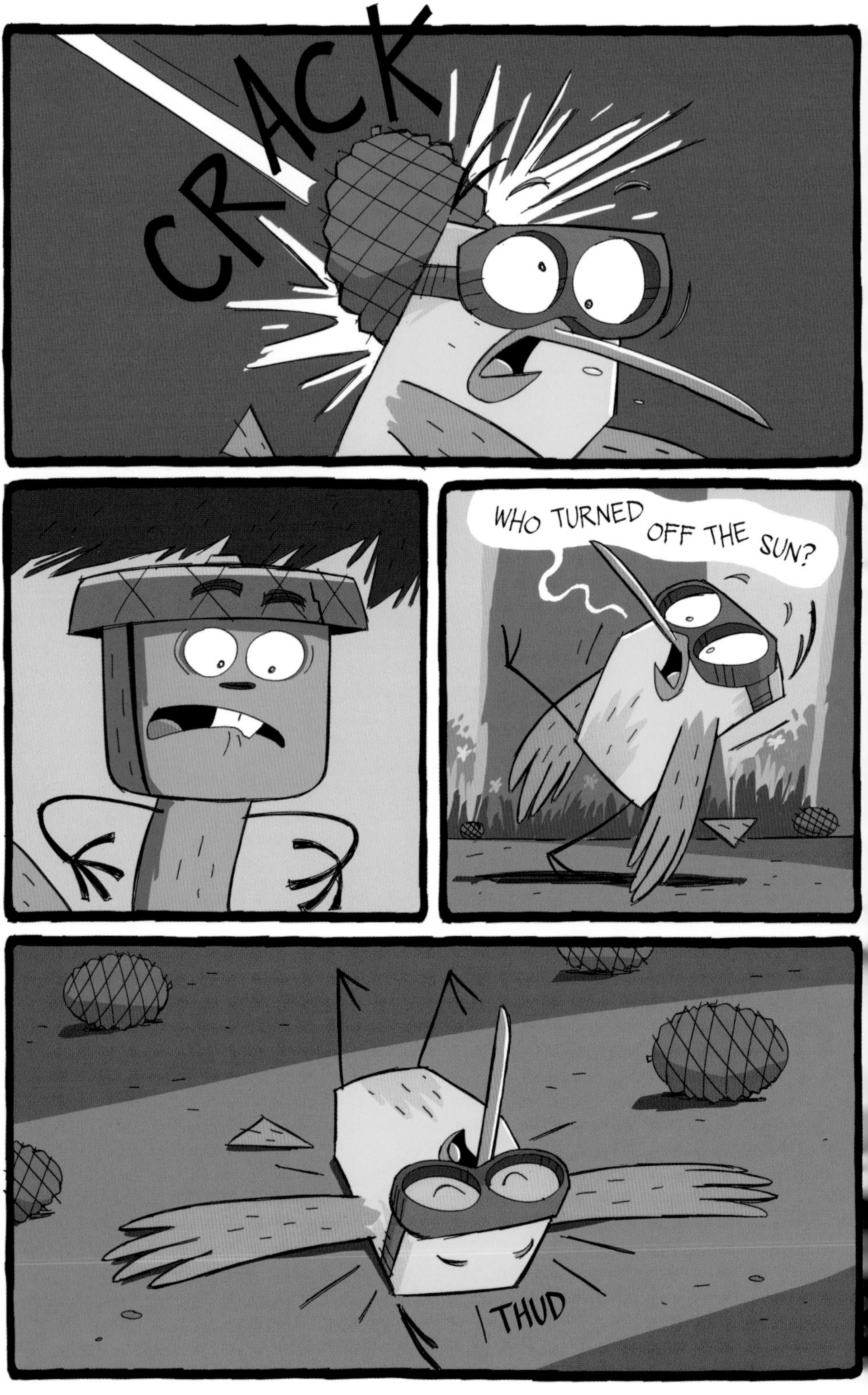
CRACK
WHO TURNED OFF THE SUN?
THUD

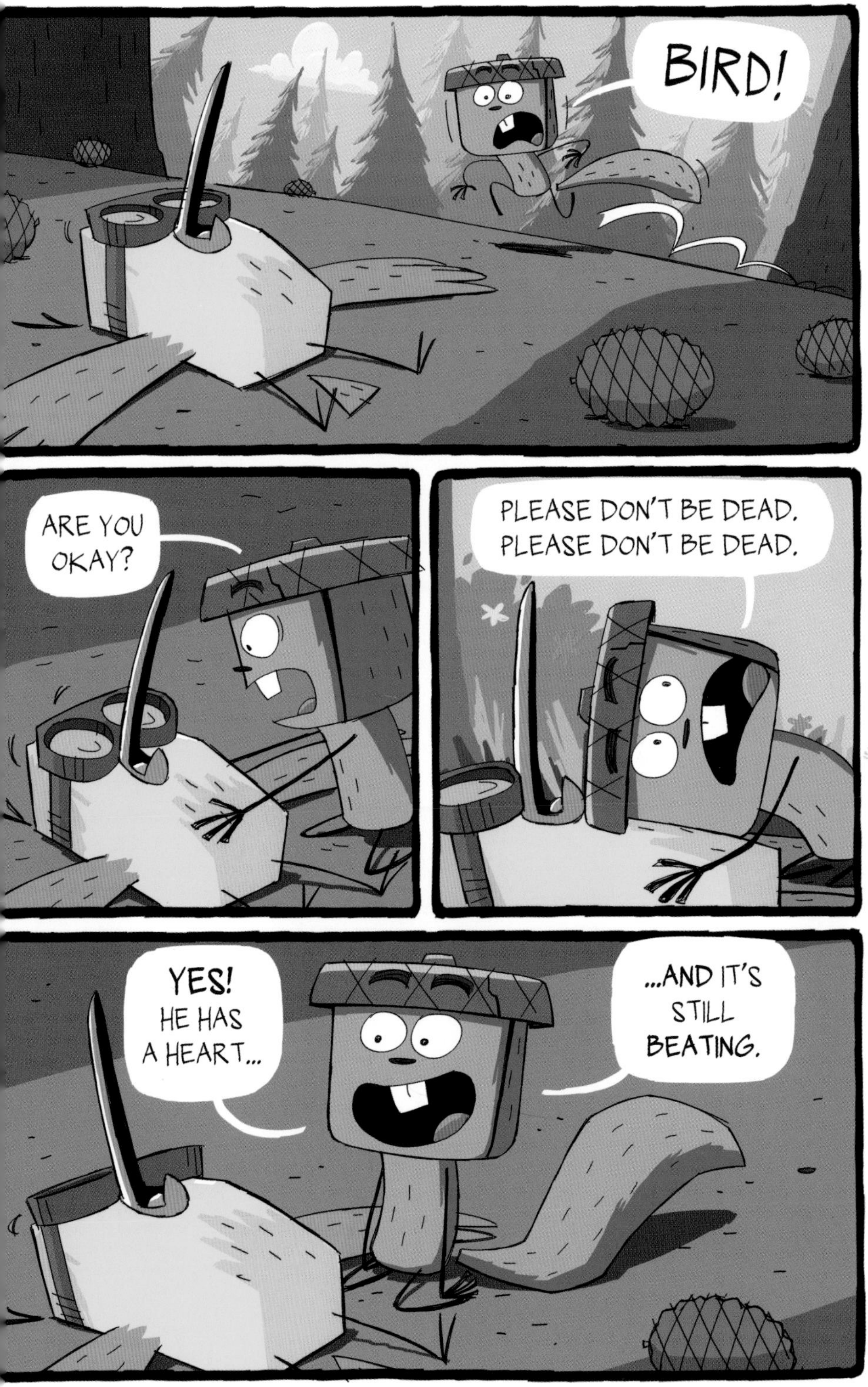
BIRD!
ARE YOU OKAY?
PLEASE DON'T BE DEAD. PLEASE DON'T BE DEAD.
YES! HE HAS A HEART...
...AND IT'S STILL BEATING.

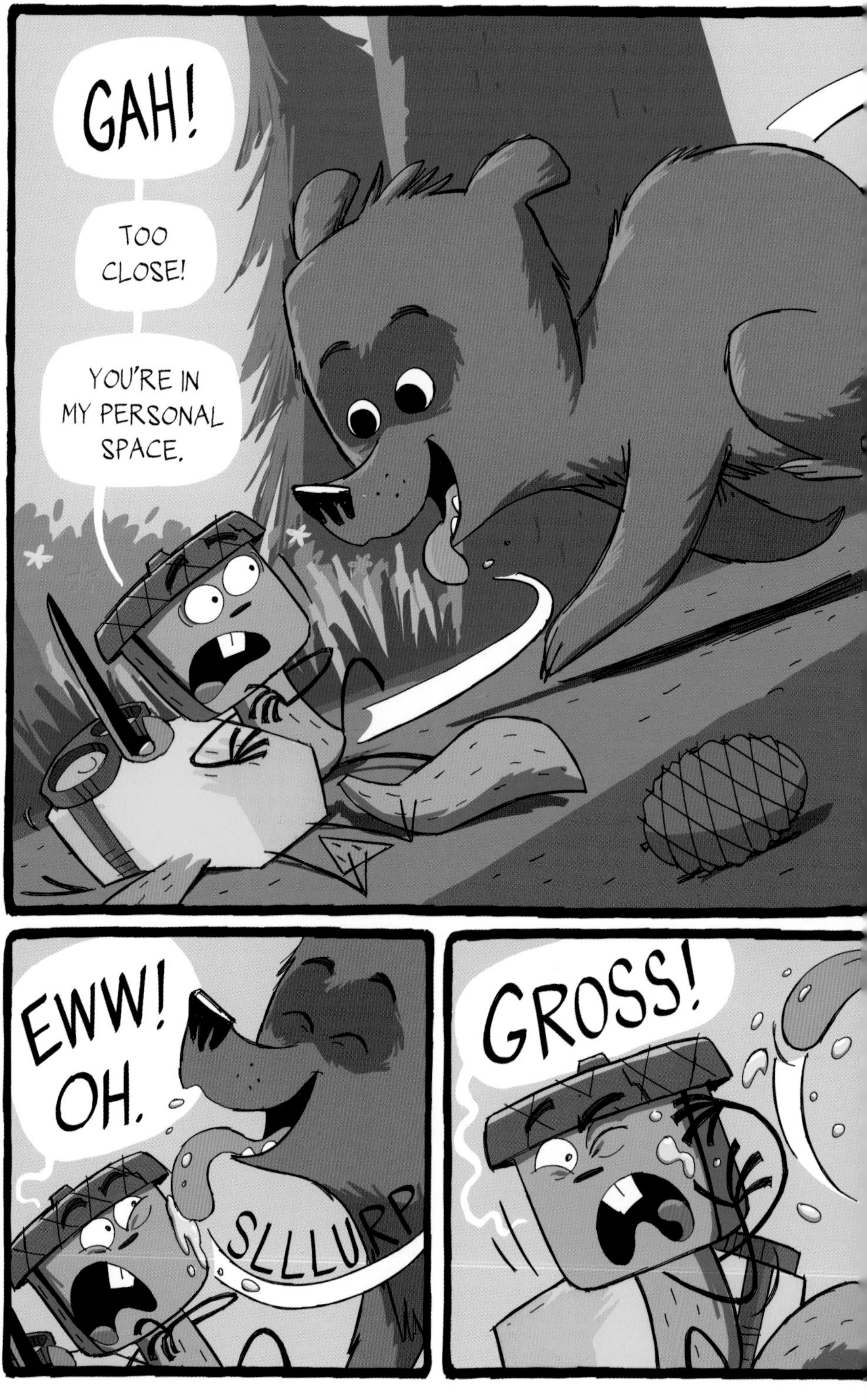
GAH!
TOO CLOSE!
YOU'RE IN MY PERSONAL SPACE.
EWW! OH.
SLLLURP
GROSS!

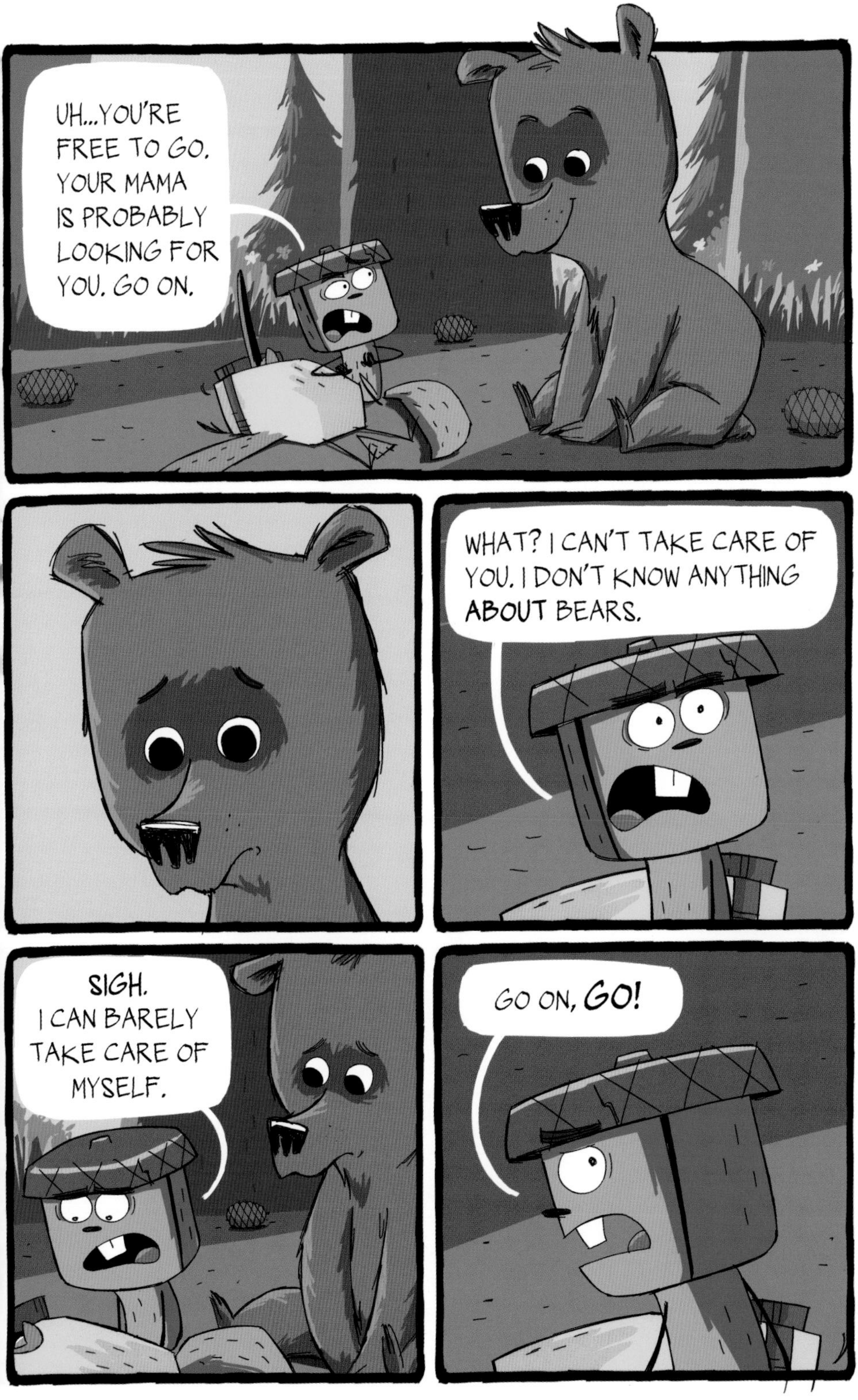
UH...YOU'RE FREE TO GO. YOUR MAMA IS PROBABLY LOOKING FOR YOU. GO ON.
WHAT? I CAN'T TAKE CARE OF YOU. I DON'T KNOW ANYTHING **ABOUT** BEARS.
SIGH. I CAN BARELY TAKE CARE OF MYSELF.
GO ON, **GO!**

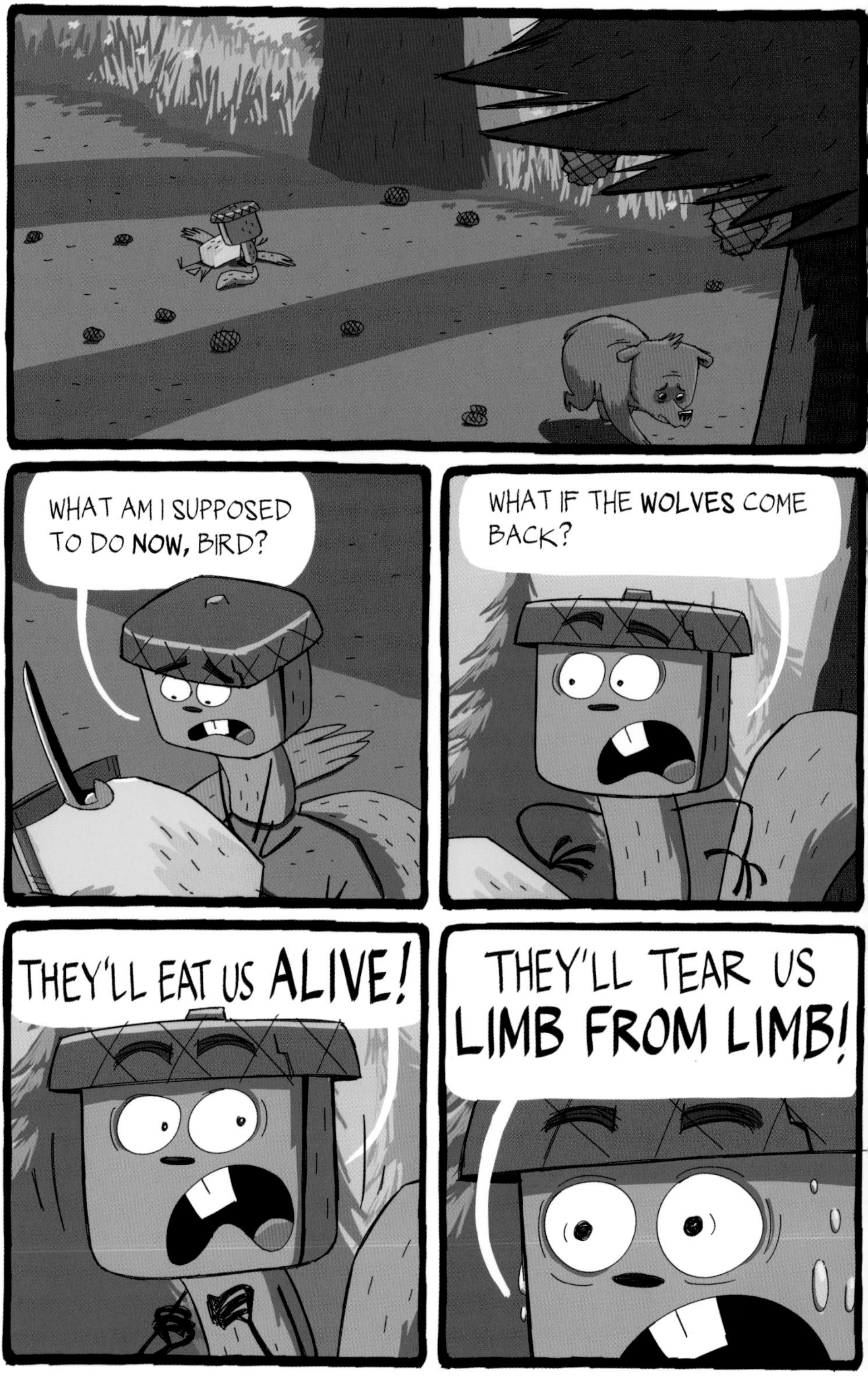
WHAT AM I SUPPOSED TO DO NOW, BIRD?
WHAT IF THE WOLVES COME BACK?
THEY'LL EAT US ALIVE!
THEY'LL TEAR US LIMB FROM LIMB!

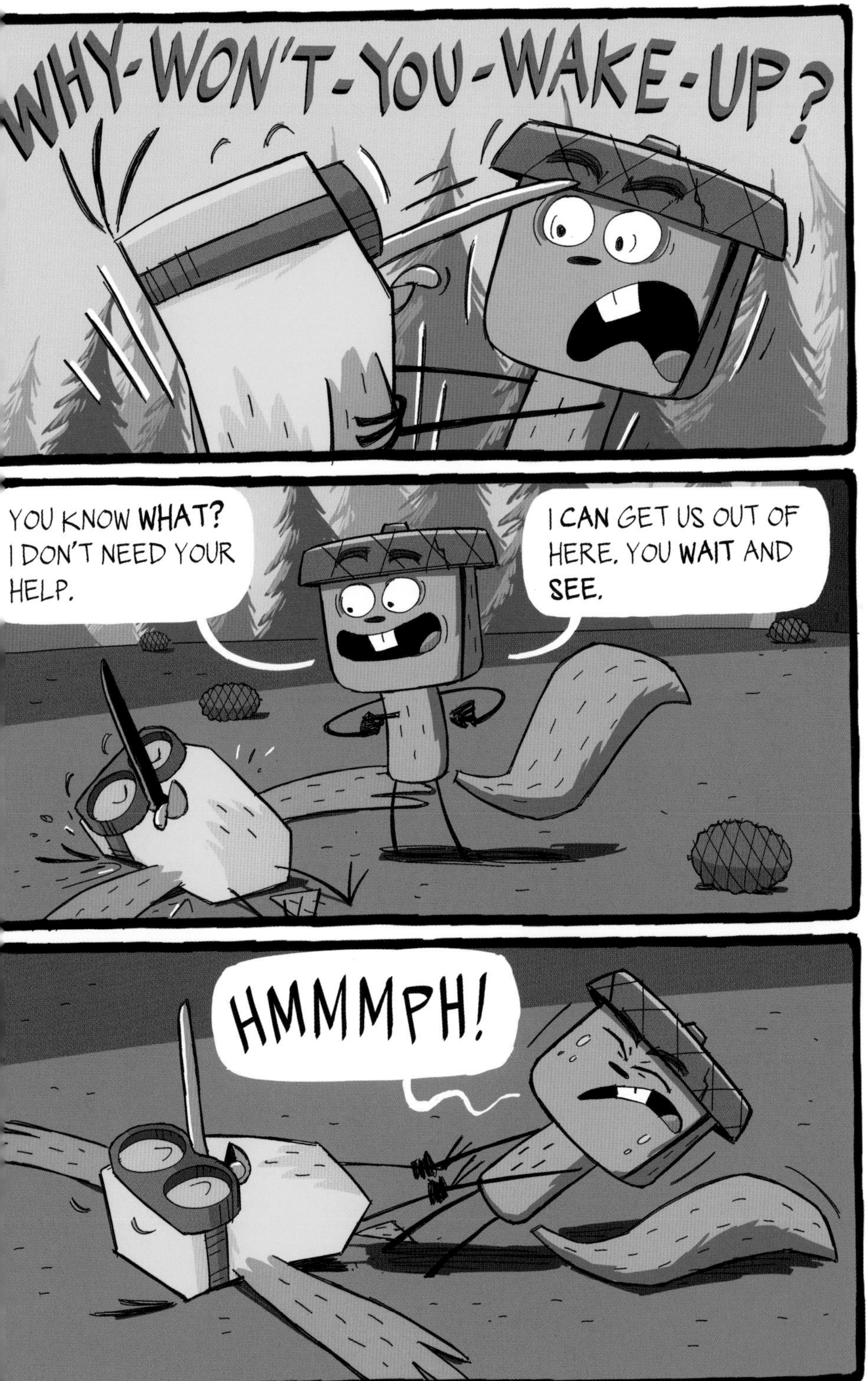
WHY-WON'T-YOU-WAKE-UP?
YOU KNOW WHAT? I DON'T NEED YOUR HELP.
I CAN GET US OUT OF HERE. YOU WAIT AND SEE.
HMMMPH!

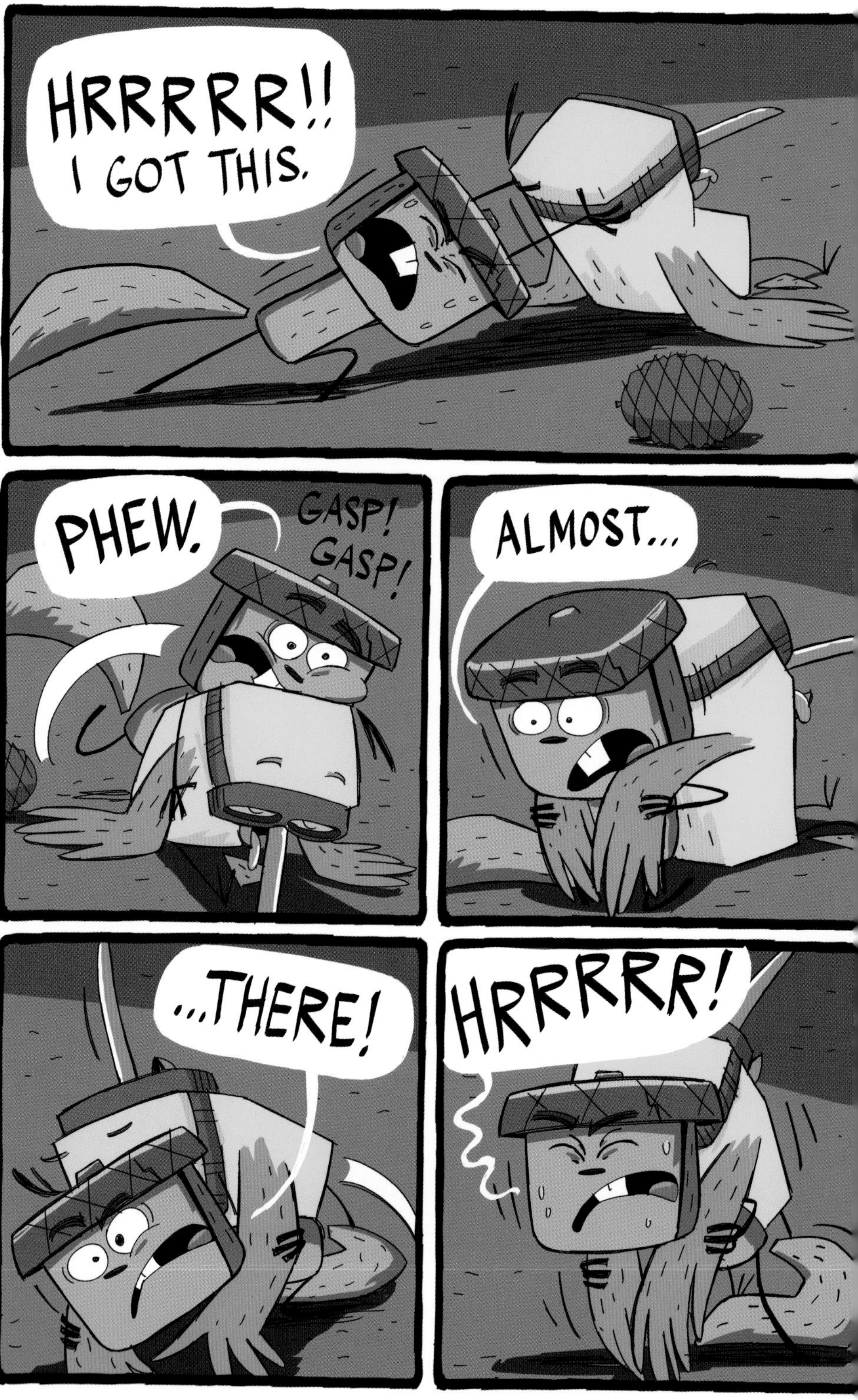
HRRRRR!! I GOT THIS.
PHEW.
GASP! GASP!
ALMOST...
...THERE!
HRRRRR!

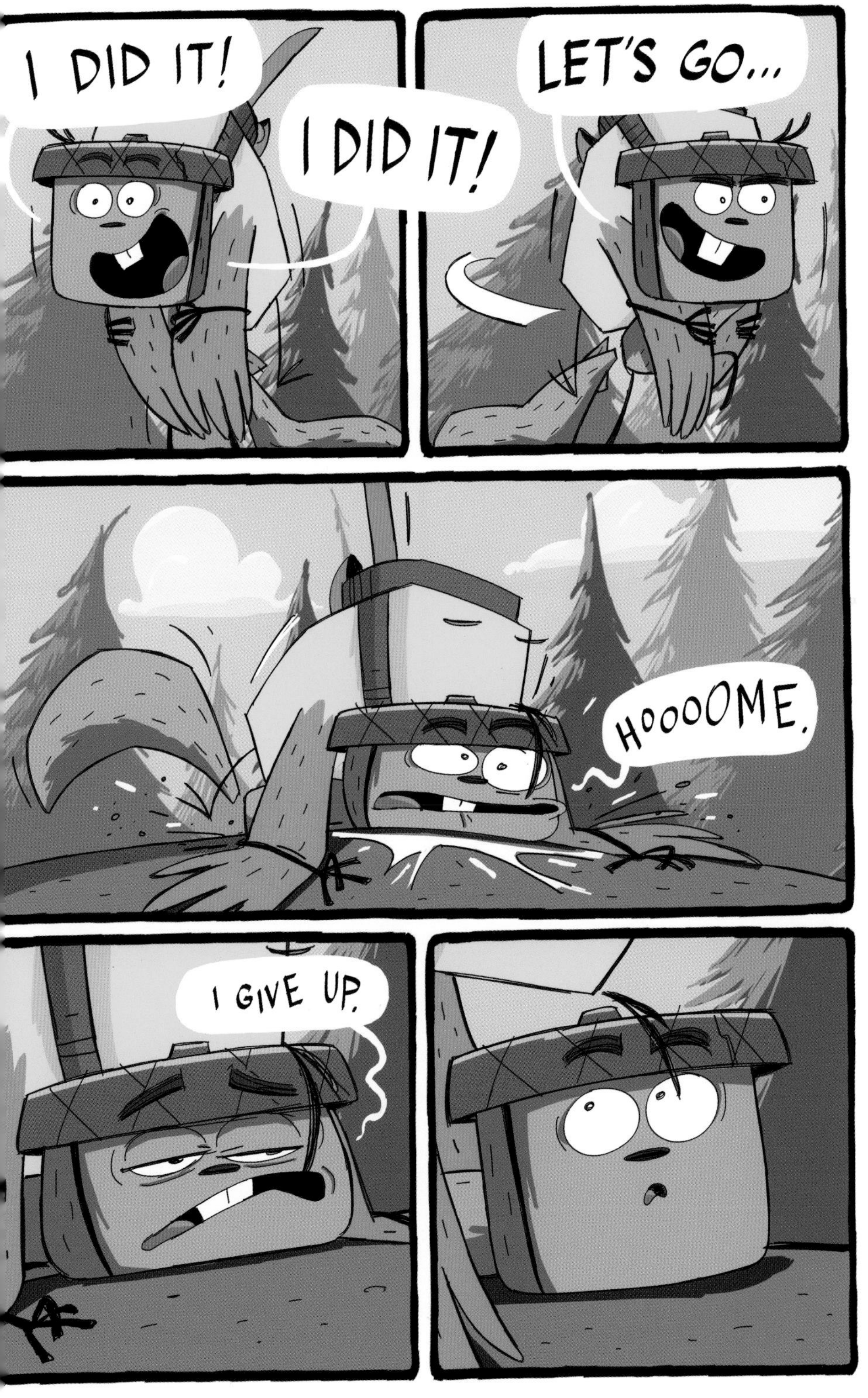
I DID IT!
I DID IT!
LET'S GO...
HOOOOME.
I GIVE UP.

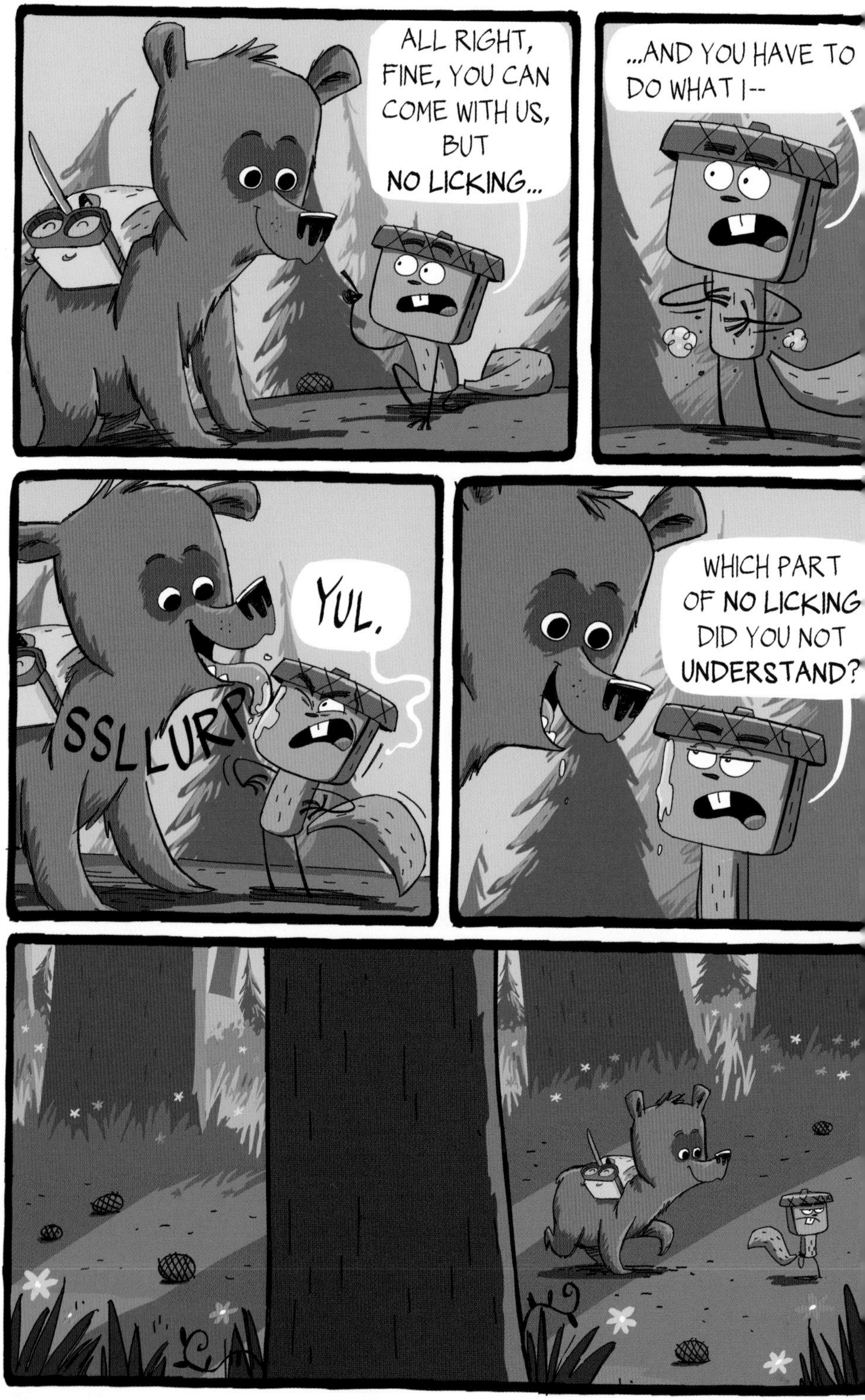
ALL RIGHT, FINE, YOU CAN COME WITH US, BUT NO LICKING...
...AND YOU HAVE TO DO WHAT I--
YUL.
SSLLURP
WHICH PART OF NO LICKING DID YOU NOT UNDERSTAND?

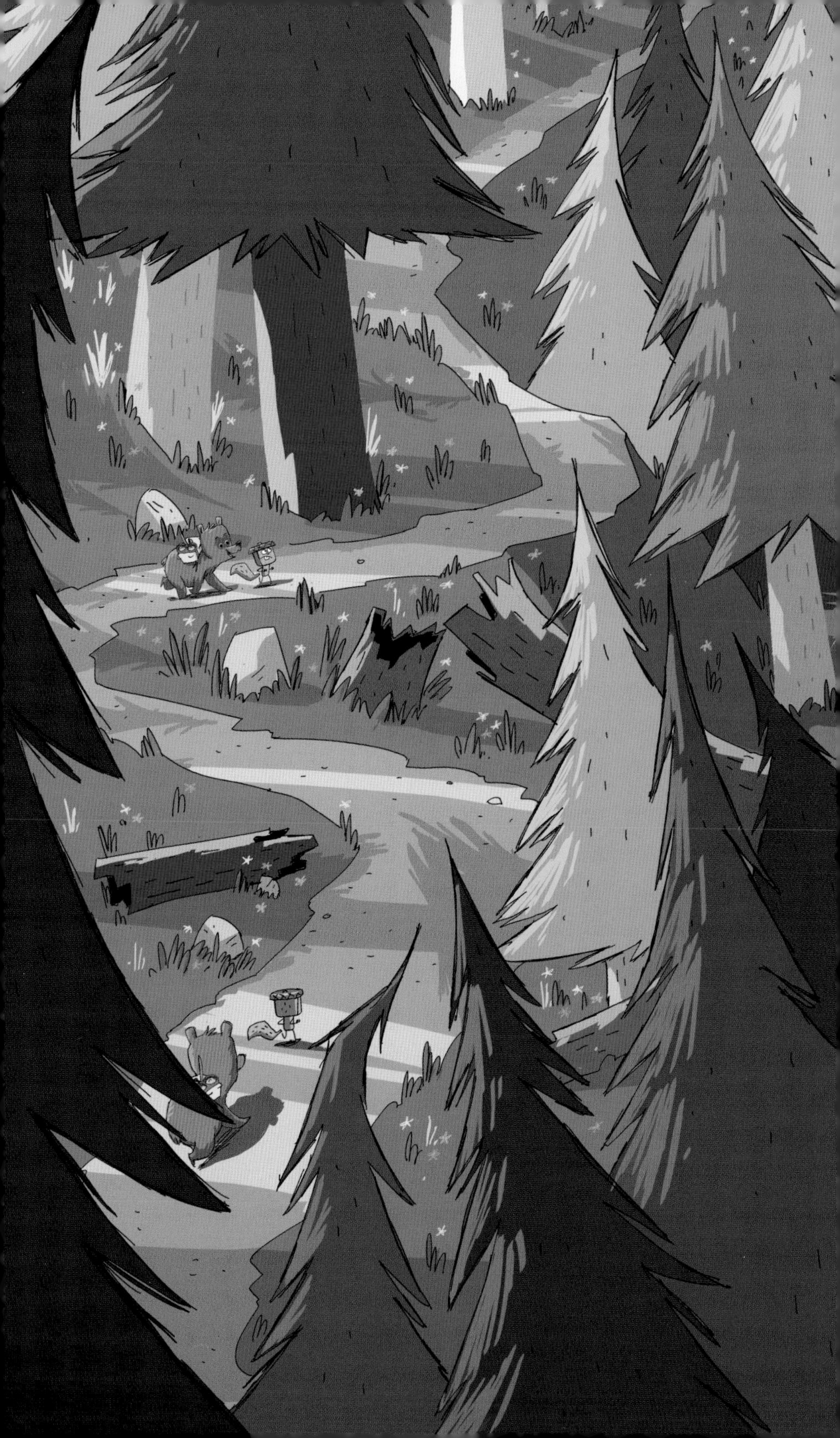

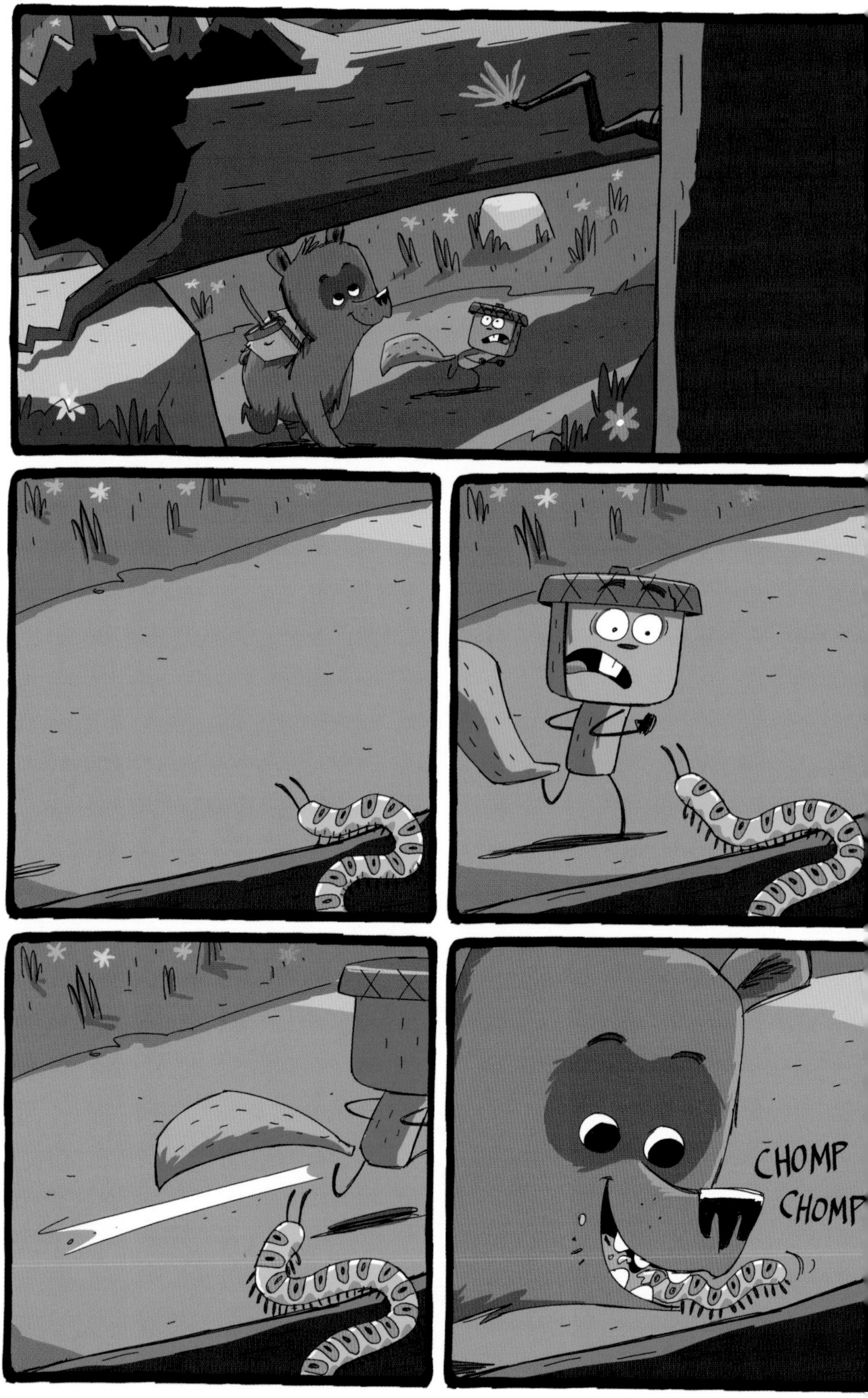
CHOMP
CHOMP

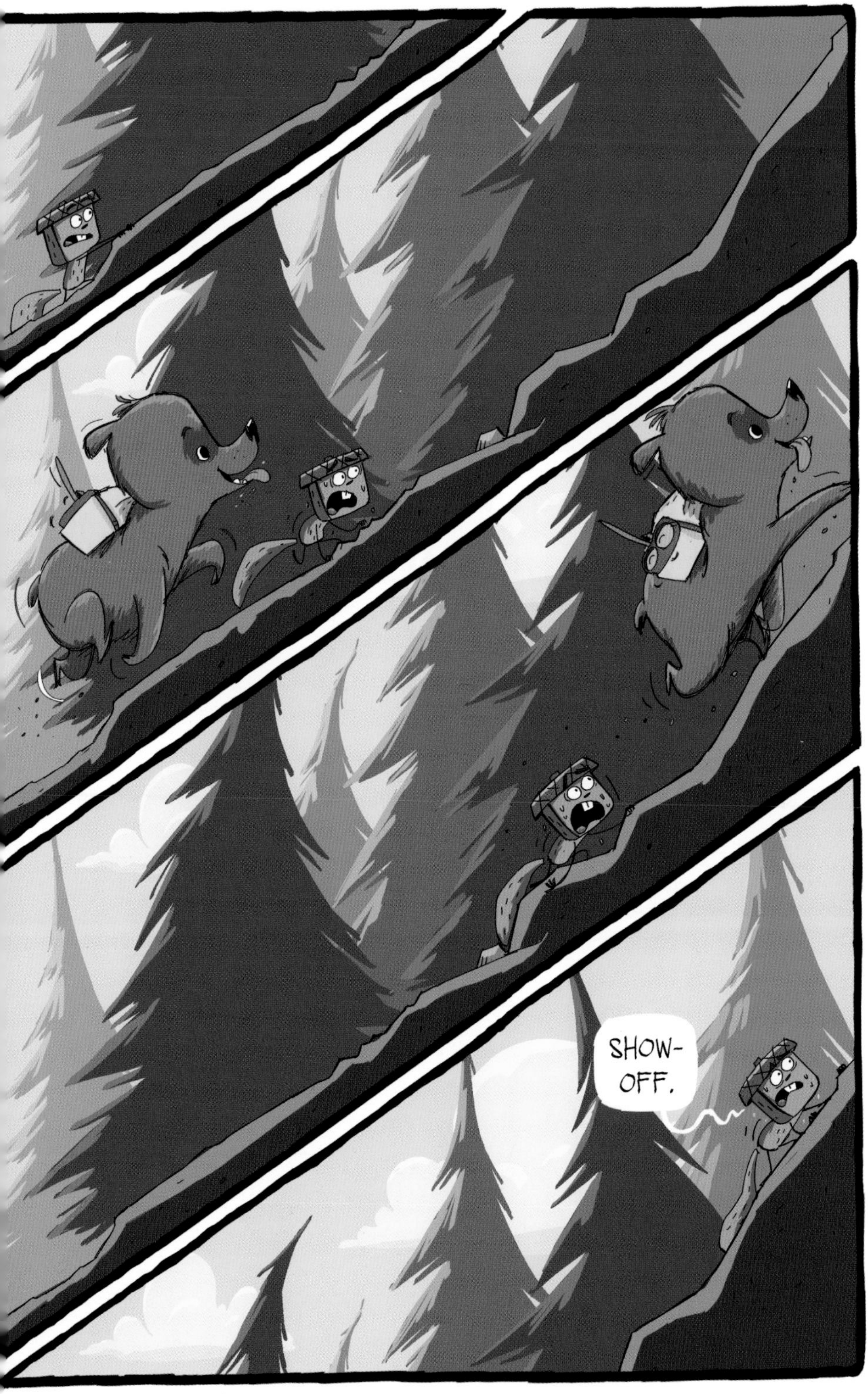
SHOW-
OFF.

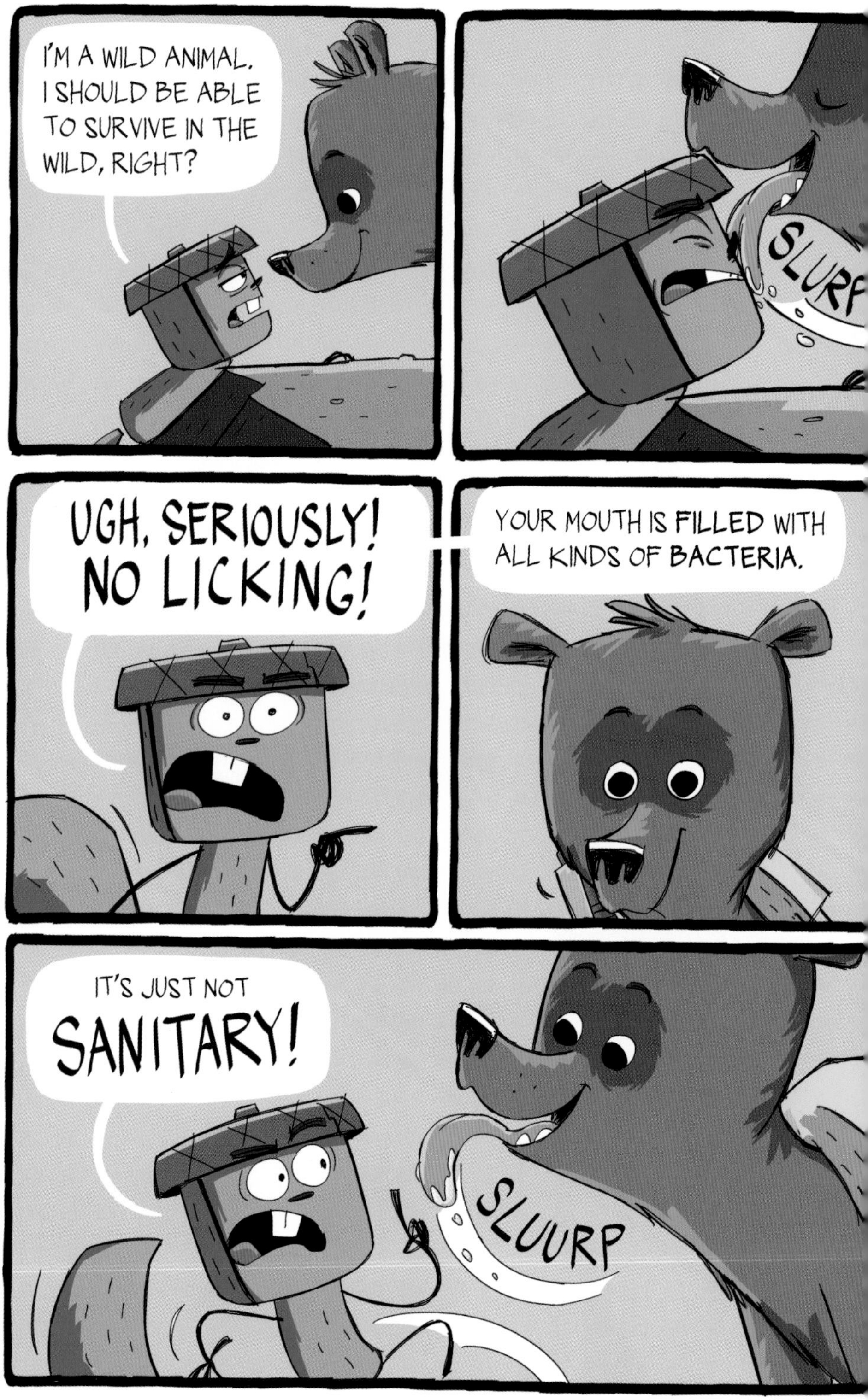
I'M A WILD ANIMAL. I SHOULD BE ABLE TO SURVIVE IN THE WILD, RIGHT?
SLURP
UGH, SERIOUSLY! NO LICKING!
YOUR MOUTH IS FILLED WITH ALL KINDS OF BACTERIA.
IT'S JUST NOT SANITARY!
SLUURP

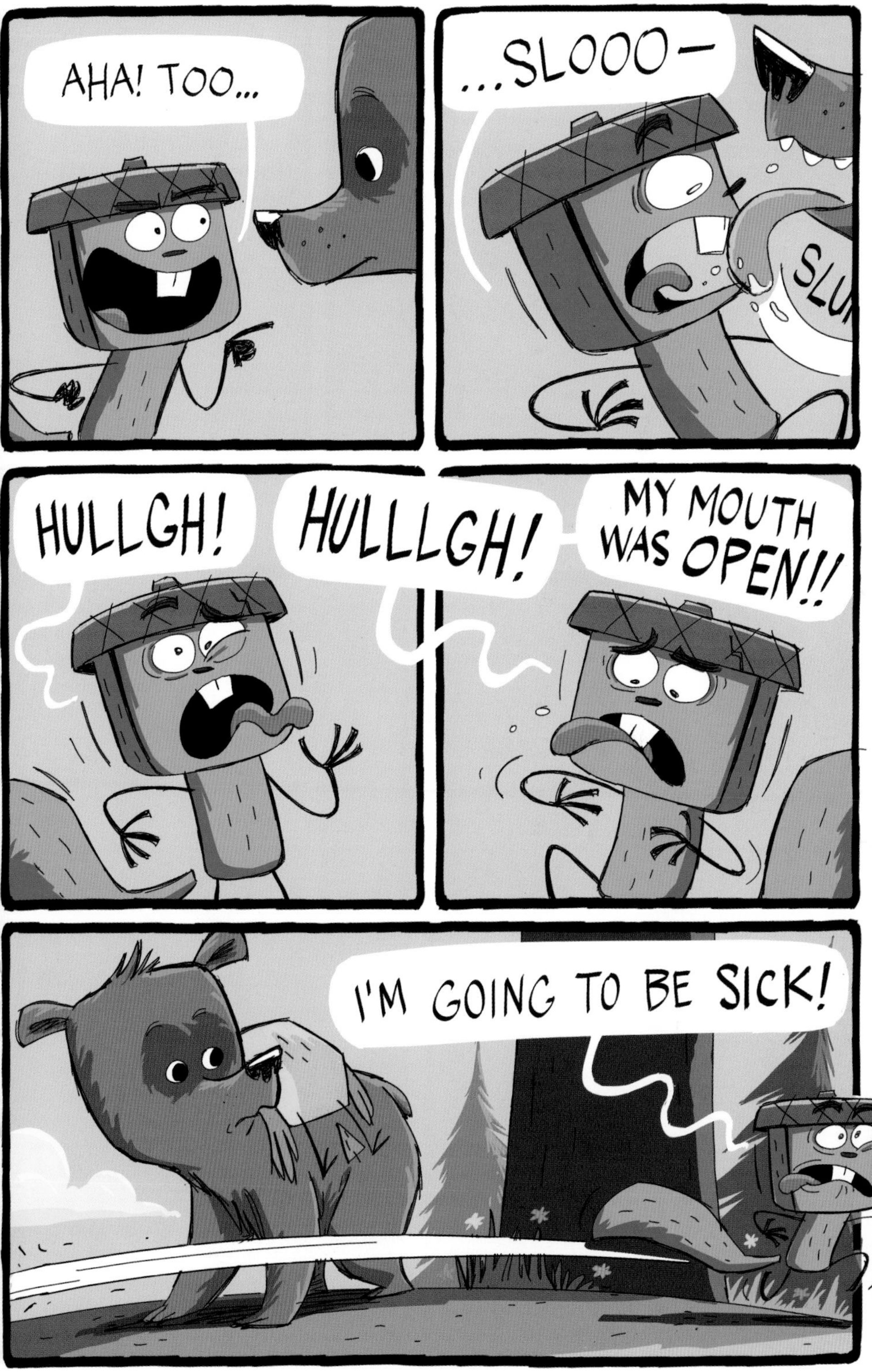
AHA! TOO...
...SLOOO-
SLU
HULLGH!
HULLLGH!
MY MOUTH WAS OPEN!!
I'M GOING TO BE SICK!

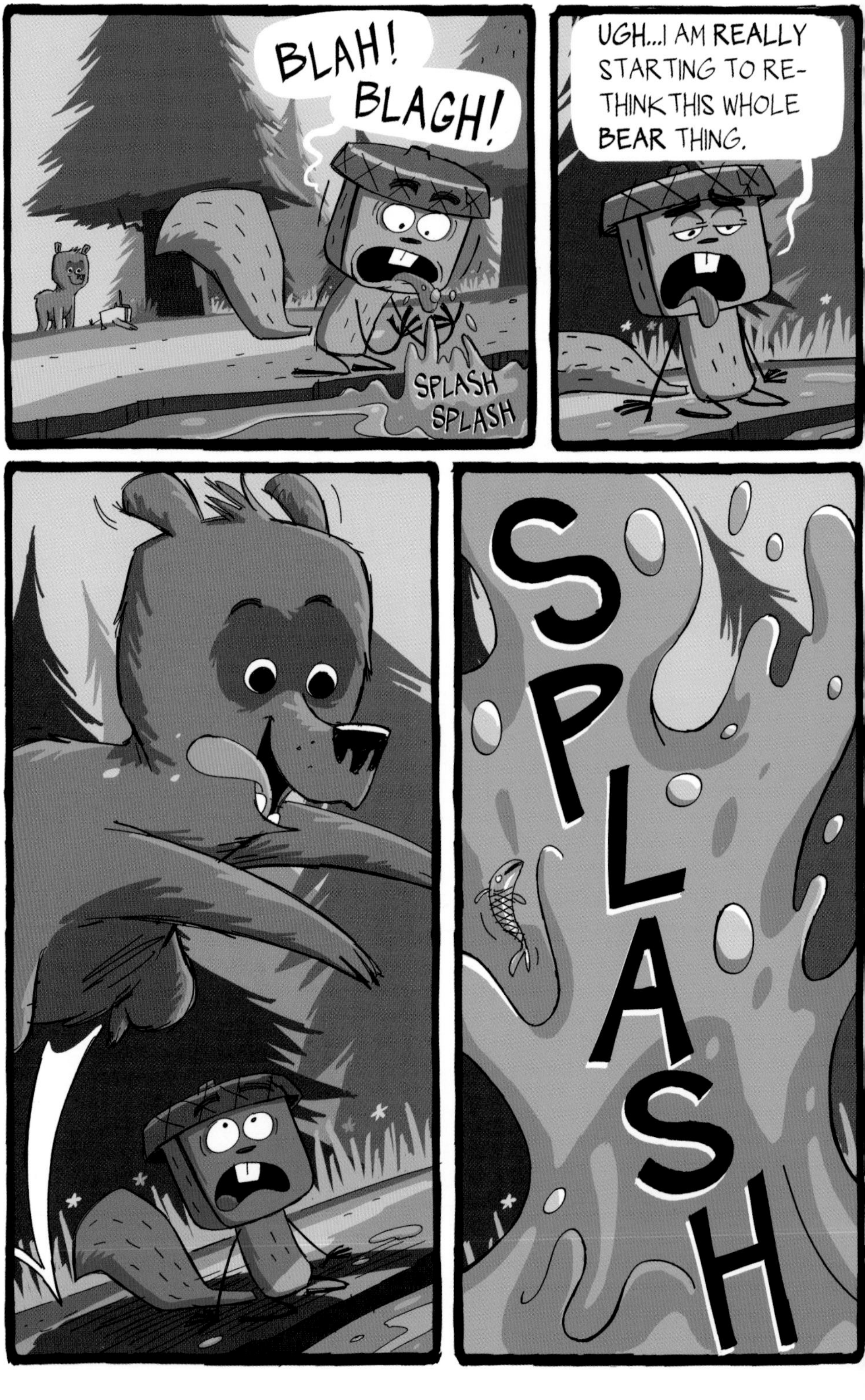
BLAH! BLAGH!
SPLASH SPLASH
UGH...I AM REALLY STARTING TO RE-THINK THIS WHOLE BEAR THING.
SPLASH

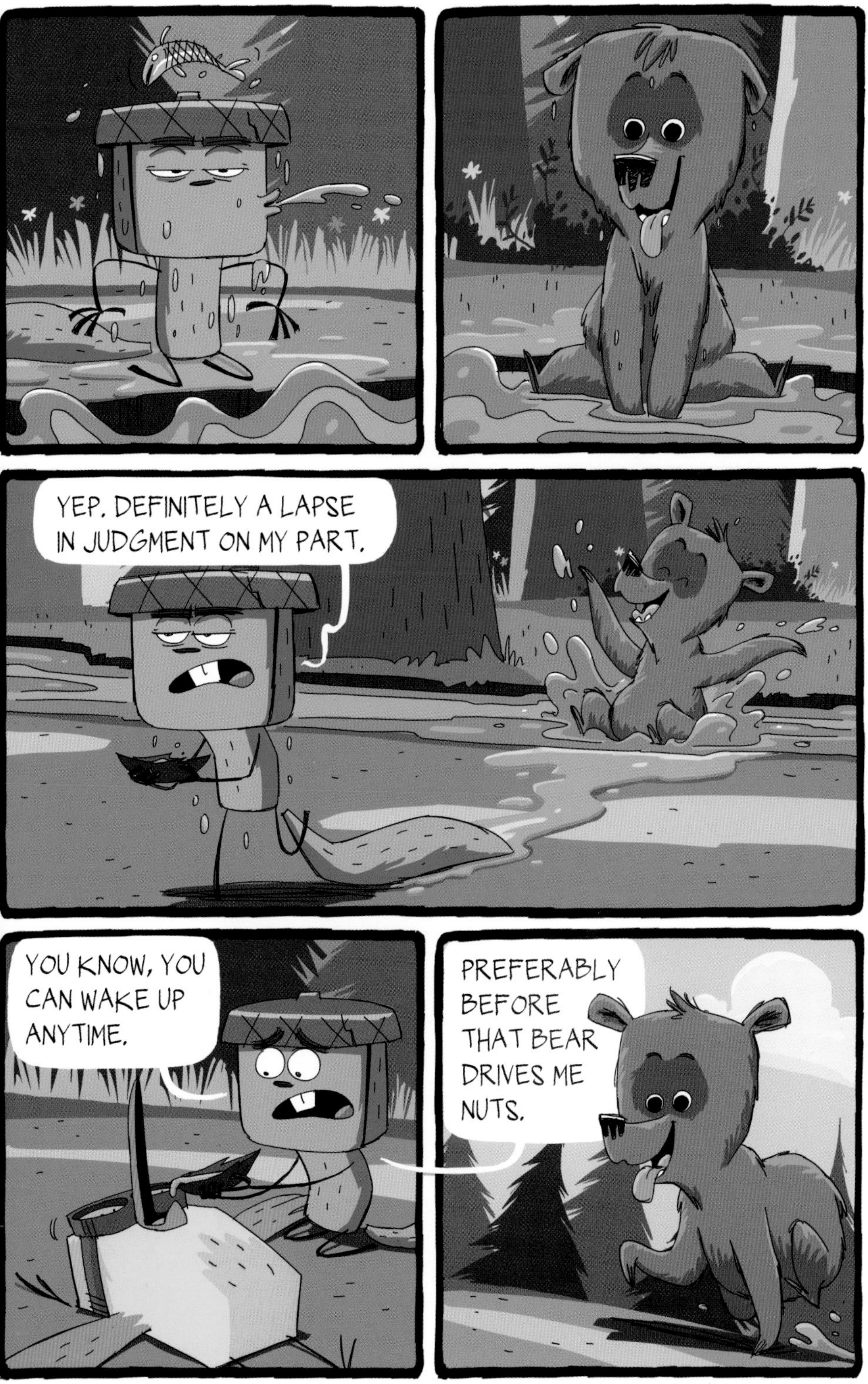
YEP. DEFINITELY A LAPSE IN JUDGMENT ON MY PART.
YOU KNOW, YOU CAN WAKE UP ANYTIME.
PREFERABLY BEFORE THAT BEAR DRIVES ME NUTS.

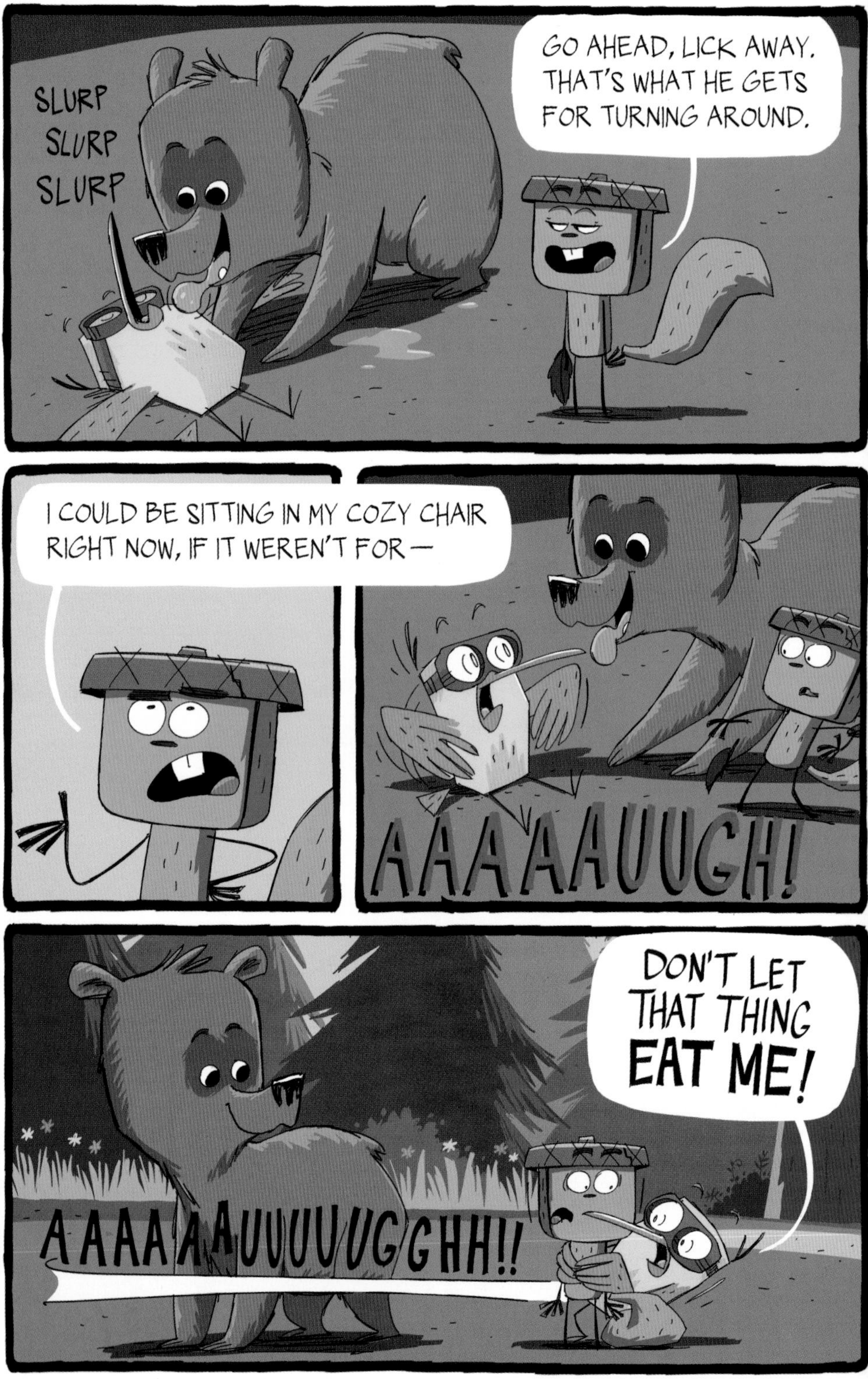
SLURP
SLURP
SLURP
GO AHEAD, LICK AWAY. THAT'S WHAT HE GETS FOR TURNING AROUND.
I COULD BE SITTING IN MY COZY CHAIR RIGHT NOW, IF IT WEREN'T FOR—
AAAAAAUUGH!
DON'T LET THAT THING EAT ME!
AAAAAAUUUUUGGHH!!

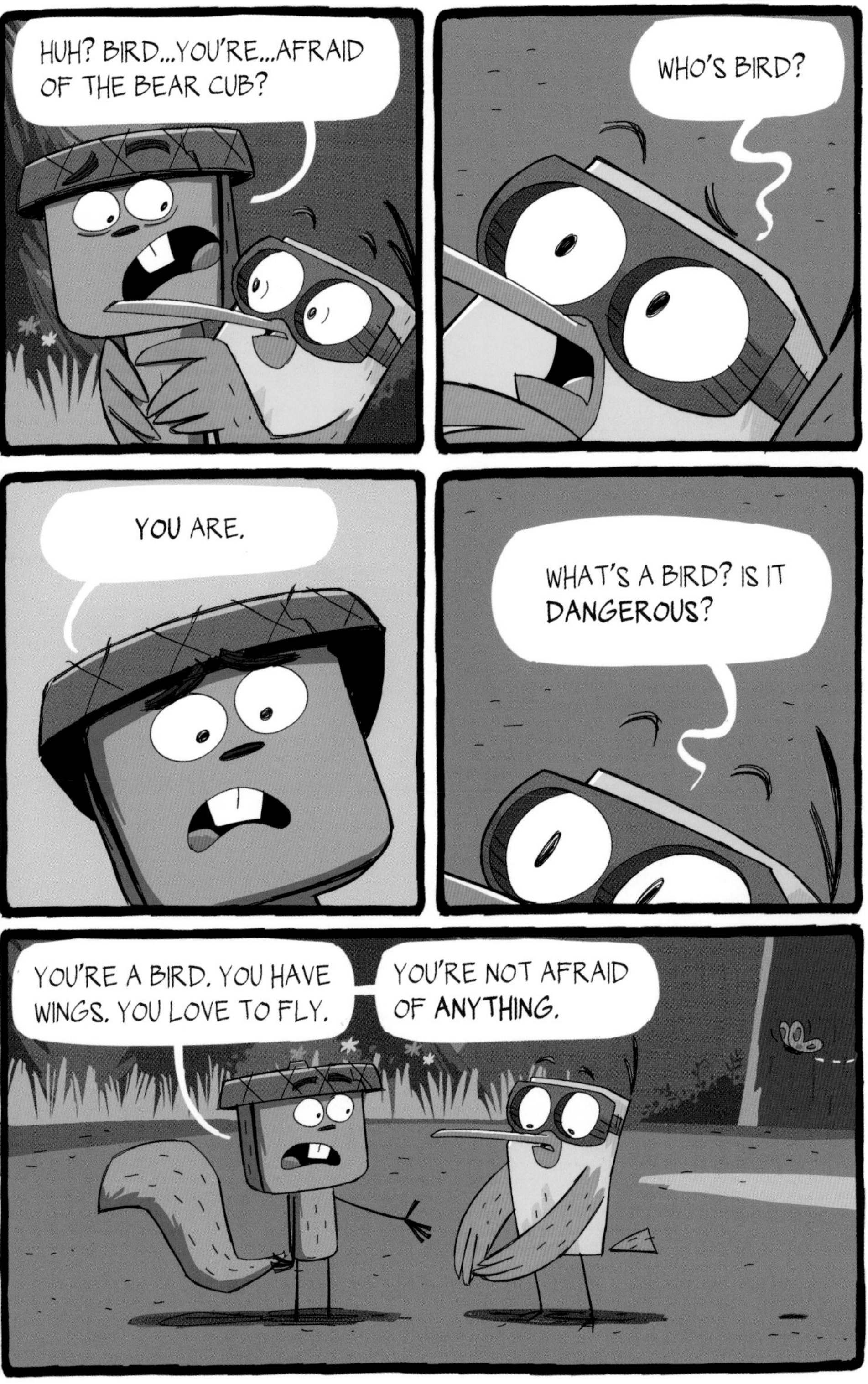
HUH? BIRD...YOU'RE...AFRAID OF THE BEAR CUB?
WHO'S BIRD?
YOU ARE.
WHAT'S A BIRD? IS IT DANGEROUS?
YOU'RE A BIRD. YOU HAVE WINGS. YOU LOVE TO FLY.
YOU'RE NOT AFRAID OF ANYTHING.

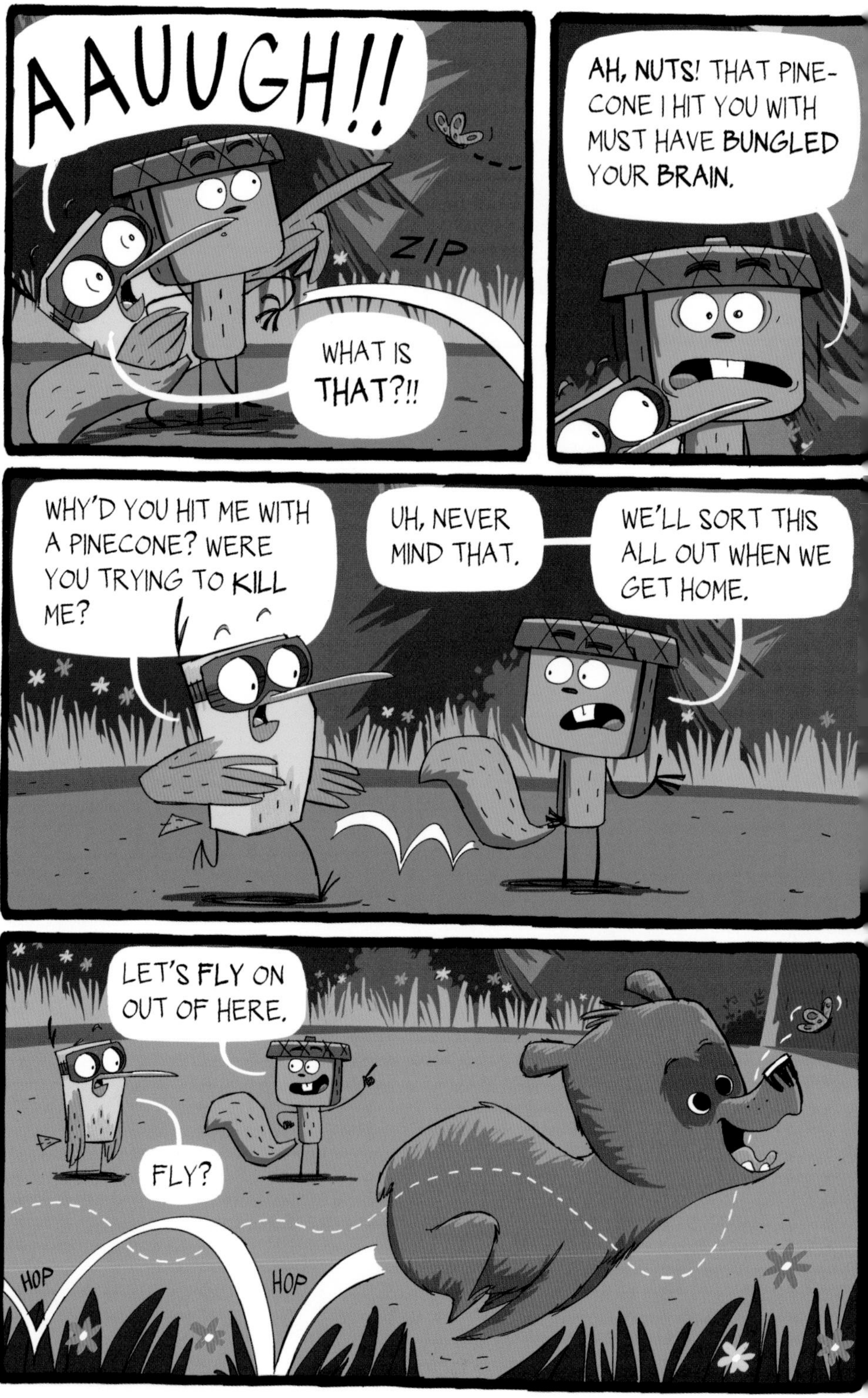
AAUUGH!!
ZIP
WHAT IS THAT?!!
AH, NUTS! THAT PINE-CONE I HIT YOU WITH MUST HAVE BUNGLED YOUR BRAIN.
WHY'D YOU HIT ME WITH A PINECONE? WERE YOU TRYING TO KILL ME?
UH, NEVER MIND THAT.
WE'LL SORT THIS ALL OUT WHEN WE GET HOME.
LET'S FLY ON OUT OF HERE.
FLY?
HOP
HOP

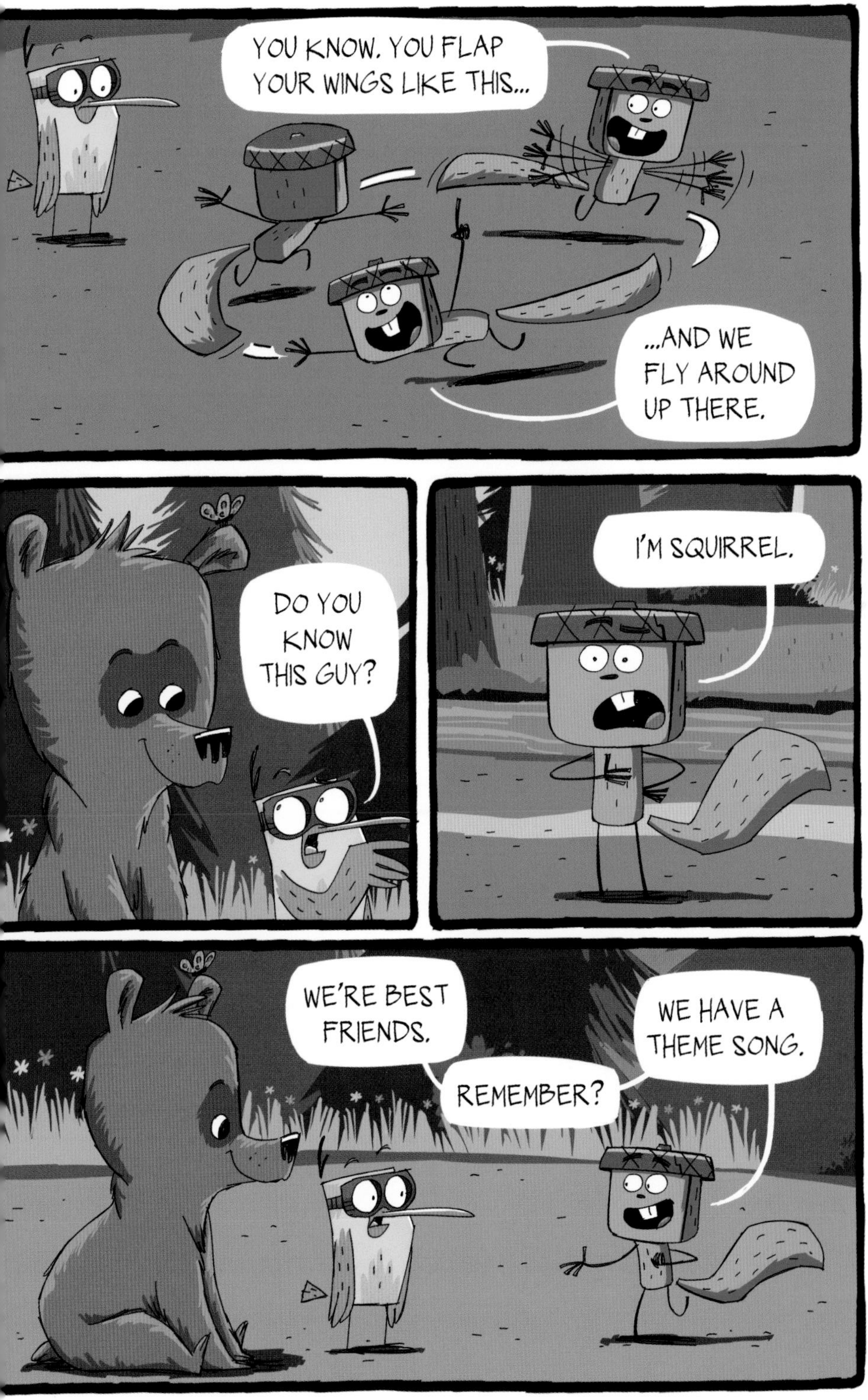
YOU KNOW. YOU FLAP YOUR WINGS LIKE THIS...
...AND WE FLY AROUND UP THERE.
DO YOU KNOW THIS GUY?
I'M SQUIRREL.
WE'RE BEST FRIENDS.
REMEMBER?
WE HAVE A THEME SONG.

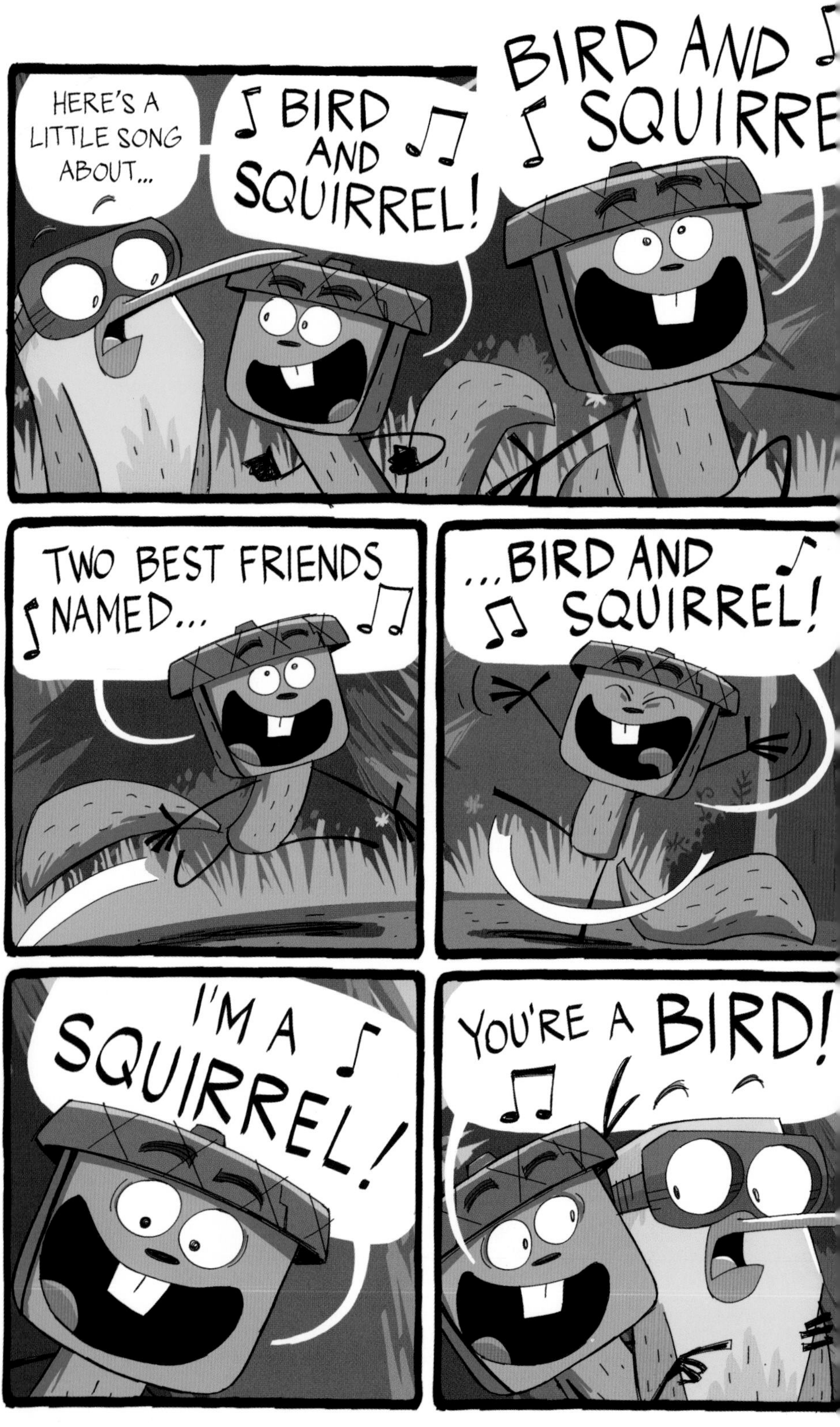
HERE'S A LITTLE SONG ABOUT...
BIRD AND SQUIRREL!
BIRD AND SQUIRRE
TWO BEST FRIENDS NAMED...
...BIRD AND SQUIRREL!
I'M A SQUIRREL!
YOU'RE A BIRD!

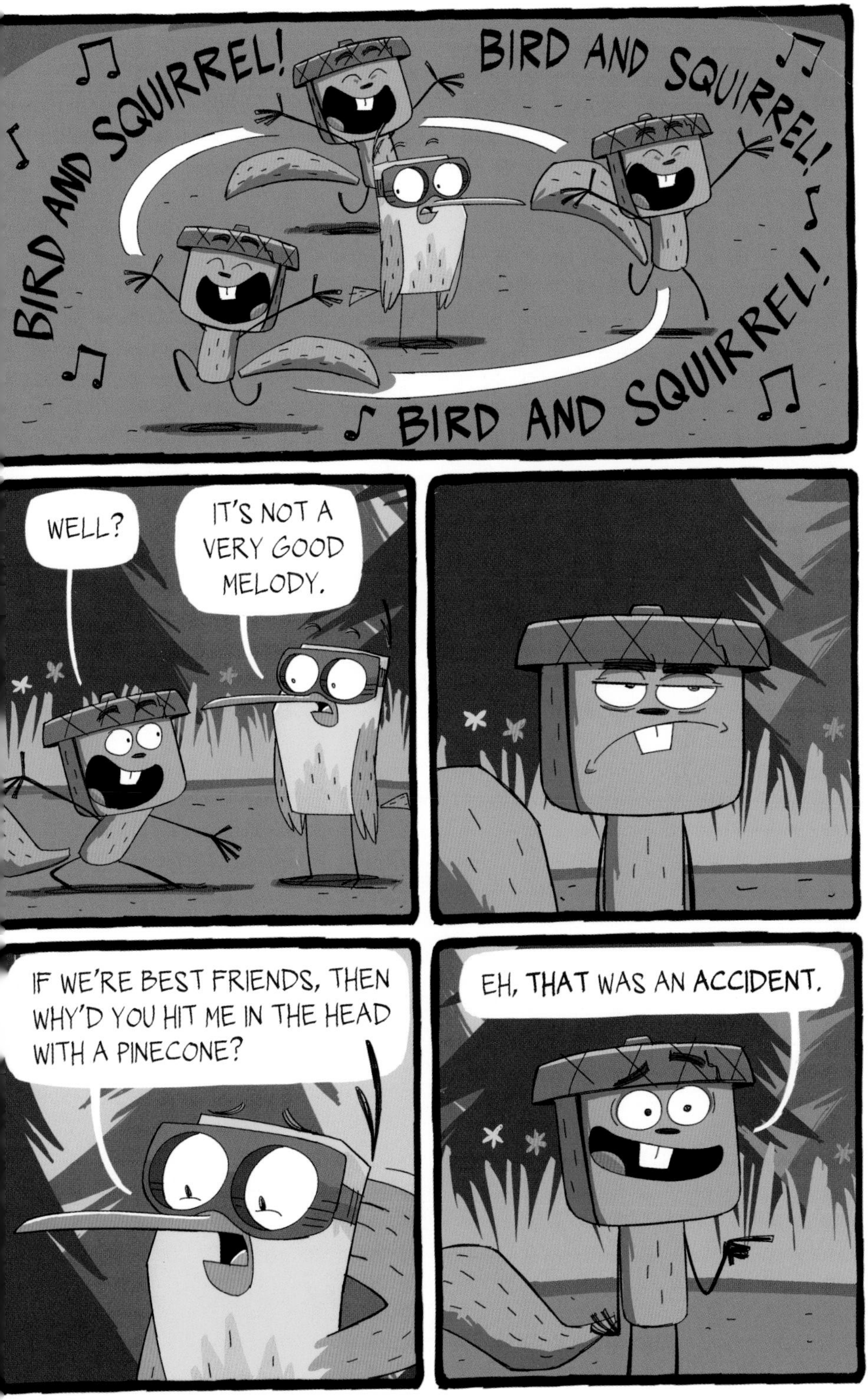
BIRD AND SQUIRREL!
BIRD AND SQUIRREL!
BIRD AND SQUIRREL!
BIRD AND SQUIRREL!
WELL?
IT'S NOT A VERY GOOD MELODY.
IF WE'RE BEST FRIENDS, THEN WHY'D YOU HIT ME IN THE HEAD WITH A PINECONE?
EH, THAT WAS AN ACCIDENT.

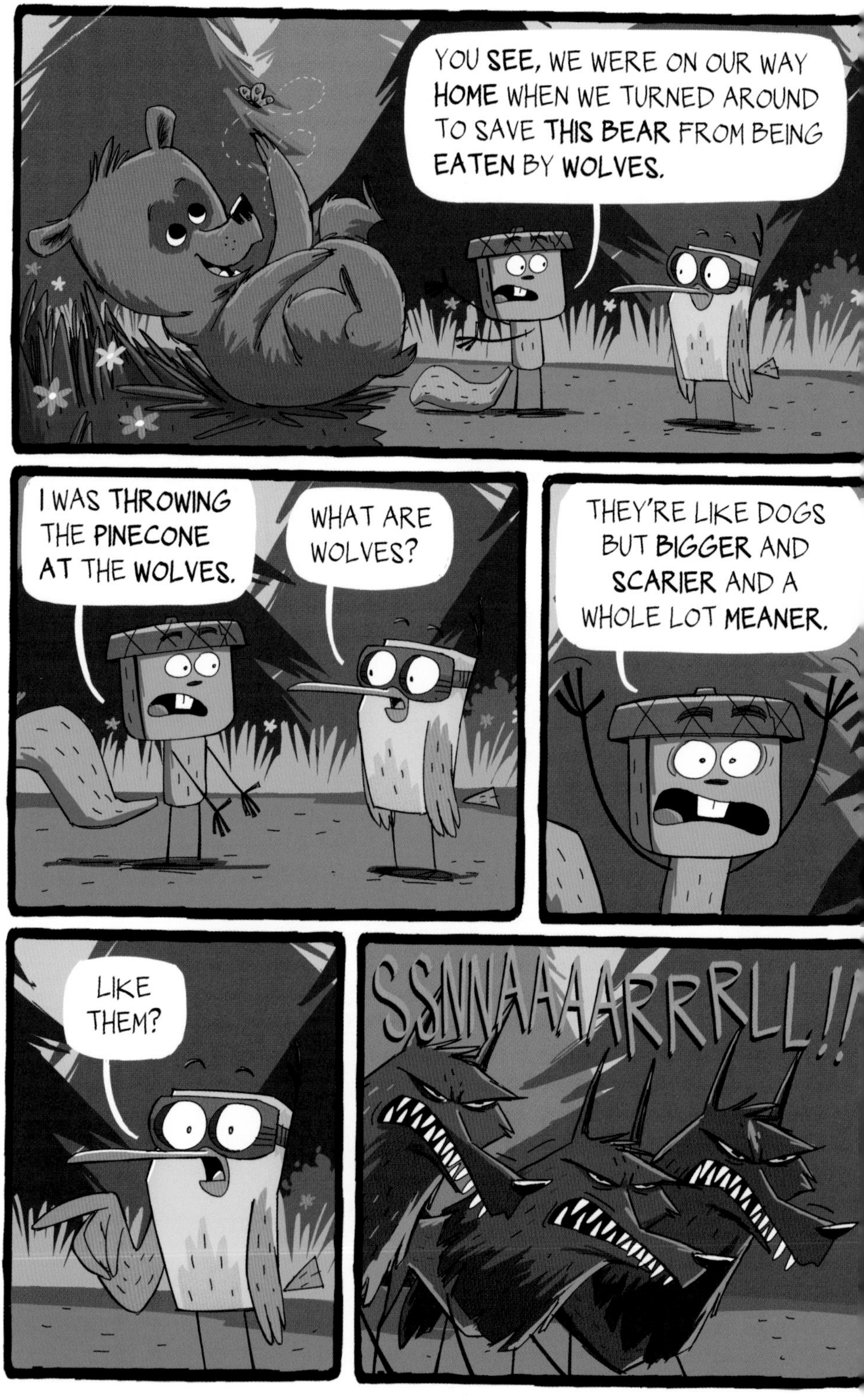

YOU SEE, WE WERE ON OUR WAY HOME WHEN WE TURNED AROUND TO SAVE THIS BEAR FROM BEING EATEN BY WOLVES.
I WAS THROWING THE PINECONE AT THE WOLVES.
WHAT ARE WOLVES?
THEY'RE LIKE DOGS BUT BIGGER AND SCARIER AND A WHOLE LOT MEANER.
LIKE THEM?
SSNNAAAARRRLL!!

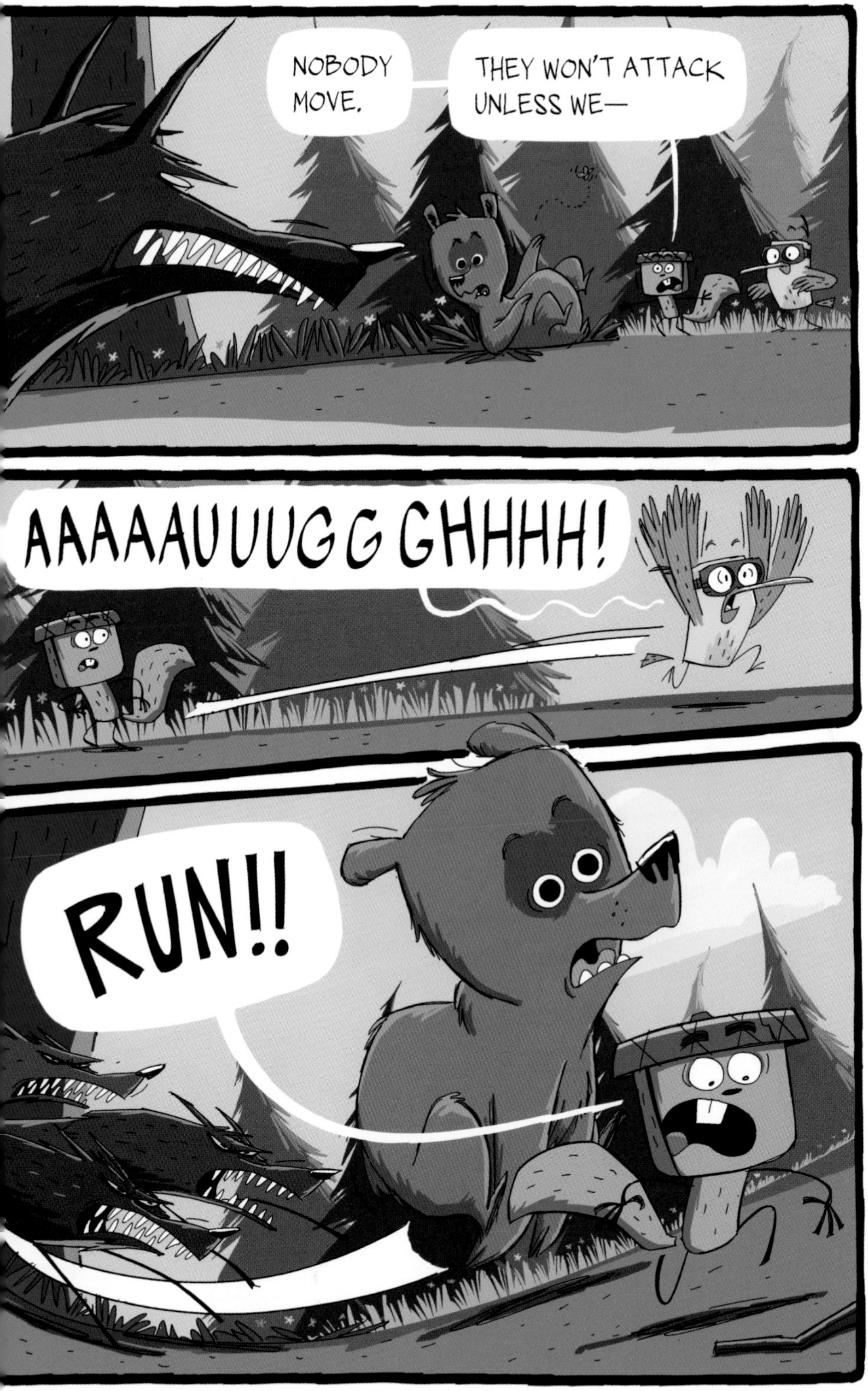

NOBODY MOVE.
THEY WON'T ATTACK UNLESS WE—
AAAAAUUUGGGHHHH!
RUN!!

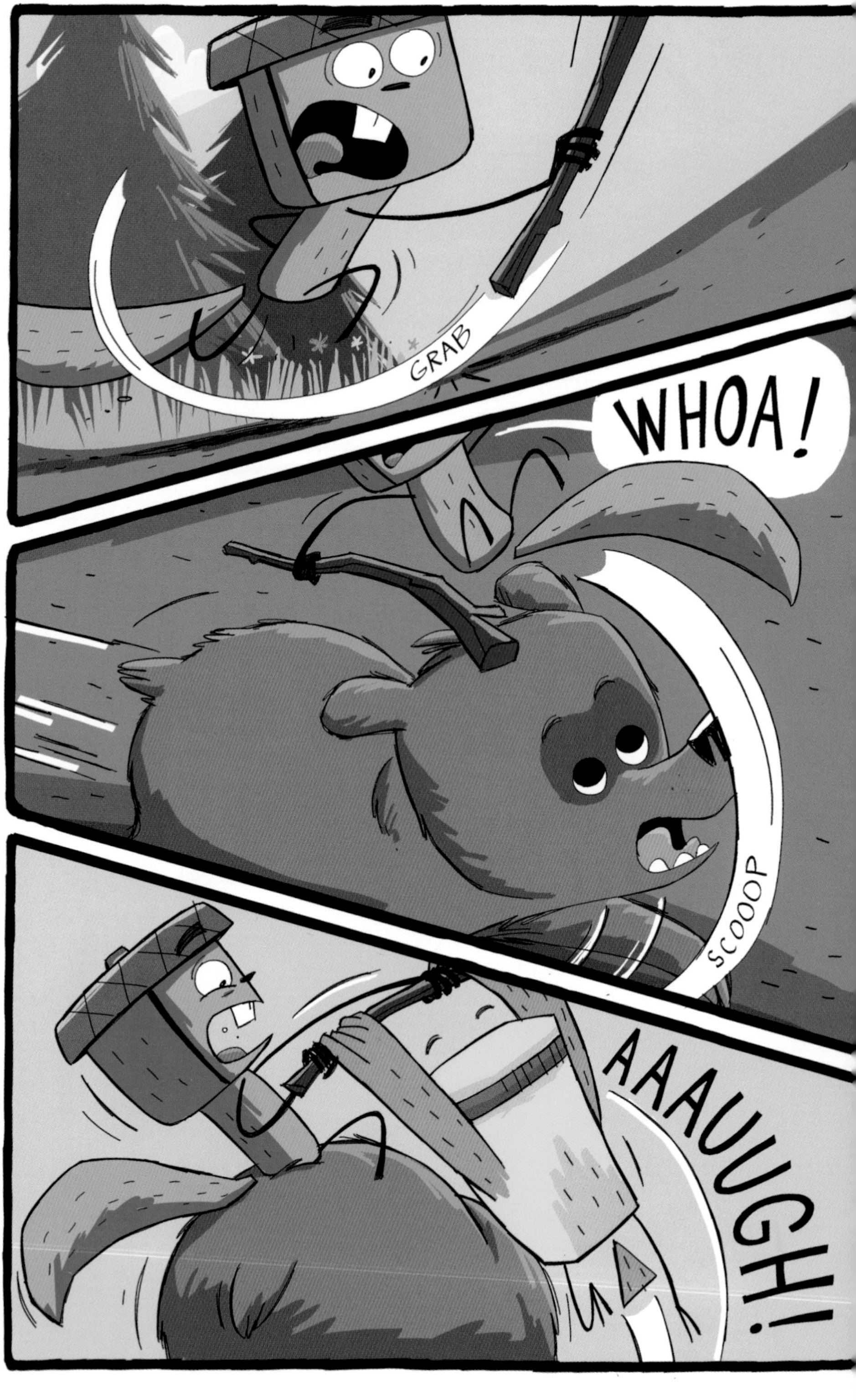
GRAB
WHOA!
SCOOOP
AAAUUGH!

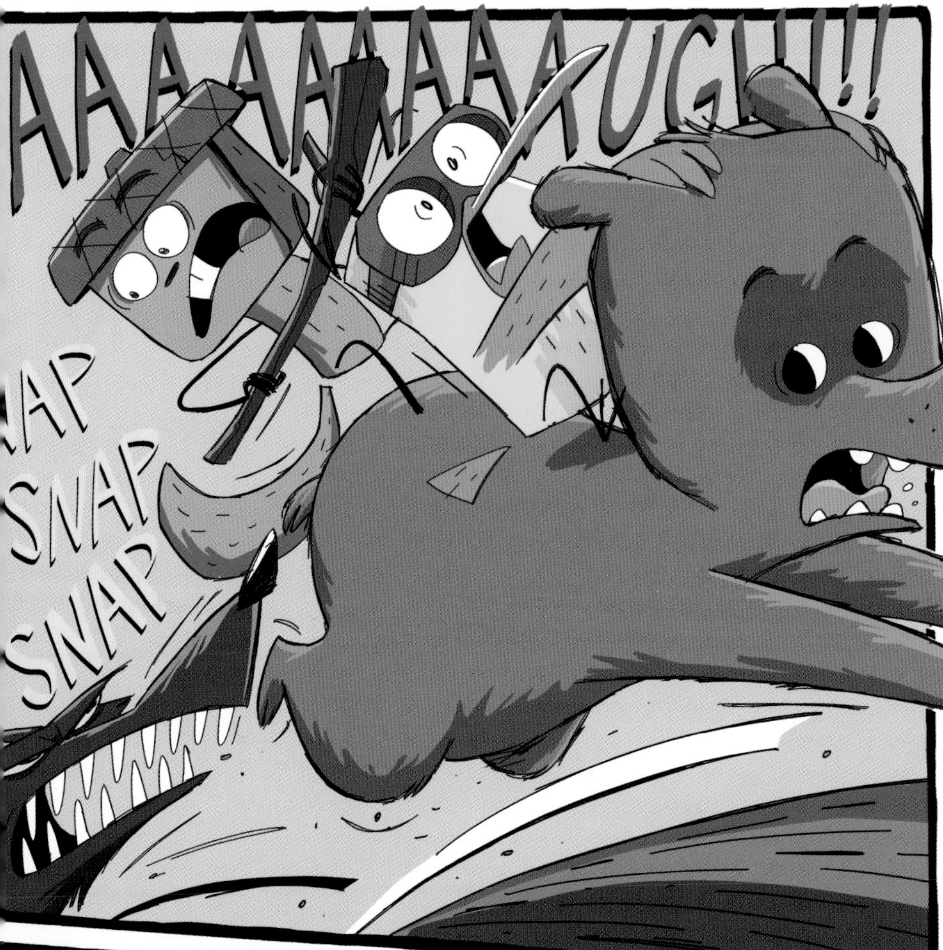
AAAAAAAAAUGH!!!
NAP
SNAP
SNAP
SNAP

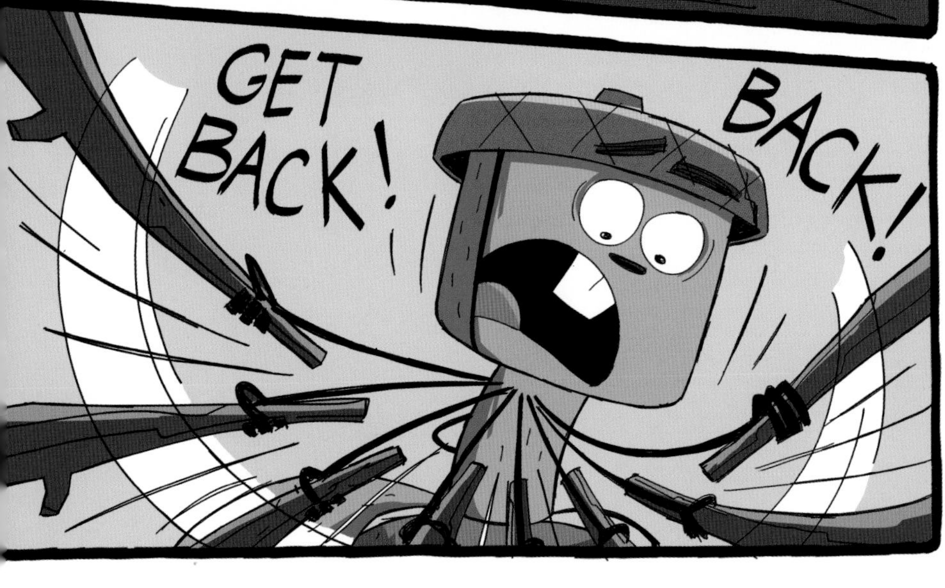
GET BACK!
BACK!

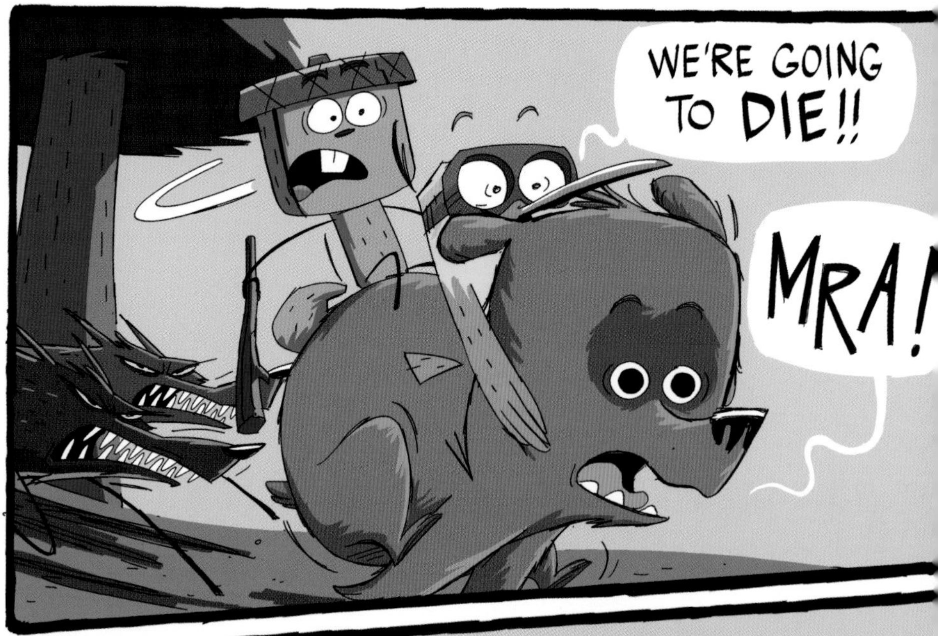
WE'RE GOING TO DIE!!
MRA!

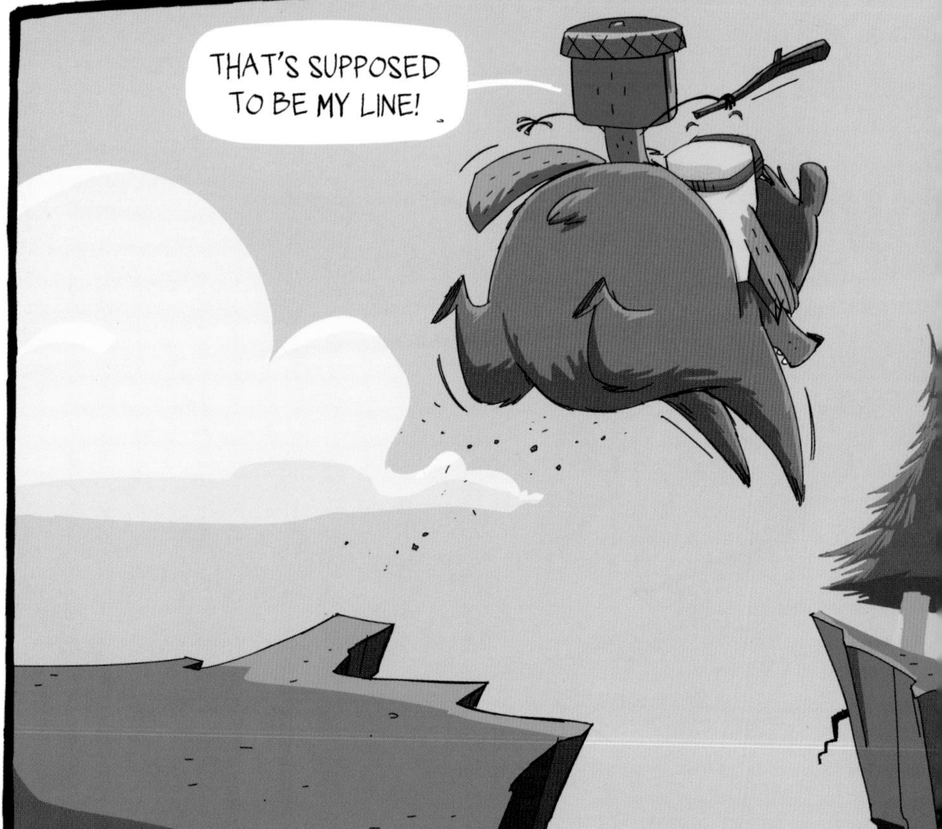
THAT'S SUPPOSED TO BE MY LINE!

CRUMBLE

HOOOOWWLLL!

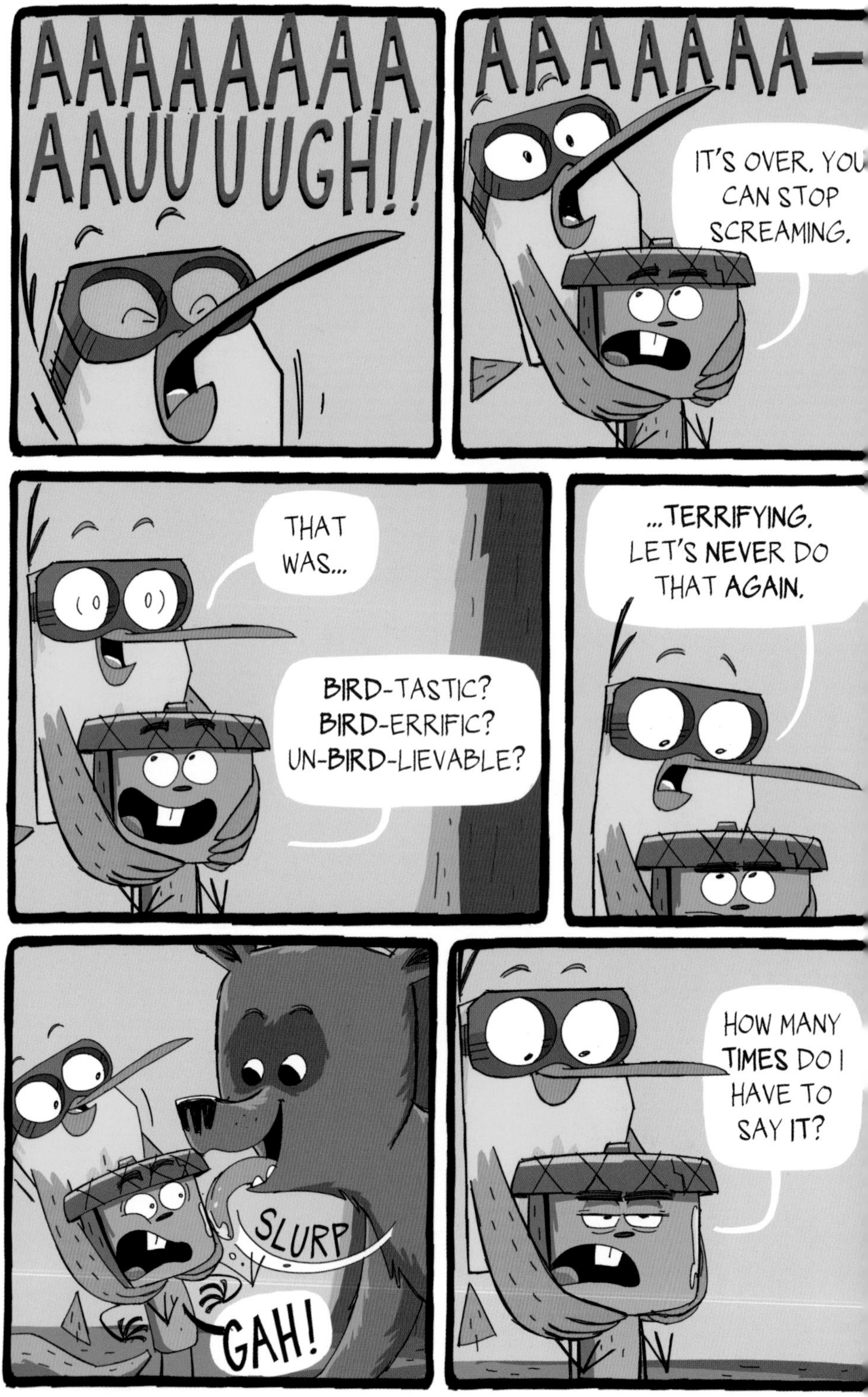
AAAAAAAA AAUUUUGH!!
AAAAAAA—
IT'S OVER. YOU CAN STOP SCREAMING.
THAT WAS...
BIRD-TASTIC? BIRD-ERRIFIC? UN-BIRD-LIEVABLE?
...TERRIFYING. LET'S NEVER DO THAT AGAIN.
SLURP
GAH!
HOW MANY TIMES DO I HAVE TO SAY IT?

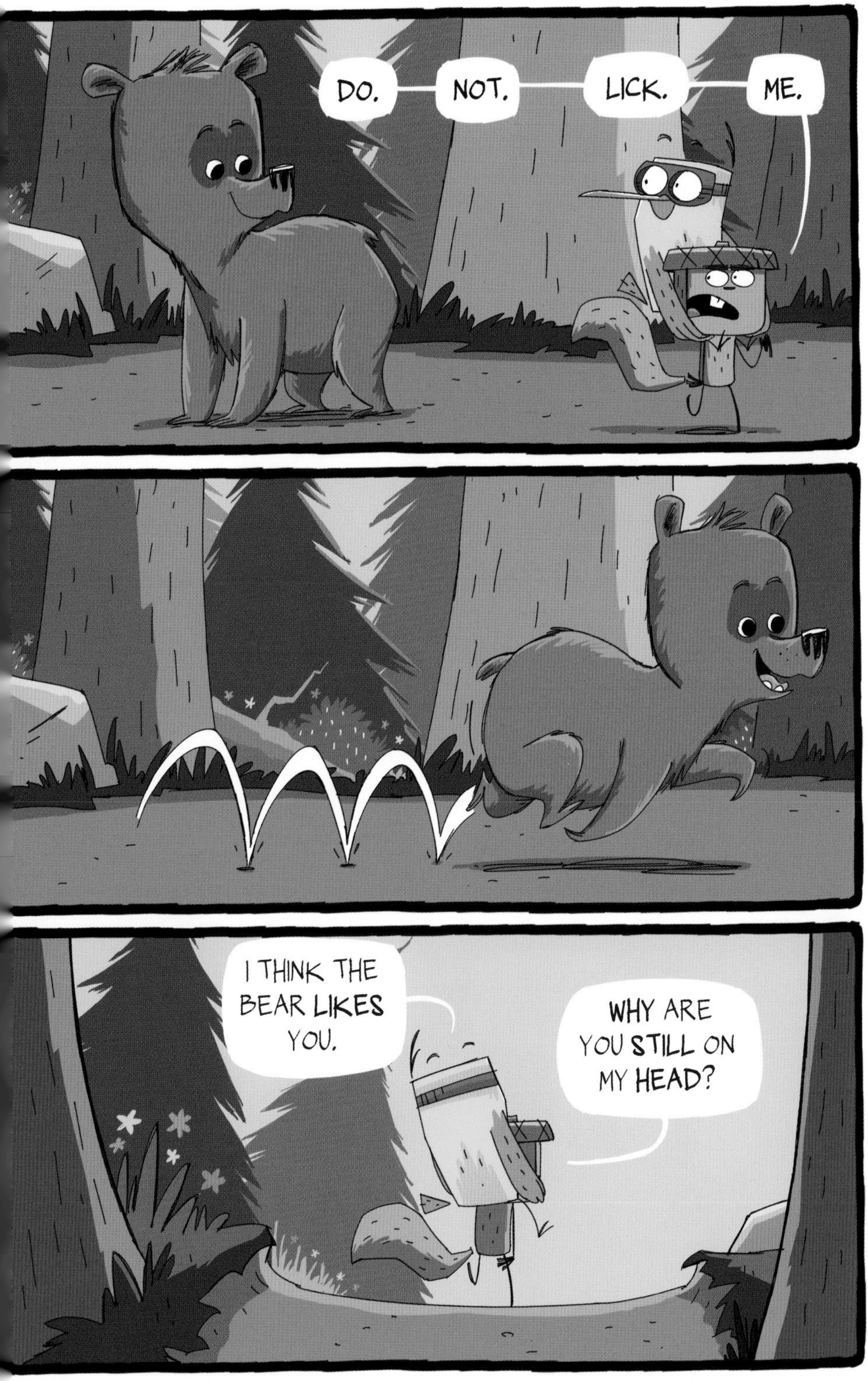
DO.
NOT.
LICK.
ME.
I THINK THE BEAR LIKES YOU.
WHY ARE YOU STILL ON MY HEAD?

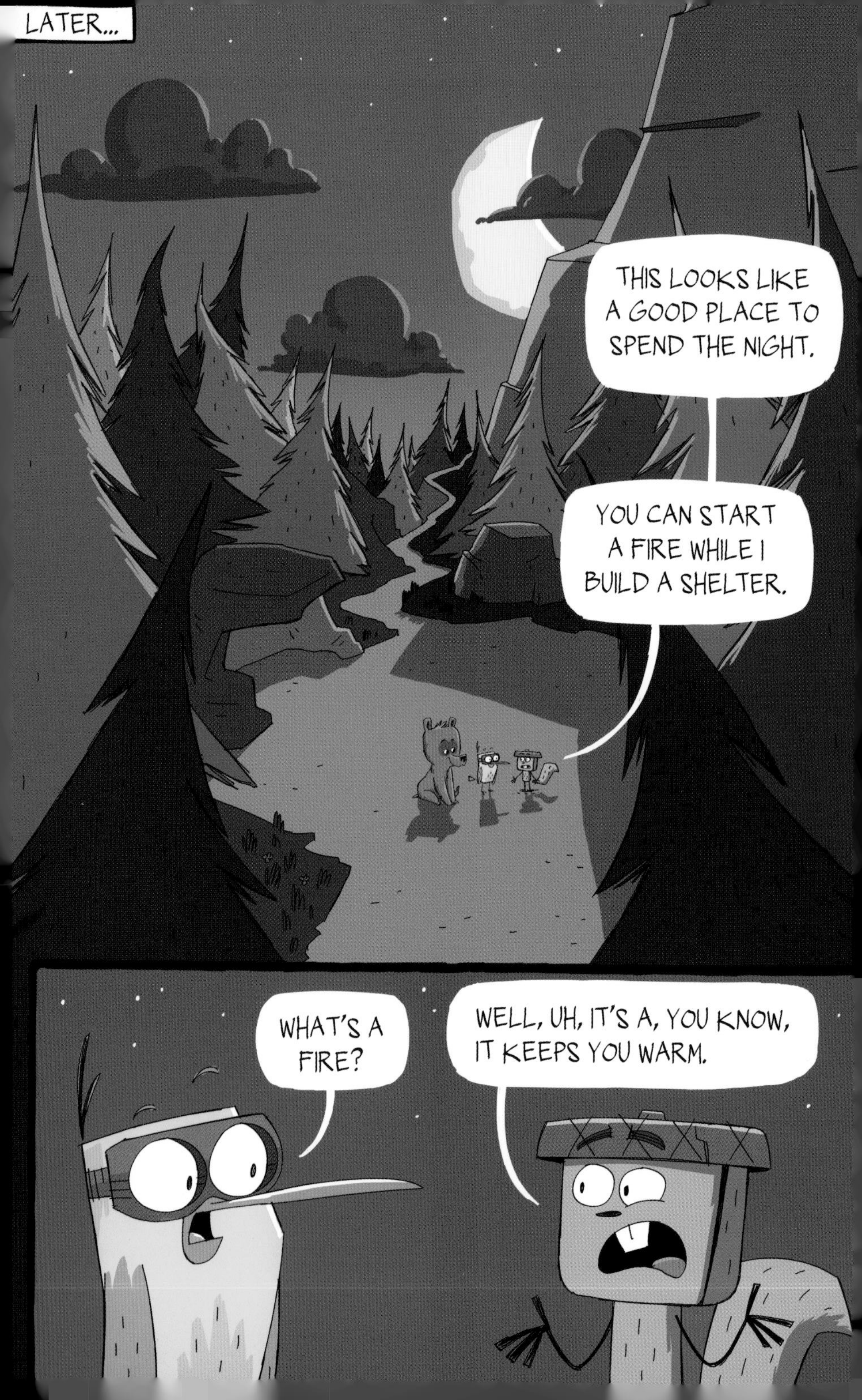
LATER...
THIS LOOKS LIKE A GOOD PLACE TO SPEND THE NIGHT.
YOU CAN START A FIRE WHILE I BUILD A SHELTER.
WHAT'S A FIRE?
WELL, UH, IT'S A, YOU KNOW, IT KEEPS YOU WARM.

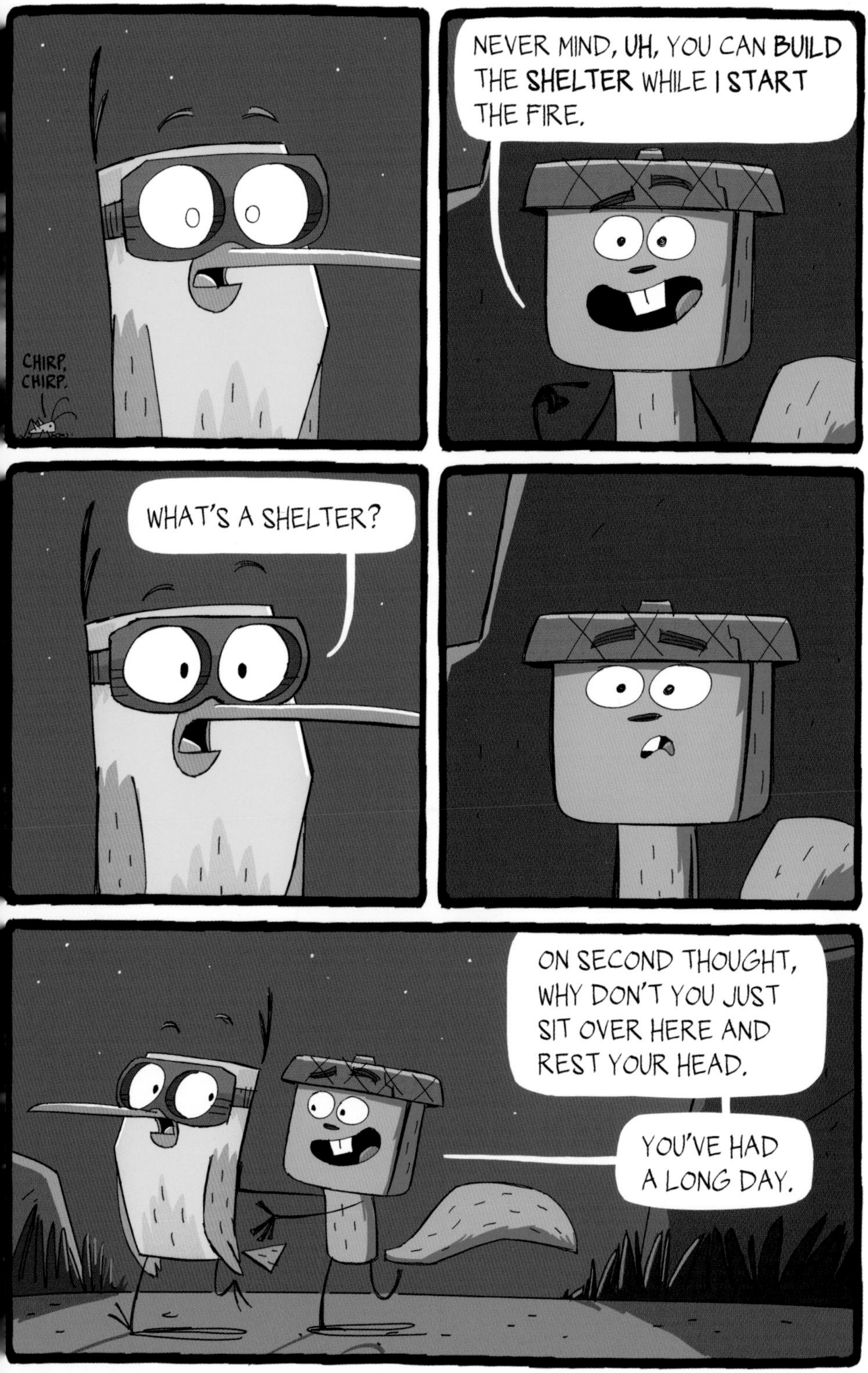
CHIRP. CHIRP.
NEVER MIND, UH, YOU CAN BUILD THE SHELTER WHILE I START THE FIRE.
WHAT'S A SHELTER?
ON SECOND THOUGHT, WHY DON'T YOU JUST SIT OVER HERE AND REST YOUR HEAD.
YOU'VE HAD A LONG DAY.

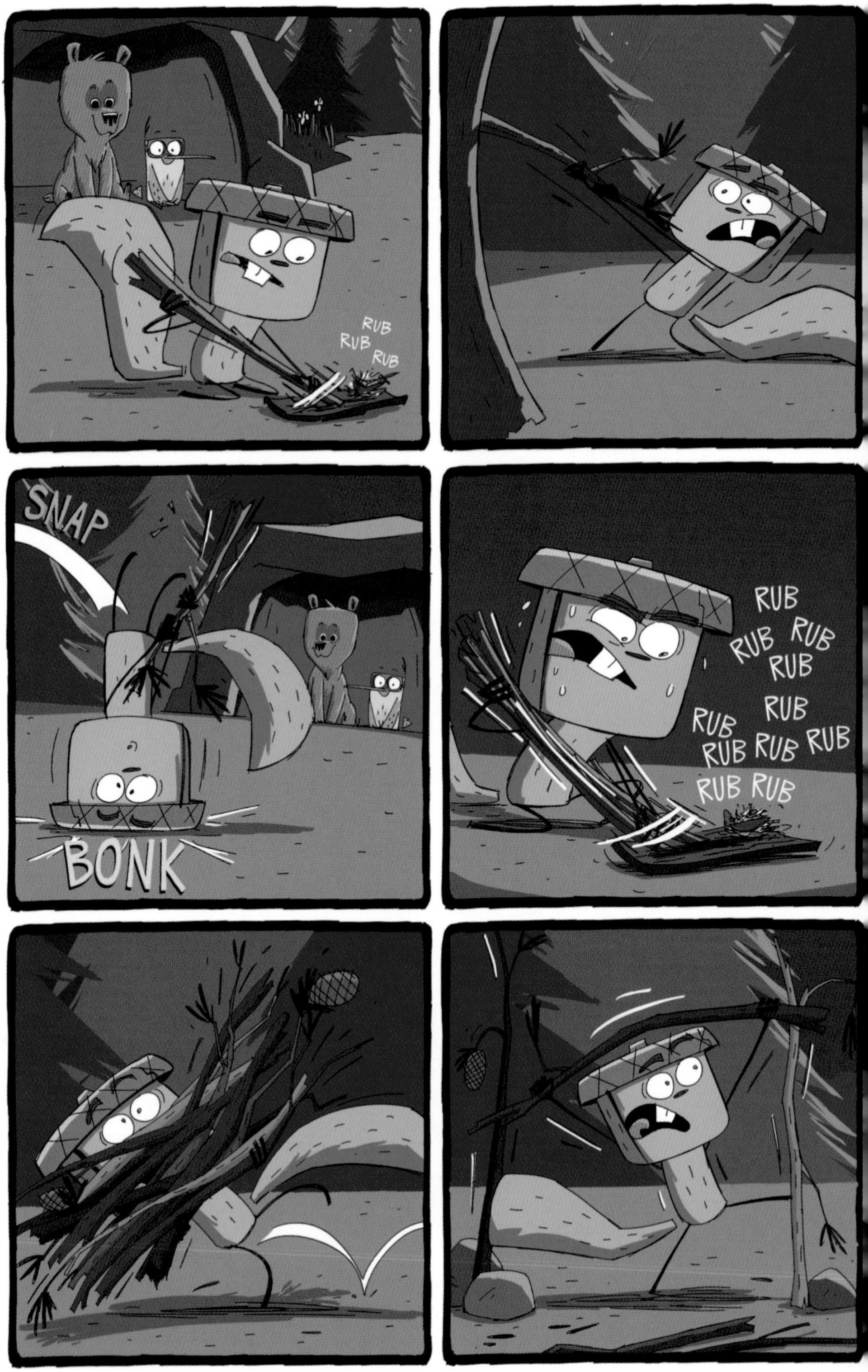
RUB
RUB
RUB
SNAP
BONK
RUB
RUB RUB
RUB
RUB
RUB
RUB RUB RUB
RUB RUB

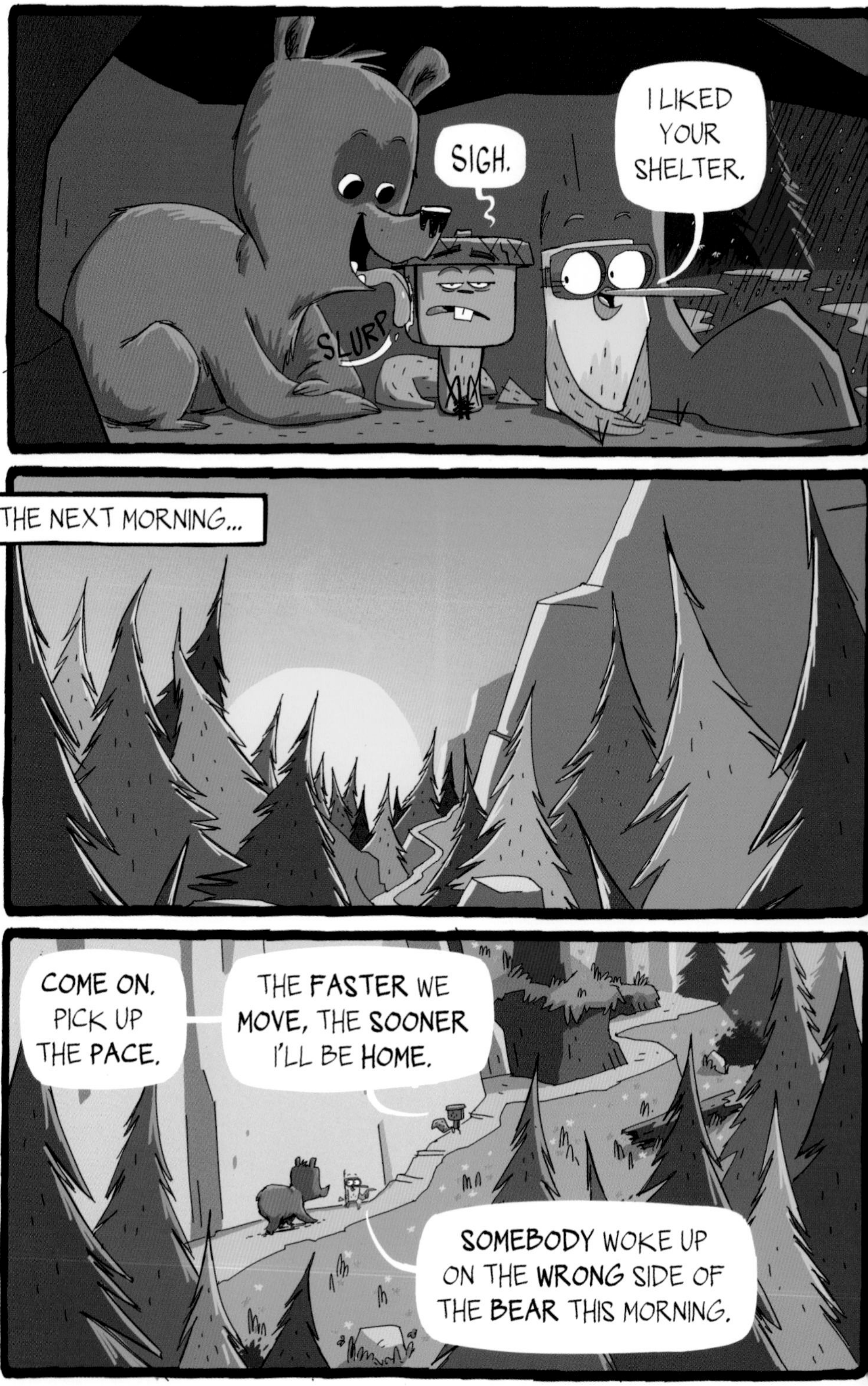

SIGH.
I LIKED YOUR SHELTER.
SLURP
THE NEXT MORNING...
COME ON. PICK UP THE PACE.
THE FASTER WE MOVE, THE SOONER I'LL BE HOME.
SOMEBODY WOKE UP ON THE WRONG SIDE OF THE BEAR THIS MORNING.

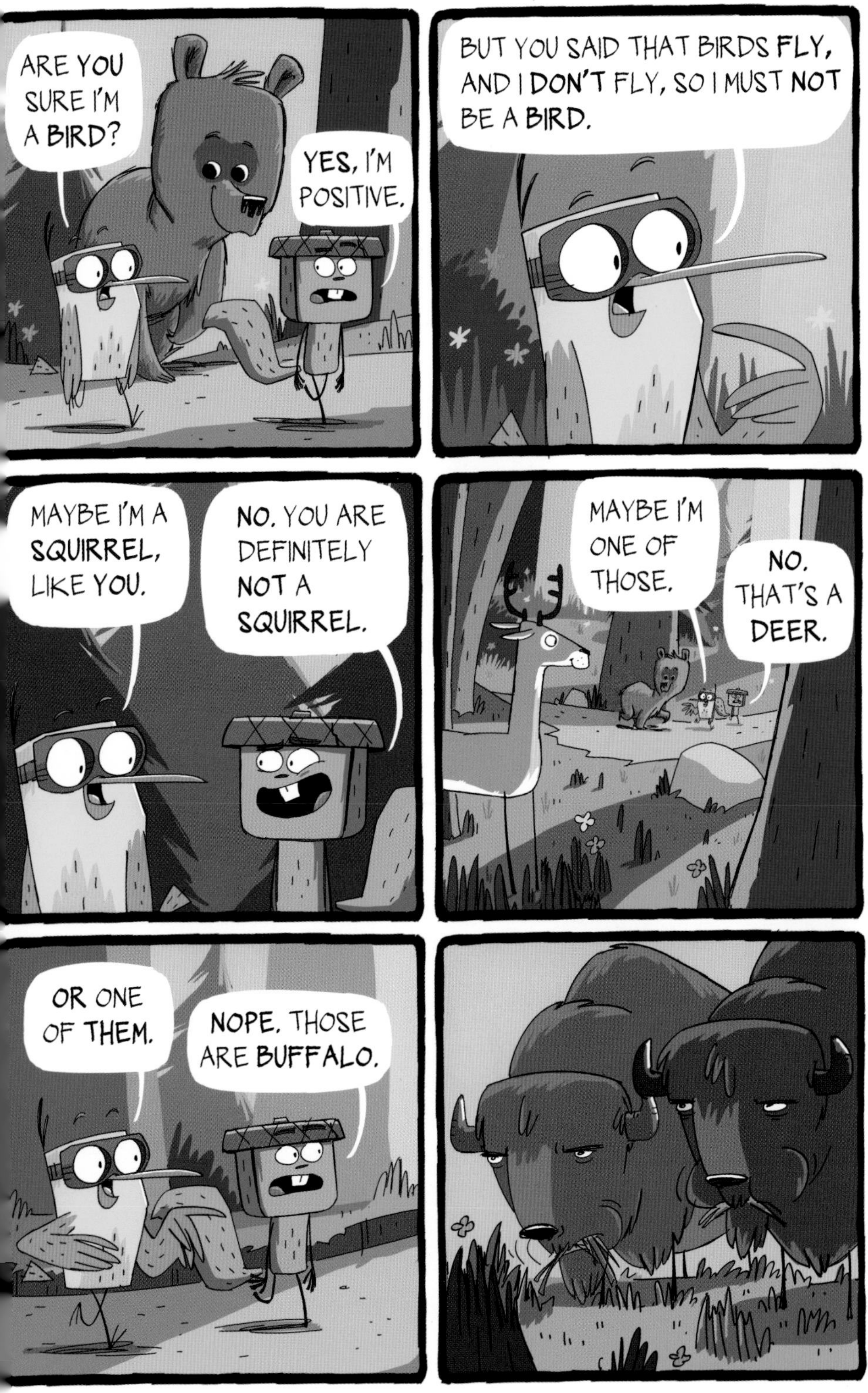
ARE YOU SURE I'M A BIRD?
YES, I'M POSITIVE.
BUT YOU SAID THAT BIRDS FLY, AND I DON'T FLY, SO I MUST NOT BE A BIRD.
MAYBE I'M A SQUIRREL, LIKE YOU.
NO. YOU ARE DEFINITELY NOT A SQUIRREL.
MAYBE I'M ONE OF THOSE.
NO. THAT'S A DEER.
OR ONE OF THEM.
NOPE. THOSE ARE BUFFALO.

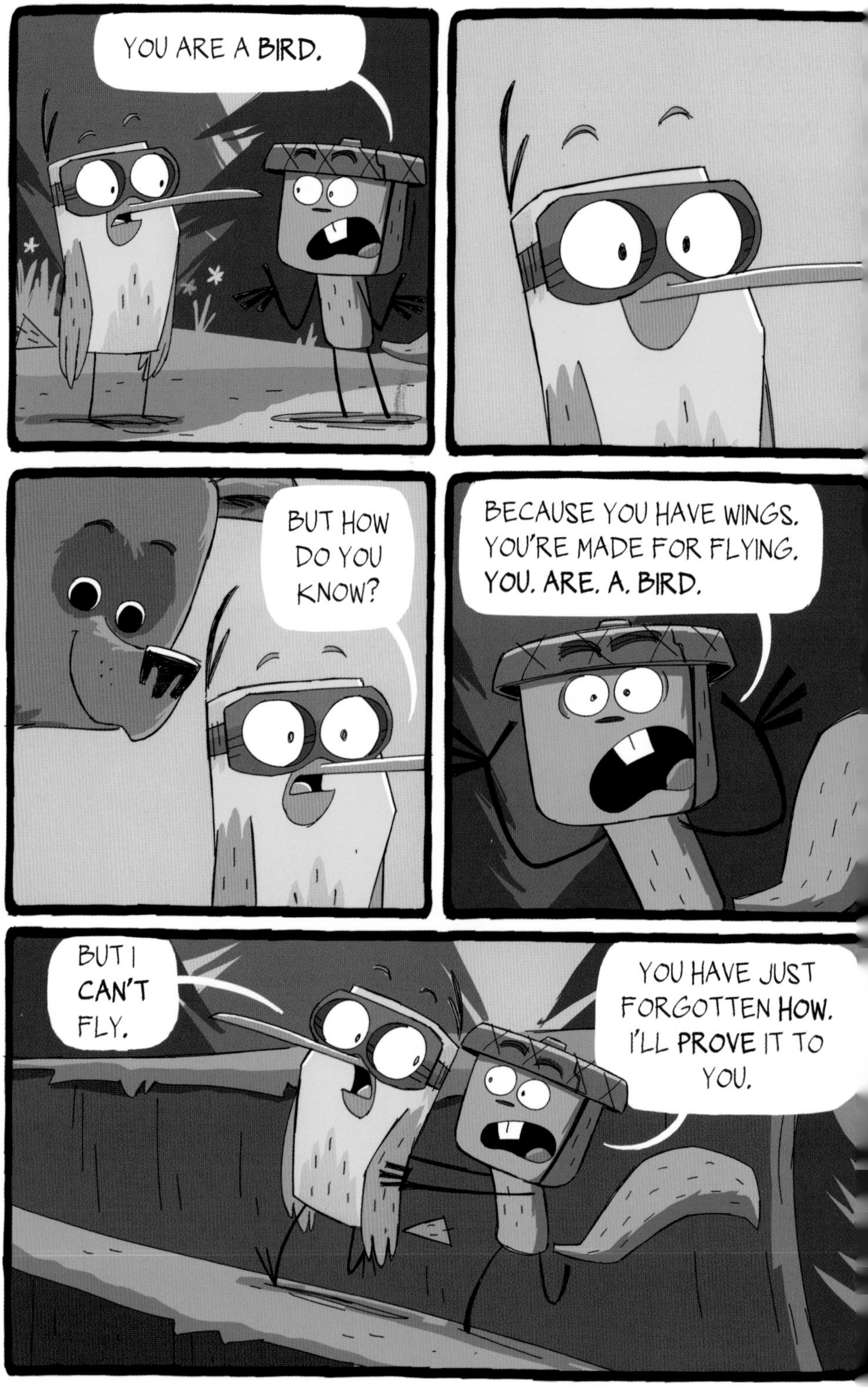
YOU ARE A **BIRD.**
BUT HOW DO YOU KNOW?
BECAUSE YOU HAVE WINGS. YOU'RE MADE FOR FLYING. **YOU. ARE. A. BIRD.**
BUT I **CAN'T** FLY.
YOU HAVE JUST FORGOTTEN **HOW.** I'LL **PROVE** IT TO YOU.

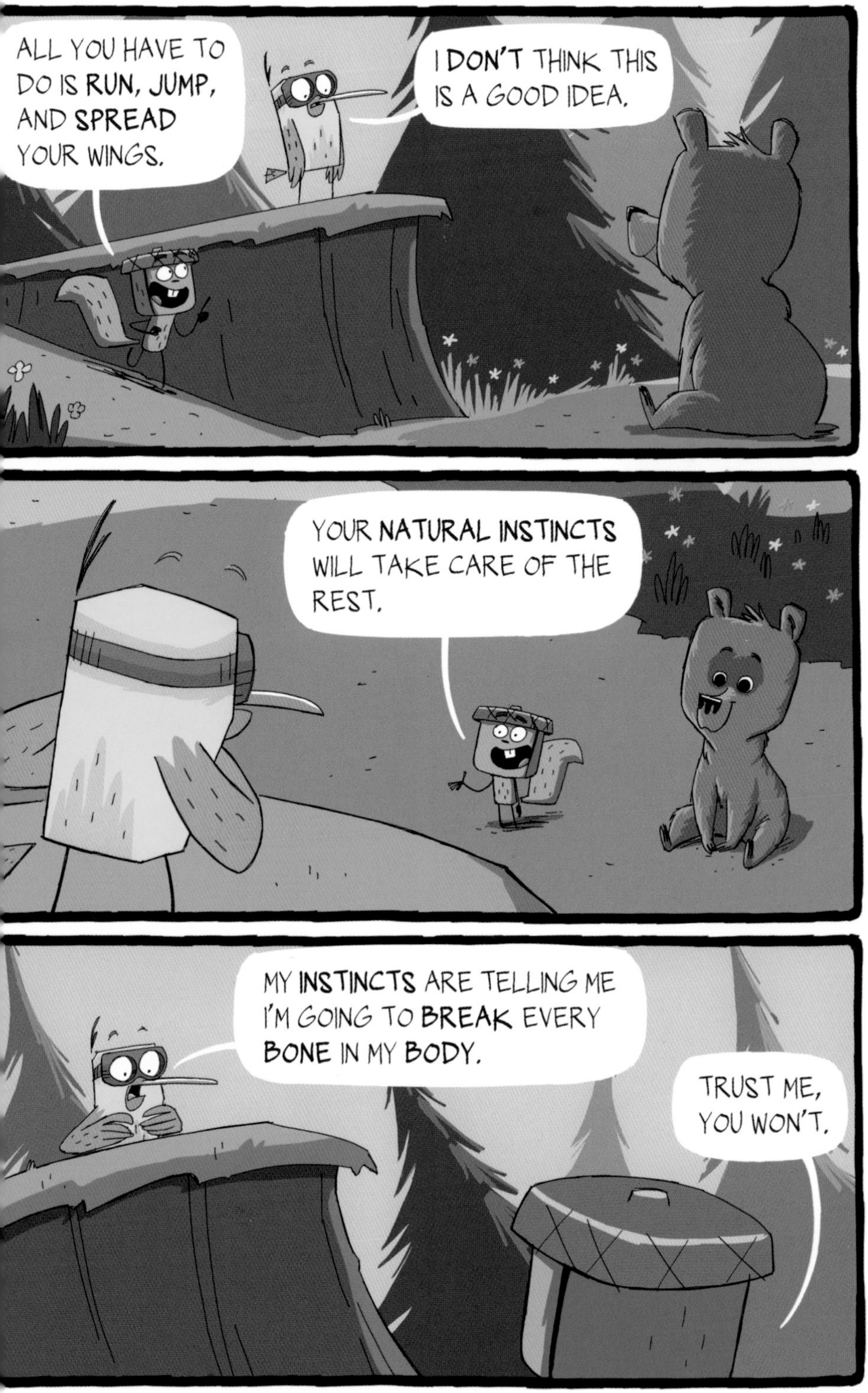
ALL YOU HAVE TO DO IS **RUN, JUMP,** AND **SPREAD** YOUR WINGS.
I **DON'T** THINK THIS IS A GOOD IDEA.
YOUR **NATURAL INSTINCTS** WILL TAKE CARE OF THE REST.
MY **INSTINCTS** ARE TELLING ME I'M GOING TO **BREAK** EVERY **BONE** IN MY **BODY**.
TRUST ME, YOU WON'T.

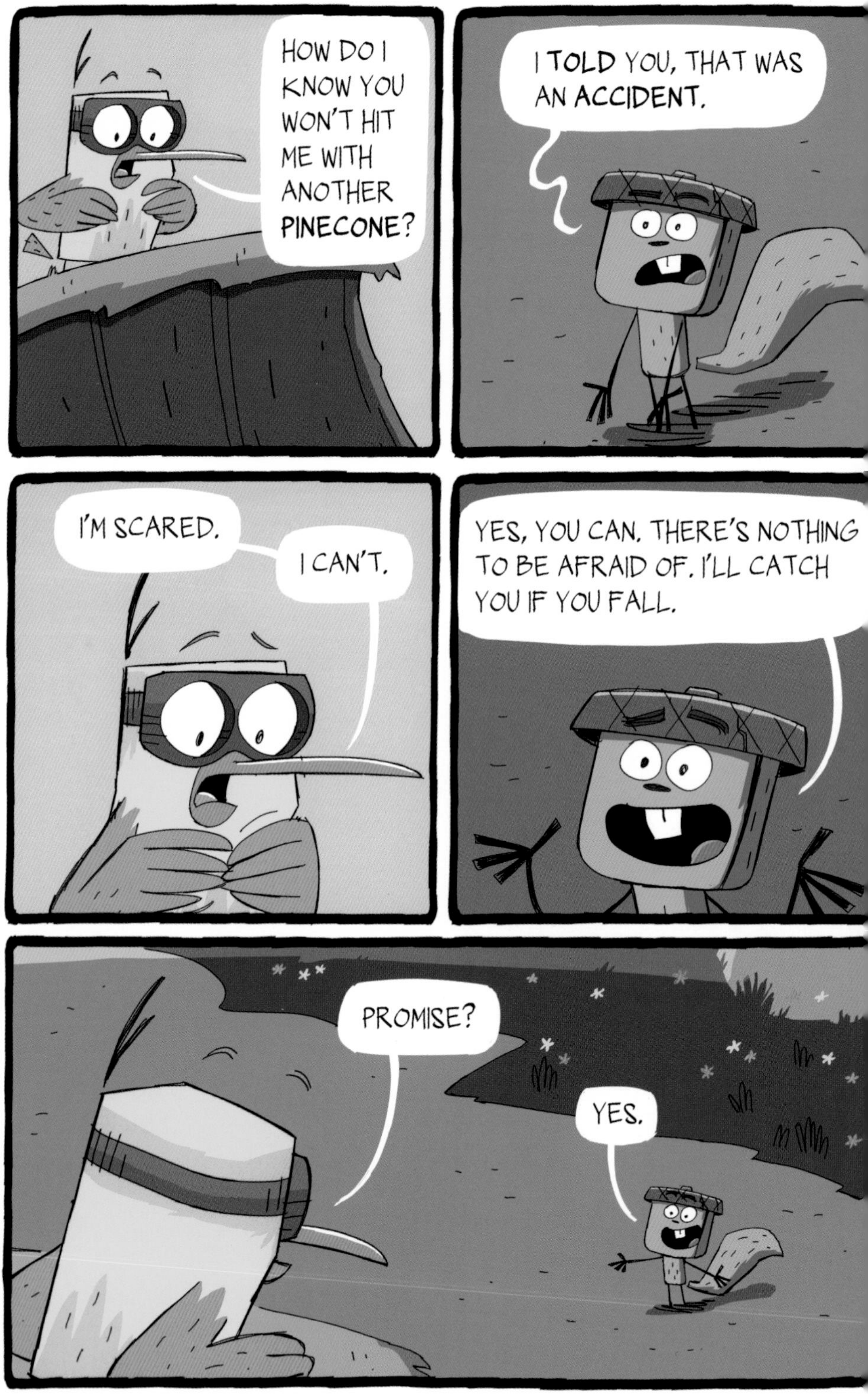
HOW DO I KNOW YOU WON'T HIT ME WITH ANOTHER PINECONE?
I TOLD YOU, THAT WAS AN ACCIDENT.
I'M SCARED.
I CAN'T.
YES, YOU CAN. THERE'S NOTHING TO BE AFRAID OF. I'LL CATCH YOU IF YOU FALL.
PROMISE?
YES.

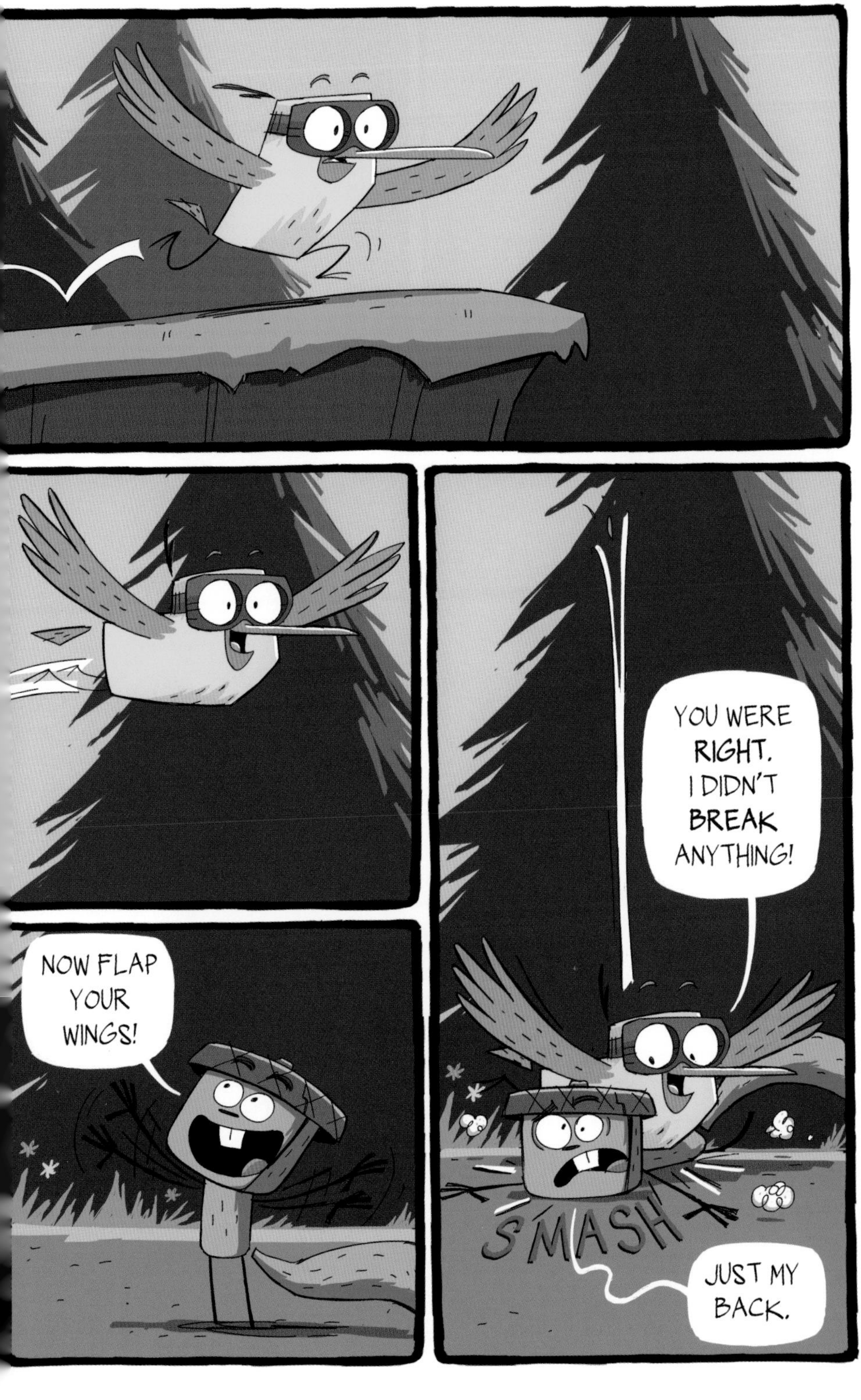
NOW FLAP YOUR WINGS!
YOU WERE RIGHT. I DIDN'T BREAK ANYTHING!
SMASH
JUST MY BACK.

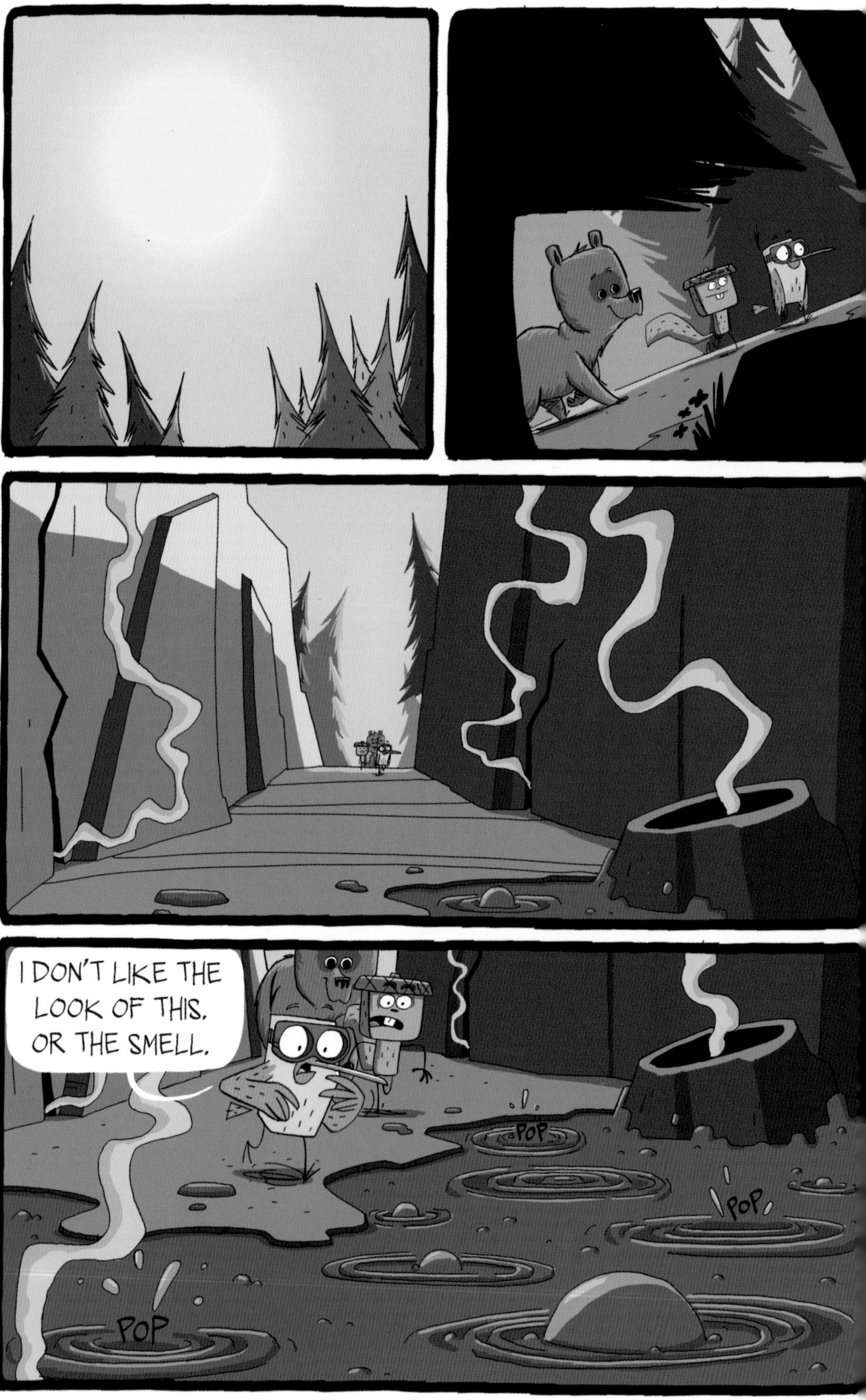
I DON'T LIKE THE LOOK OF THIS. OR THE SMELL.
POP
POP
POP

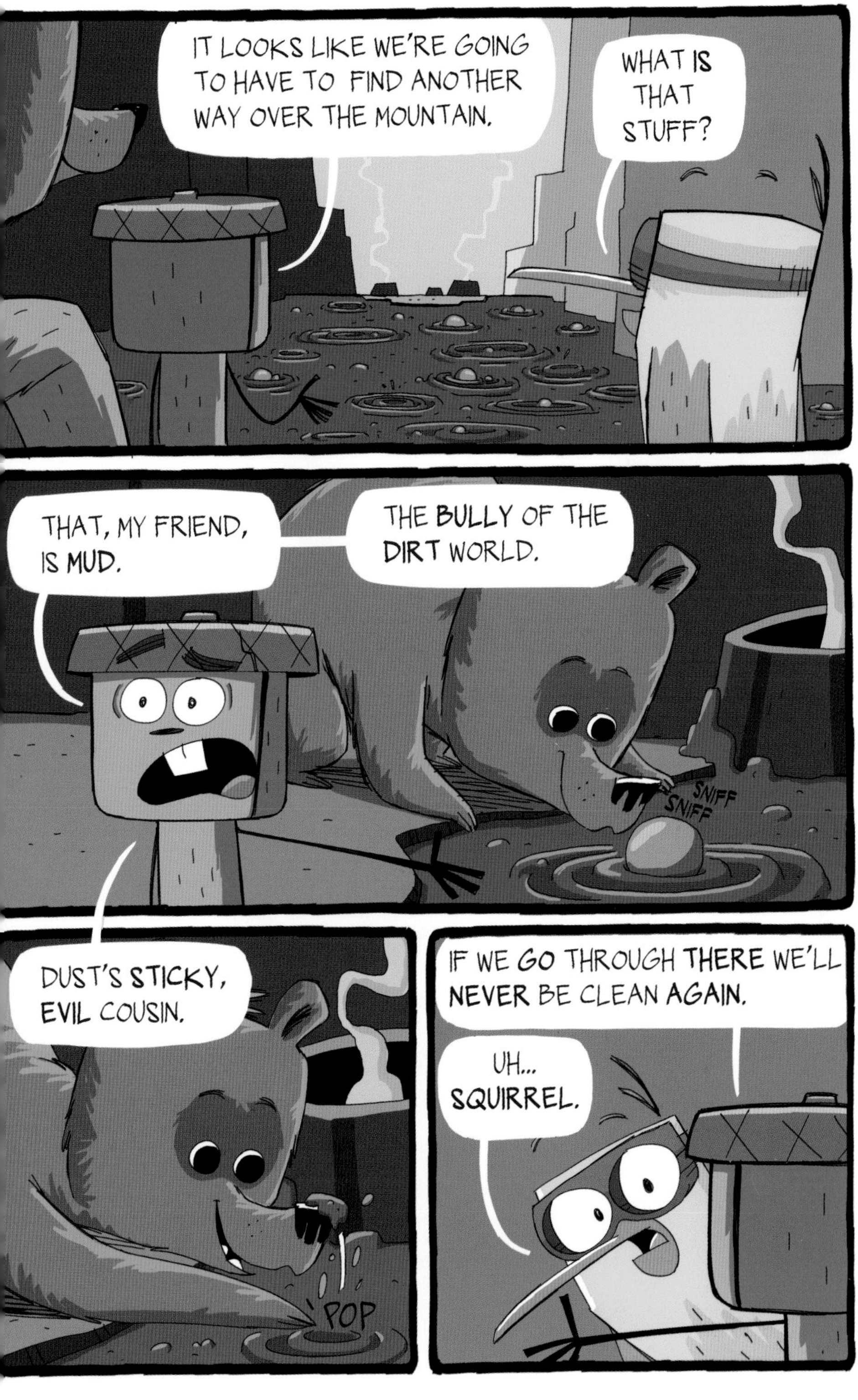
IT LOOKS LIKE WE'RE GOING TO HAVE TO FIND ANOTHER WAY OVER THE MOUNTAIN.
WHAT IS THAT STUFF?
THAT, MY FRIEND, IS MUD.
THE BULLY OF THE DIRT WORLD.
SNIFF SNIFF
DUST'S STICKY, EVIL COUSIN.
POP
IF WE GO THROUGH THERE WE'LL NEVER BE CLEAN AGAIN.
UH... SQUIRREL.

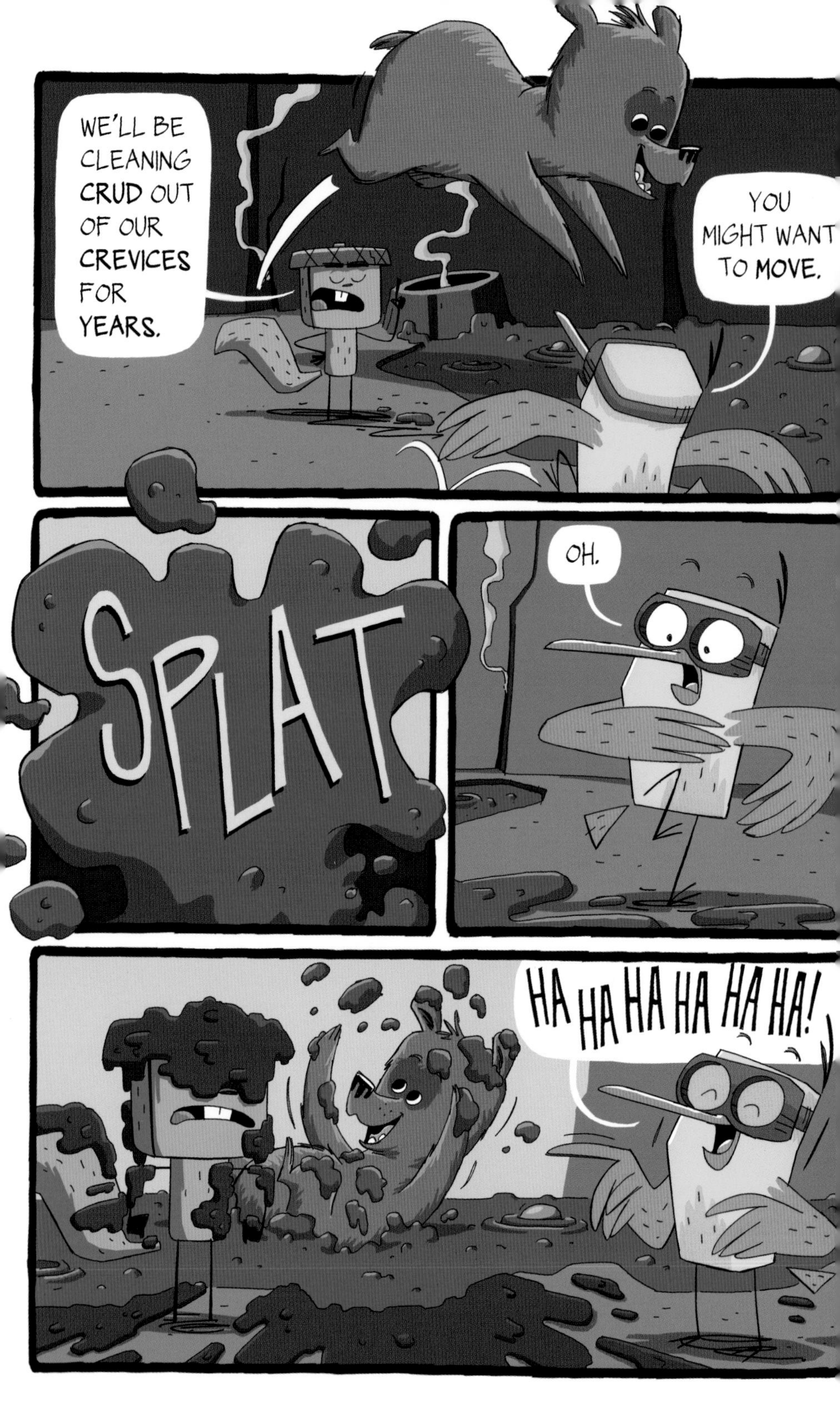
WE'LL BE CLEANING CRUD OUT OF OUR CREVICES FOR YEARS.
YOU MIGHT WANT TO MOVE.
SPLAT
OH.
HA HA HA HA HA HA!

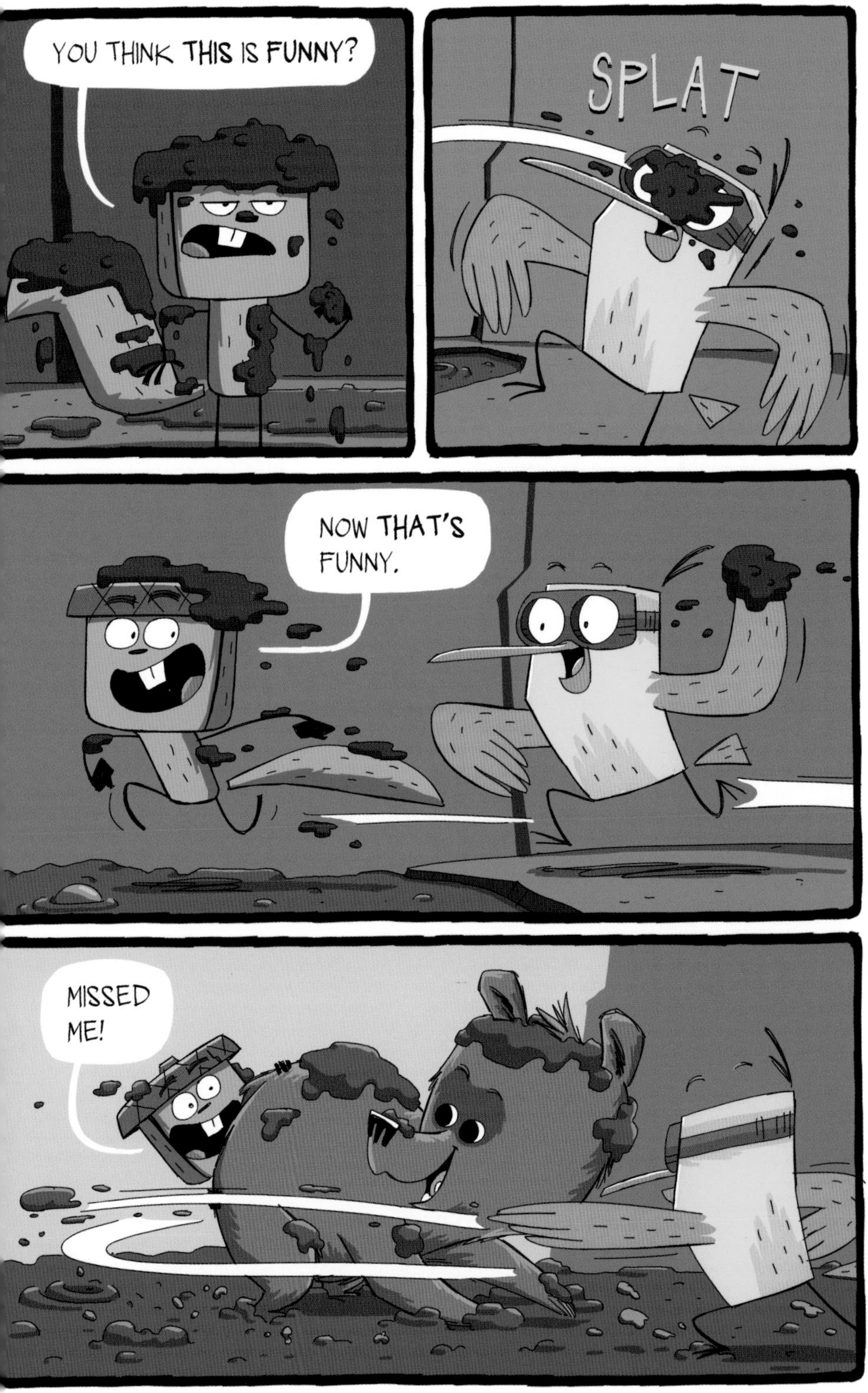
YOU THINK THIS IS FUNNY?
SPLAT
NOW THAT'S FUNNY.
MISSED ME!

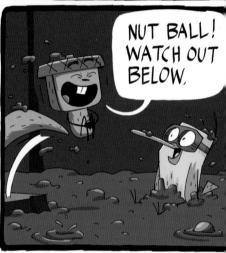

NUT BALL! WATCH OUT BELOW.

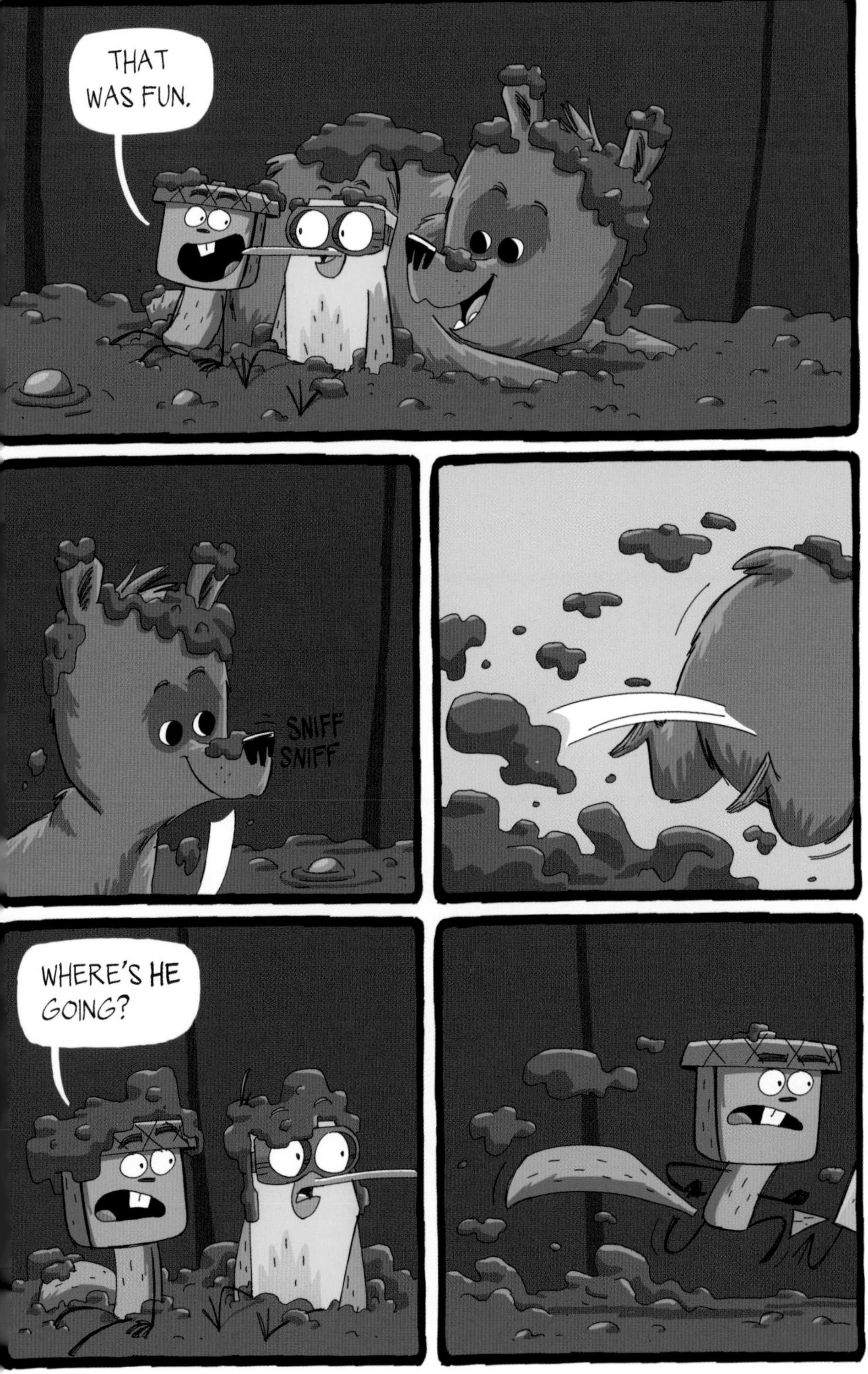
THAT WAS FUN.
SNIFF SNIFF
WHERE'S HE GOING?

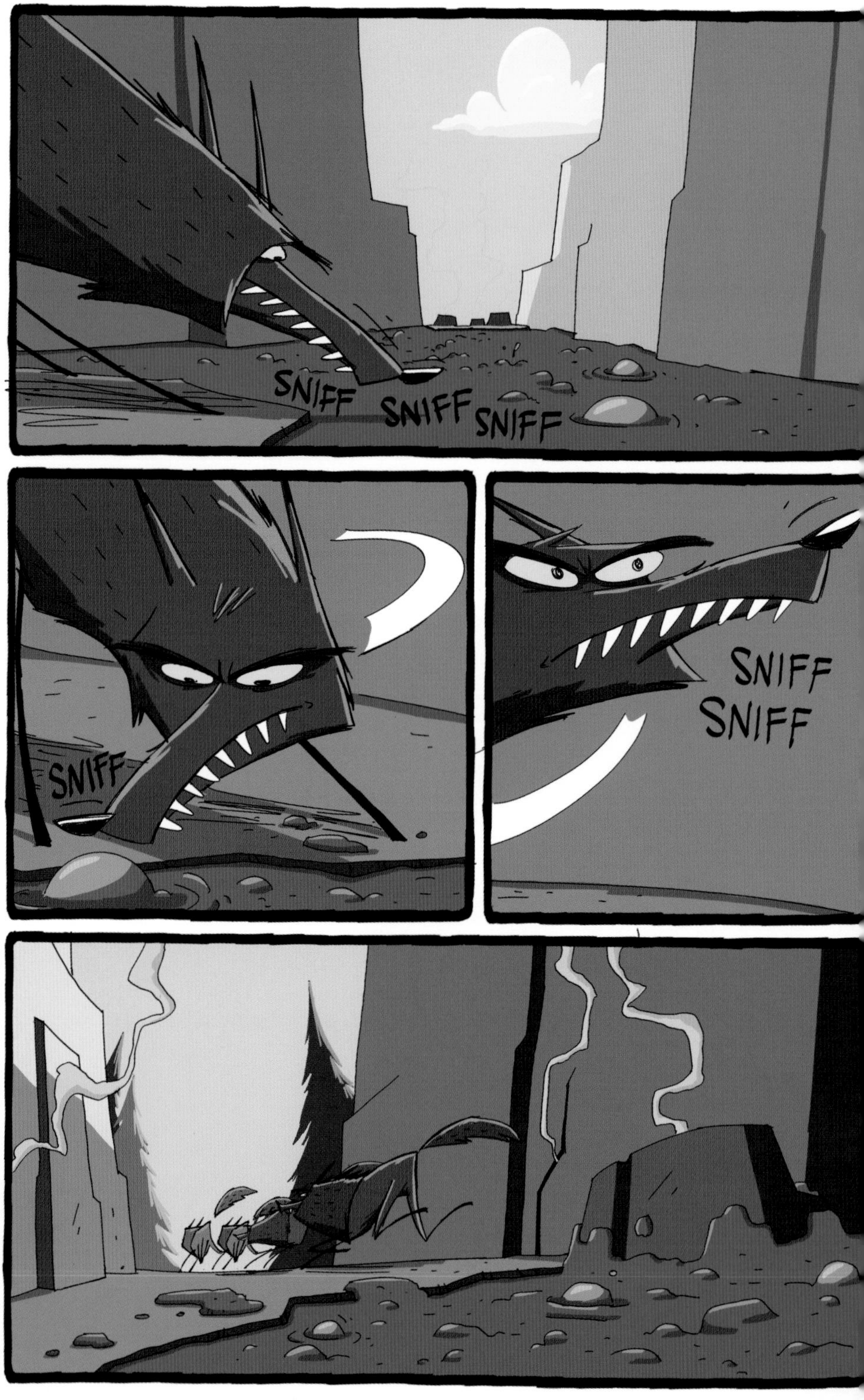
SNIFF
SNIFF
SNIFF
SNIFF
SNIFF
SNIFF

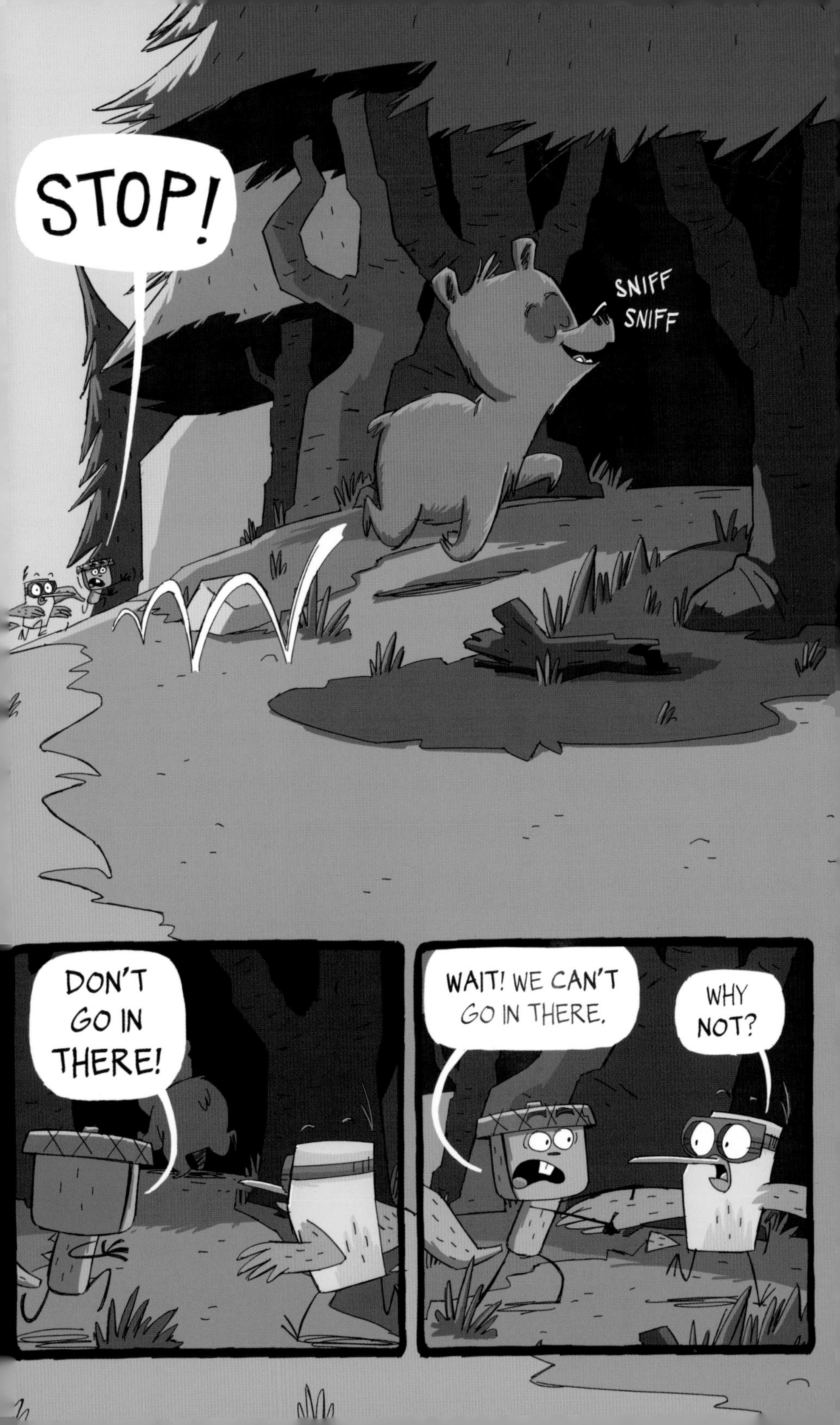
STOP!
SNIFF
SNIFF
DON'T GO IN THERE!
WAIT! WE CAN'T GO IN THERE.
WHY NOT?

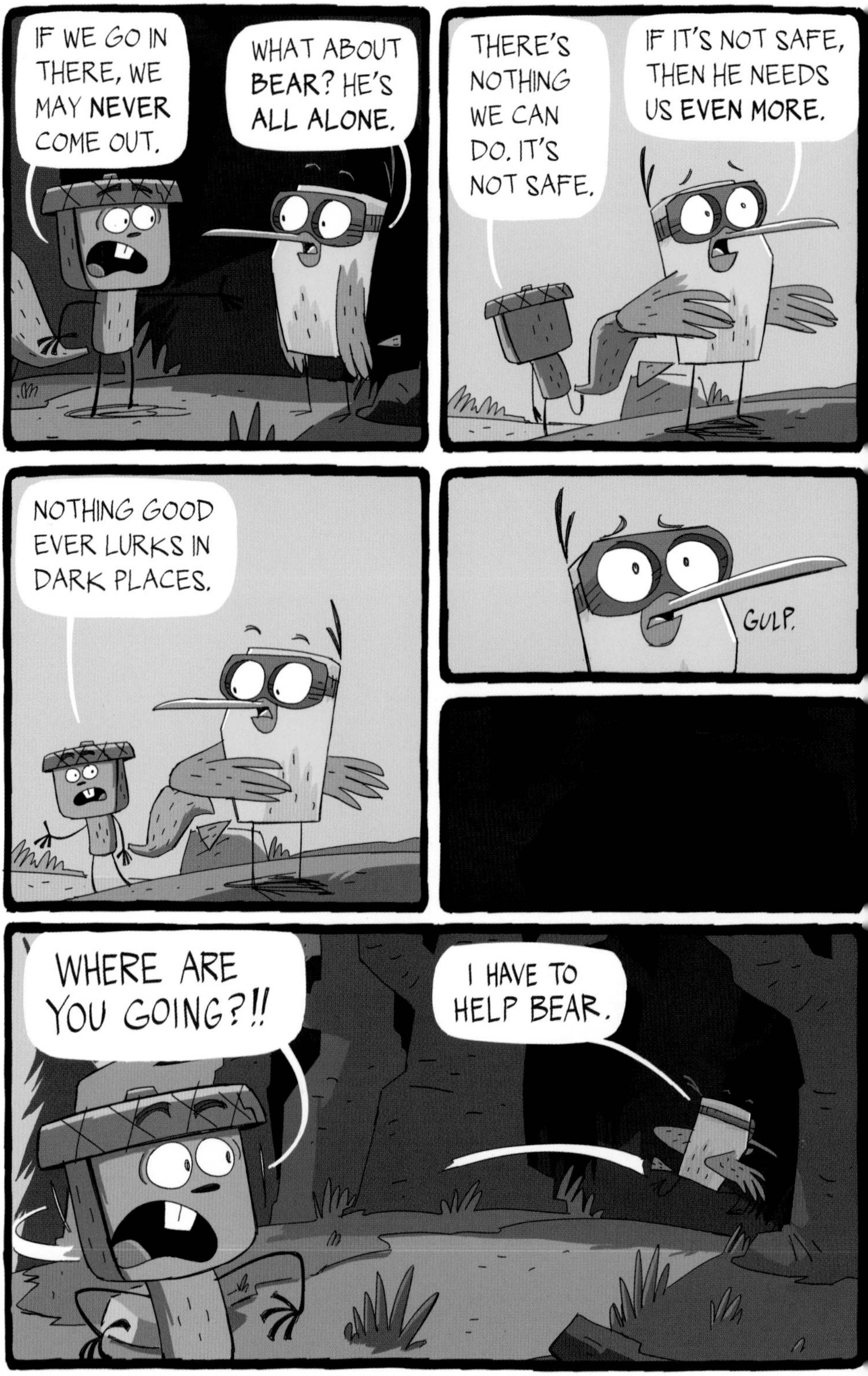
IF WE GO IN THERE, WE MAY NEVER COME OUT.
WHAT ABOUT BEAR? HE'S ALL ALONE.
THERE'S NOTHING WE CAN DO. IT'S NOT SAFE.
IF IT'S NOT SAFE, THEN HE NEEDS US EVEN MORE.
NOTHING GOOD EVER LURKS IN DARK PLACES.
GULP.
WHERE ARE YOU GOING?!!
I HAVE TO HELP BEAR.

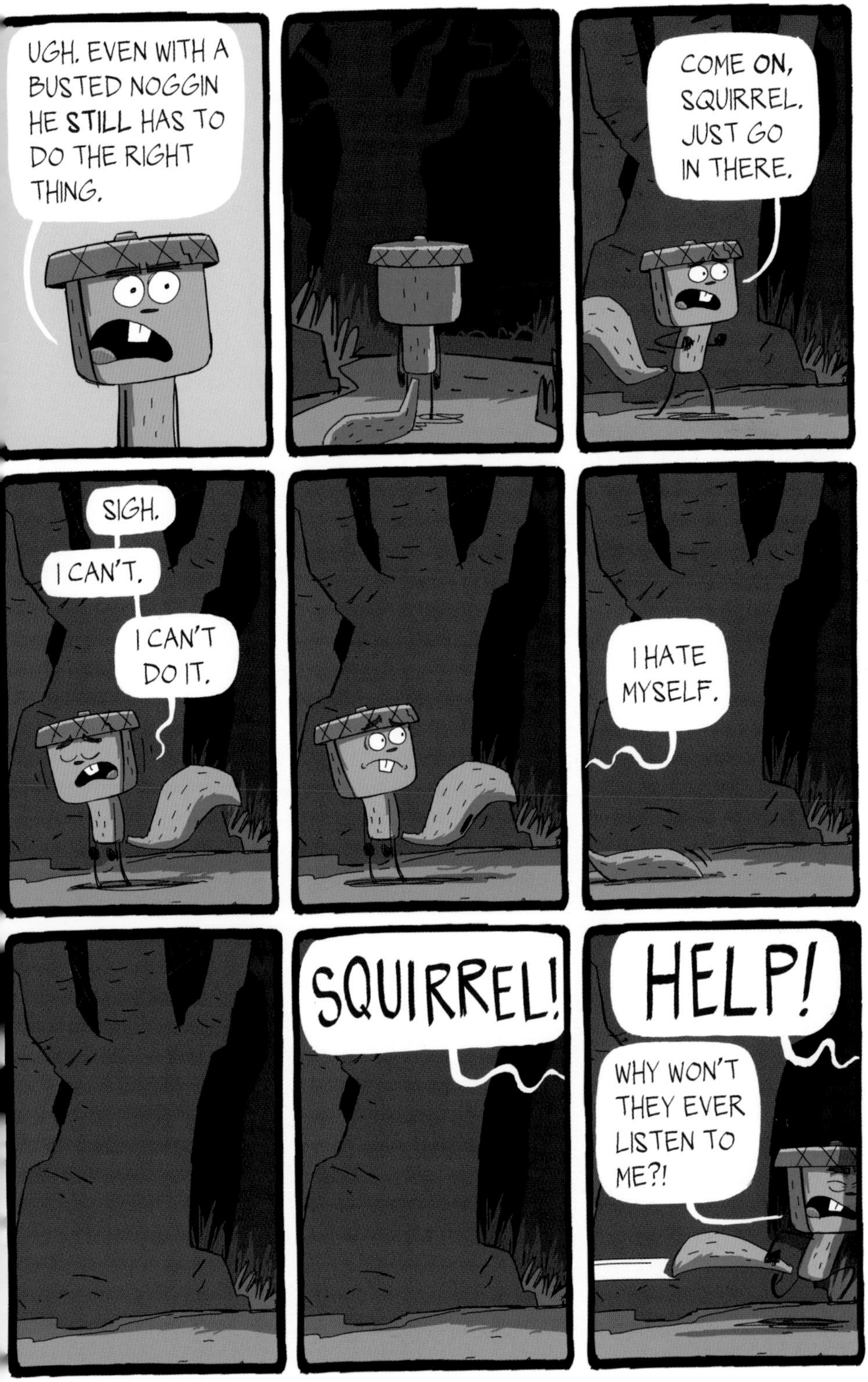
UGH. EVEN WITH A BUSTED NOGGIN HE STILL HAS TO DO THE RIGHT THING.
COME ON, SQUIRREL. JUST GO IN THERE.
SIGH.
I CAN'T.
I CAN'T DO IT.
I HATE MYSELF.
SQUIRREL!
HELP!
WHY WON'T THEY EVER LISTEN TO ME?!

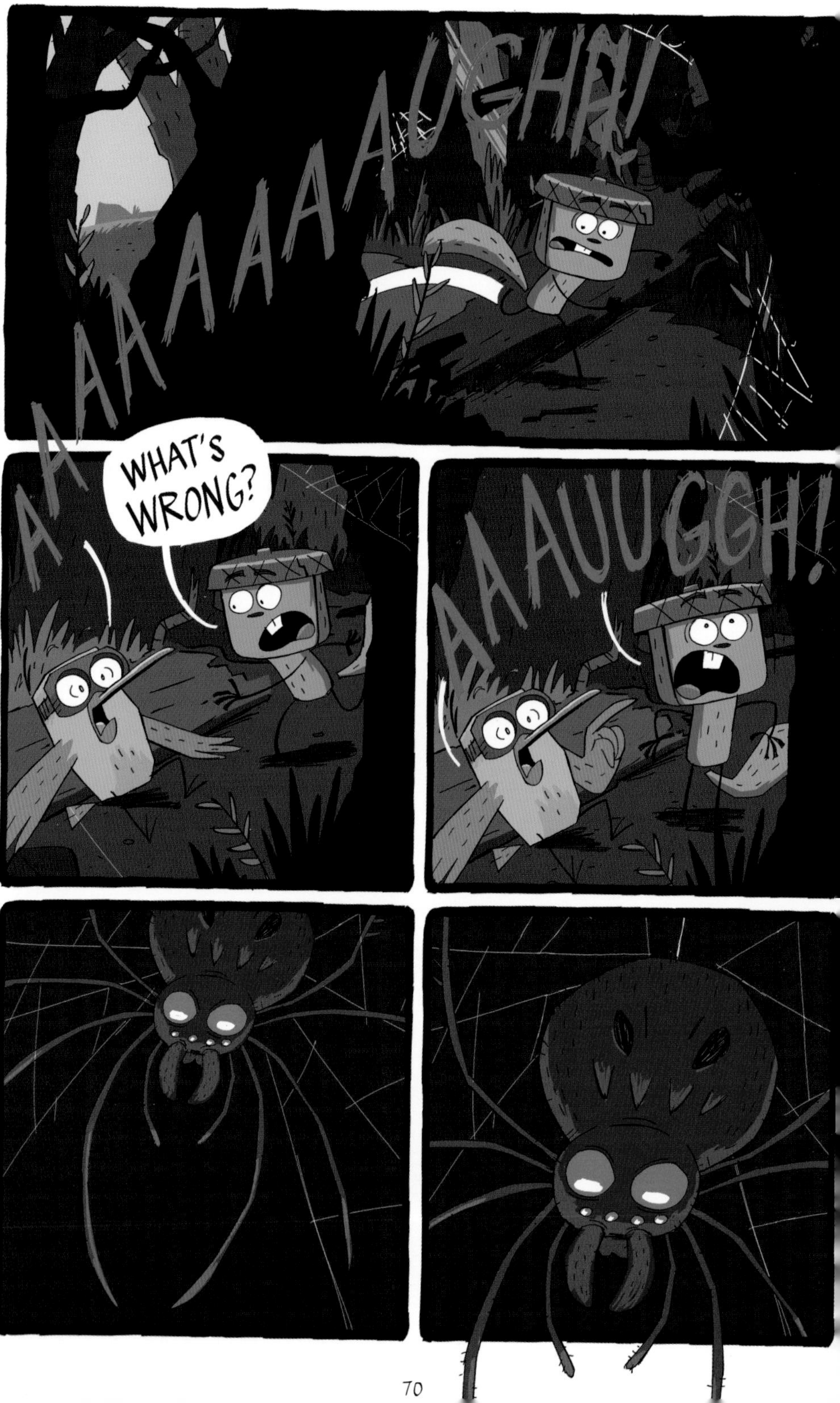
AAAAAAAAAUGHH!
WHAT'S WRONG?
AAAUUGGH!

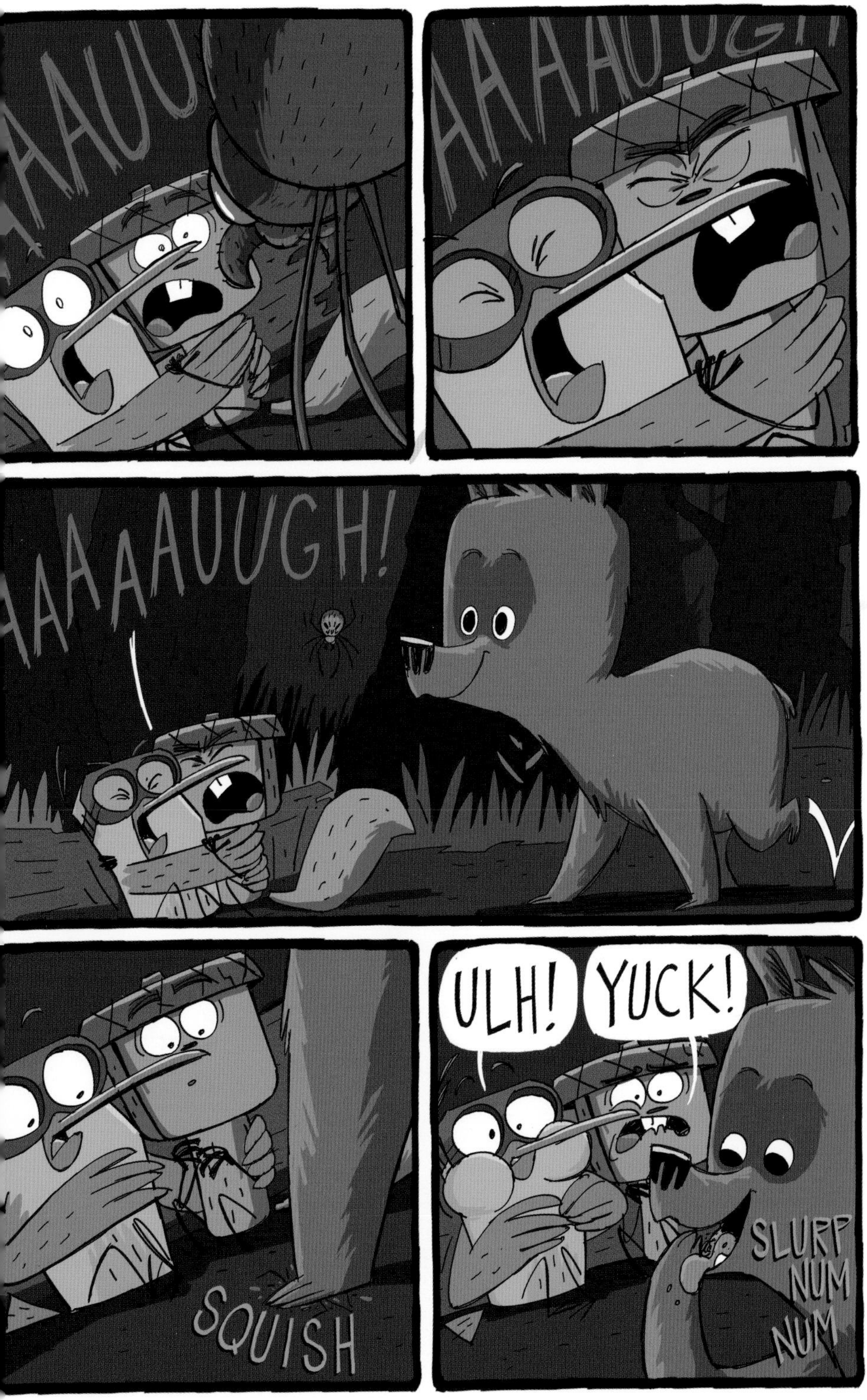
AAUU
AAAAUUGH
AAAAAUUGH!
SQUISH
ULH!
YUCK!
SLURP
NUM
NUM

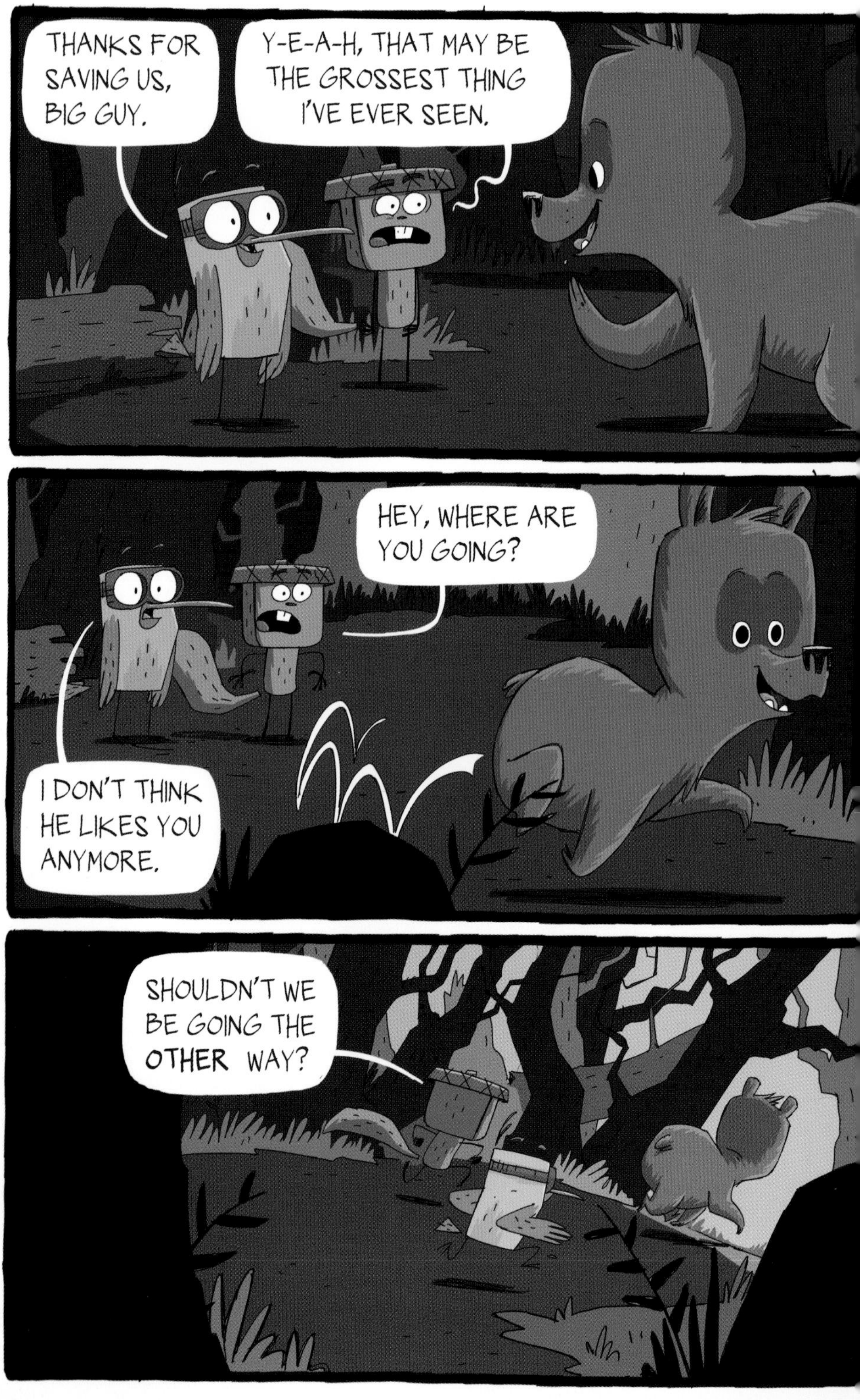
THANKS FOR SAVING US, BIG GUY.
Y-E-A-H, THAT MAY BE THE GROSSEST THING I'VE EVER SEEN.
HEY, WHERE ARE YOU GOING?
I DON'T THINK HE LIKES YOU ANYMORE.
SHOULDN'T WE BE GOING THE OTHER WAY?

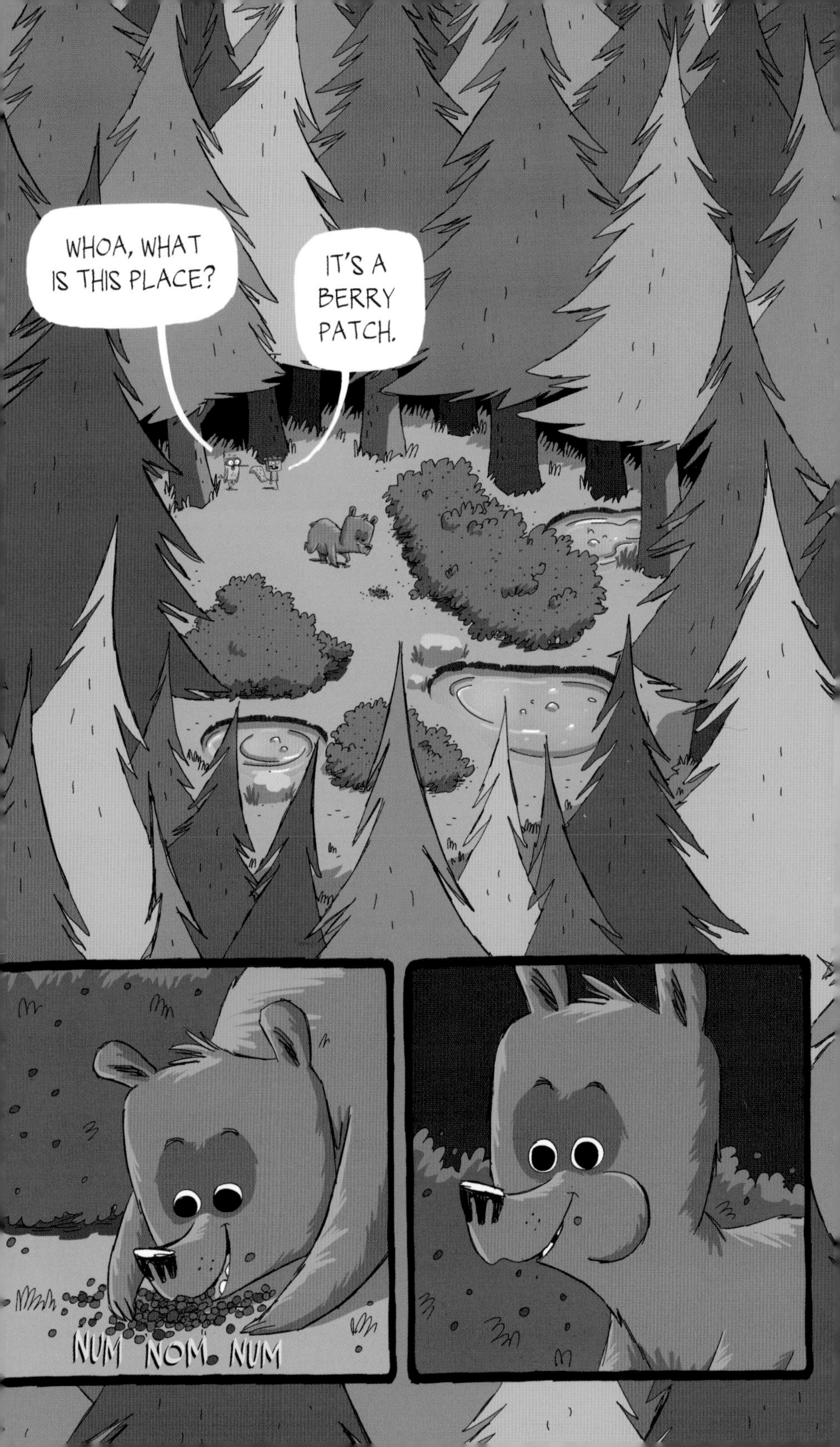
WHOA, WHAT IS THIS PLACE?
IT'S A BERRY PATCH.
NUM NOM NUM

HOW DID YOU KNOW THESE WERE IN HERE?

SNIFF SNIFF

WOW, THAT'S ONE IMPRESSIVE SENSE OF SMELL.

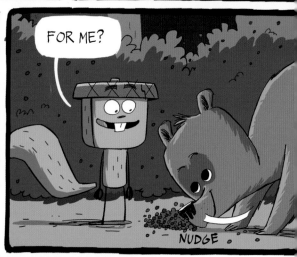
FOR ME?

NUDGE

THANKS.

NUM...YUM... MMM...YUM... NUM...NUM.

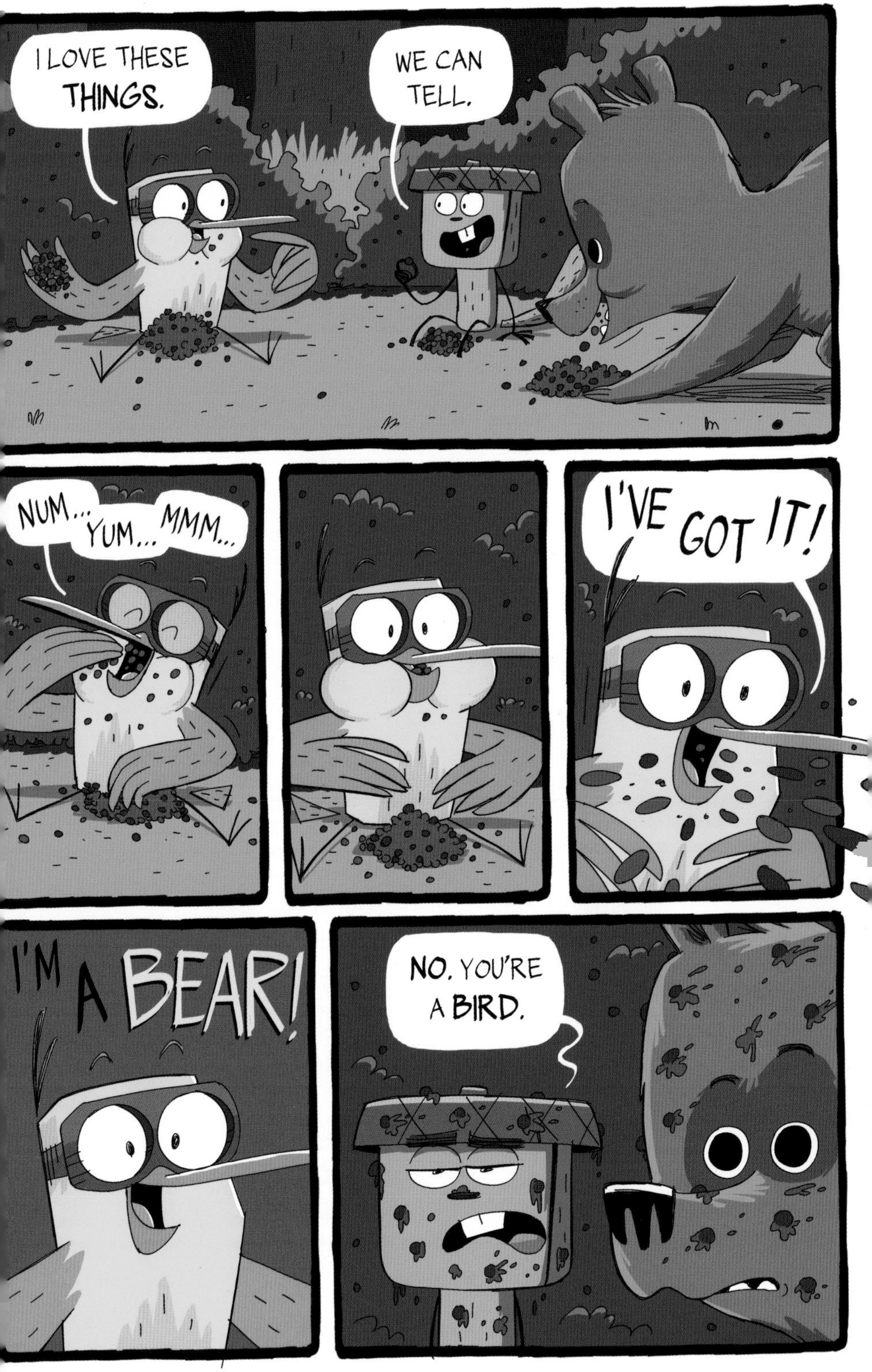
I LOVE THESE THINGS.
WE CAN TELL.
NUM... YUM... MMM...
I'VE GOT IT!
I'M A BEAR!
NO. YOU'RE A BIRD.

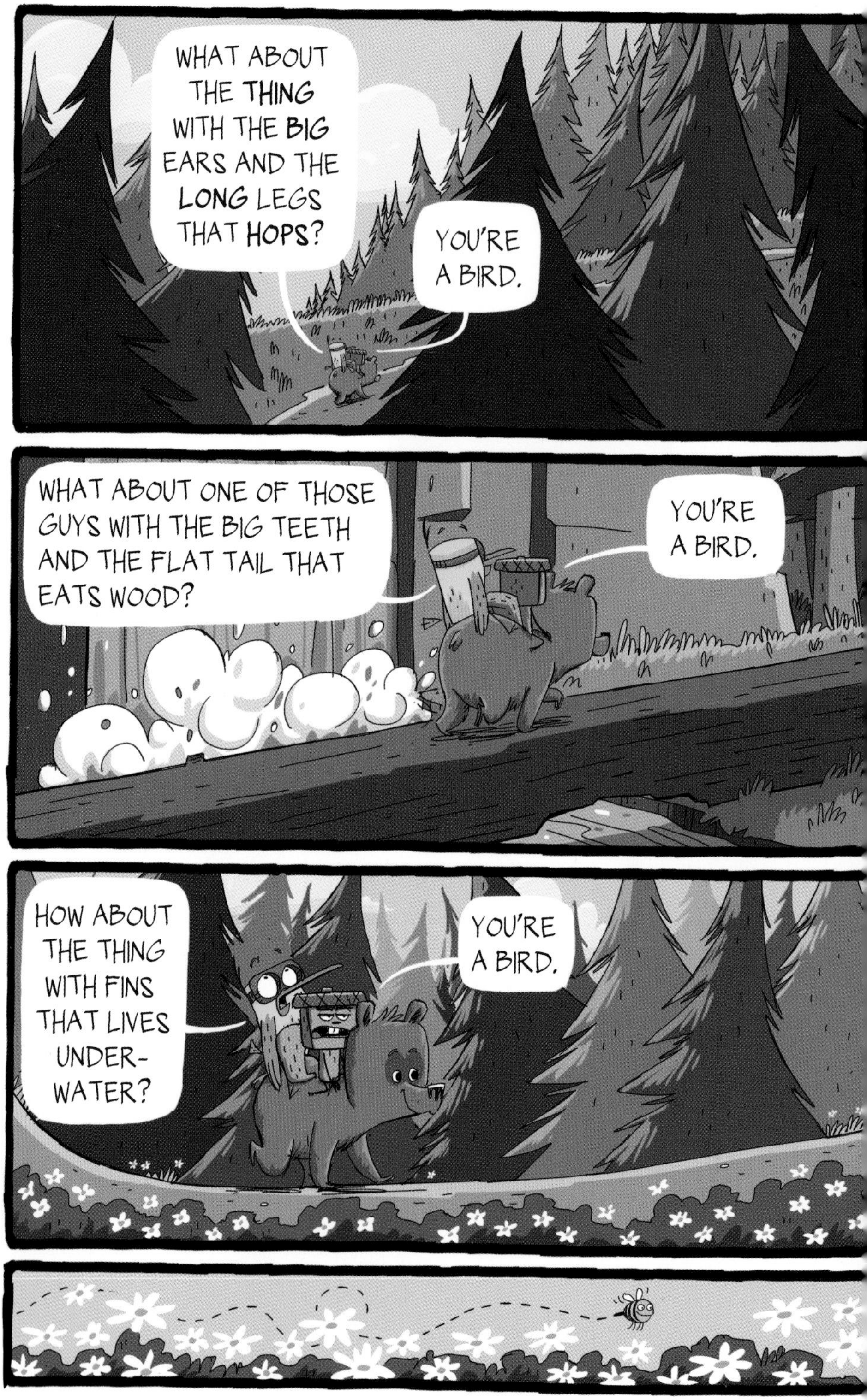
WHAT ABOUT THE **THING** WITH THE **BIG** EARS AND THE **LONG** LEGS THAT **HOPS**?
YOU'RE A BIRD.
WHAT ABOUT ONE OF THOSE GUYS WITH THE BIG TEETH AND THE FLAT TAIL THAT EATS WOOD?
YOU'RE A BIRD.
HOW ABOUT THE THING WITH FINS THAT LIVES UNDER-WATER?
YOU'RE A BIRD.

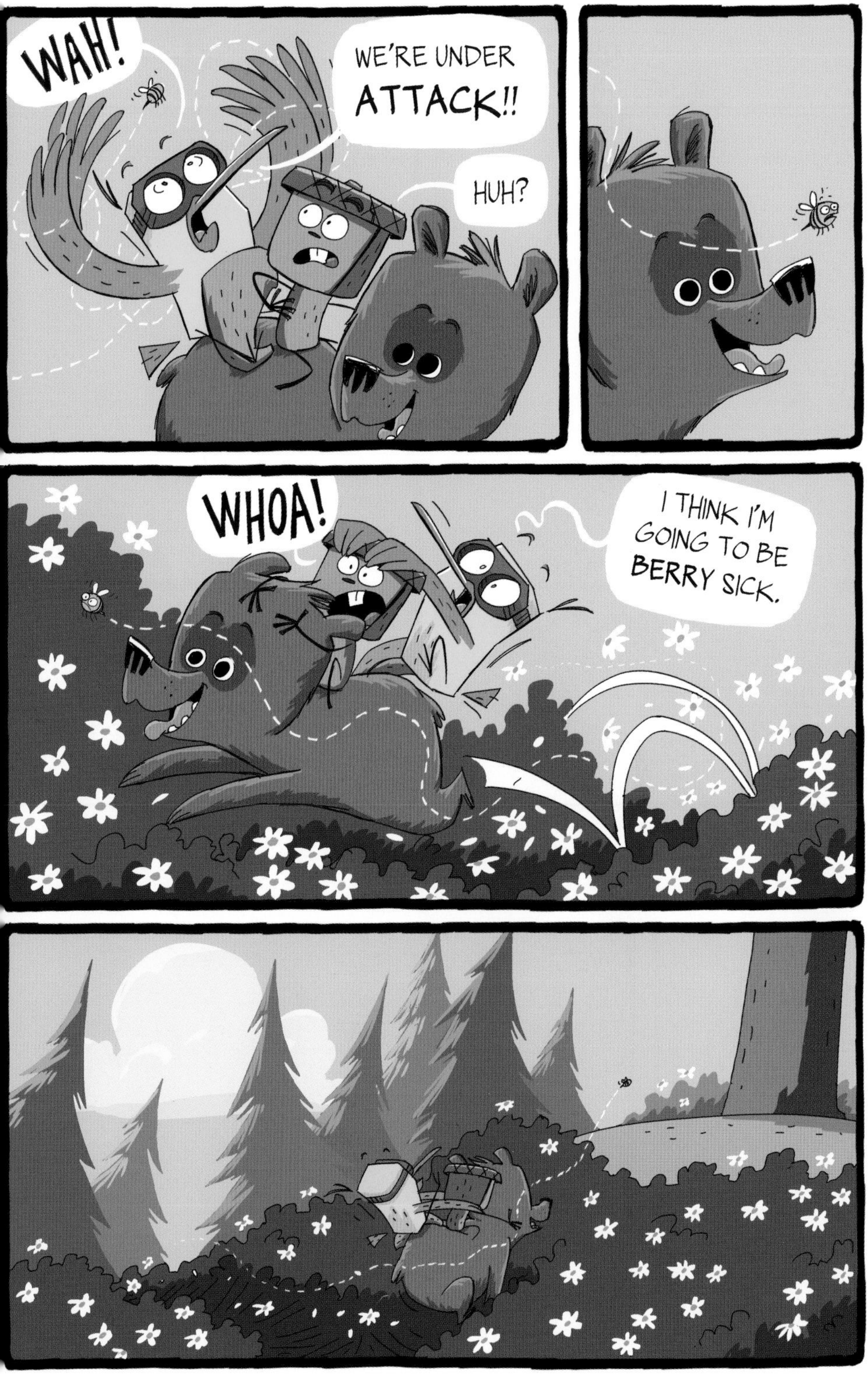
WAH!
WE'RE UNDER ATTACK!!
HUH?
WHOA!
I THINK I'M GOING TO BE BERRY SICK.

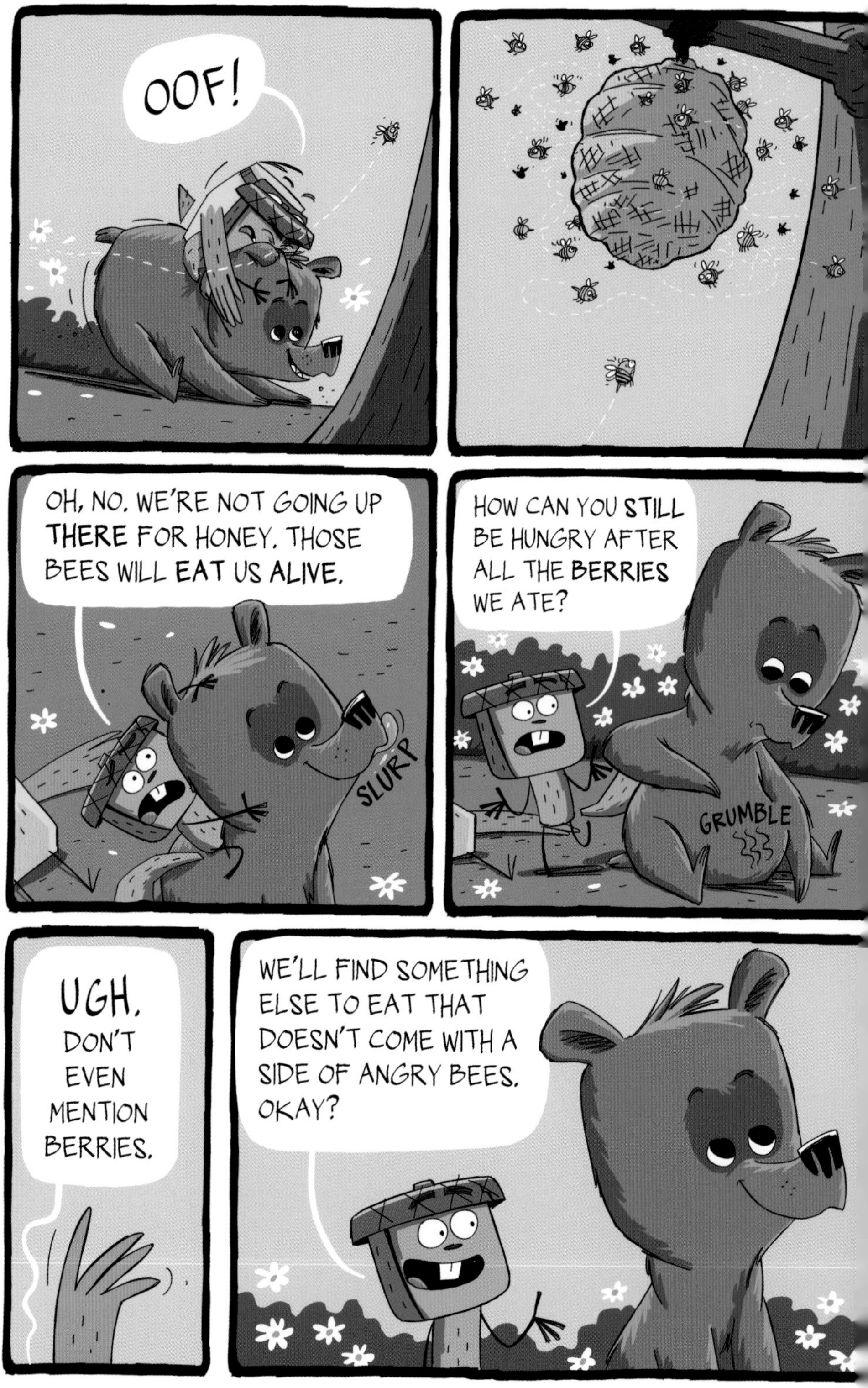
OOF!
OH, NO. WE'RE NOT GOING UP THERE FOR HONEY. THOSE BEES WILL EAT US ALIVE.
SLURP
HOW CAN YOU STILL BE HUNGRY AFTER ALL THE BERRIES WE ATE?
GRUMBLE
UGH. DON'T EVEN MENTION BERRIES.
WE'LL FIND SOMETHING ELSE TO EAT THAT DOESN'T COME WITH A SIDE OF ANGRY BEES. OKAY?

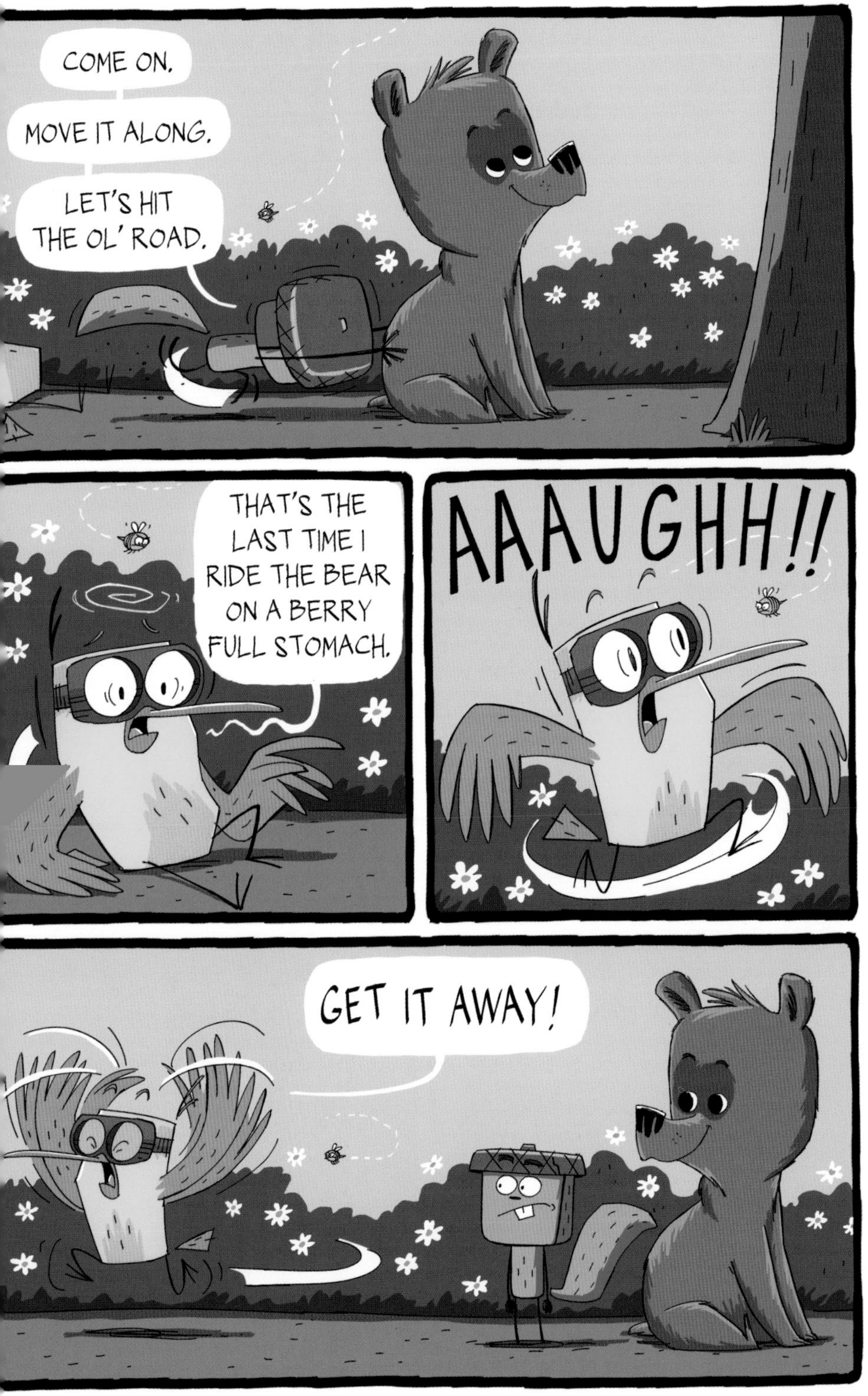
COME ON.
MOVE IT ALONG.
LET'S HIT THE OL' ROAD.
THAT'S THE LAST TIME I RIDE THE BEAR ON A BERRY FULL STOMACH.
AAAUGHH!!
GET IT AWAY!

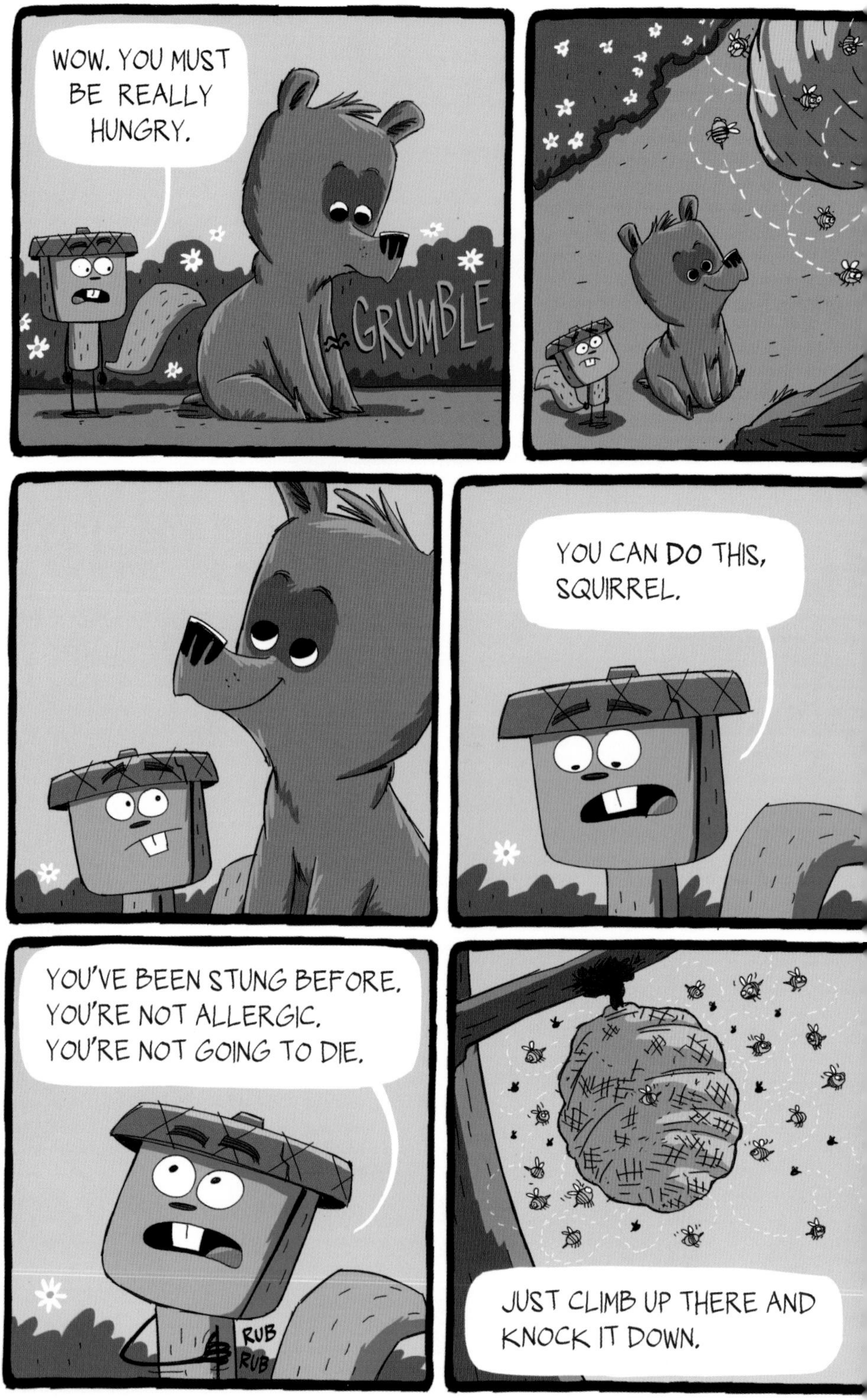

WOW. YOU MUST BE REALLY HUNGRY.
GRUMBLE
YOU CAN DO THIS, SQUIRREL.
YOU'VE BEEN STUNG BEFORE. YOU'RE NOT ALLERGIC. YOU'RE NOT GOING TO DIE.
RUB RUB
JUST CLIMB UP THERE AND KNOCK IT DOWN.

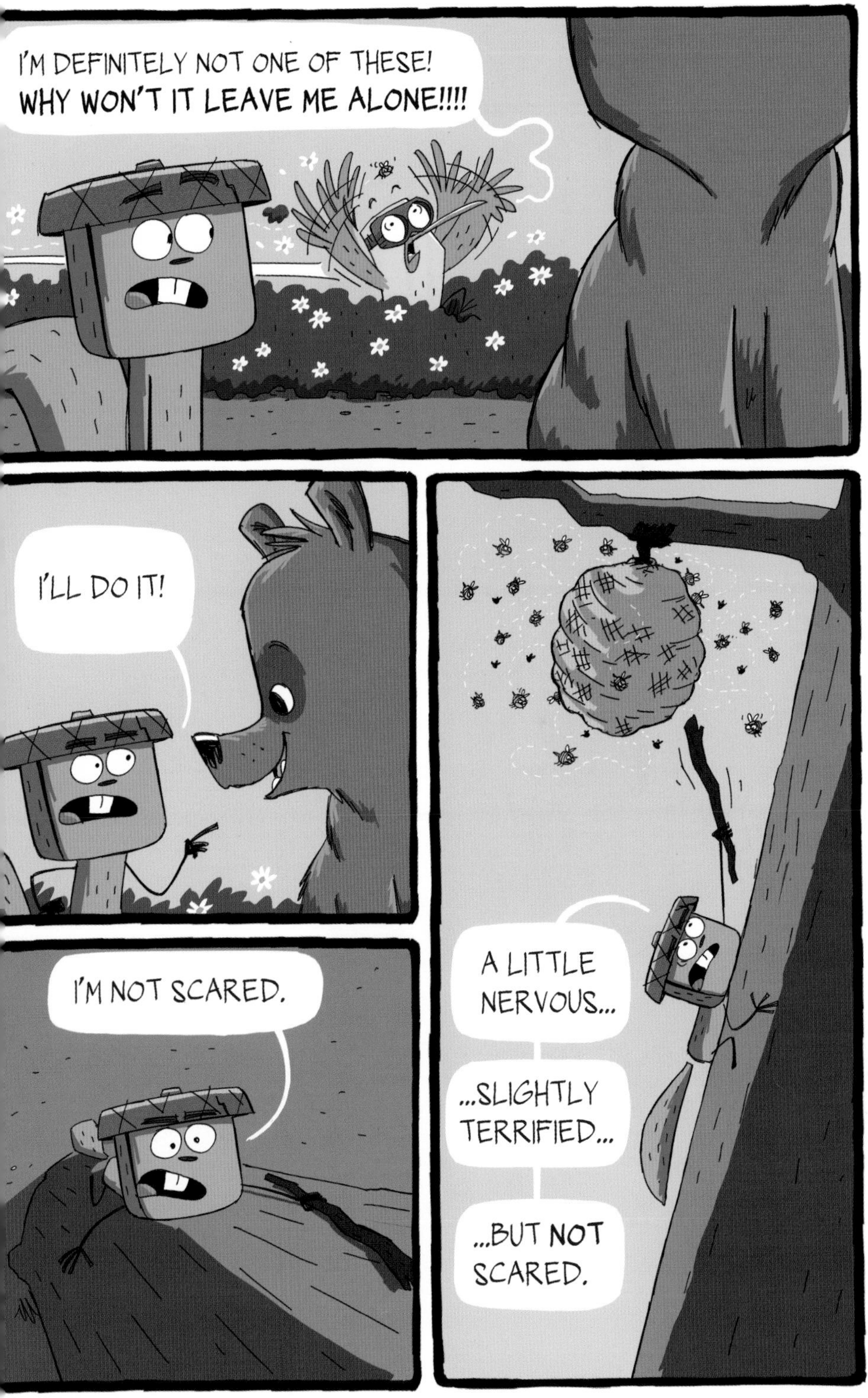
I'M DEFINITELY NOT ONE OF THESE!
WHY WON'T IT LEAVE ME ALONE!!!!
I'LL DO IT!
I'M NOT SCARED.
A LITTLE NERVOUS...
...SLIGHTLY TERRIFIED...
...BUT NOT SCARED.

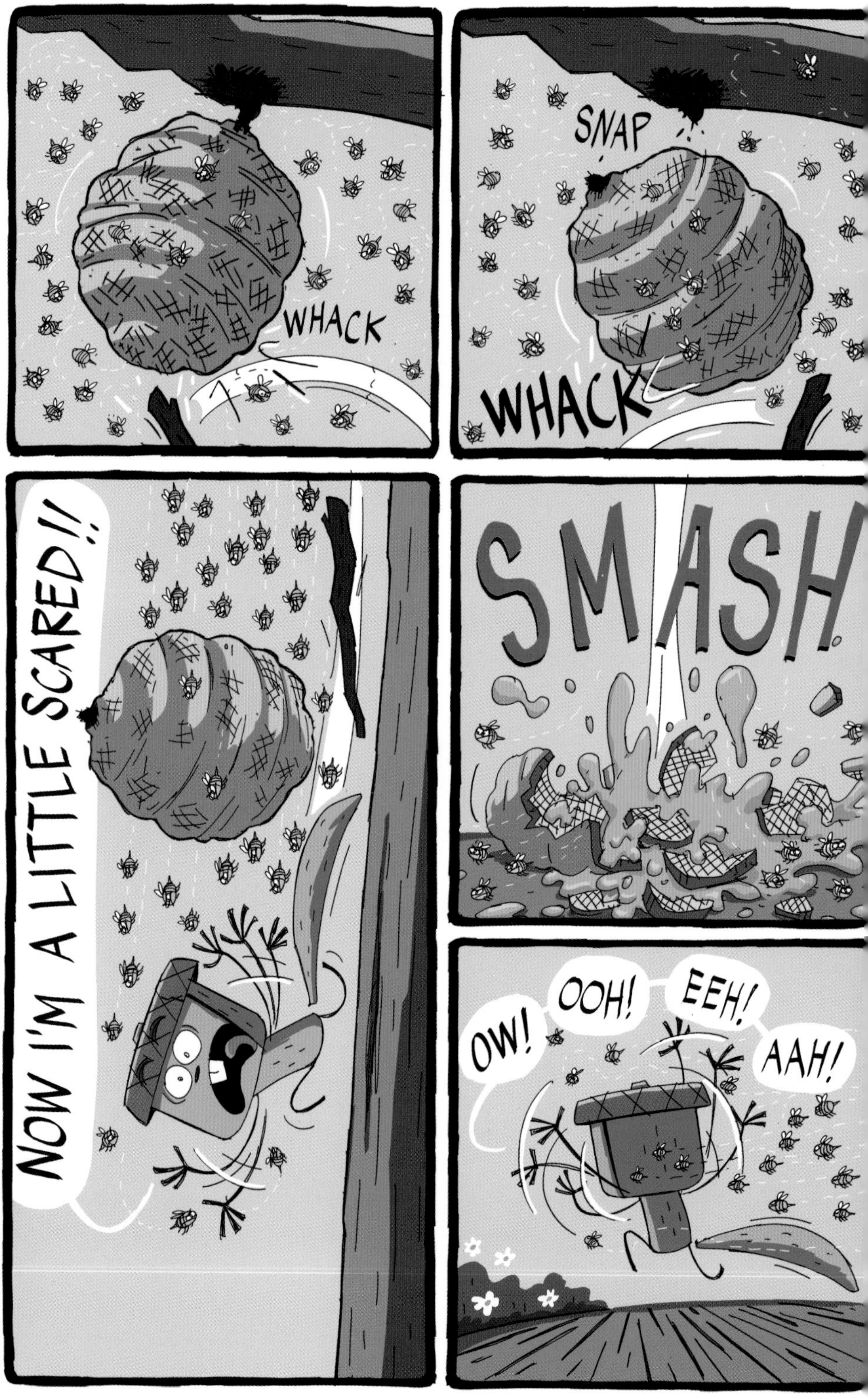
WHACK
SNAP
WHACK
NOW I'M A LITTLE SCARED!!
SMASH
OW!
OOH!
EEH!
AAH!

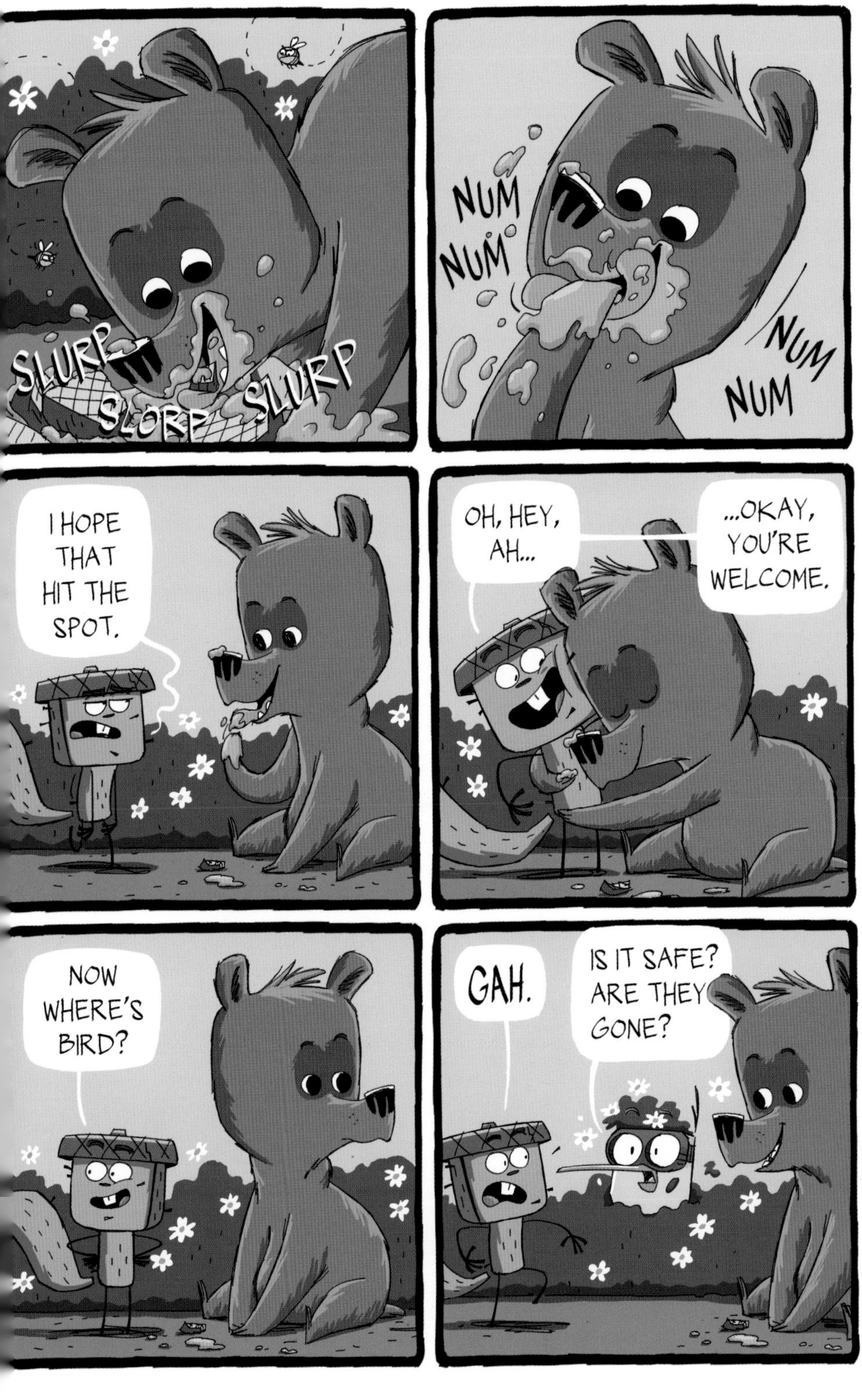
SLURP
SLORP
SLURP
NUM
NUM
NUM
NUM
I HOPE THAT HIT THE SPOT.
OH, HEY, AH...
...OKAY, YOU'RE WELCOME.
NOW WHERE'S BIRD?
GAH.
IS IT SAFE? ARE THEY GONE?

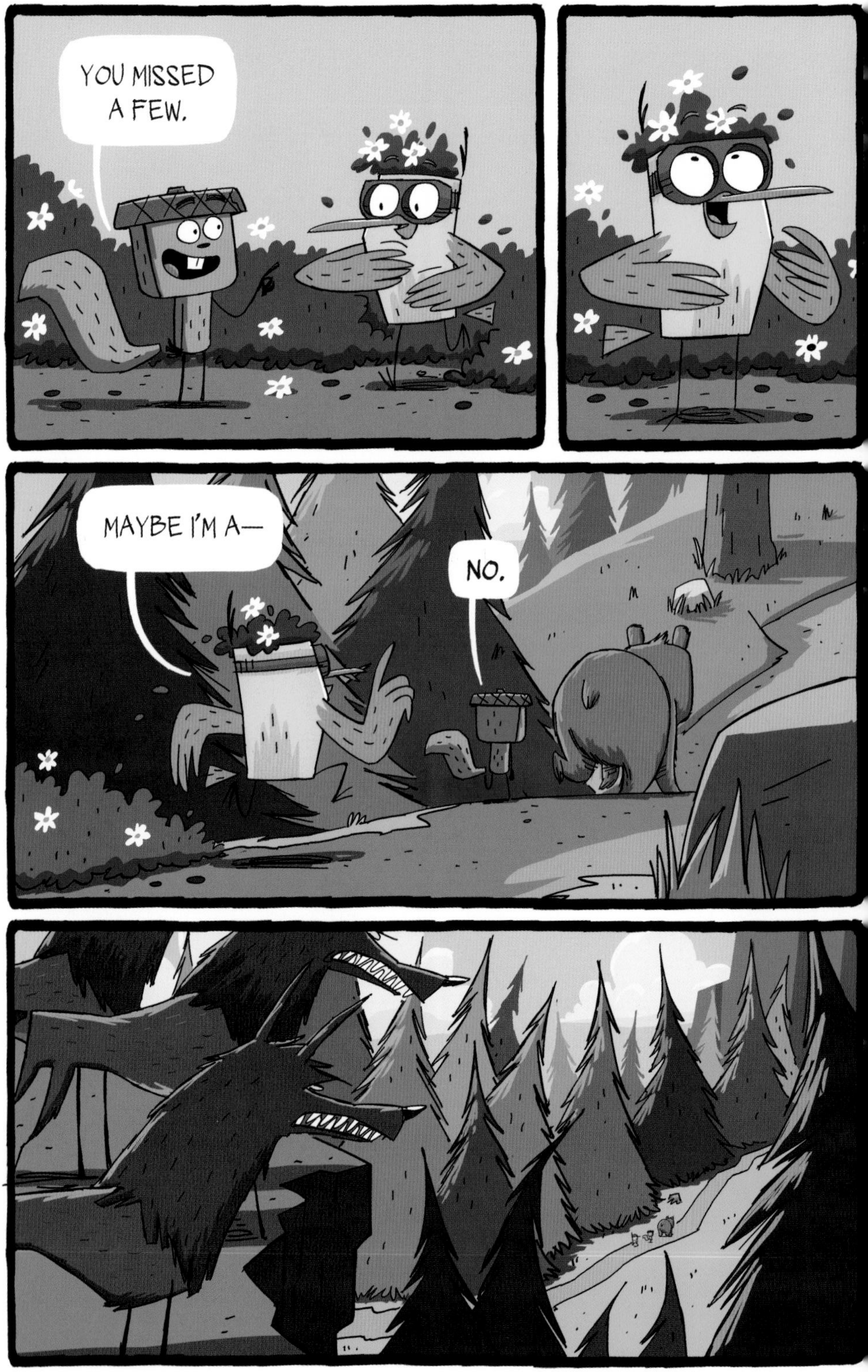
YOU MISSED A FEW.
MAYBE I'M A—
NO.

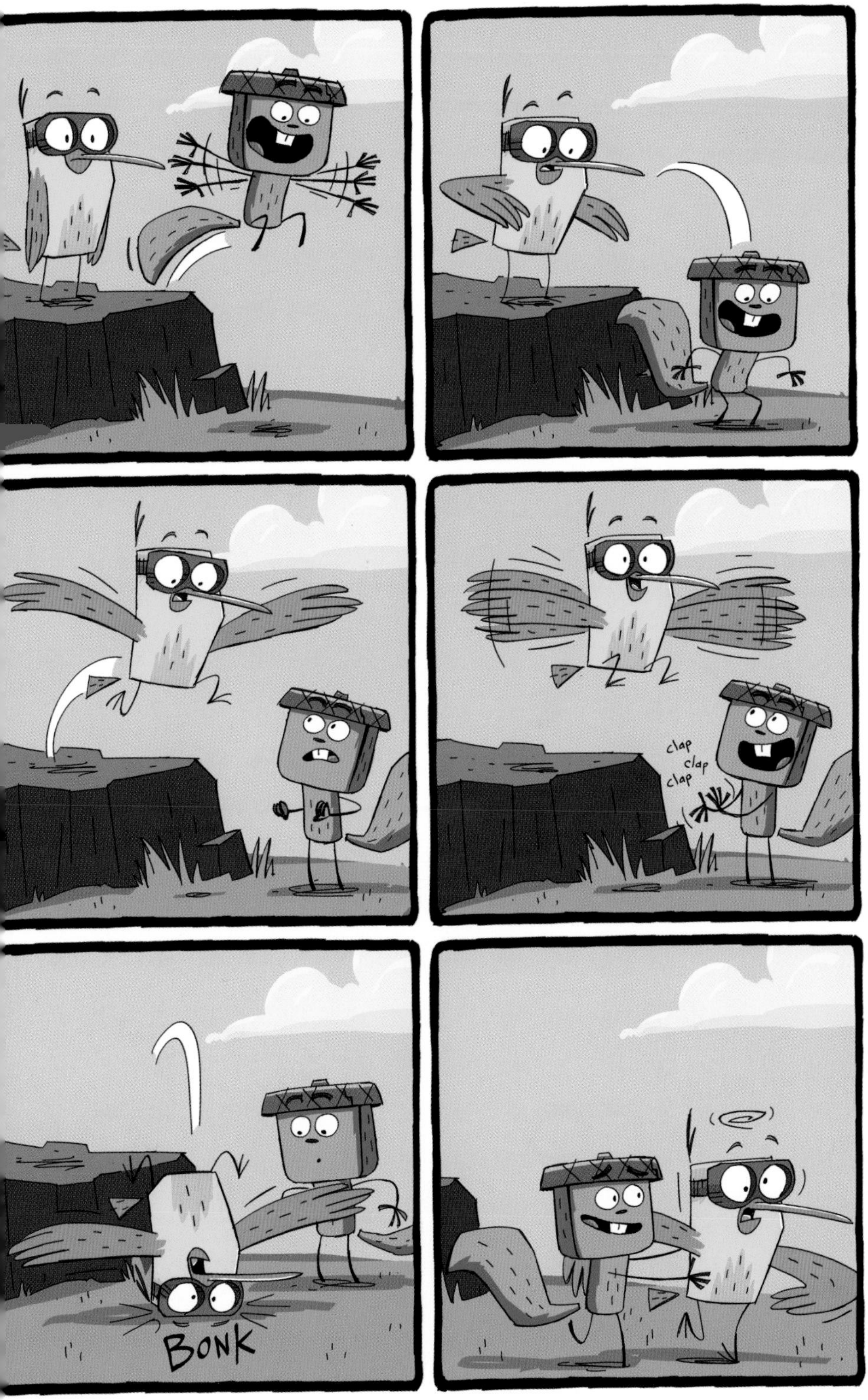
clap
clap
clap
BONK

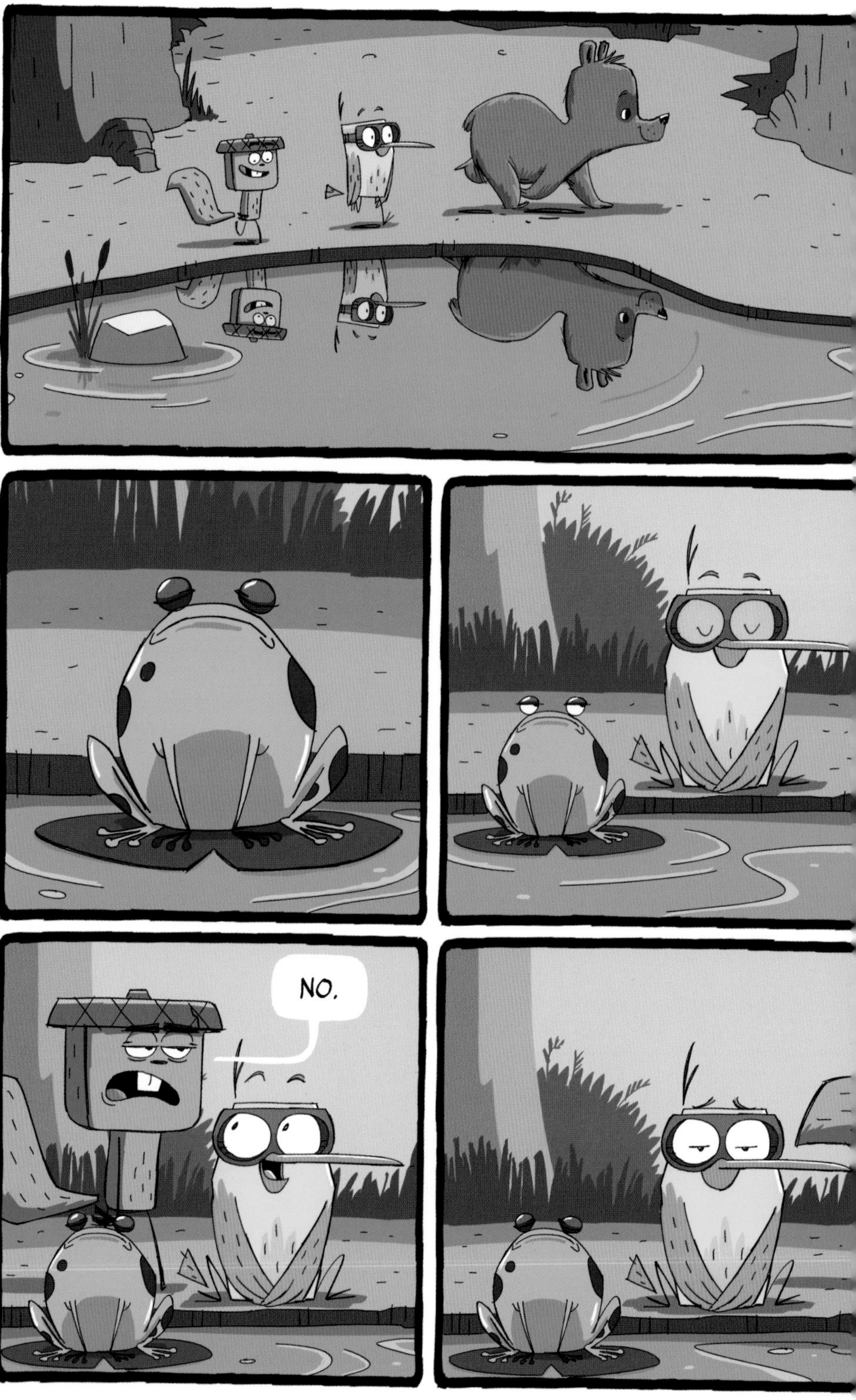
NO.

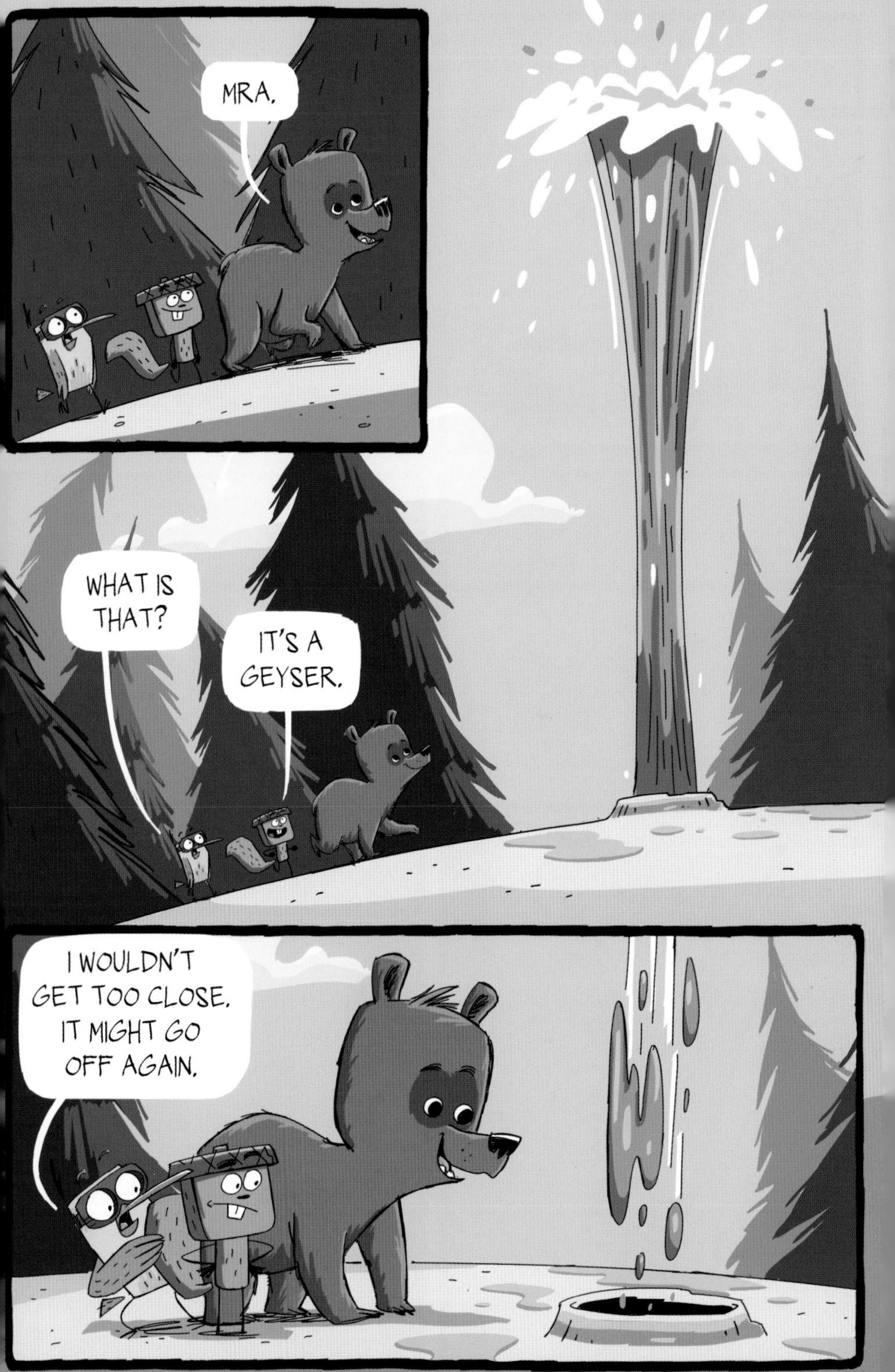
MRA.
WHAT IS THAT?
IT'S A GEYSER.
I WOULDN'T GET TOO CLOSE. IT MIGHT GO OFF AGAIN.

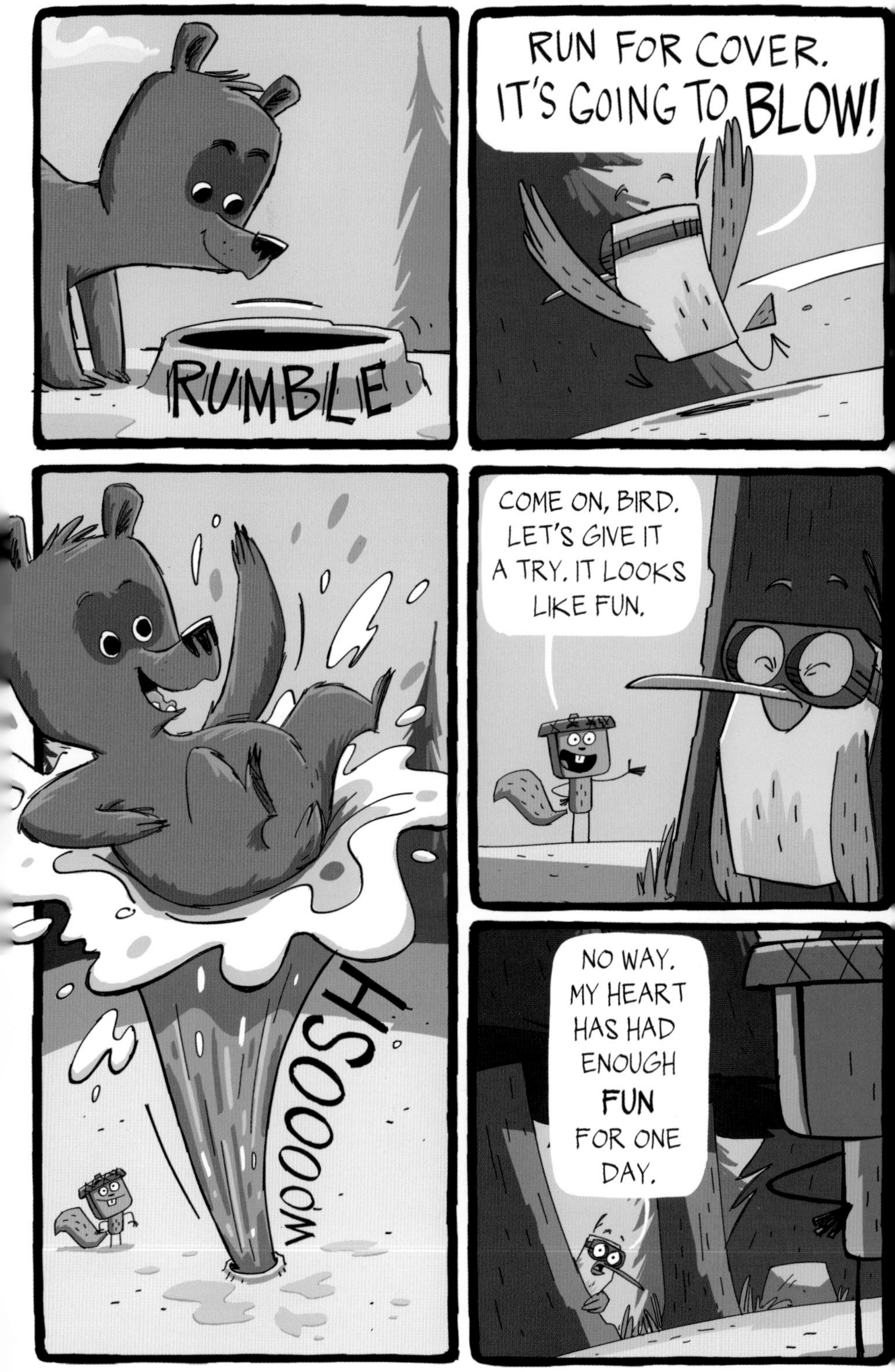
RUMBLE
RUN FOR COVER. IT'S GOING TO BLOW!
WOOOOOSH
COME ON, BIRD. LET'S GIVE IT A TRY. IT LOOKS LIKE FUN.
NO WAY. MY HEART HAS HAD ENOUGH FUN FOR ONE DAY.

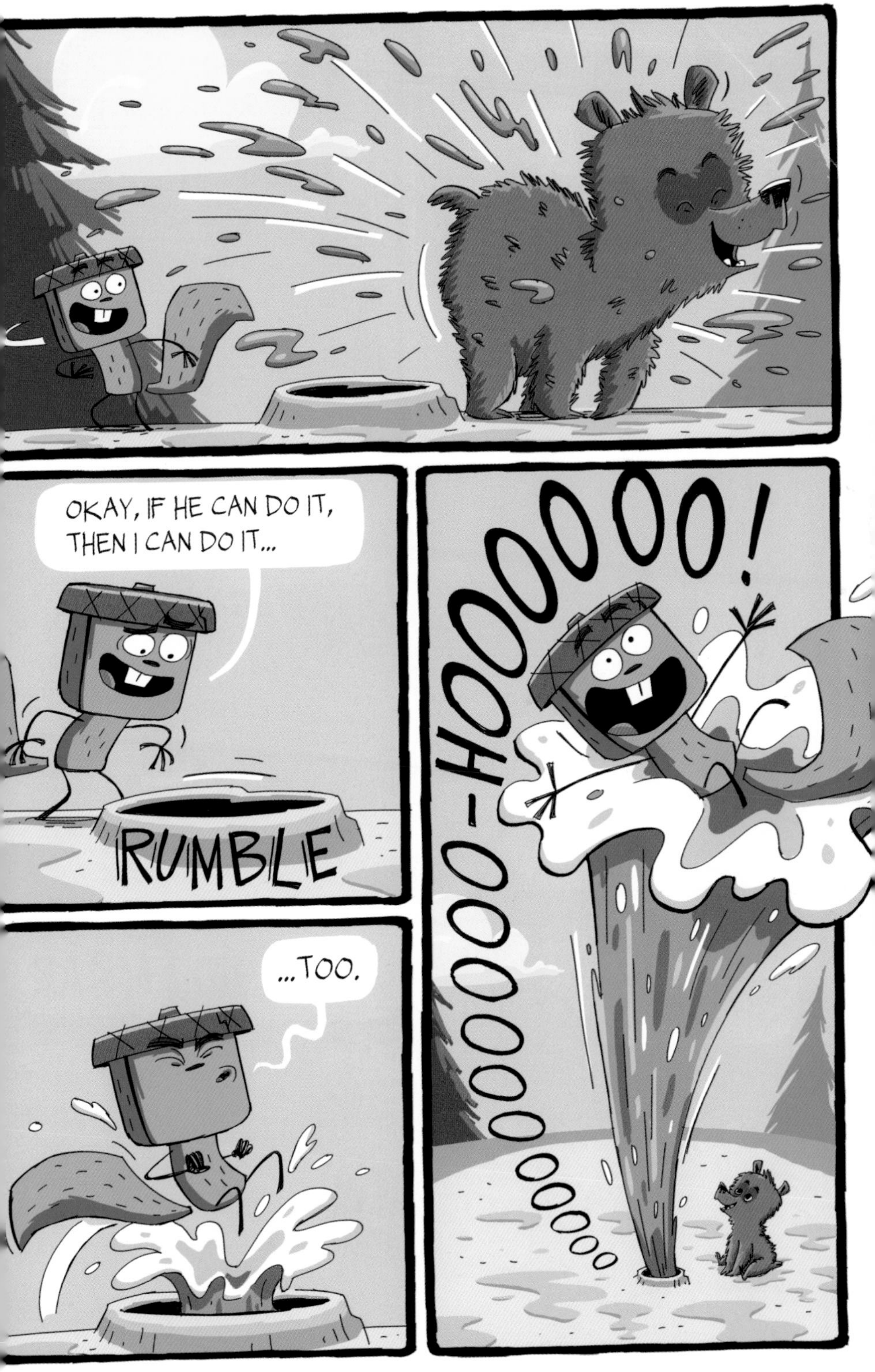
OKAY, IF HE CAN DO IT, THEN I CAN DO IT...
RUMBLE
...TOO.
HOOOOOOO!
O-OOOOOOOOOOO

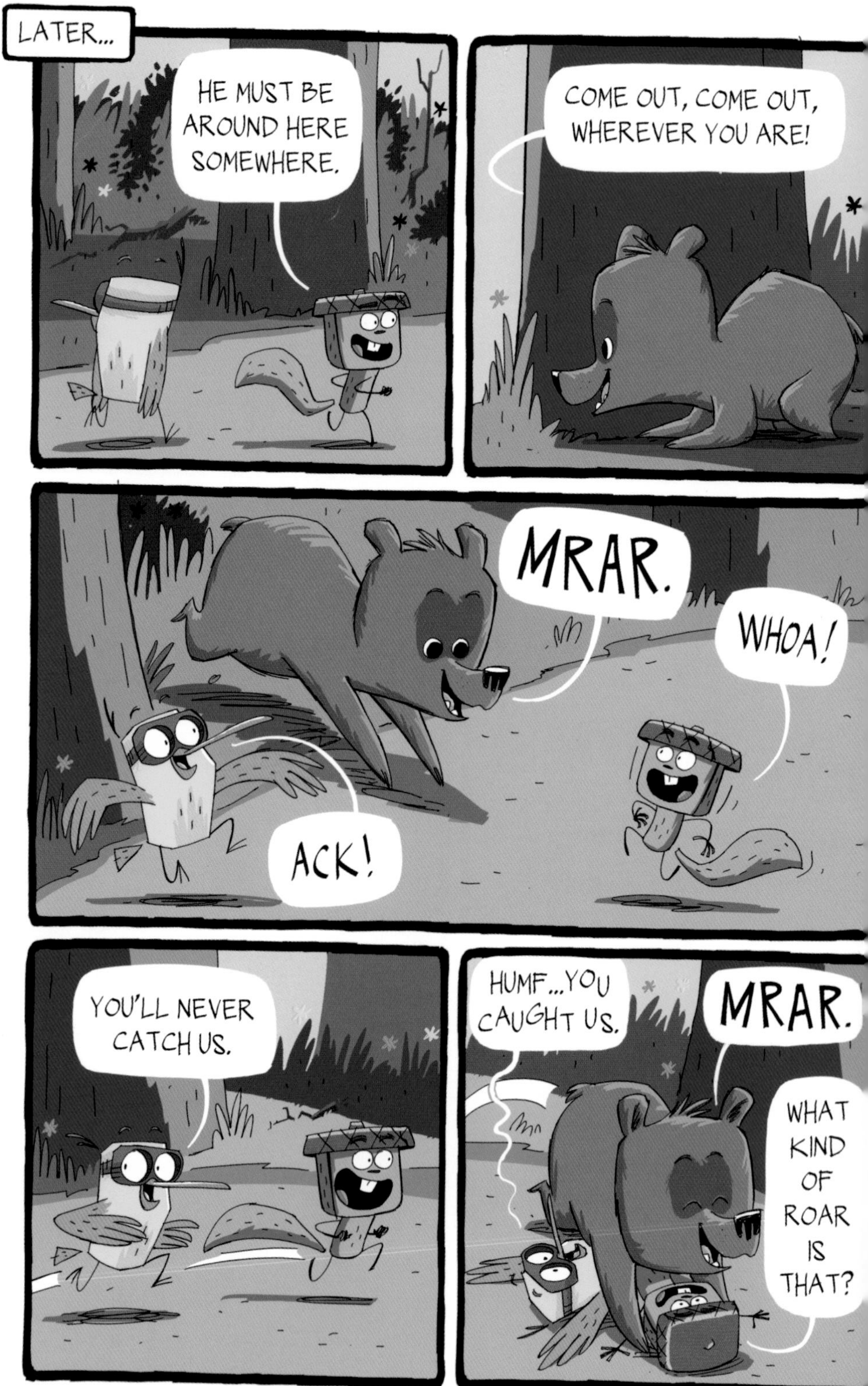
LATER...
HE MUST BE AROUND HERE SOMEWHERE.
COME OUT, COME OUT, WHEREVER YOU ARE!
MRAR.
WHOA!
ACK!
YOU'LL NEVER CATCH US.
HUMF...YOU CAUGHT US.
MRAR.
WHAT KIND OF ROAR IS THAT?

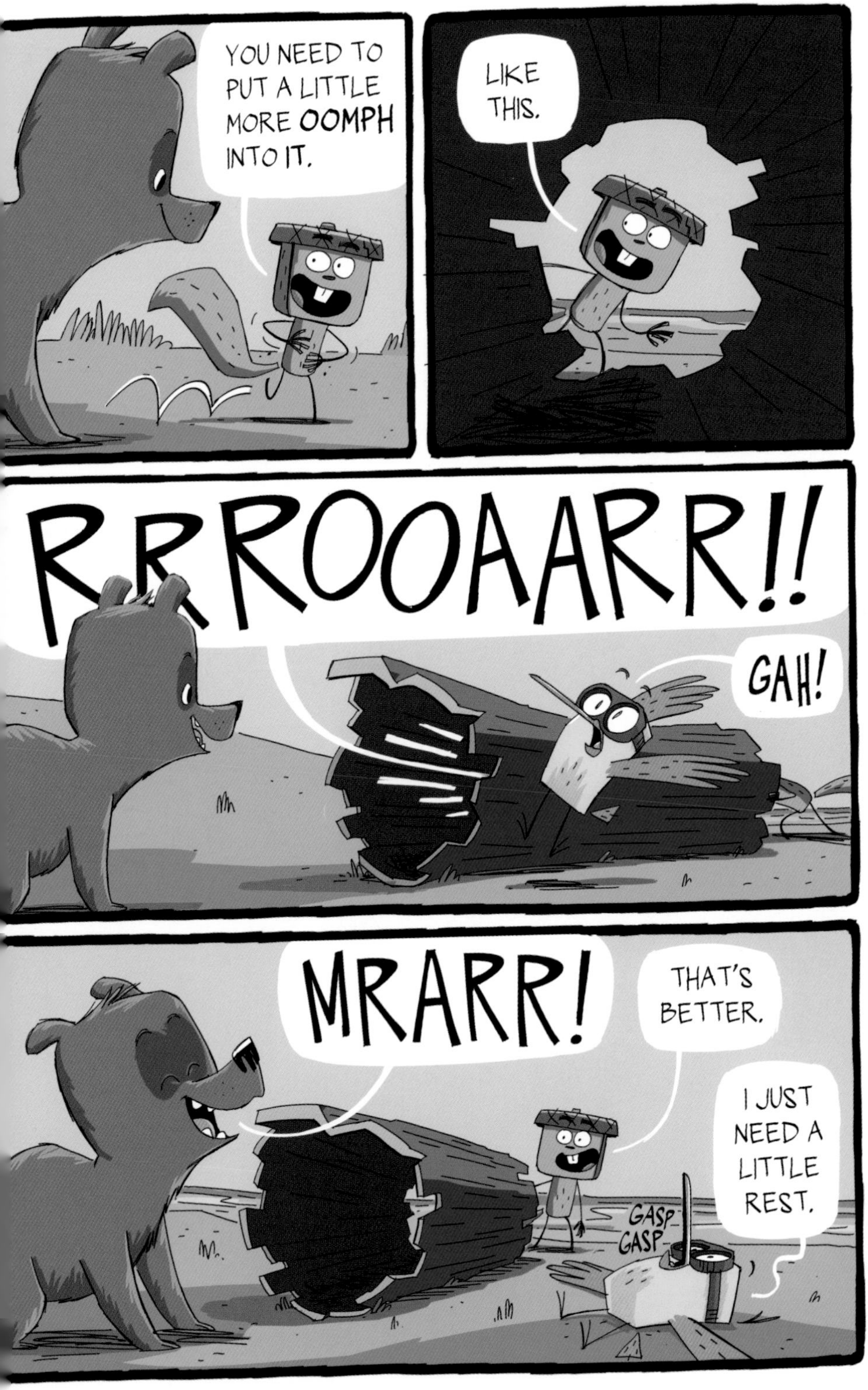
YOU NEED TO PUT A LITTLE MORE OOMPH INTO IT.
LIKE THIS.
RRROOAARR!!
GAH!
MRARR!
THAT'S BETTER.
I JUST NEED A LITTLE REST.
GASP GASP

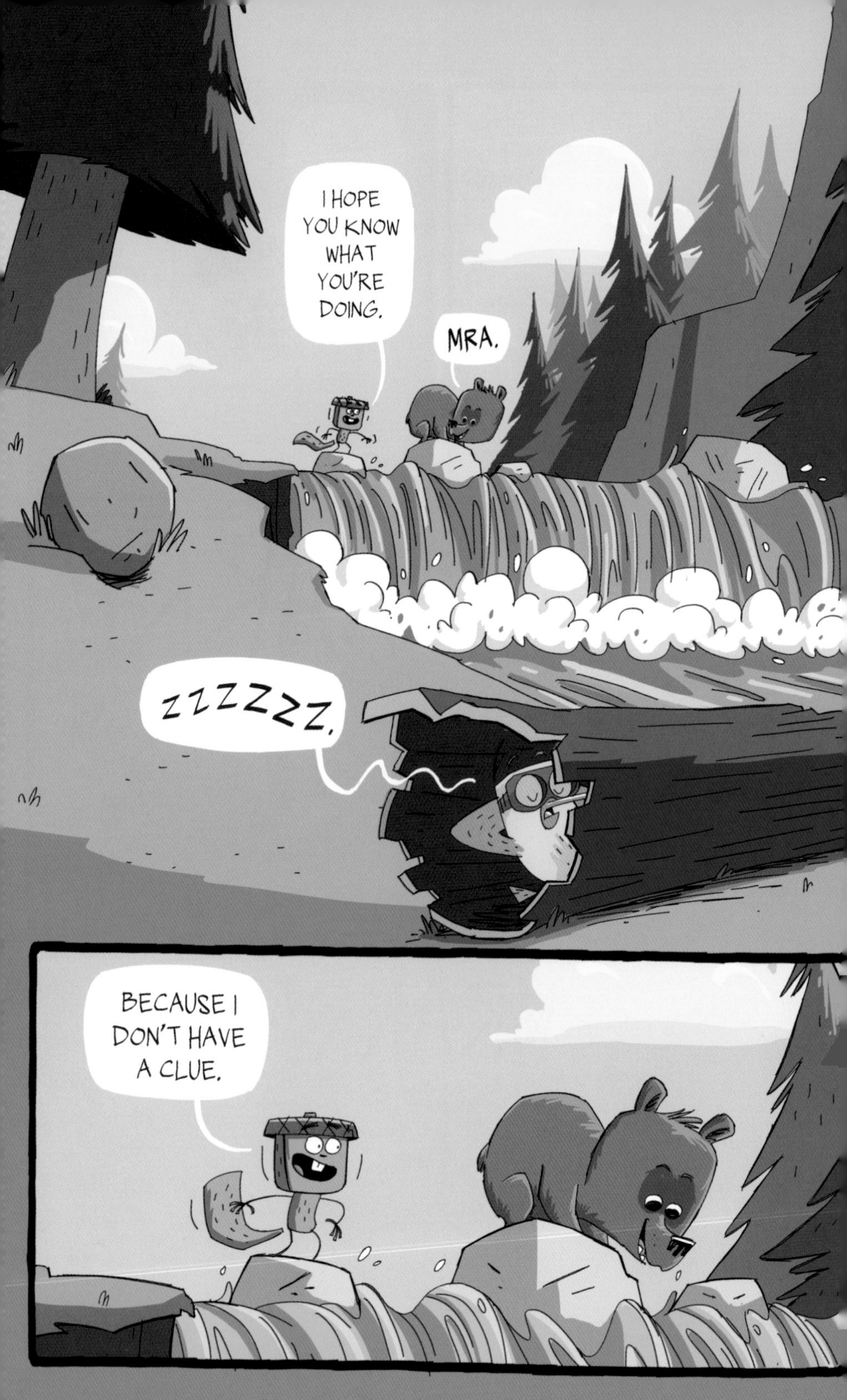
I HOPE YOU KNOW WHAT YOU'RE DOING.
MRA.
ZZZZZZ.
BECAUSE I DON'T HAVE A CLUE.

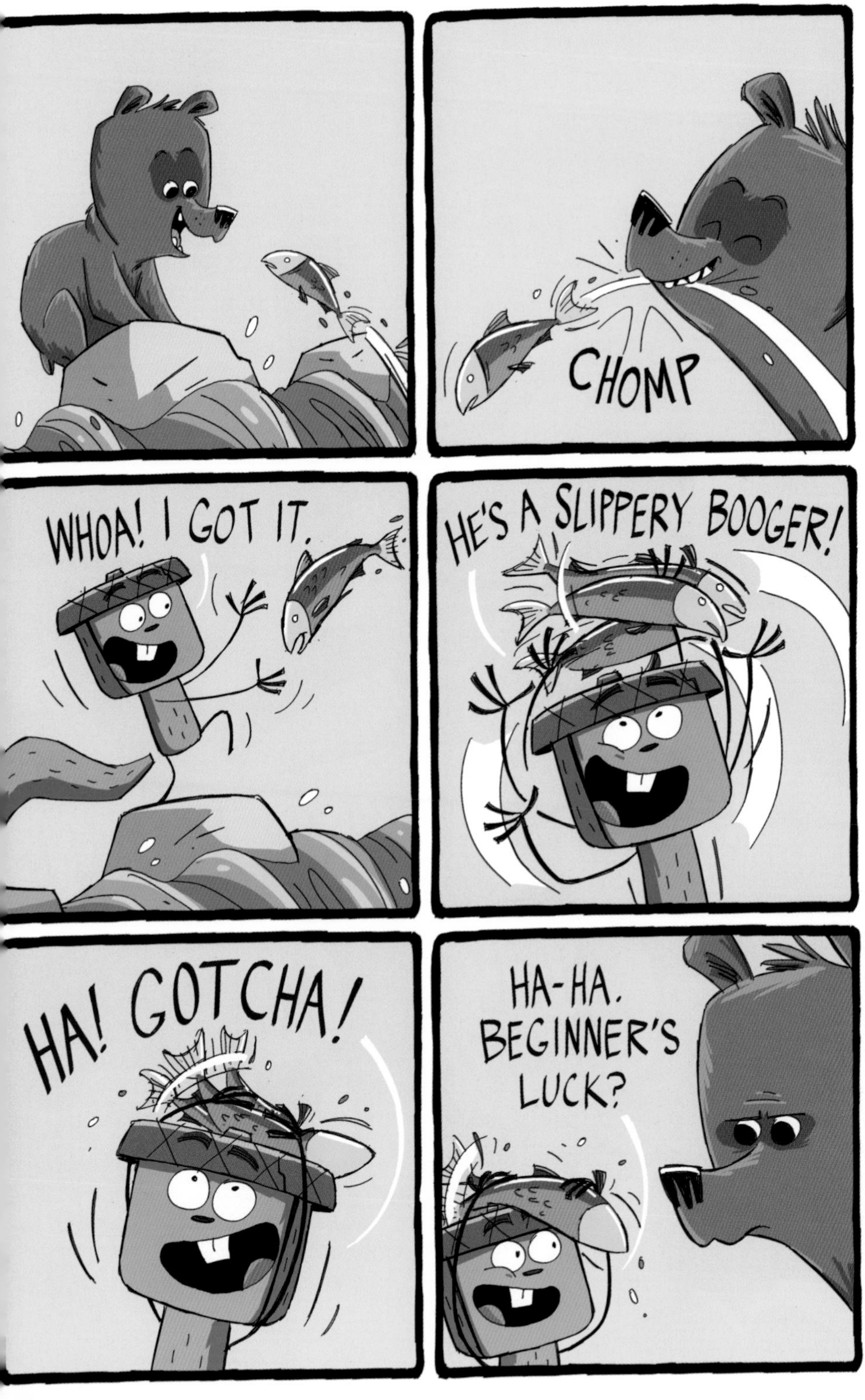
CHOMP
WHOA! I GOT IT.
HE'S A SLIPPERY BOOGER!
HA! GOTCHA!
HA-HA. BEGINNER'S LUCK?

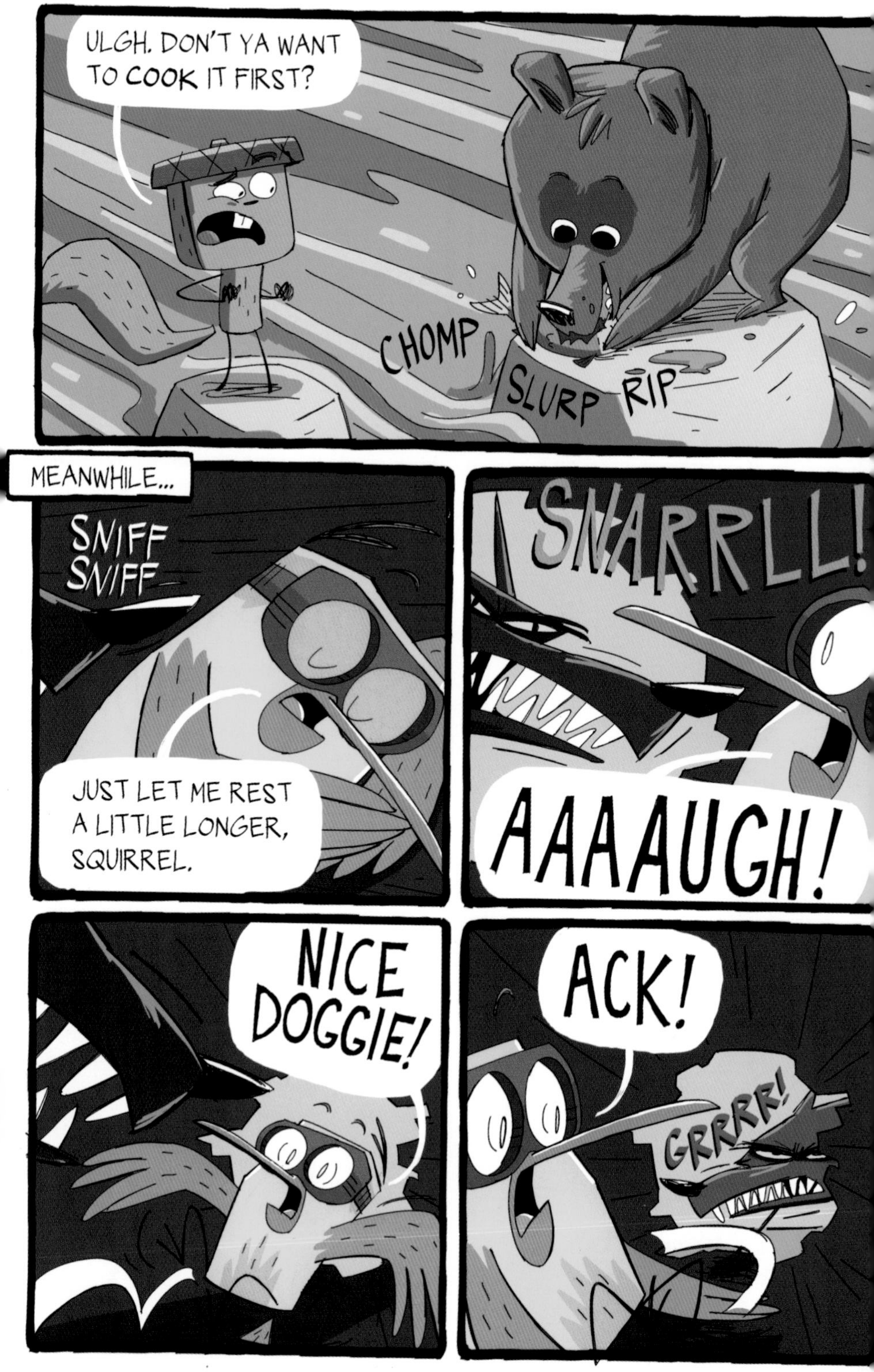
ULGH. DON'T YA WANT TO COOK IT FIRST?
CHOMP
SLURP
RIP
MEANWHILE...
SNIFF SNIFF
JUST LET ME REST A LITTLE LONGER, SQUIRREL.
SNARRLL!
AAAAUGH!
NICE DOGGIE!
ACK!
GRRRR!

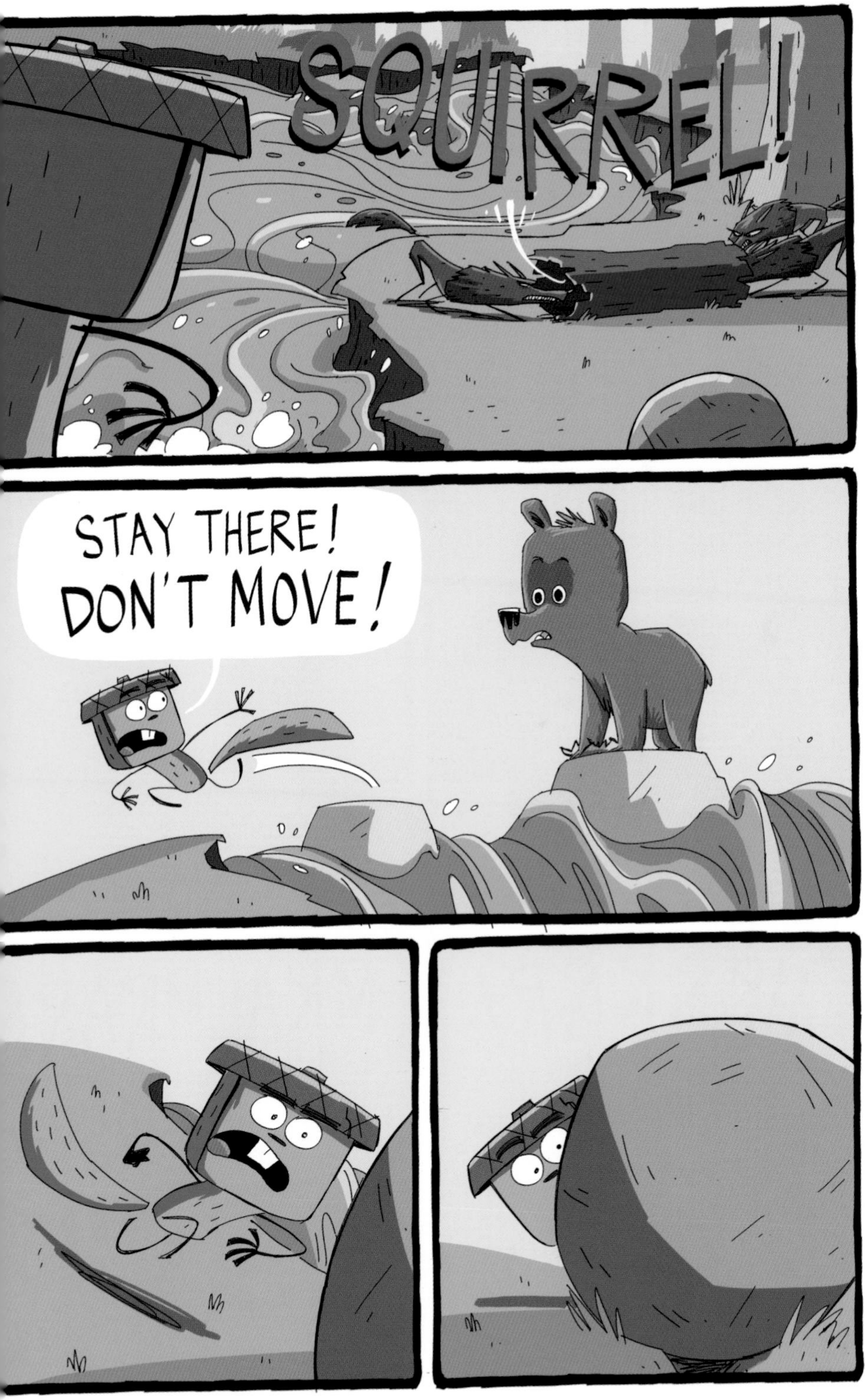
SQUIRREL!
STAY THERE! DON'T MOVE!

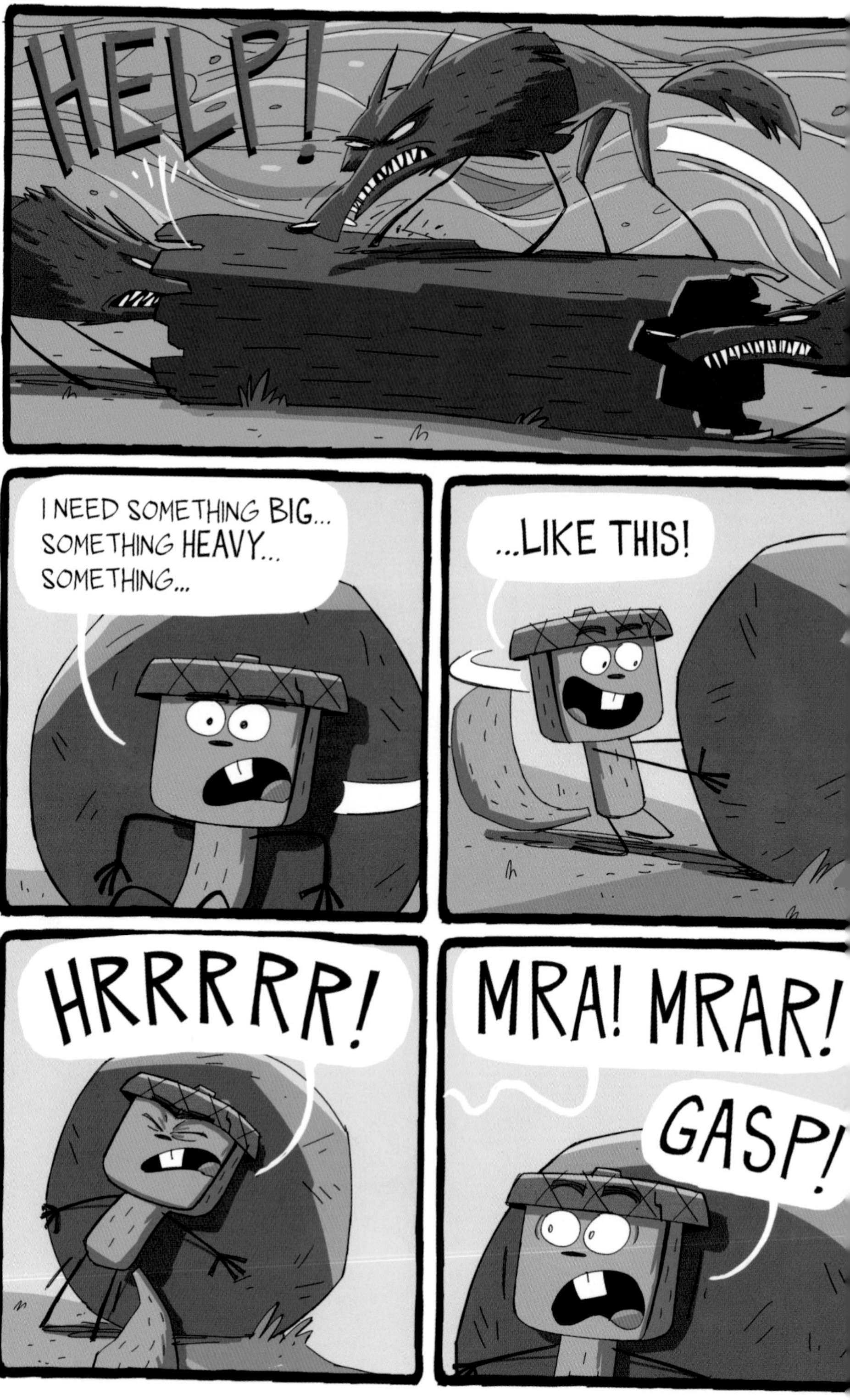
HELP!
I NEED SOMETHING BIG... SOMETHING HEAVY... SOMETHING...
...LIKE THIS!
HRRRRR!
MRA! MRAR!
GASP!

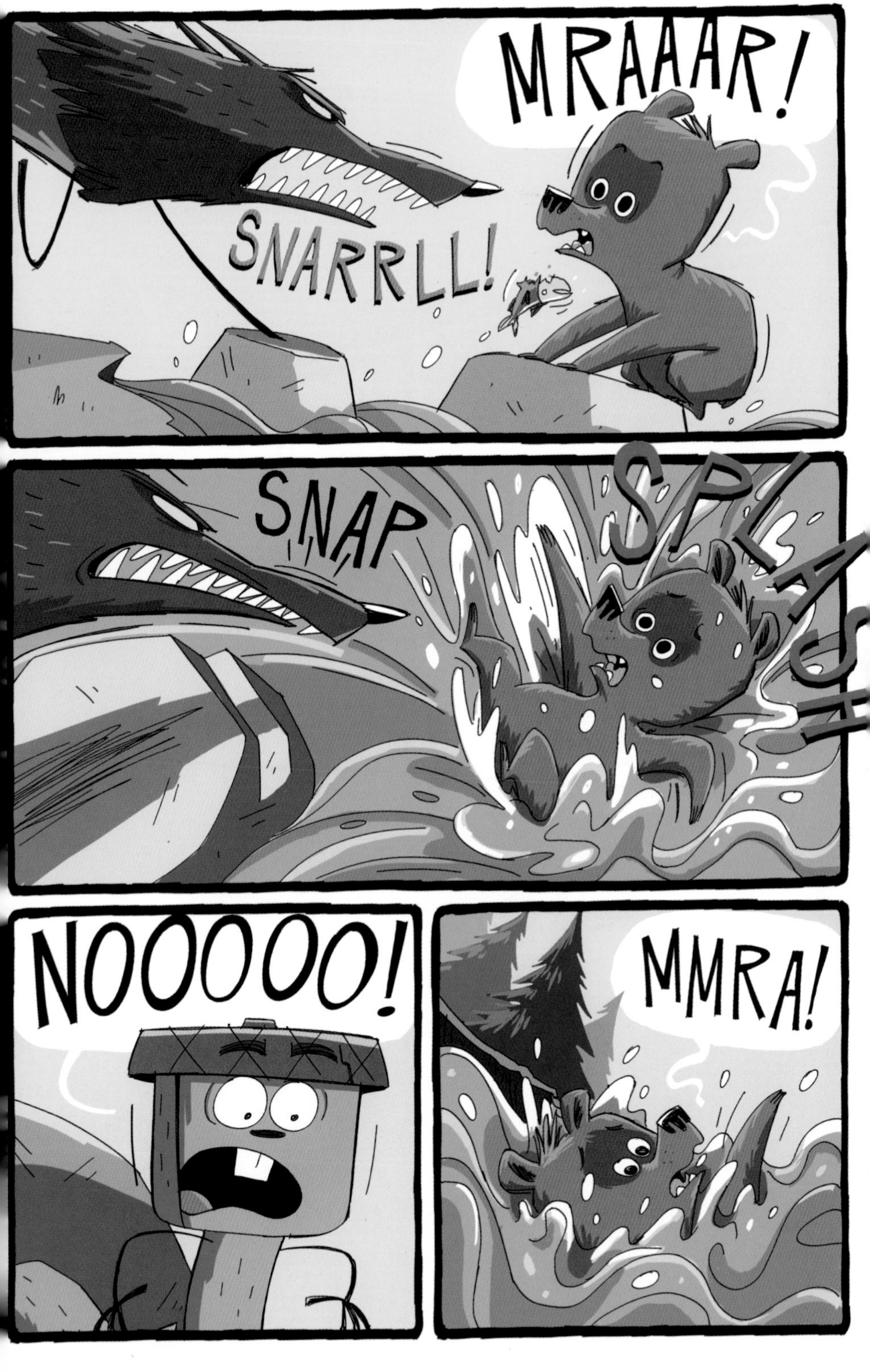
MRAAAR!
SNARRLL!
SNAP
SPLASH
NOOOOO!
MMRA!

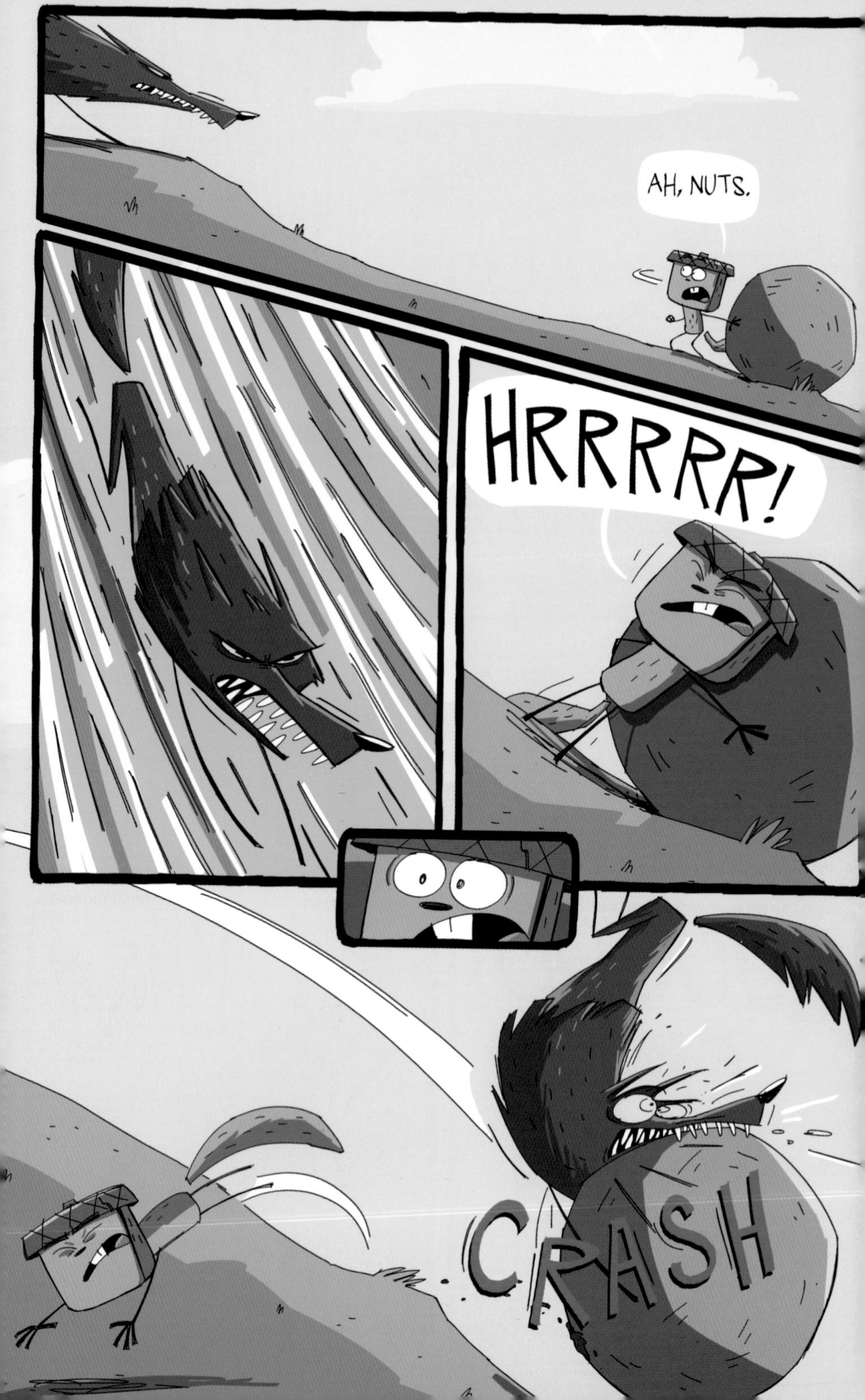
AH, NUTS.
HRRRRR!
CRASH

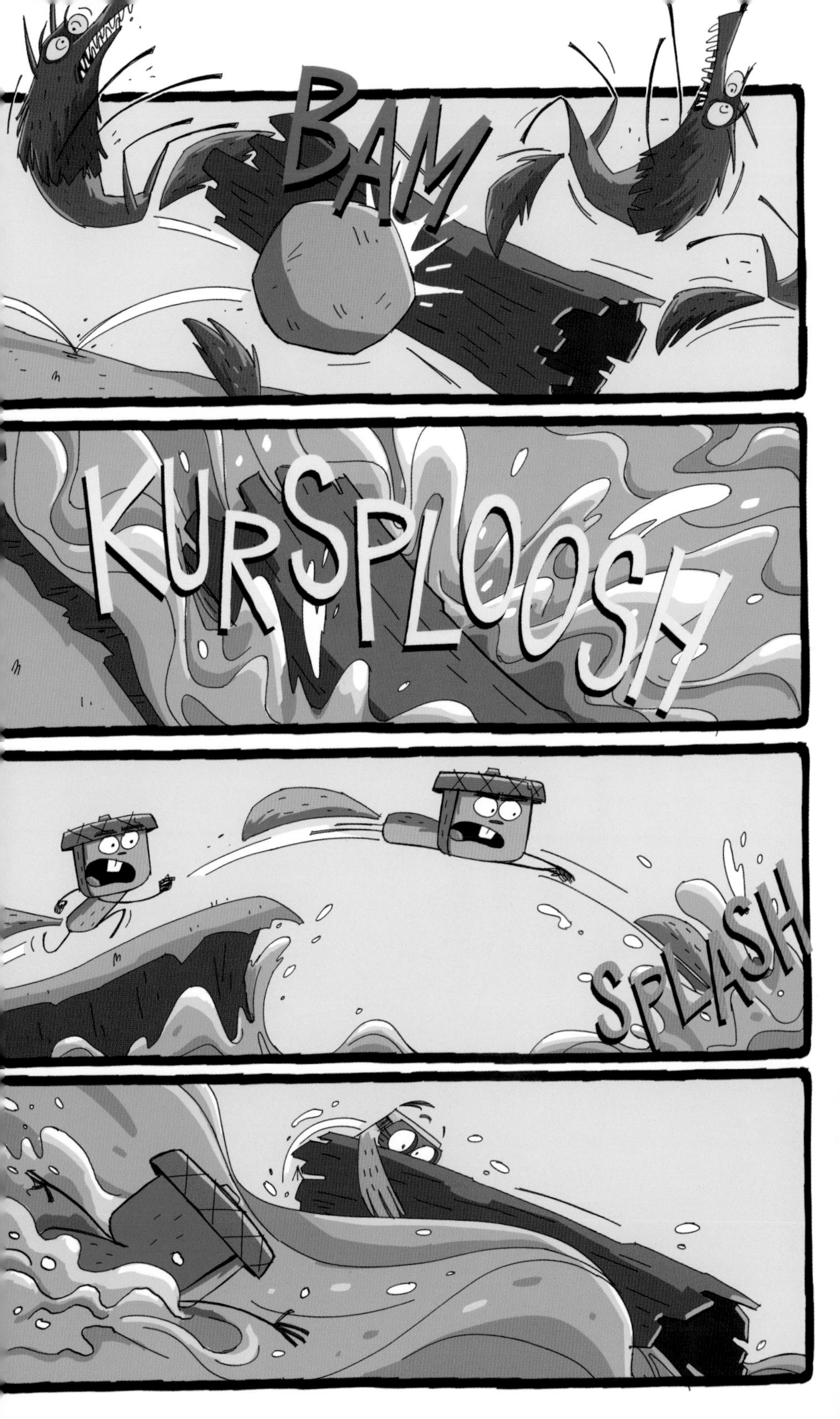
BAM
KURSPLOOSH
SPLASH

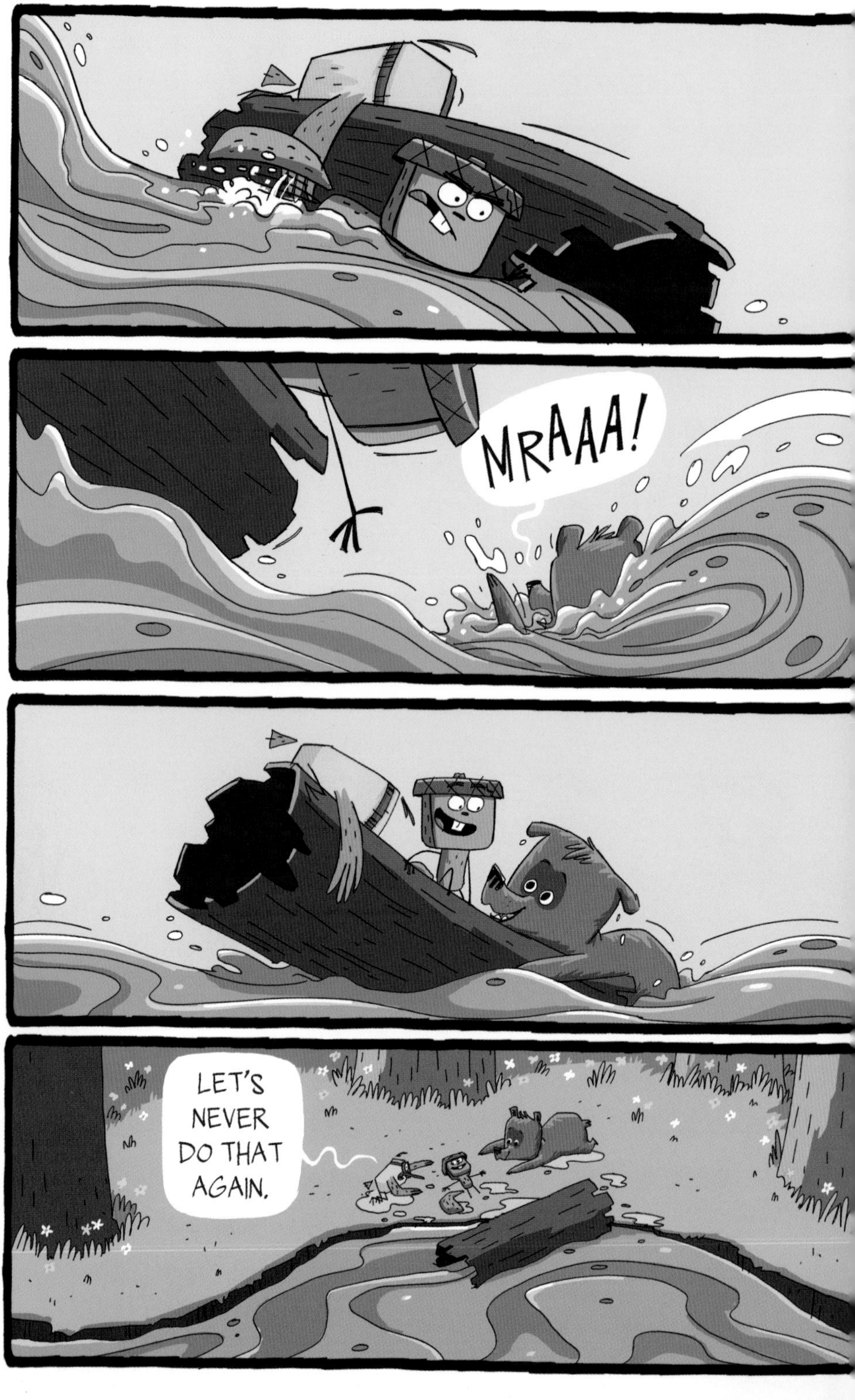
MRAAA!
LET'S NEVER DO THAT AGAIN.

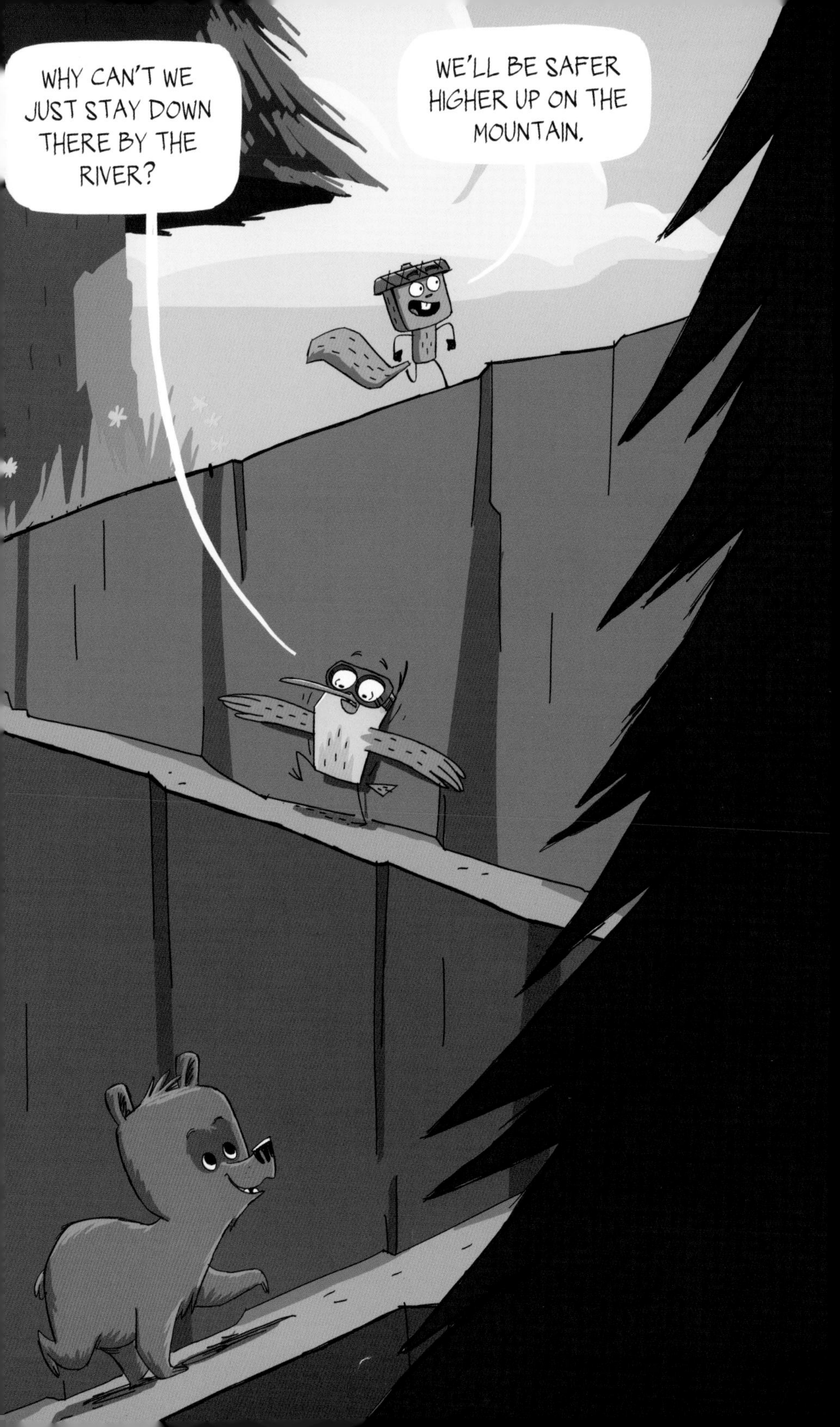
WHY CAN'T WE JUST STAY DOWN THERE BY THE RIVER?
WE'LL BE SAFER HIGHER UP ON THE MOUNTAIN.

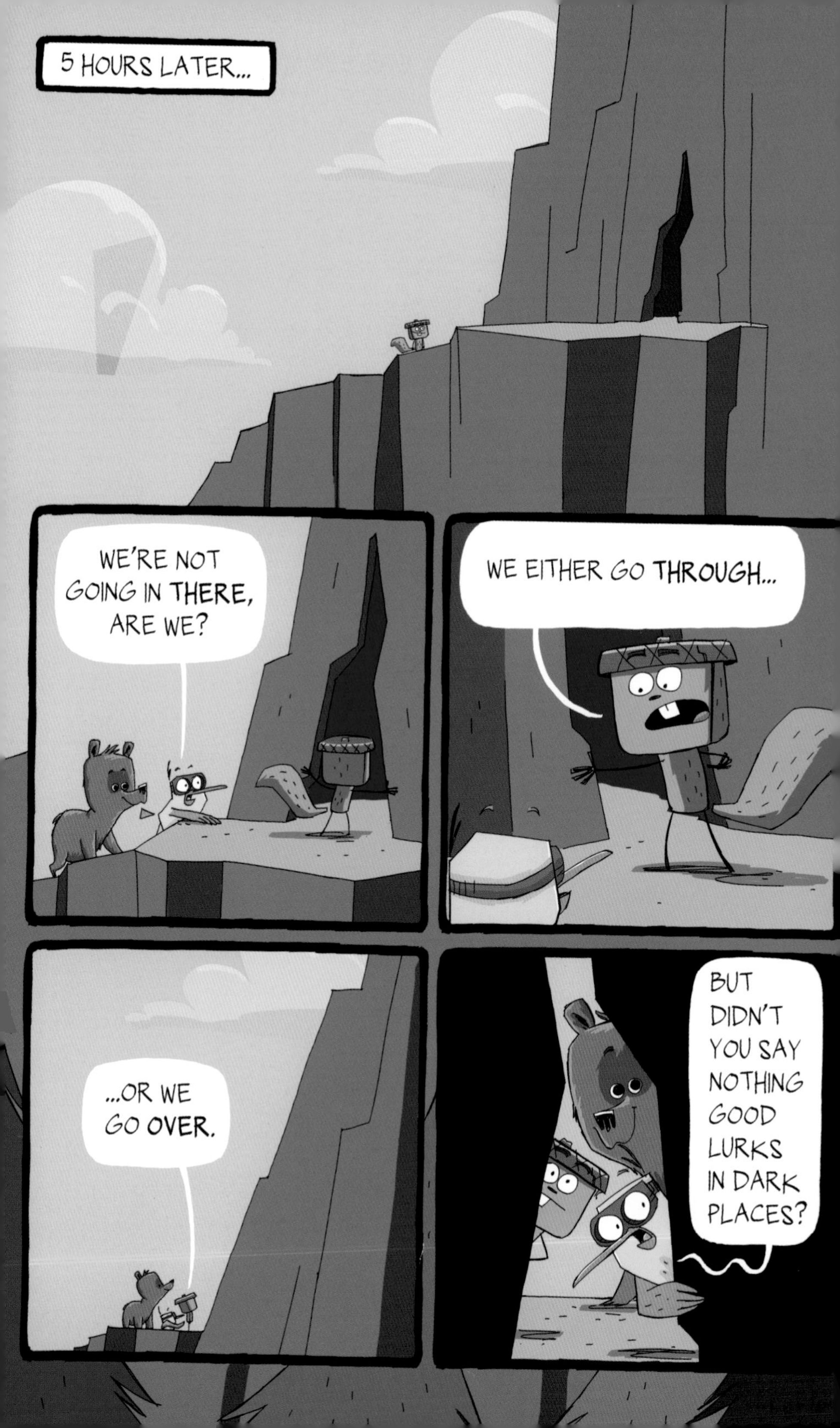
5 HOURS LATER...
WE'RE NOT GOING IN THERE, ARE WE?
WE EITHER GO THROUGH...
...OR WE GO OVER.
BUT DIDN'T YOU SAY NOTHING GOOD LURKS IN DARK PLACES?

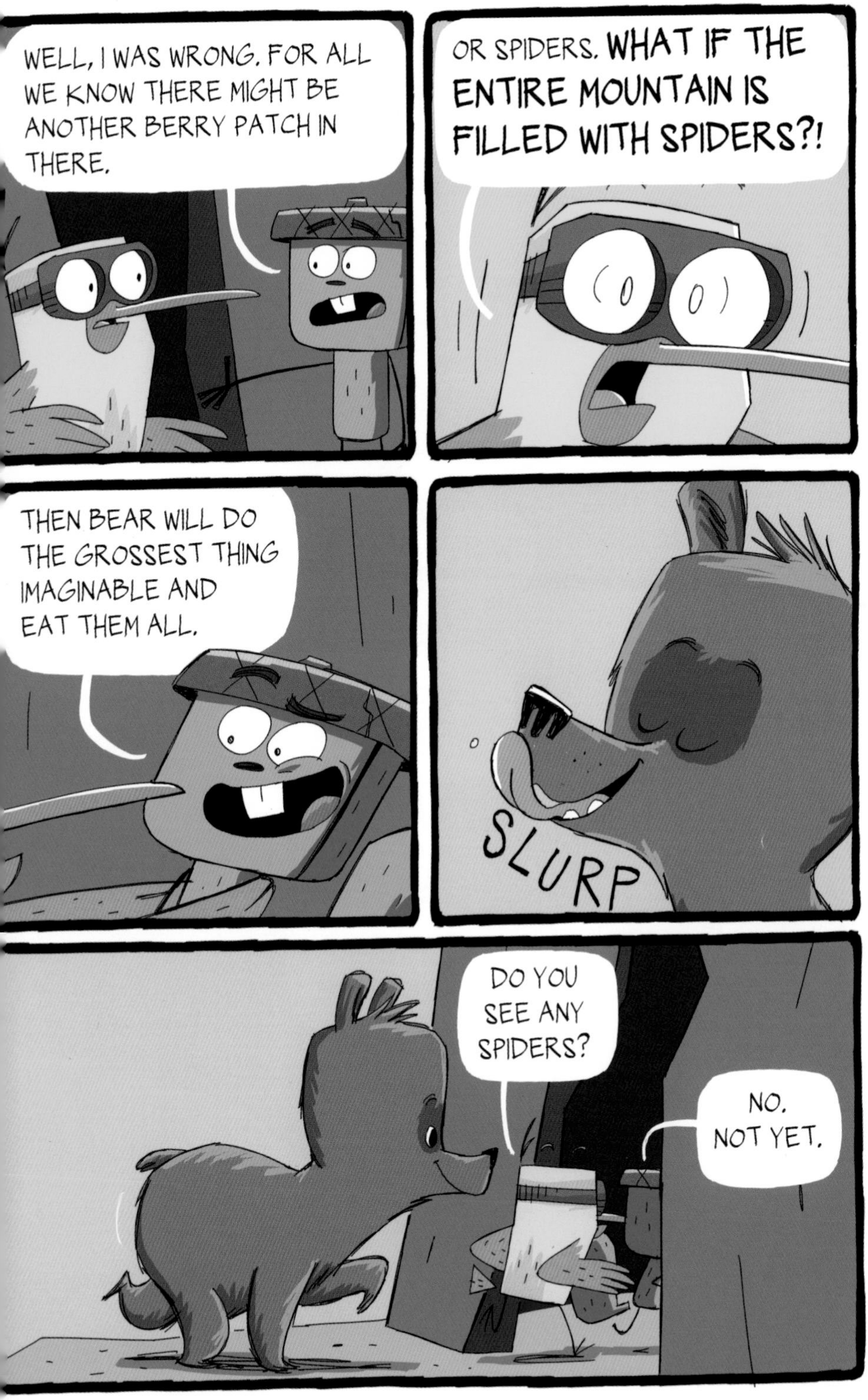
WELL, I WAS WRONG. FOR ALL WE KNOW THERE MIGHT BE ANOTHER BERRY PATCH IN THERE.
OR SPIDERS. WHAT IF THE ENTIRE MOUNTAIN IS FILLED WITH SPIDERS?!
THEN BEAR WILL DO THE GROSSEST THING IMAGINABLE AND EAT THEM ALL.
SLURP
DO YOU SEE ANY SPIDERS?
NO. NOT YET.

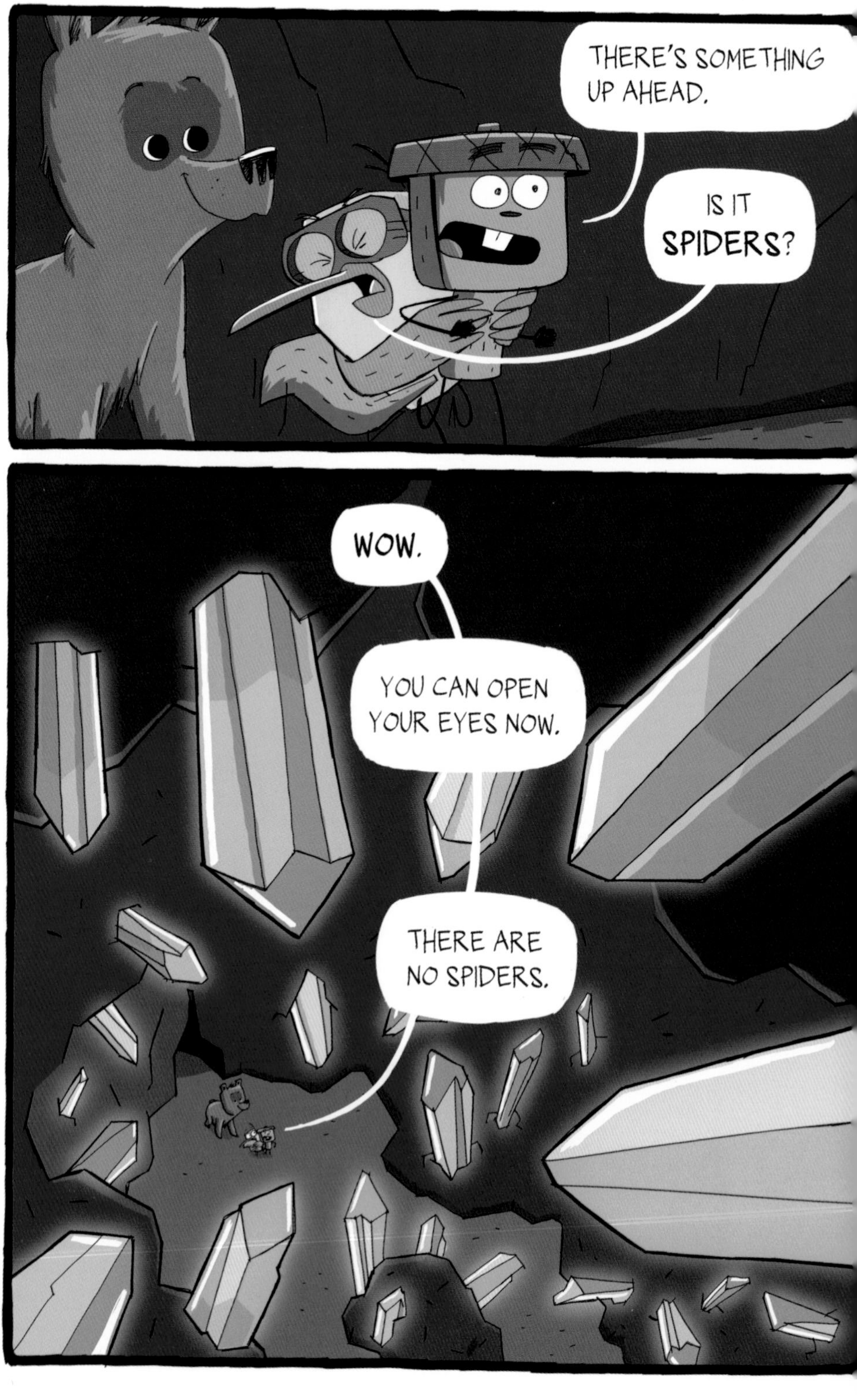
THERE'S SOMETHING UP AHEAD.
IS IT SPIDERS?
WOW.
YOU CAN OPEN YOUR EYES NOW.
THERE ARE NO SPIDERS.

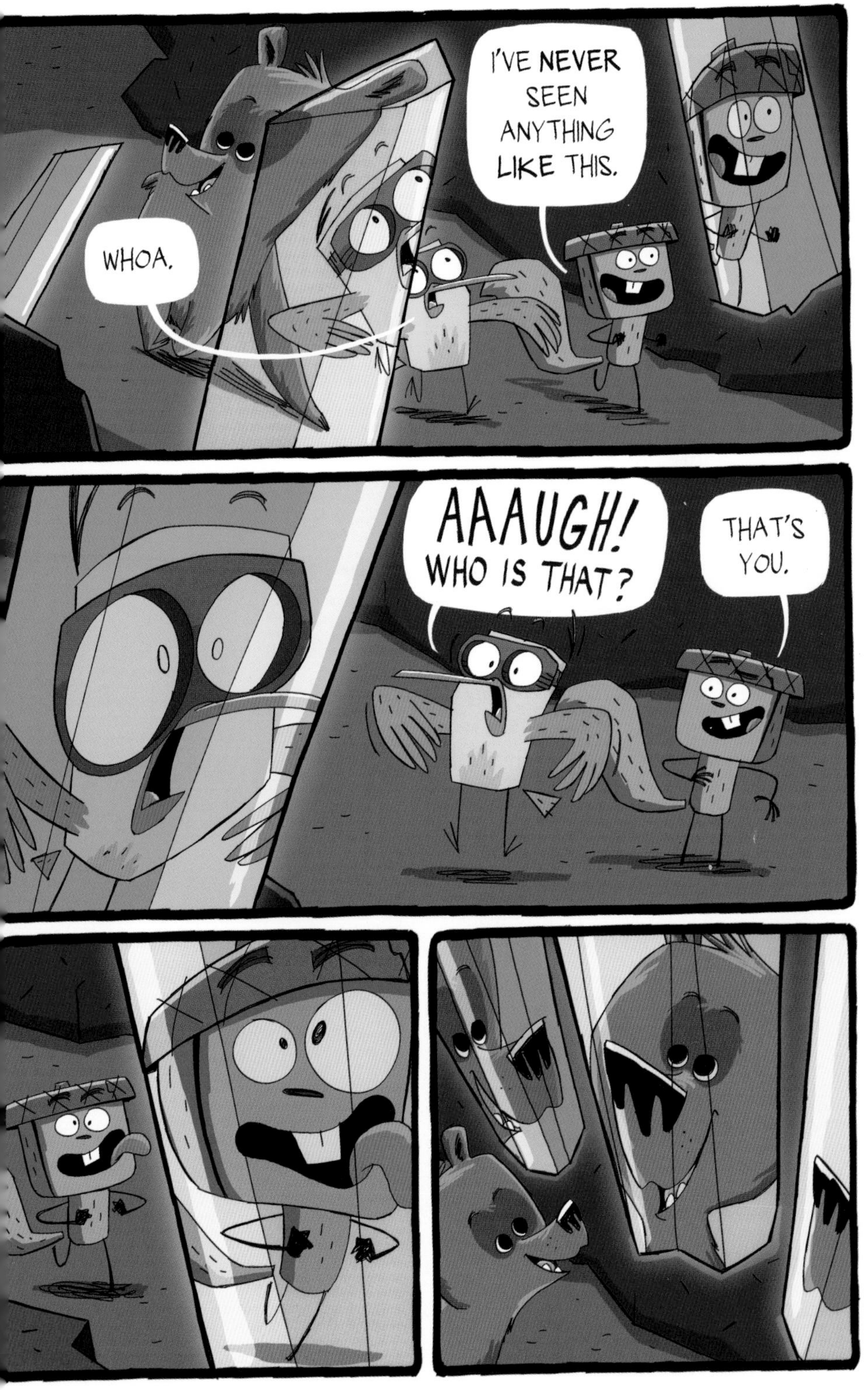
I'VE NEVER SEEN ANYTHING LIKE THIS.
WHOA.
AAAUGH! WHO IS THAT?
THAT'S YOU.

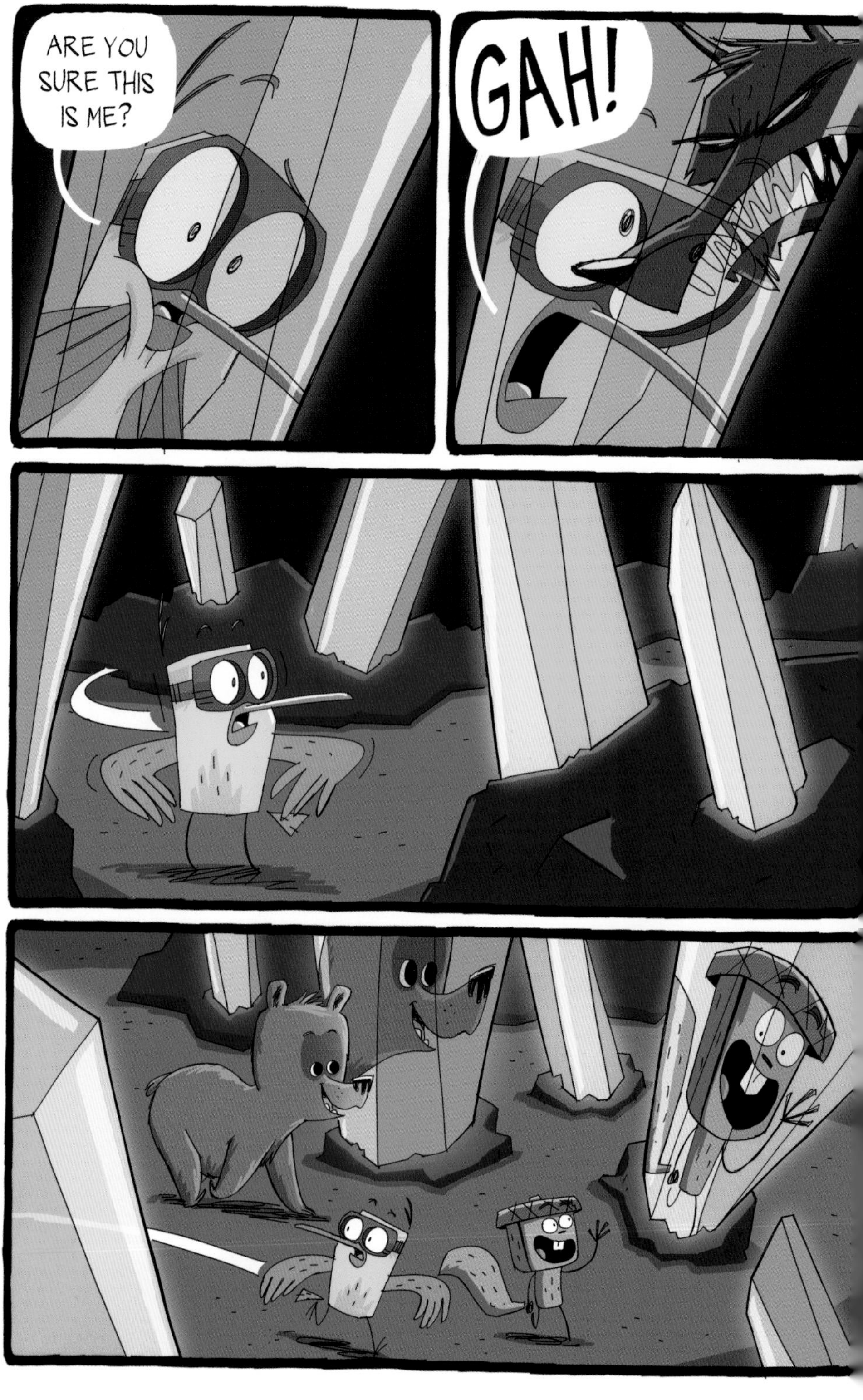
ARE YOU SURE THIS IS ME?
GAH!

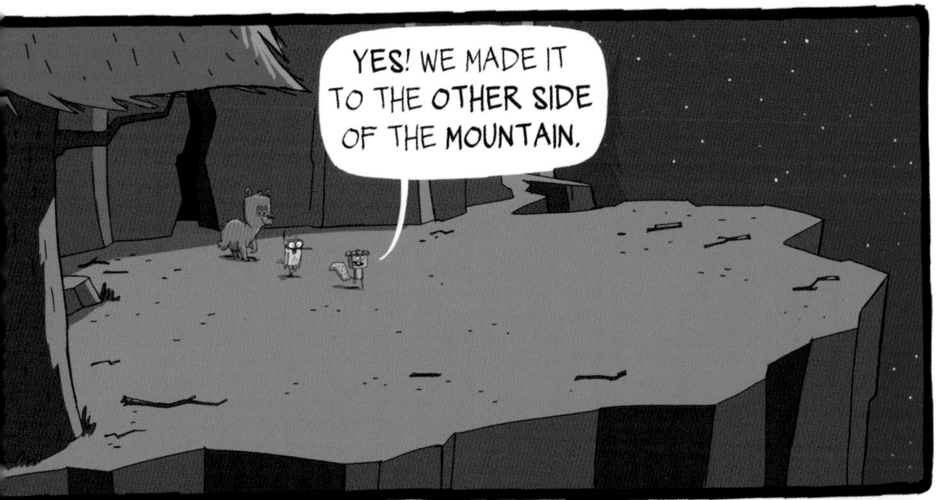
YES! WE MADE IT TO THE OTHER SIDE OF THE MOUNTAIN.

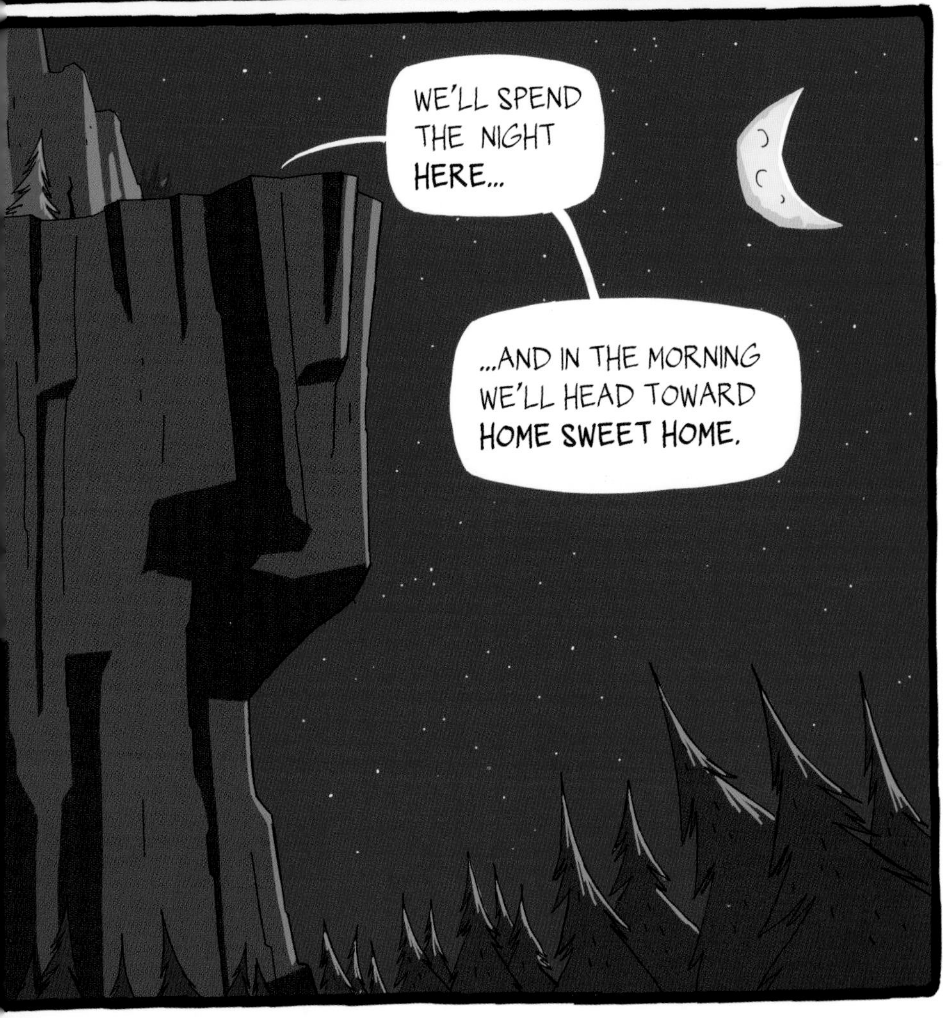
WE'LL SPEND THE NIGHT HERE...
...AND IN THE MORNING WE'LL HEAD TOWARD HOME SWEET HOME.

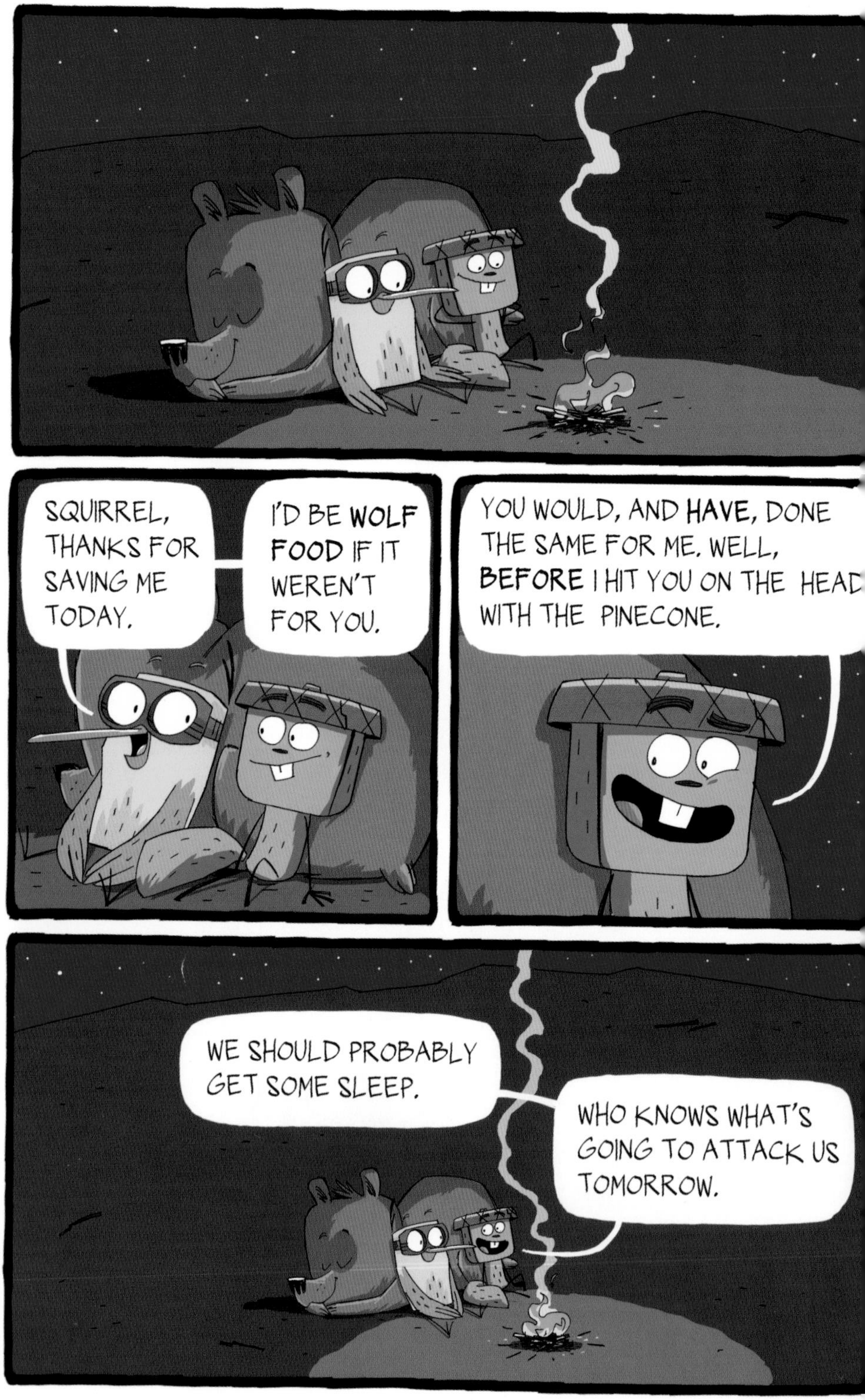
SQUIRREL, THANKS FOR SAVING ME TODAY.
I'D BE **WOLF FOOD** IF IT WEREN'T FOR YOU.
YOU WOULD, AND **HAVE,** DONE THE SAME FOR ME. WELL, **BEFORE** I HIT YOU ON THE HEAD WITH THE PINECONE.
WE SHOULD PROBABLY GET SOME SLEEP.
WHO KNOWS WHAT'S GOING TO ATTACK US TOMORROW.

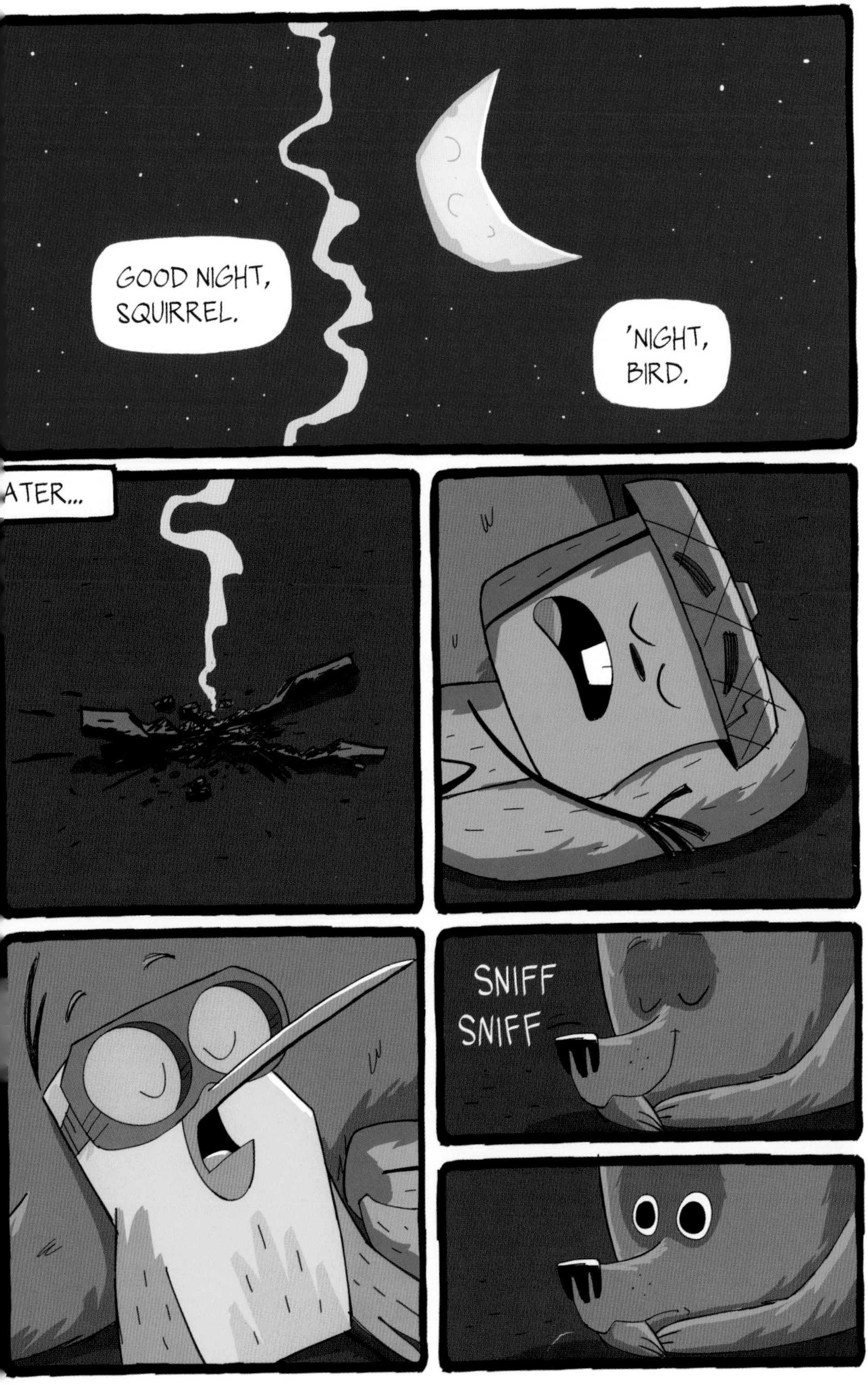
GOOD NIGHT, SQUIRREL.
'NIGHT, BIRD.
ATER...
SNIFF SNIFF

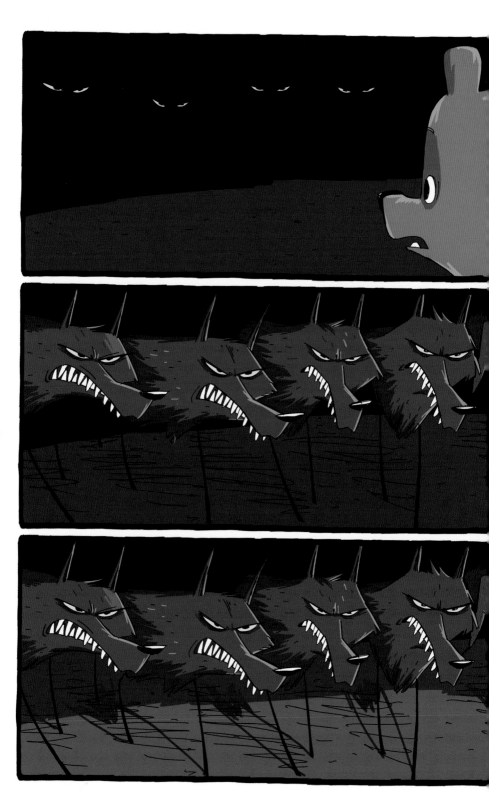

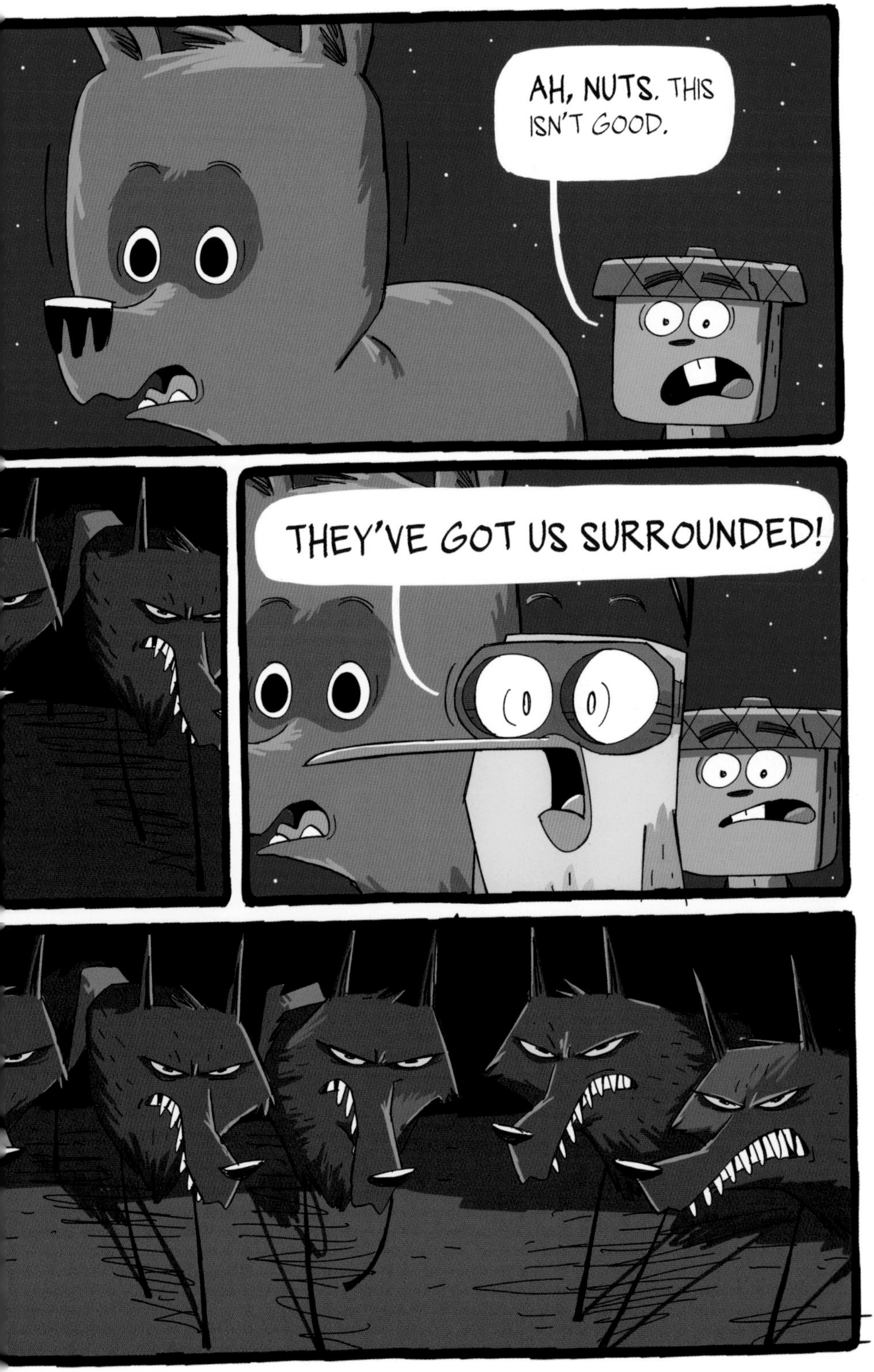
AH, NUTS. THIS ISN'T GOOD.
THEY'VE GOT US SURROUNDED!

THERE'S NOWHERE FOR US TO RUN.
WE'RE DEAD.
WE'RE DEAD!
WHAT ARE WE GOING TO DO? THERE'S NOTHING WE CAN DO!
THIS IS THE END.
IT'S THE END!
YOU'RE RIGHT.
WHAT? I AM?!!
THIS IS THE END.

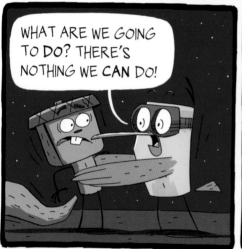

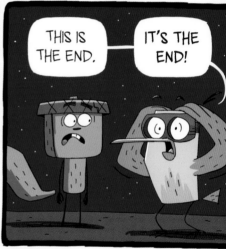

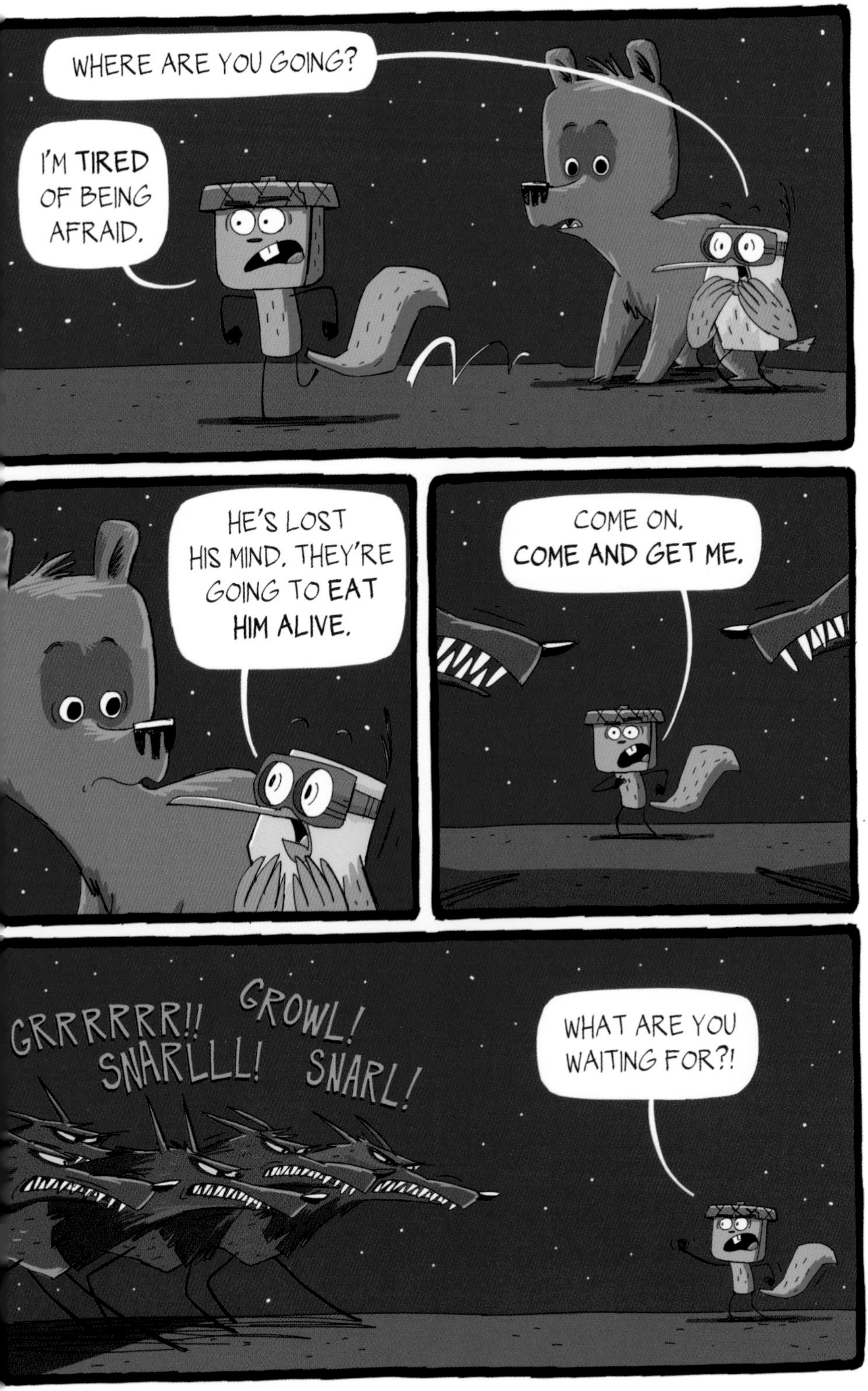
WHERE ARE YOU GOING?
I'M TIRED OF BEING AFRAID.
HE'S LOST HIS MIND. THEY'RE GOING TO EAT HIM ALIVE.
COME ON. COME AND GET ME.
GRRRRRR!! GROWL! SNARLLL! SNARL!
WHAT ARE YOU WAITING FOR?!

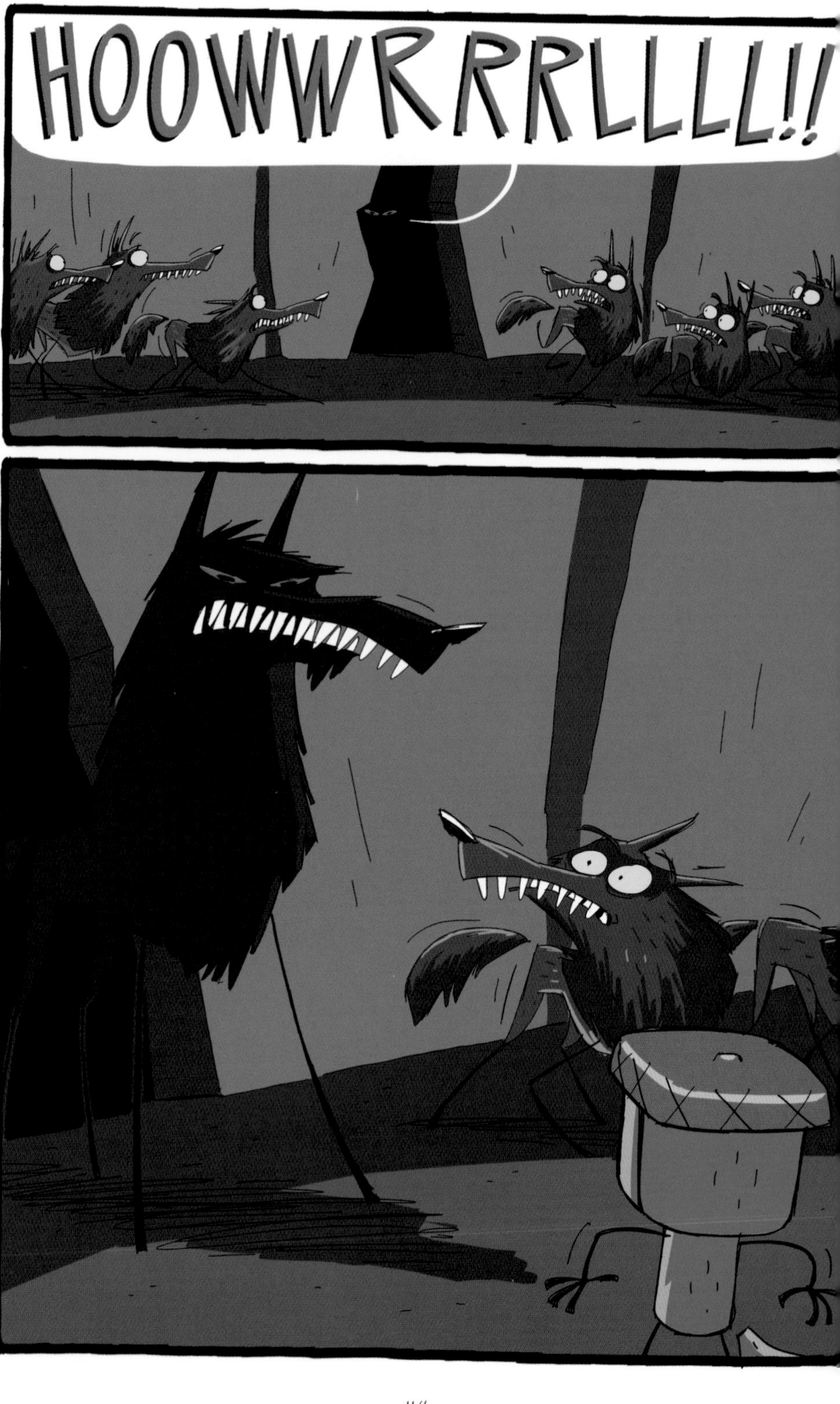
HOOWWRRRLLLLL!!

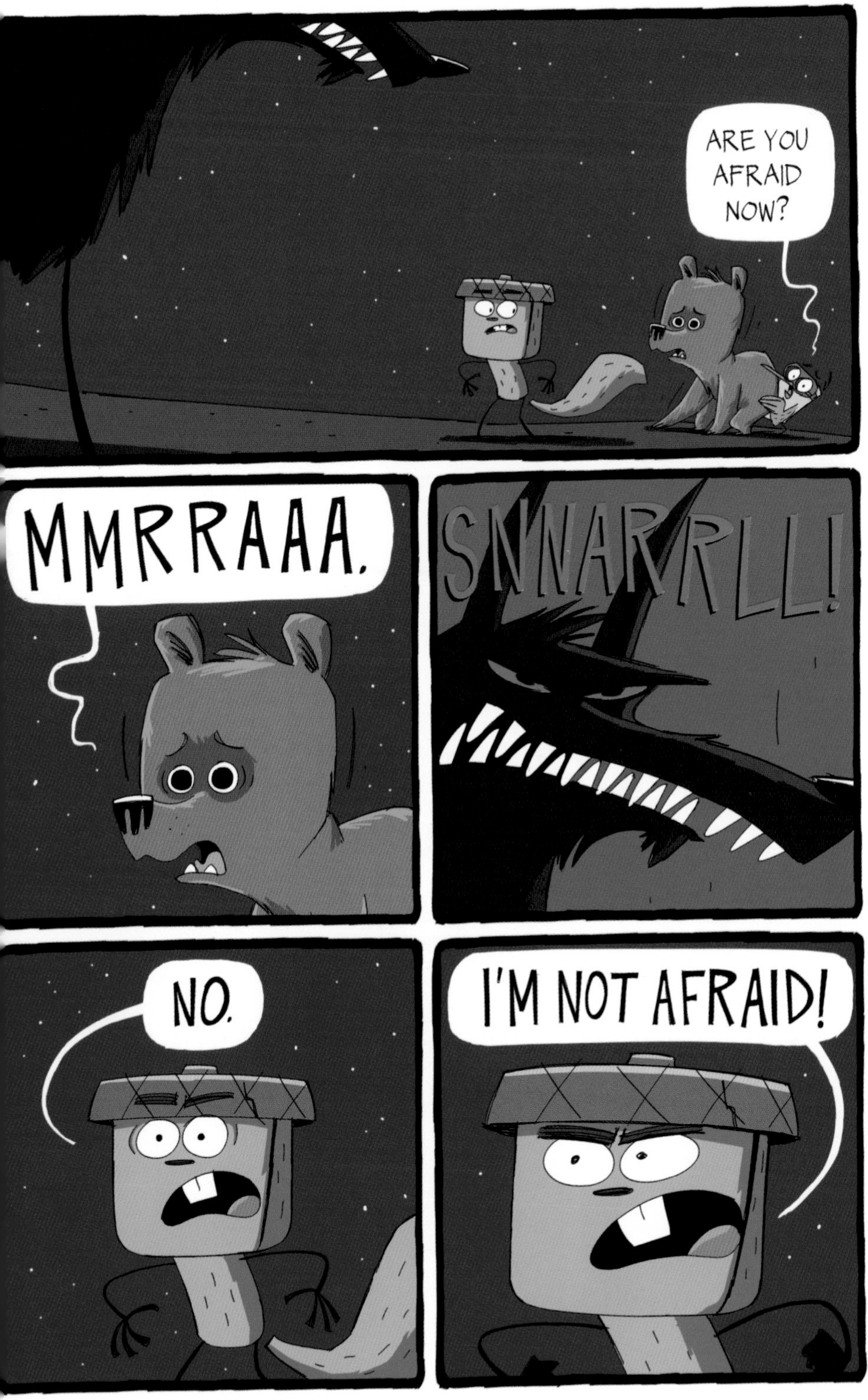
ARE YOU AFRAID NOW?
MMRRAAA.
SNNARRLL!
NO.
I'M NOT AFRAID!

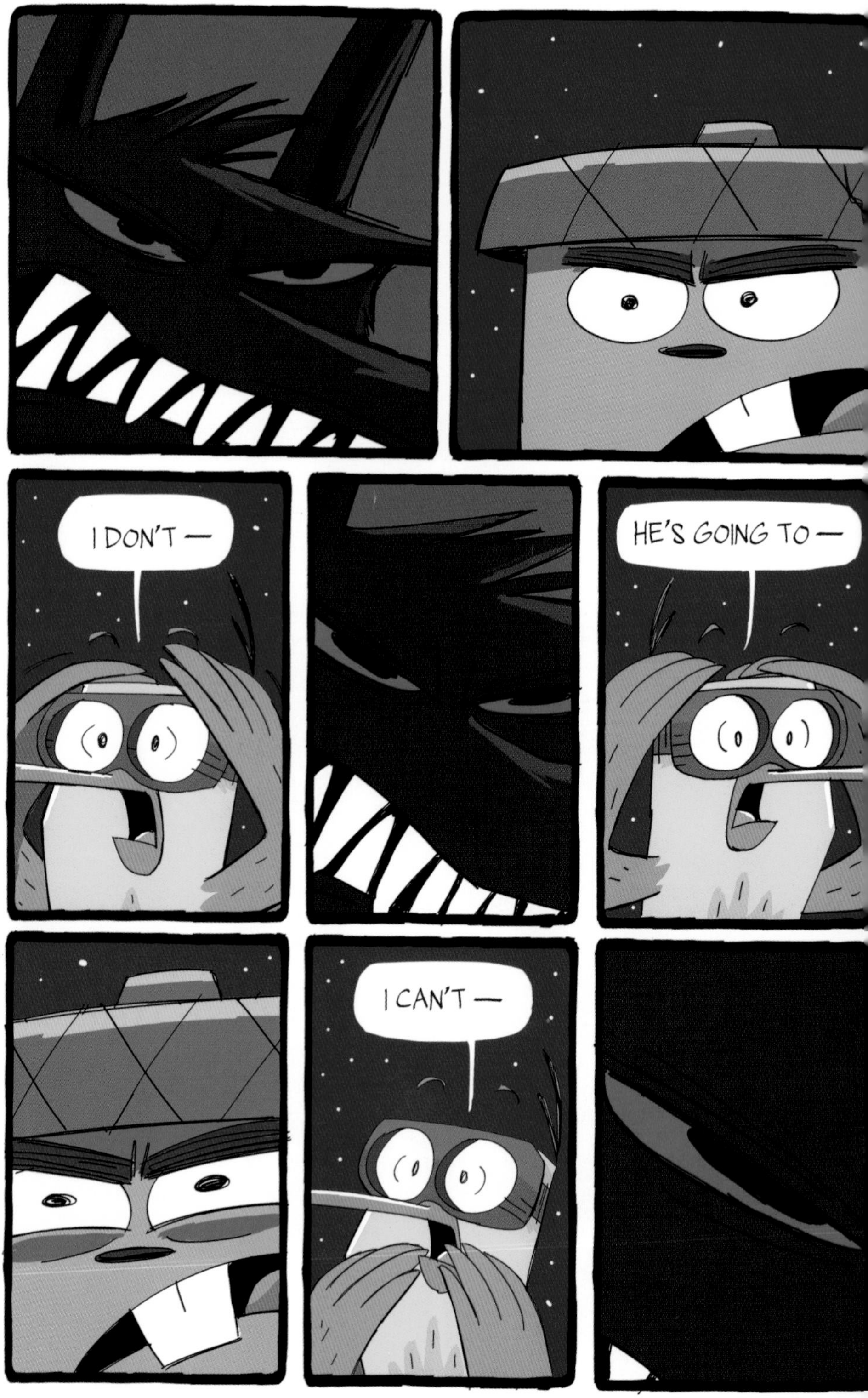
I DON'T —
HE'S GOING TO —
I CAN'T —

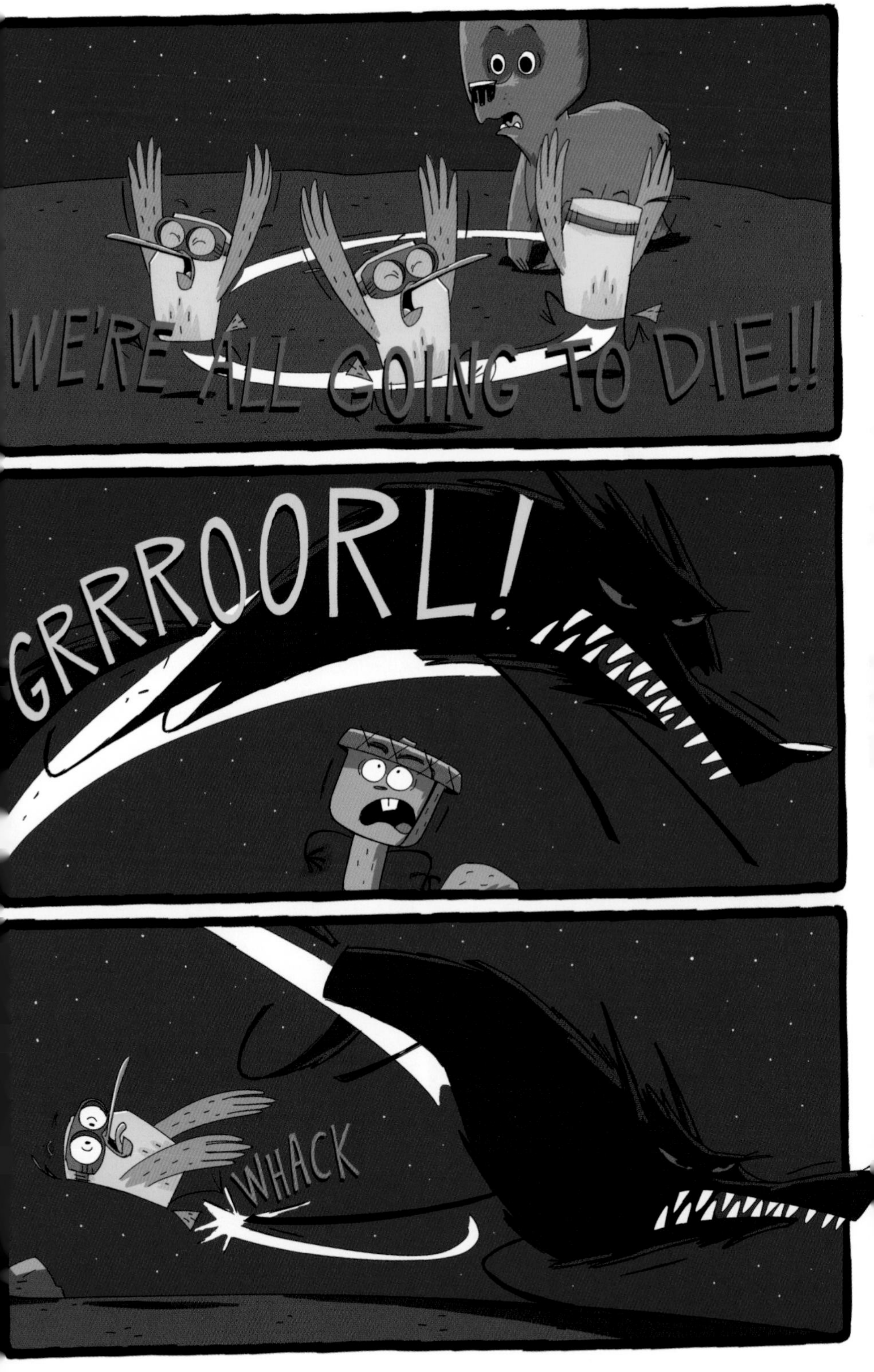
WE'RE ALL GOING TO DIE!!
GRRROORL!
WHACK

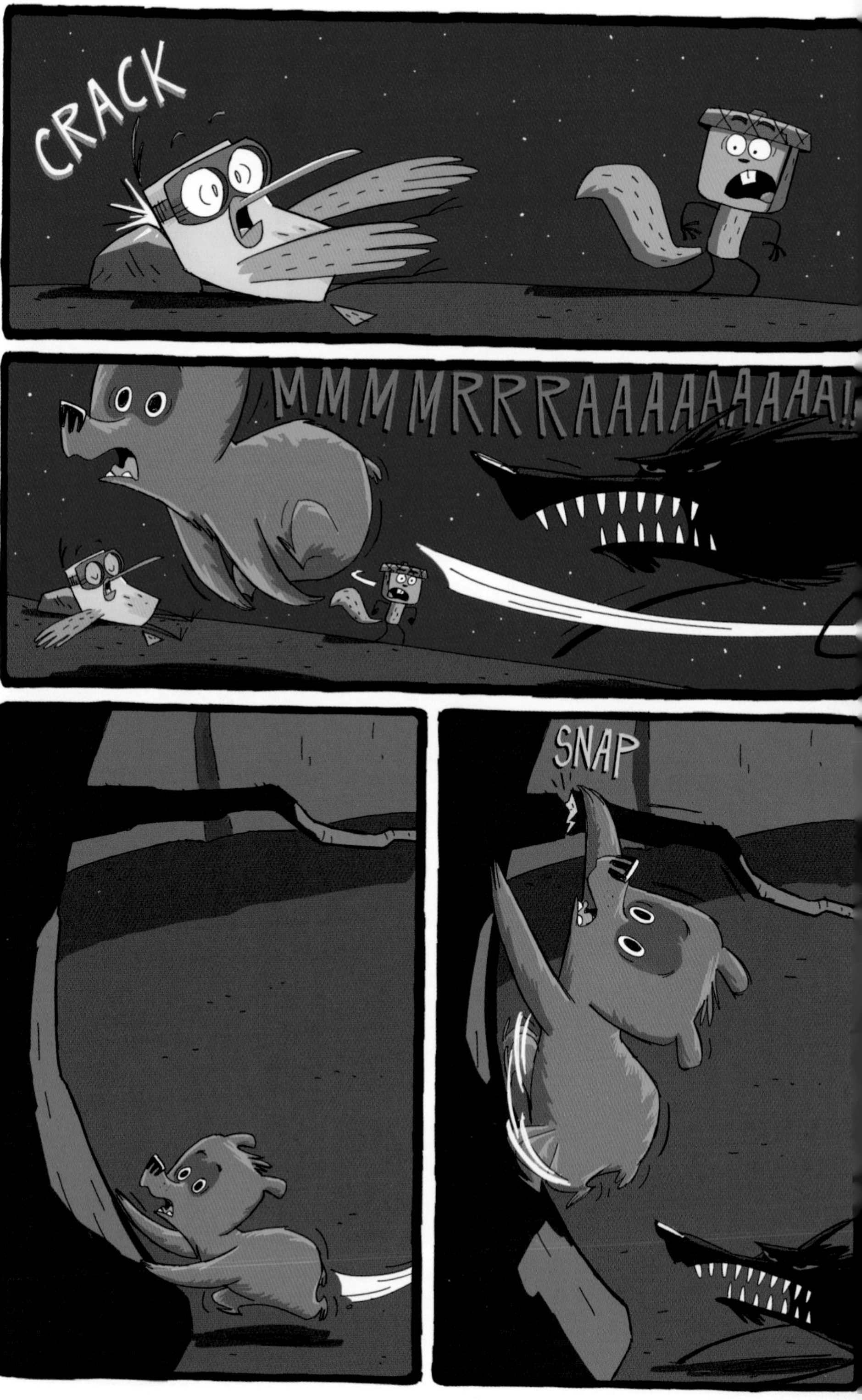
CRACK
MMMMRRRRAAAAAAAAAA!!
SNAP

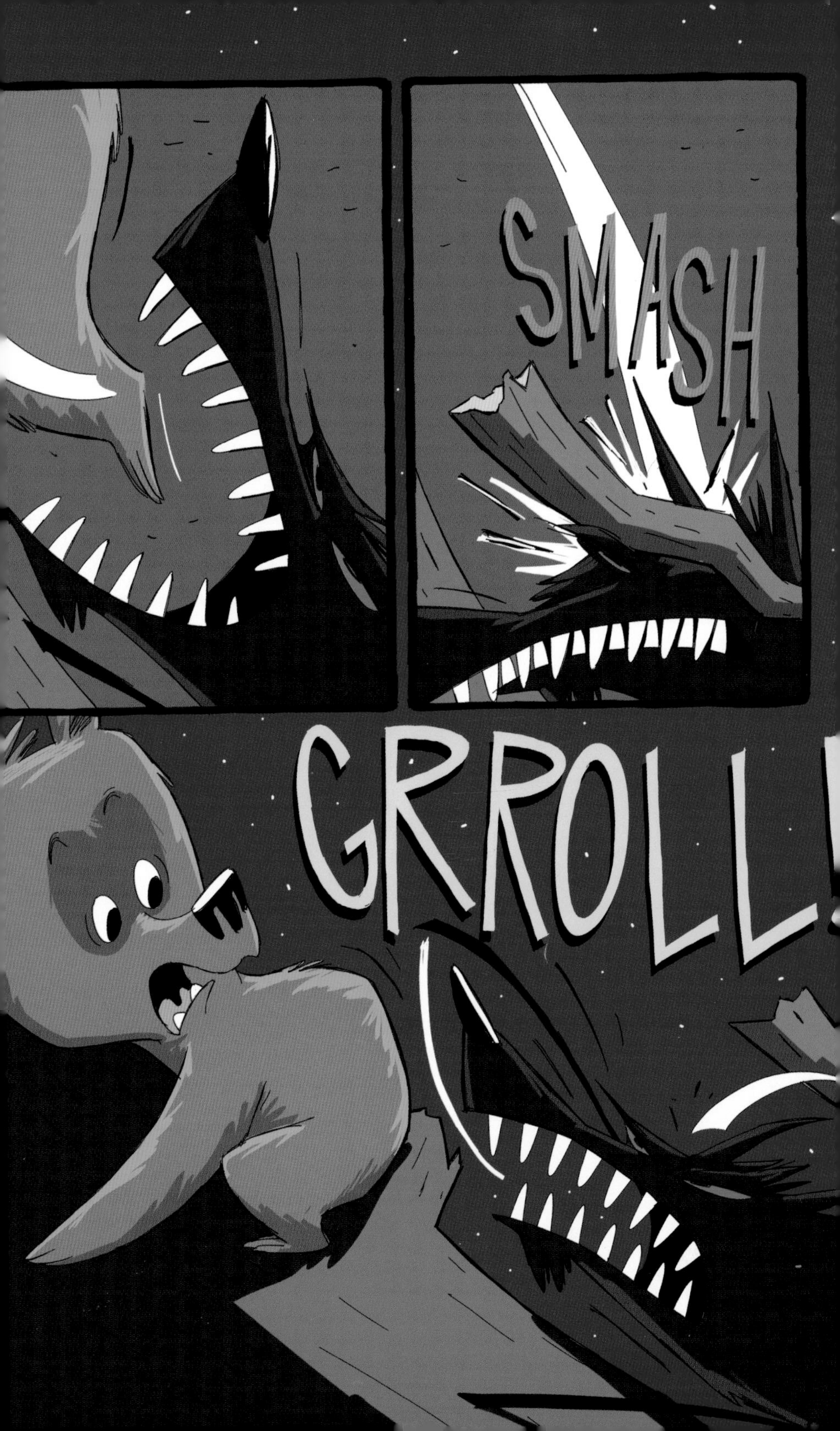
SMASH
GRROLL!

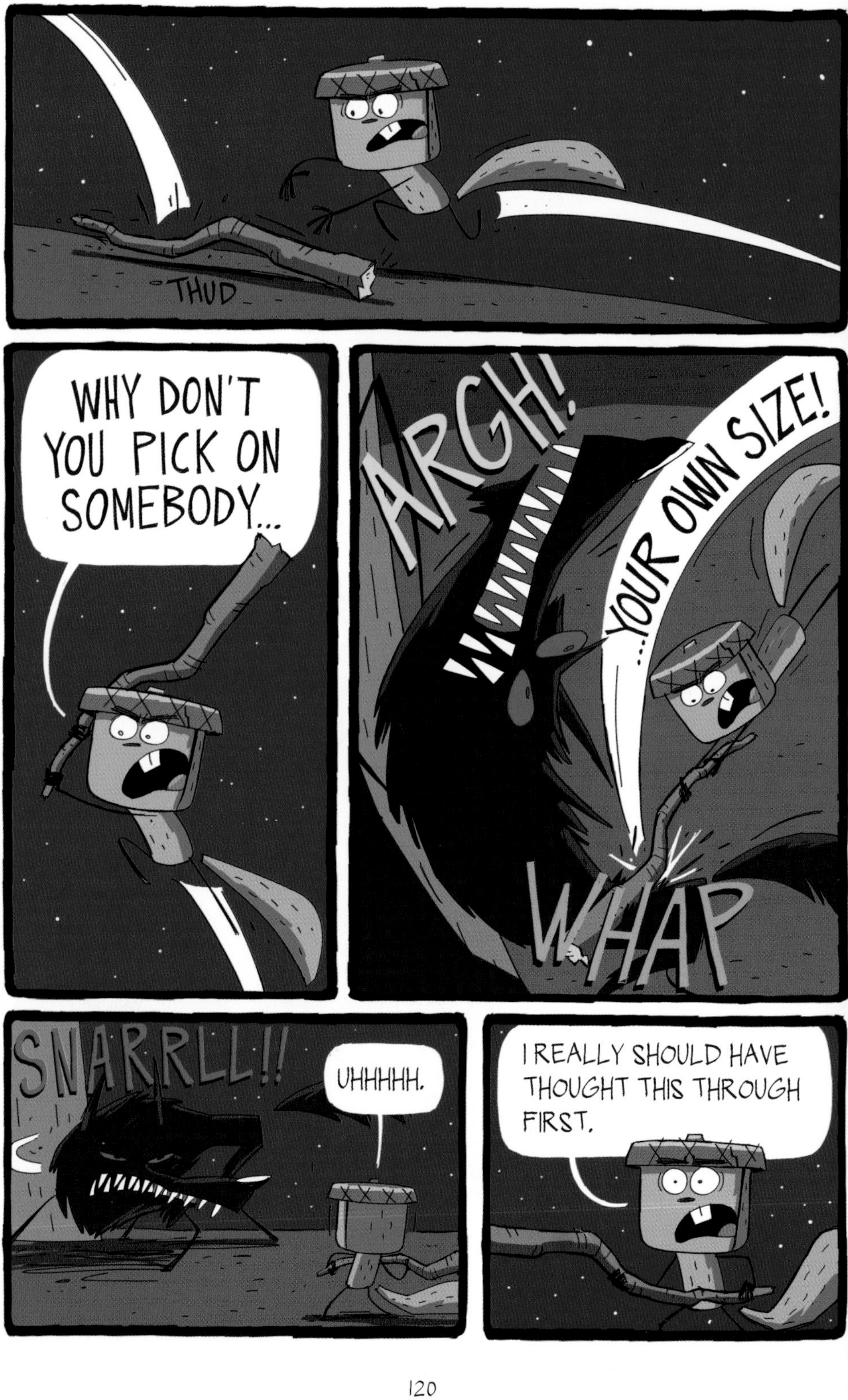

THUD
WHY DON'T YOU PICK ON SOMEBODY...
ARGH!
...YOUR OWN SIZE!
WHAP
SNARRLL!!
UHHHHH.
I REALLY SHOULD HAVE THOUGHT THIS THROUGH FIRST.

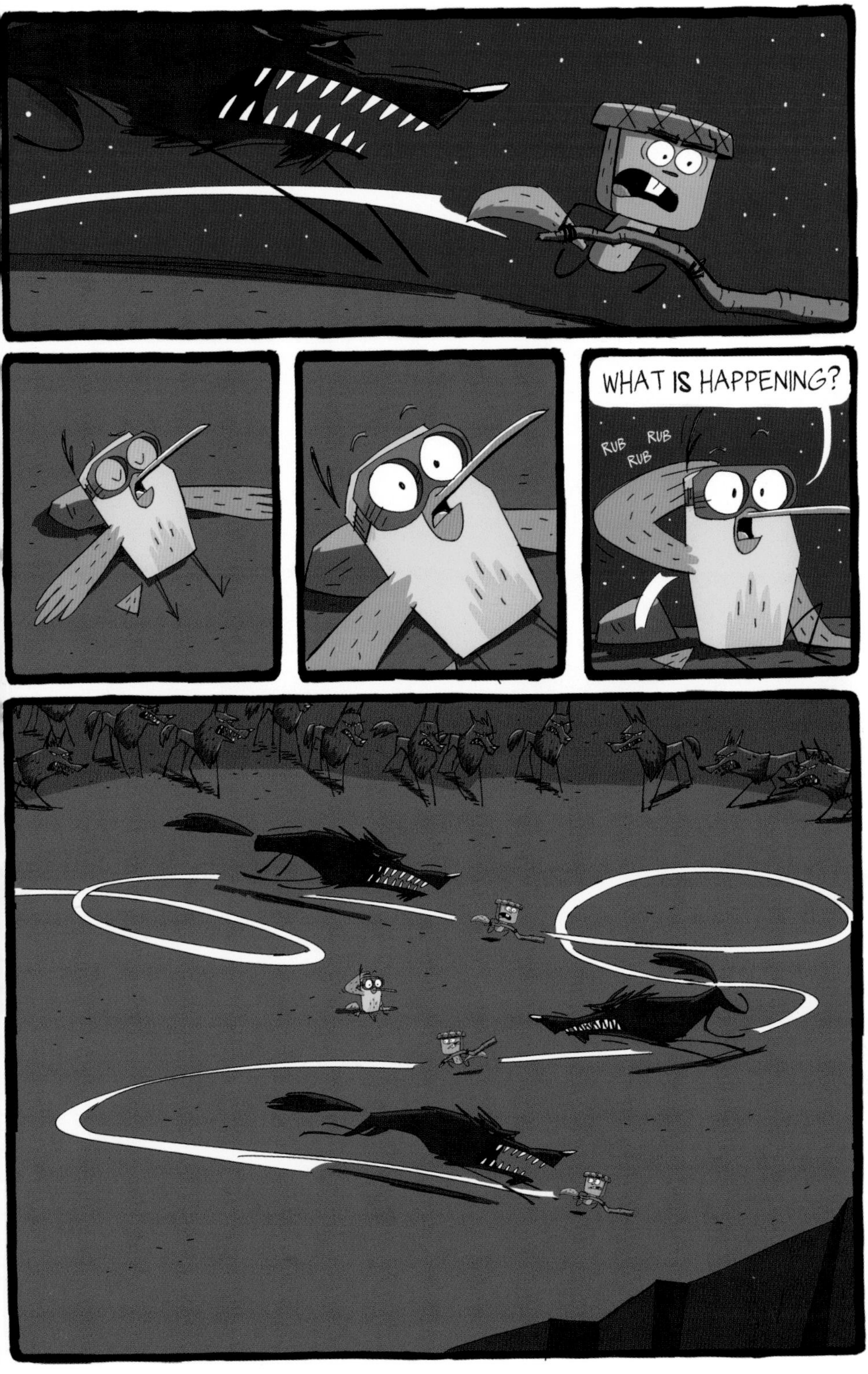
WHAT IS HAPPENING?
RUB RUB RUB

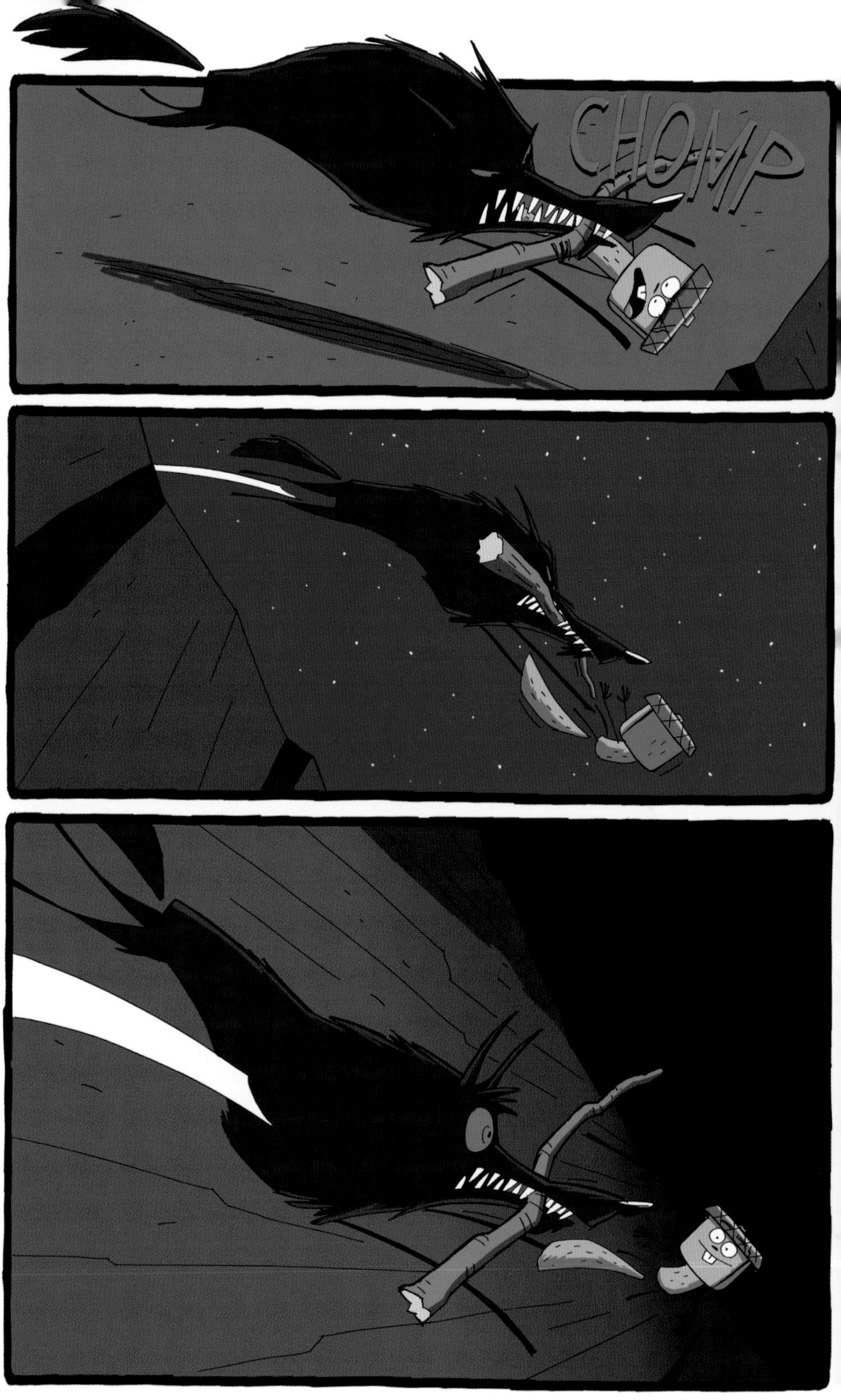
CHOMP

I AM NOT AFRAID.

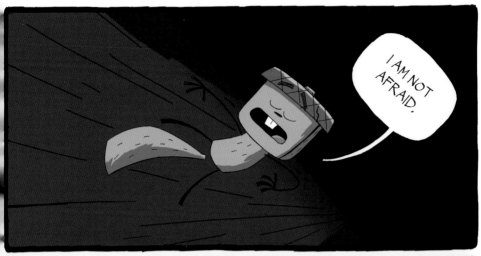

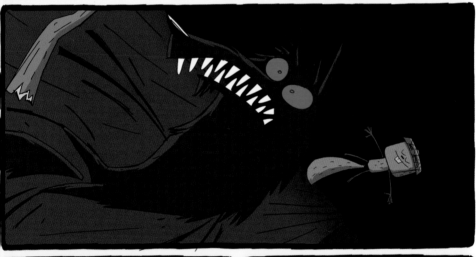

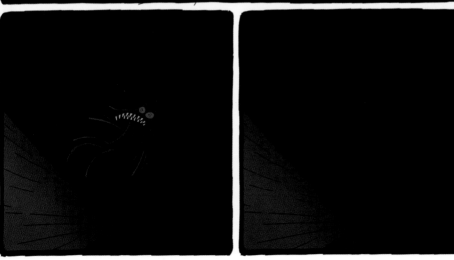

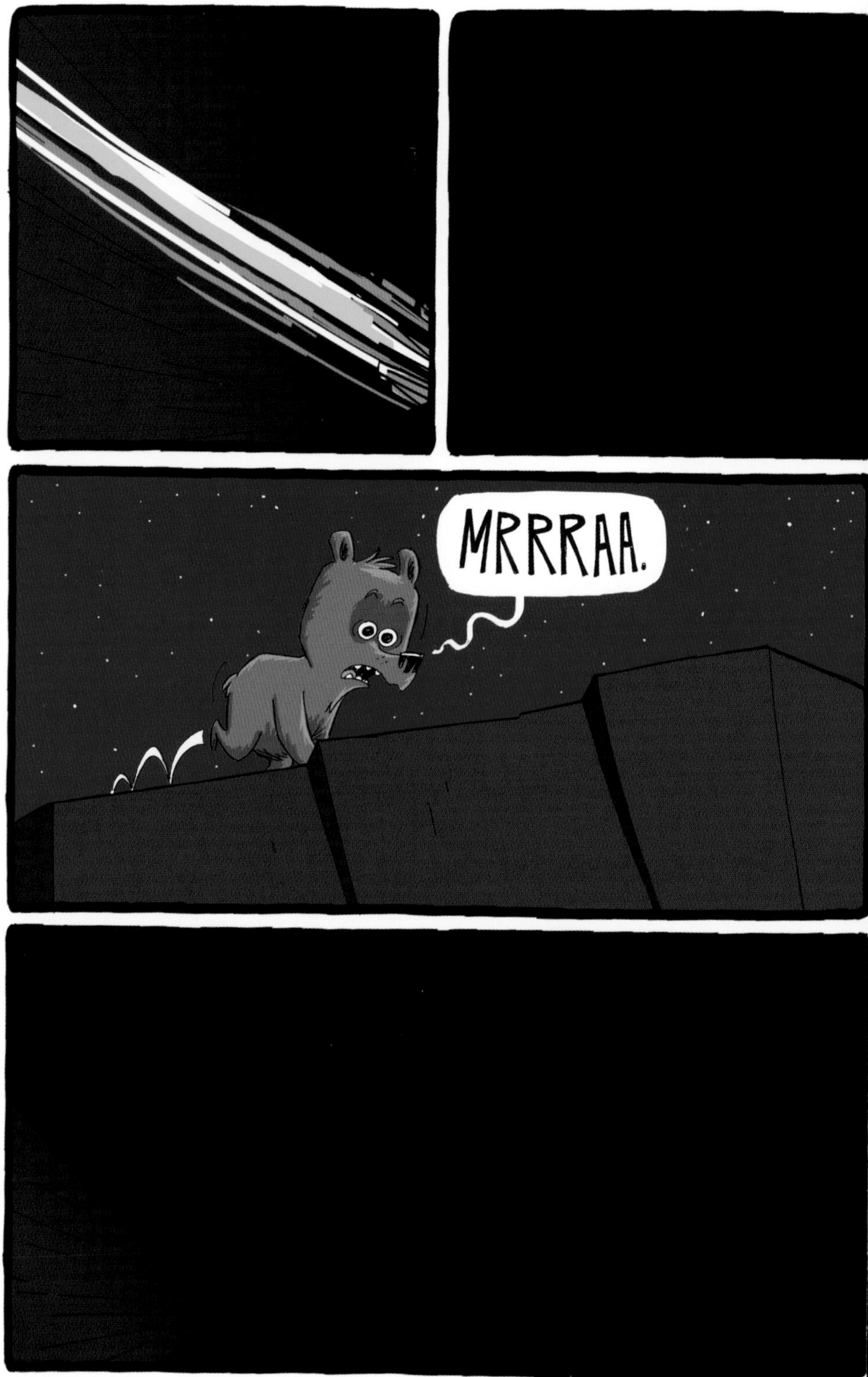
MRRRAA.

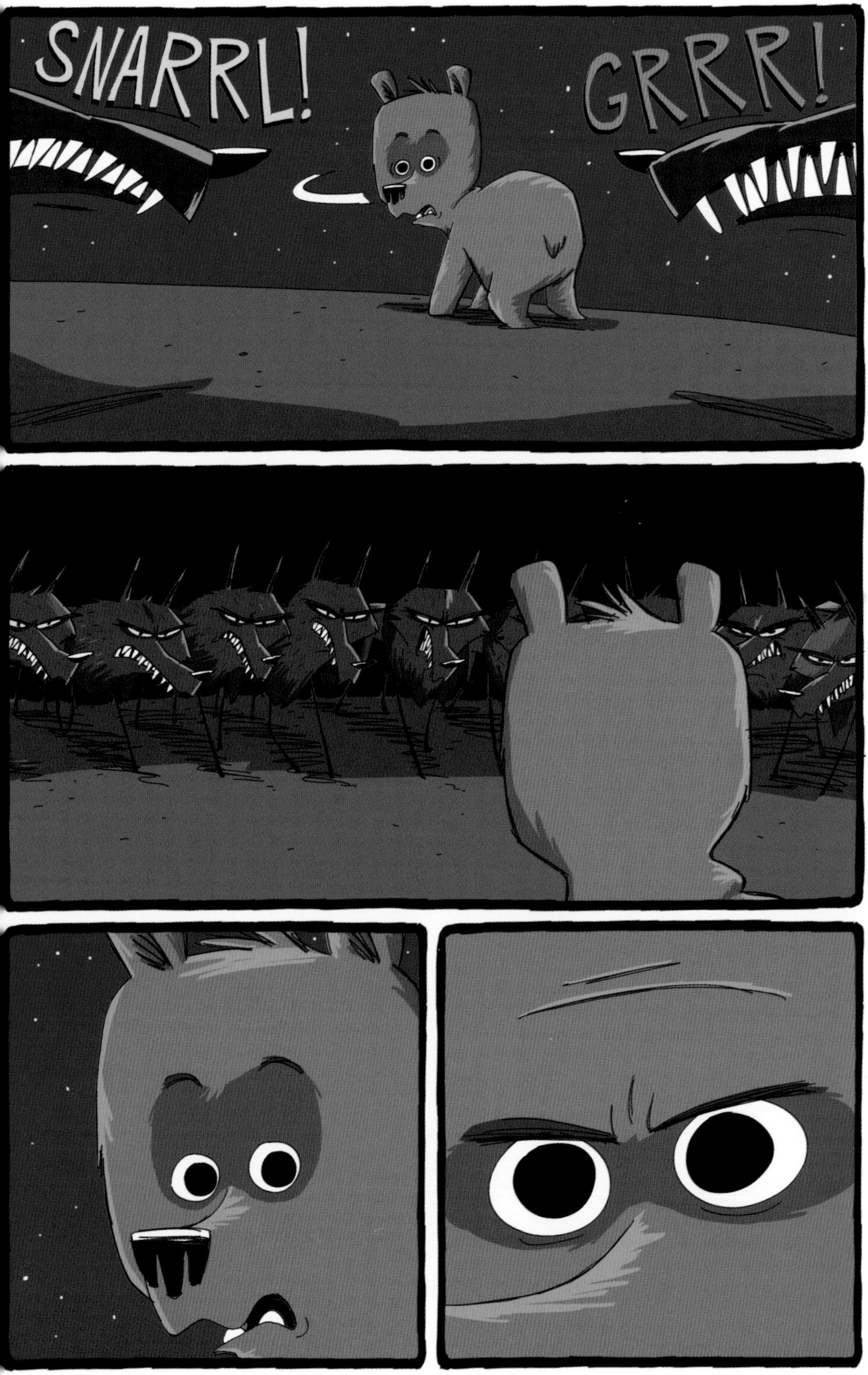
SNARRL!
GRRR!

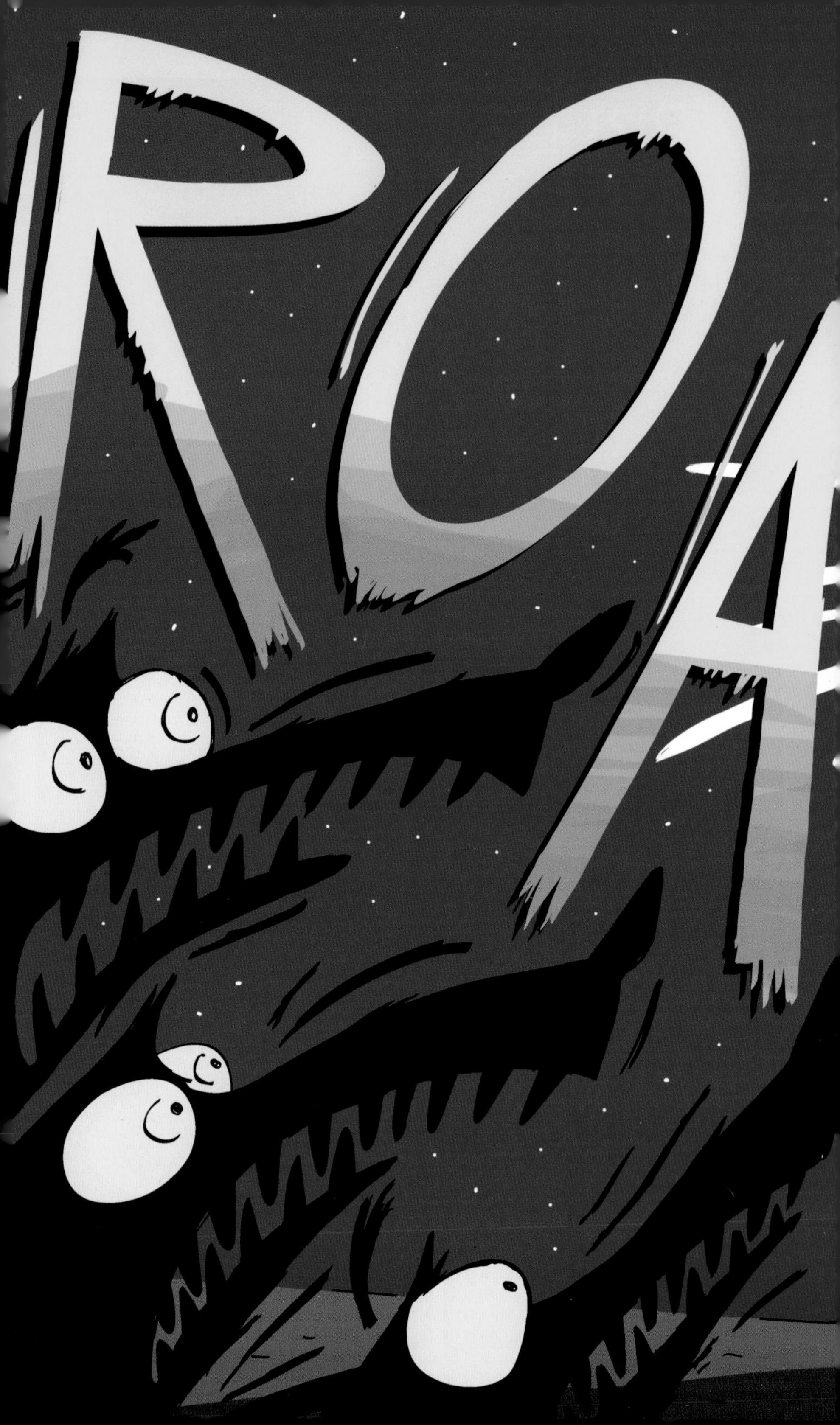
ROA

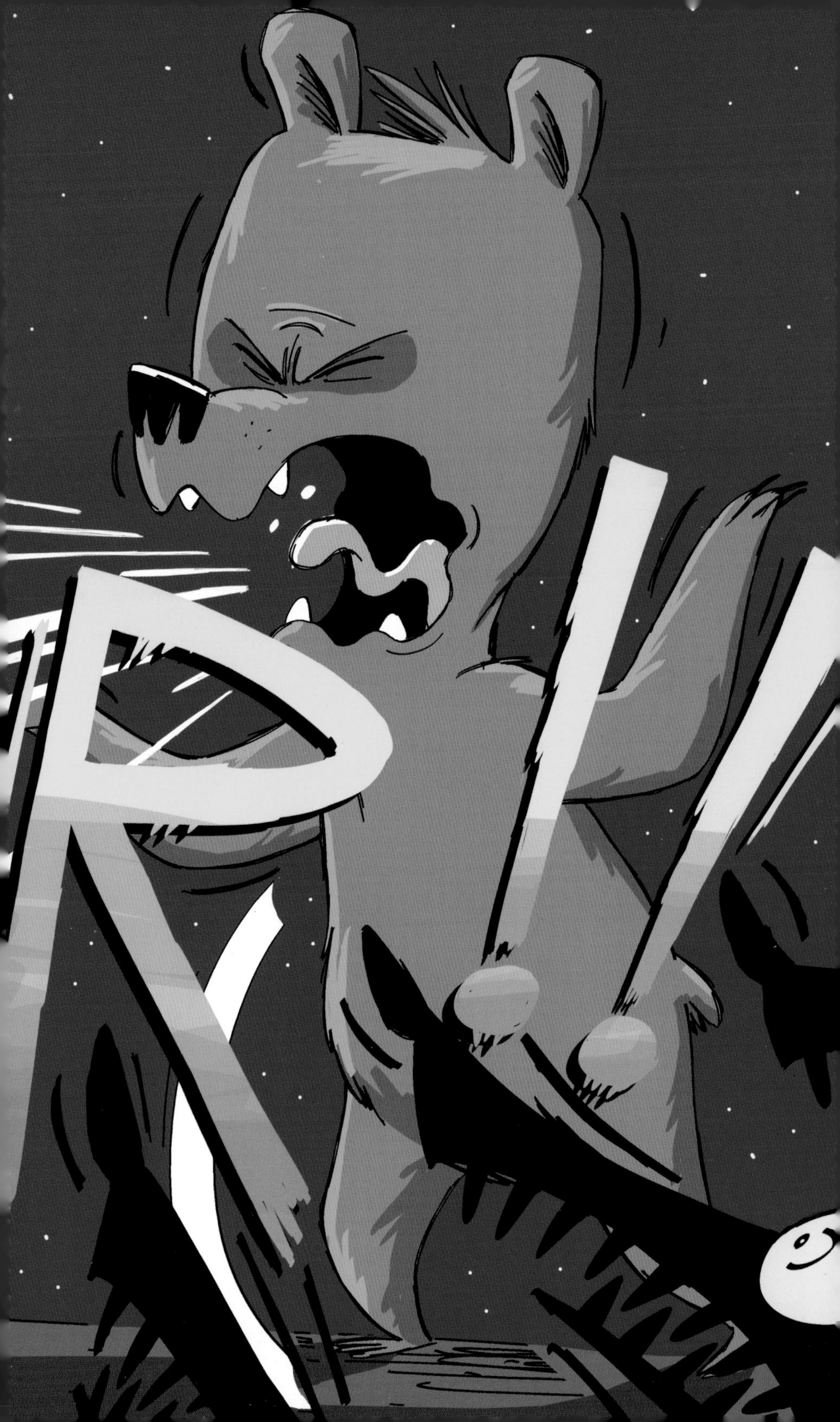
R!!

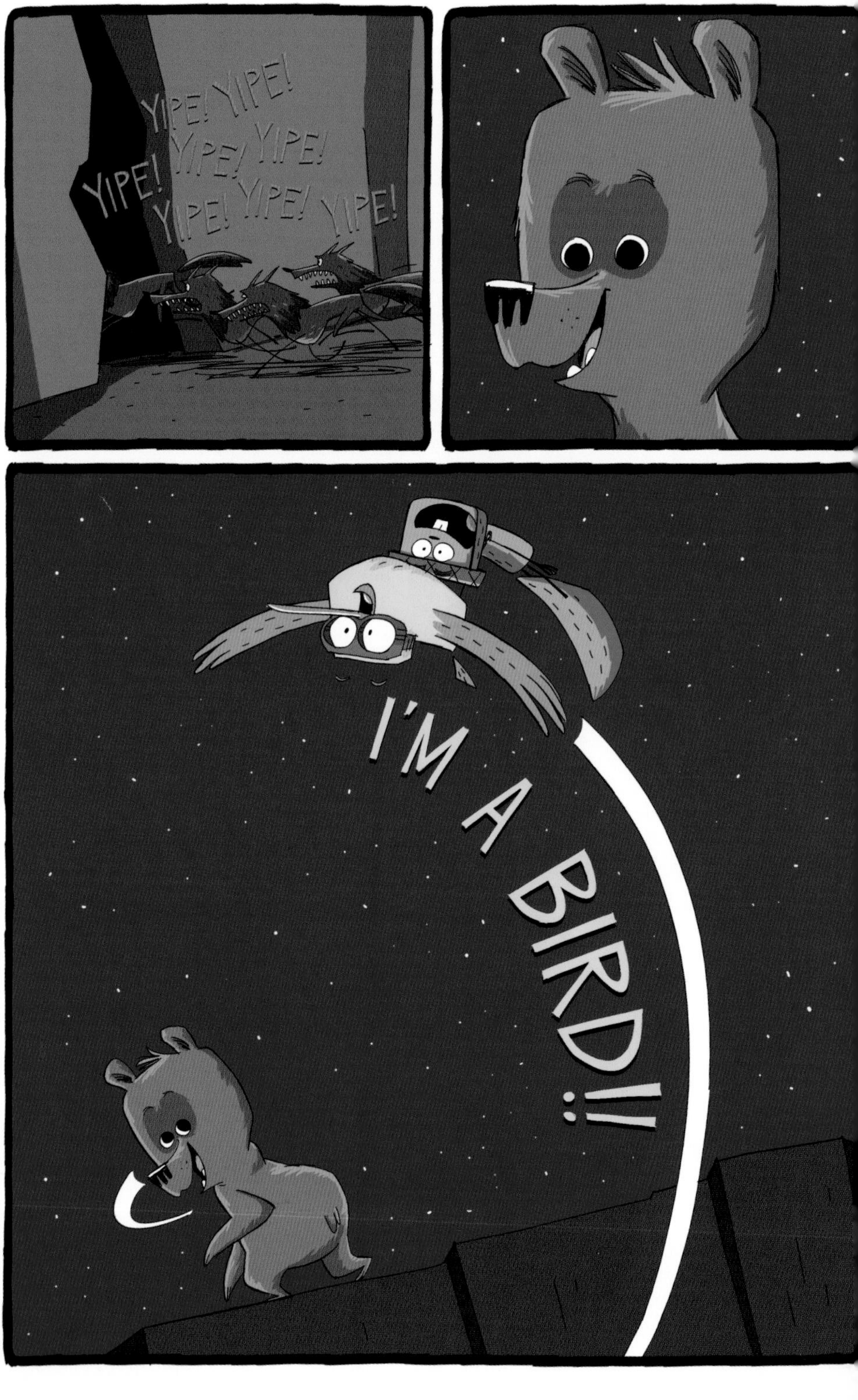
YIPE! YIPE!
YIPE! YIPE! YIPE!
YIPE! YIPE! YIPE!
I'M A BIRD!!!

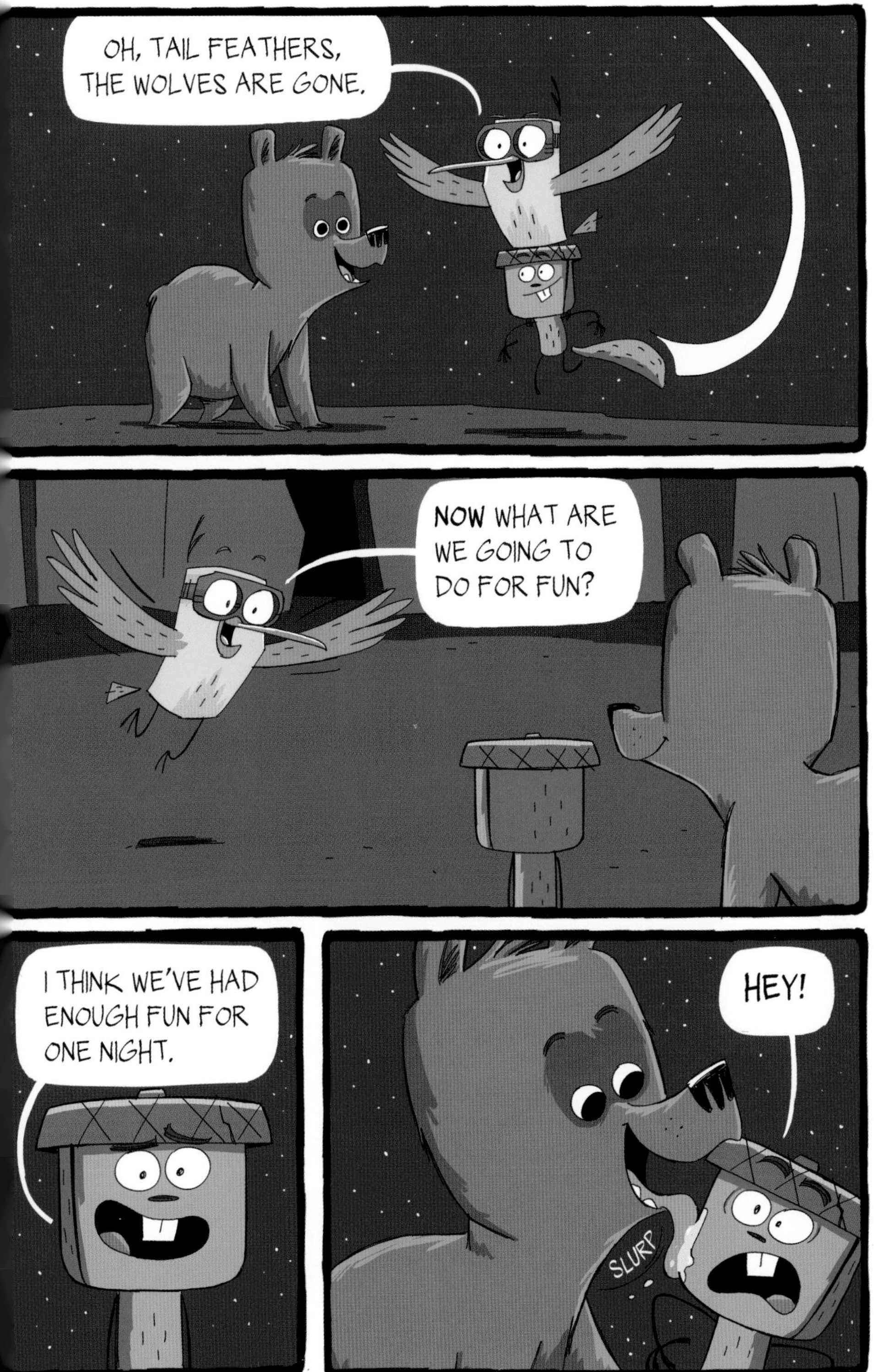
OH, TAIL FEATHERS, THE WOLVES ARE GONE.
NOW WHAT ARE WE GOING TO DO FOR FUN?
I THINK WE'VE HAD ENOUGH FUN FOR ONE NIGHT.
HEY!
SLURP

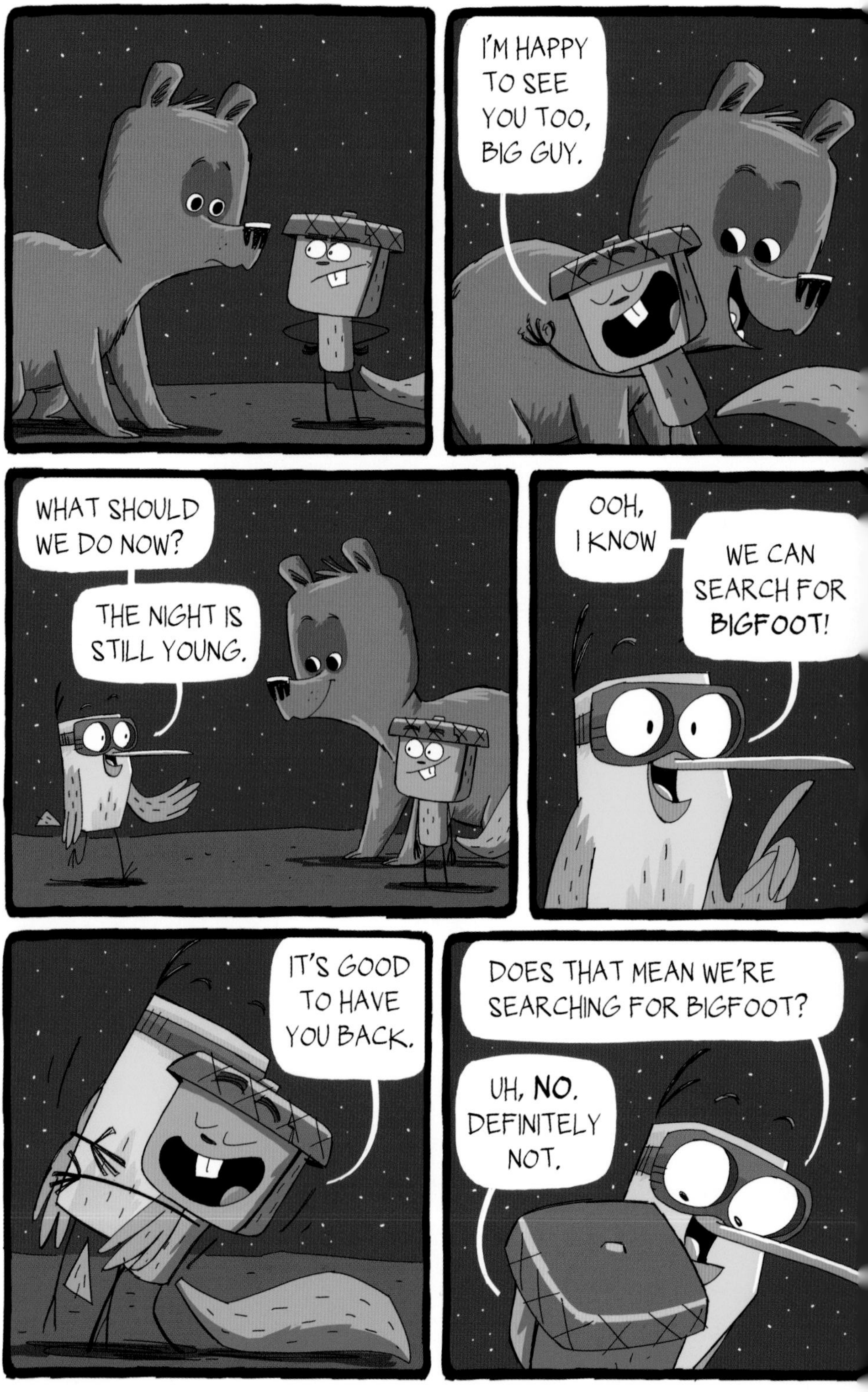
I'M HAPPY TO SEE YOU TOO, BIG GUY.
WHAT SHOULD WE DO NOW?
THE NIGHT IS STILL YOUNG.
OOH, I KNOW
WE CAN SEARCH FOR **BIGFOOT**!
IT'S GOOD TO HAVE YOU BACK.
DOES THAT MEAN WE'RE SEARCHING FOR BIGFOOT?
UH, **NO**. DEFINITELY NOT.

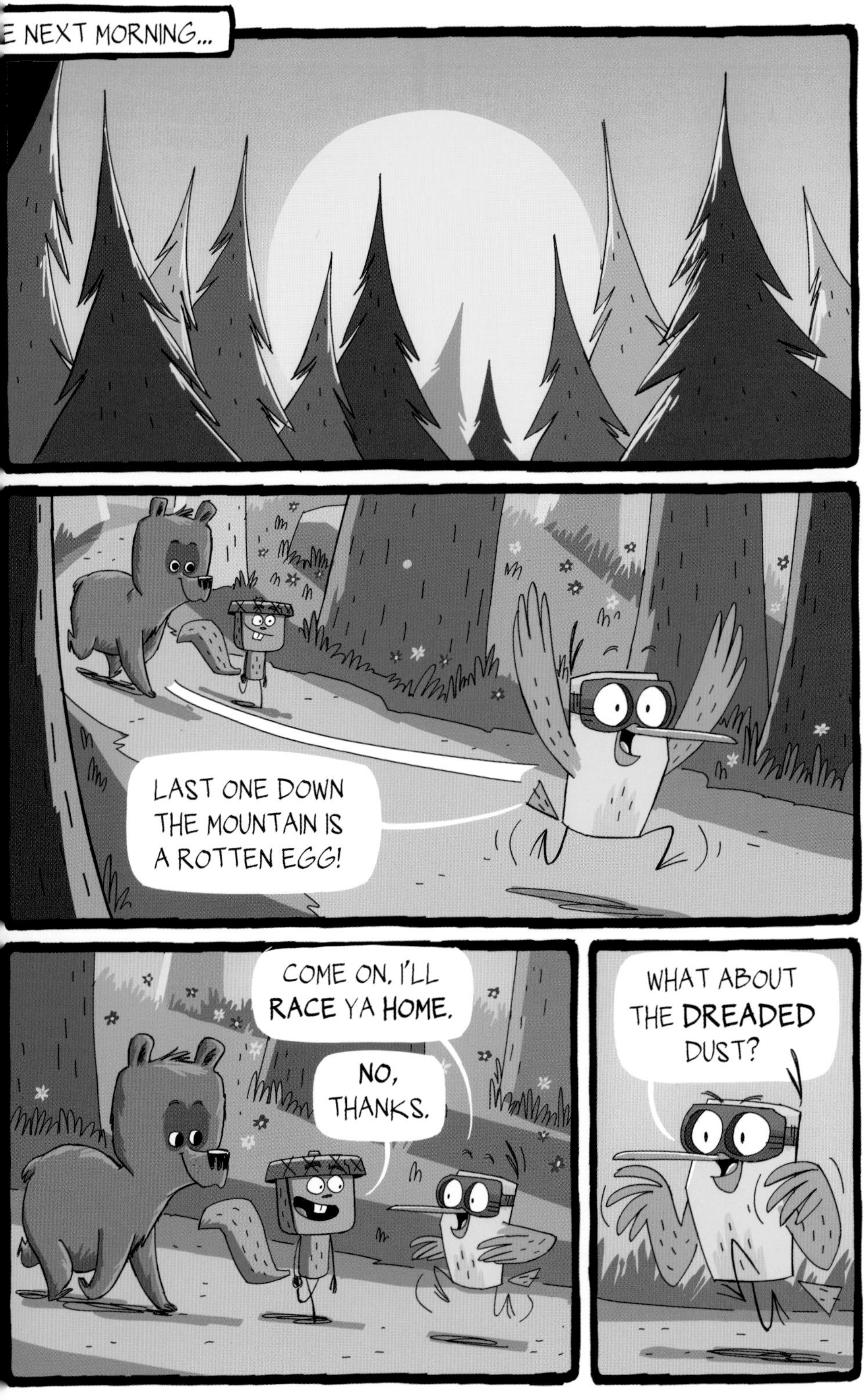
E NEXT MORNING...
LAST ONE DOWN THE MOUNTAIN IS A ROTTEN EGG!
COME ON. I'LL RACE YA HOME.
NO, THANKS.
WHAT ABOUT THE DREADED DUST?

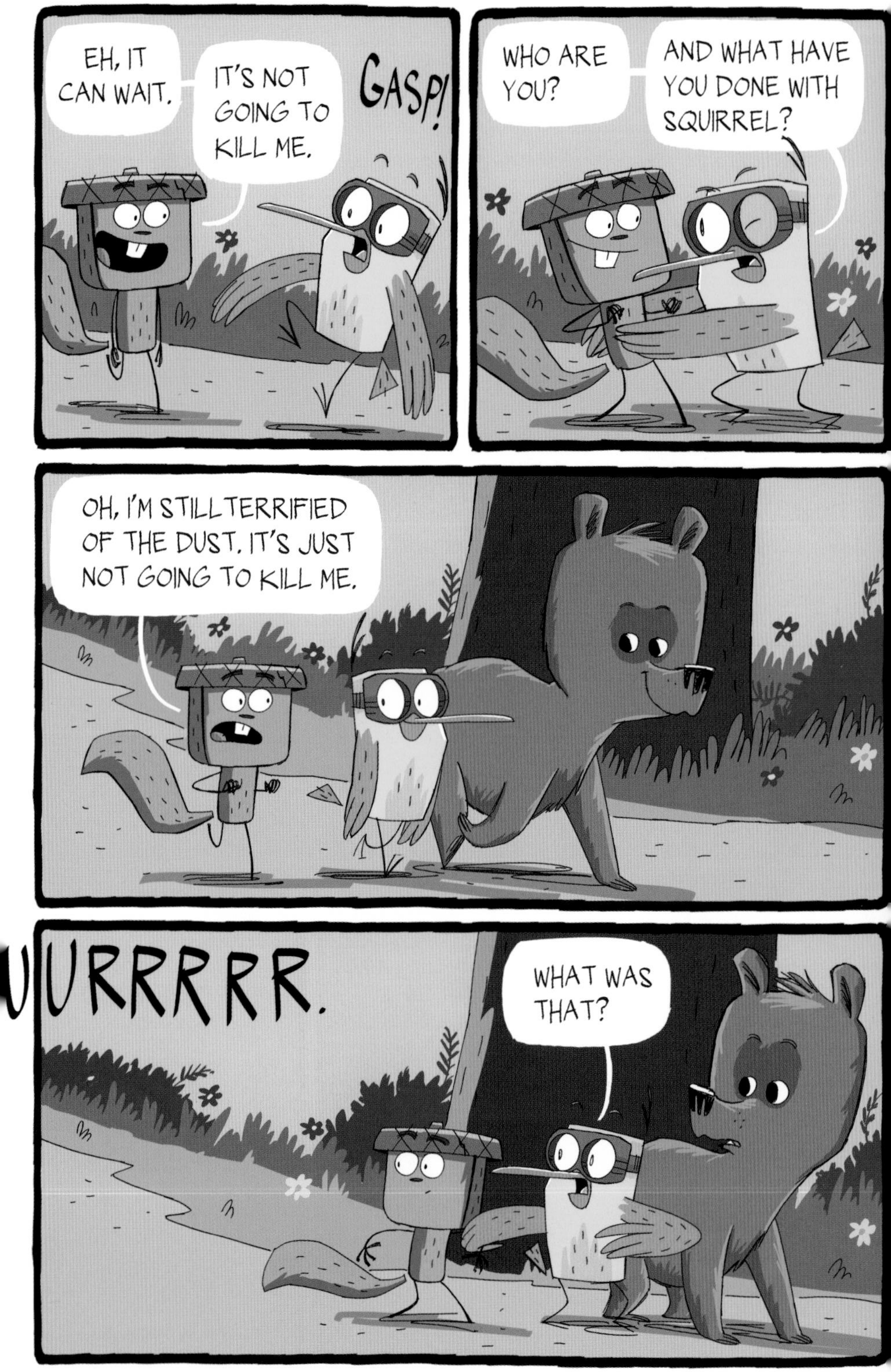
EH, IT CAN WAIT.
IT'S NOT GOING TO KILL ME.
GASP!
WHO ARE YOU?
AND WHAT HAVE YOU DONE WITH SQUIRREL?
OH, I'M STILL TERRIFIED OF THE DUST. IT'S JUST NOT GOING TO KILL ME.
URRRRRR.
WHAT WAS THAT?

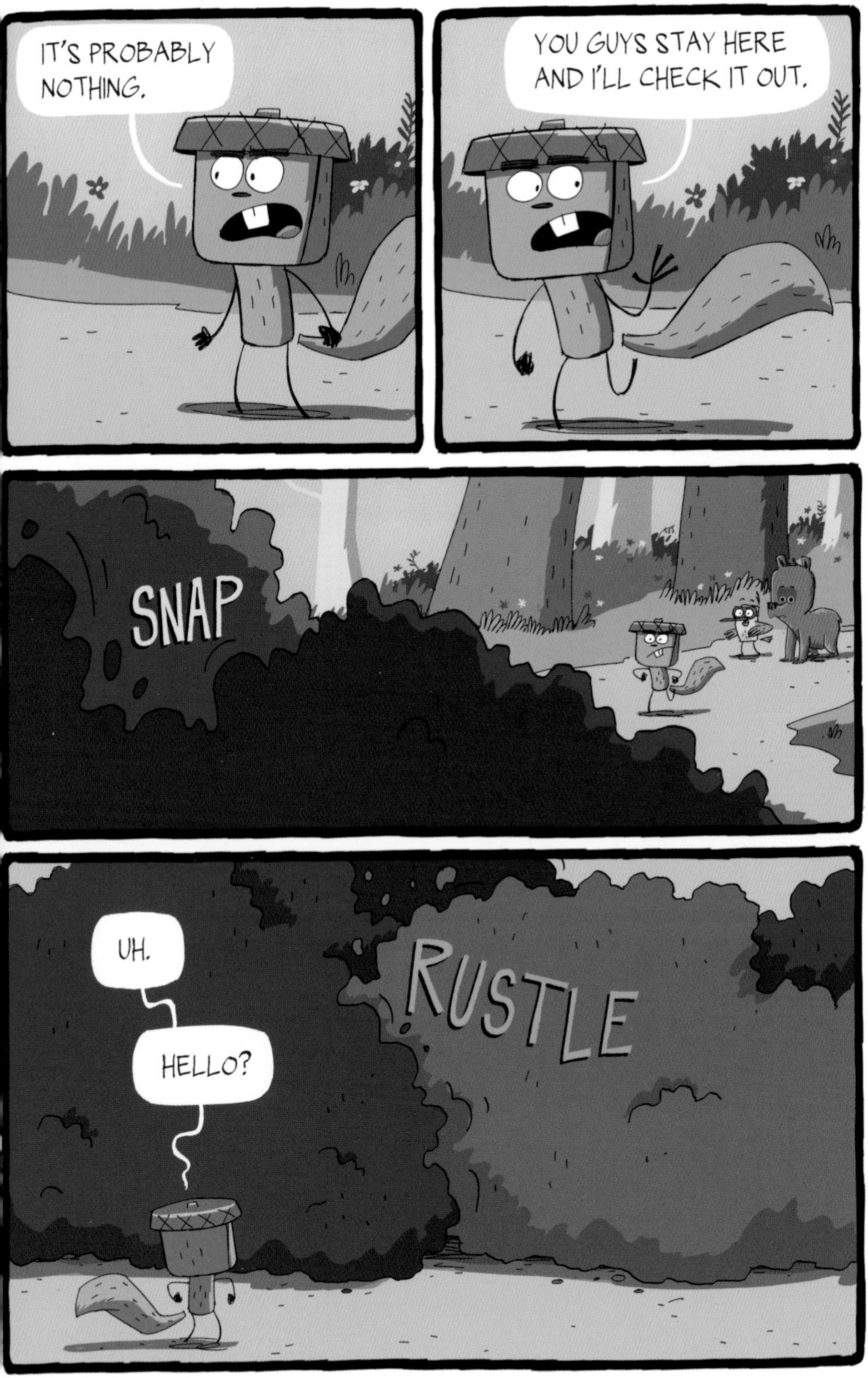
IT'S PROBABLY NOTHING.
YOU GUYS STAY HERE AND I'LL CHECK IT OUT.
SNAP
UH.
HELLO?
RUSTLE

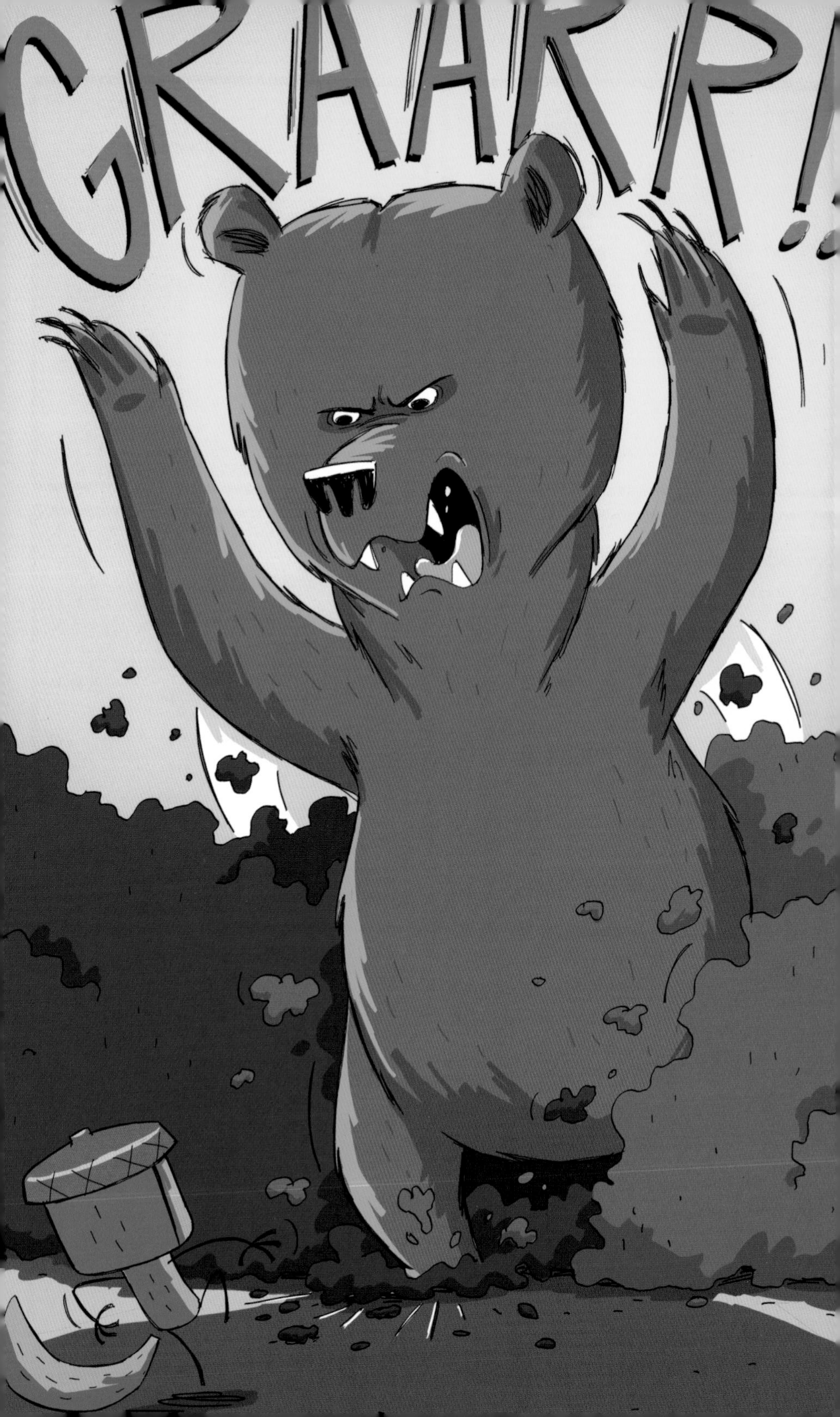
GRAARR!!

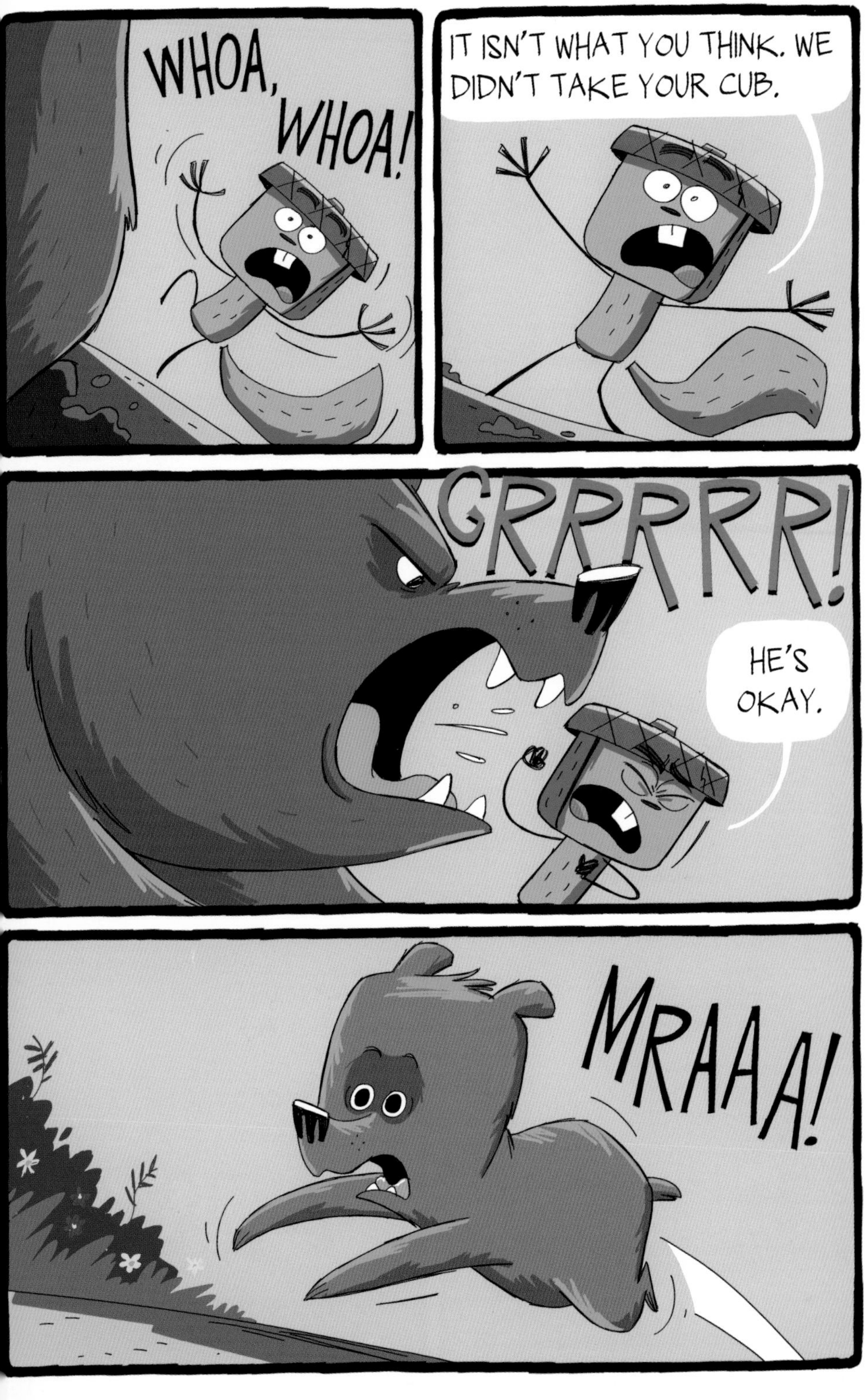
WHOA, WHOA!
IT ISN'T WHAT YOU THINK. WE DIDN'T TAKE YOUR CUB.
GRRRRRR!
HE'S OKAY.
MRAAA!

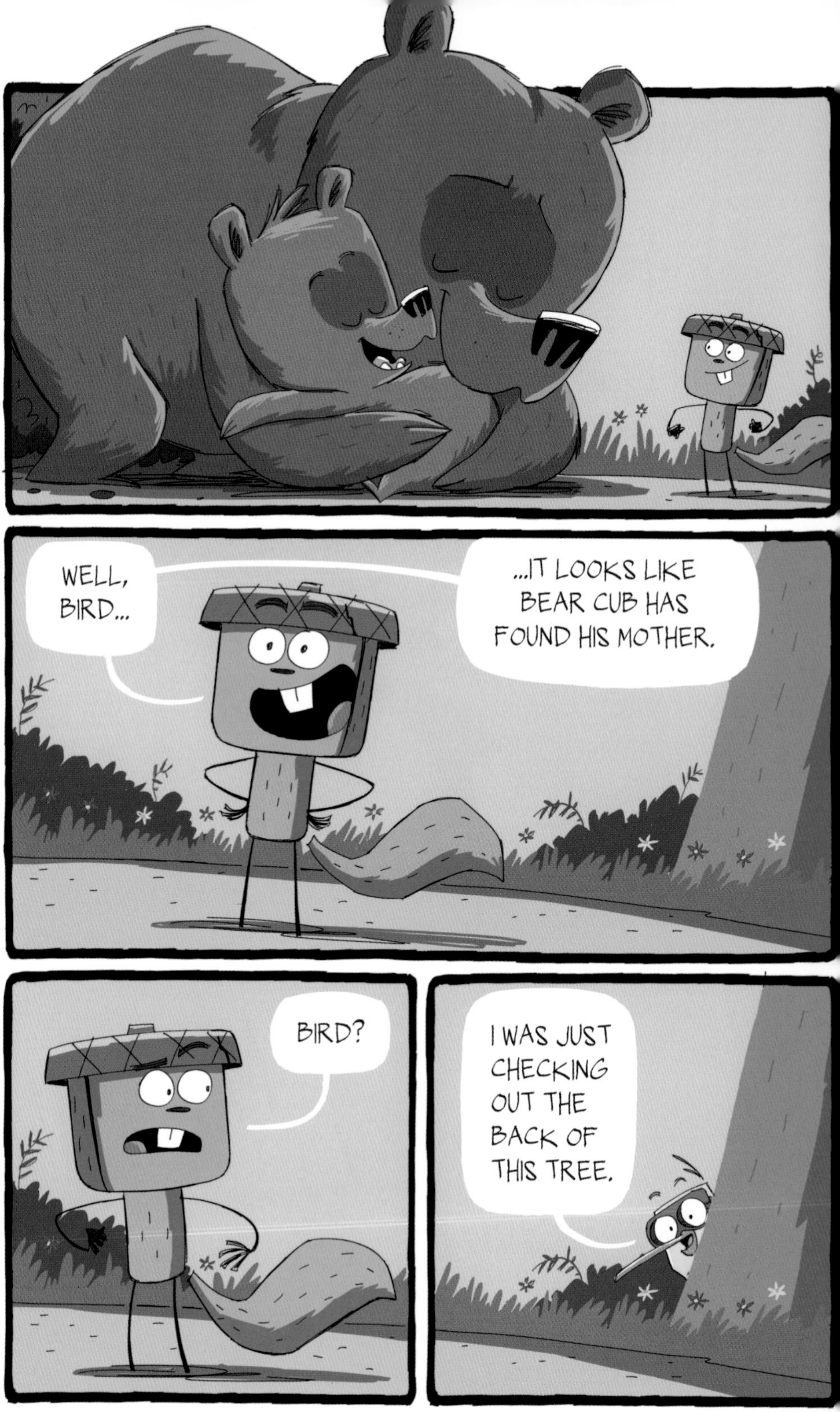
WELL, BIRD...
...IT LOOKS LIKE BEAR CUB HAS FOUND HIS MOTHER.
BIRD?
I WAS JUST CHECKING OUT THE BACK OF THIS TREE.

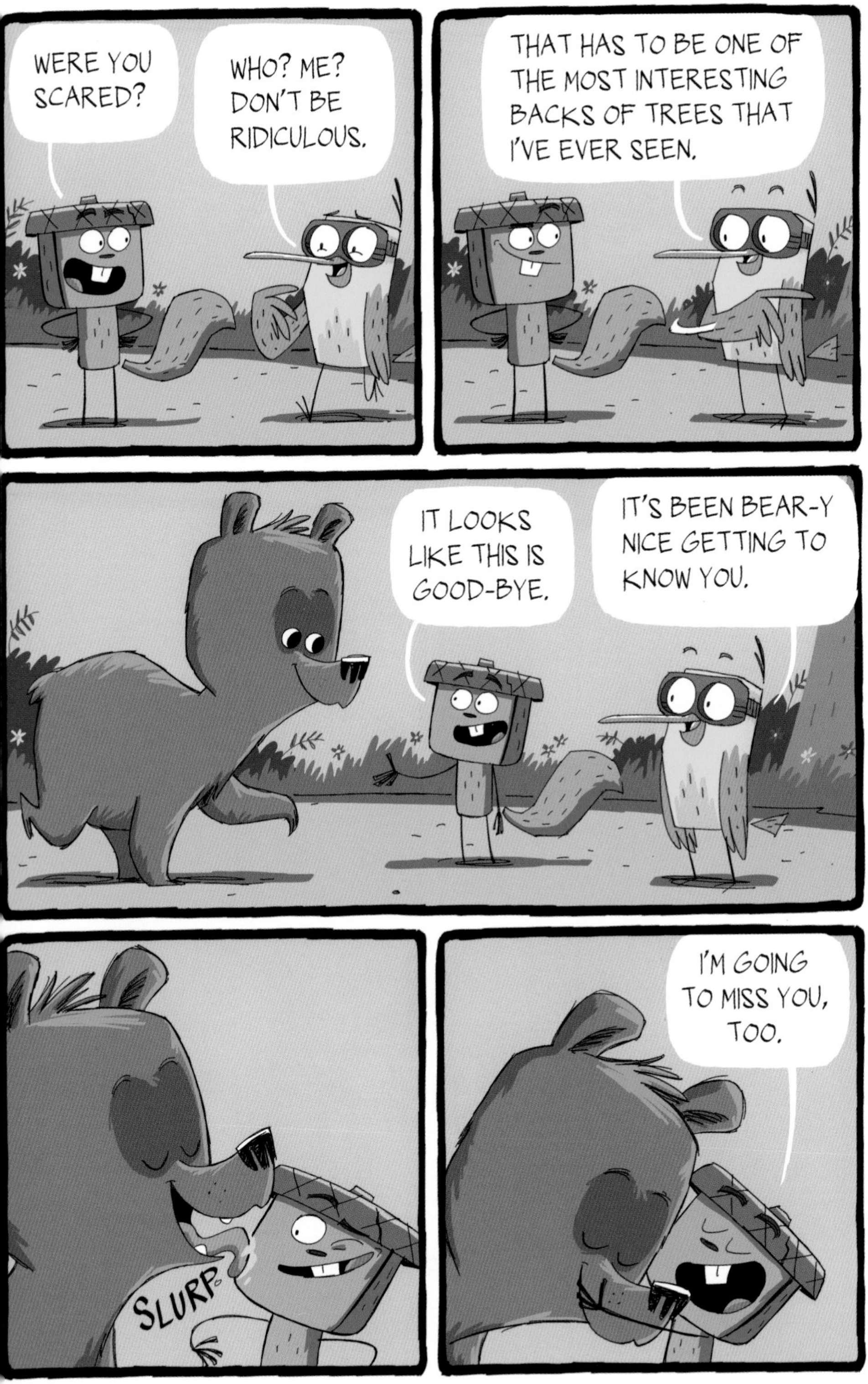
WERE YOU SCARED?
WHO? ME? DON'T BE RIDICULOUS.
THAT HAS TO BE ONE OF THE MOST INTERESTING BACKS OF TREES THAT I'VE EVER SEEN.
IT LOOKS LIKE THIS IS GOOD-BYE.
IT'S BEEN BEAR-Y NICE GETTING TO KNOW YOU.
SLURP
I'M GOING TO MISS YOU, TOO.

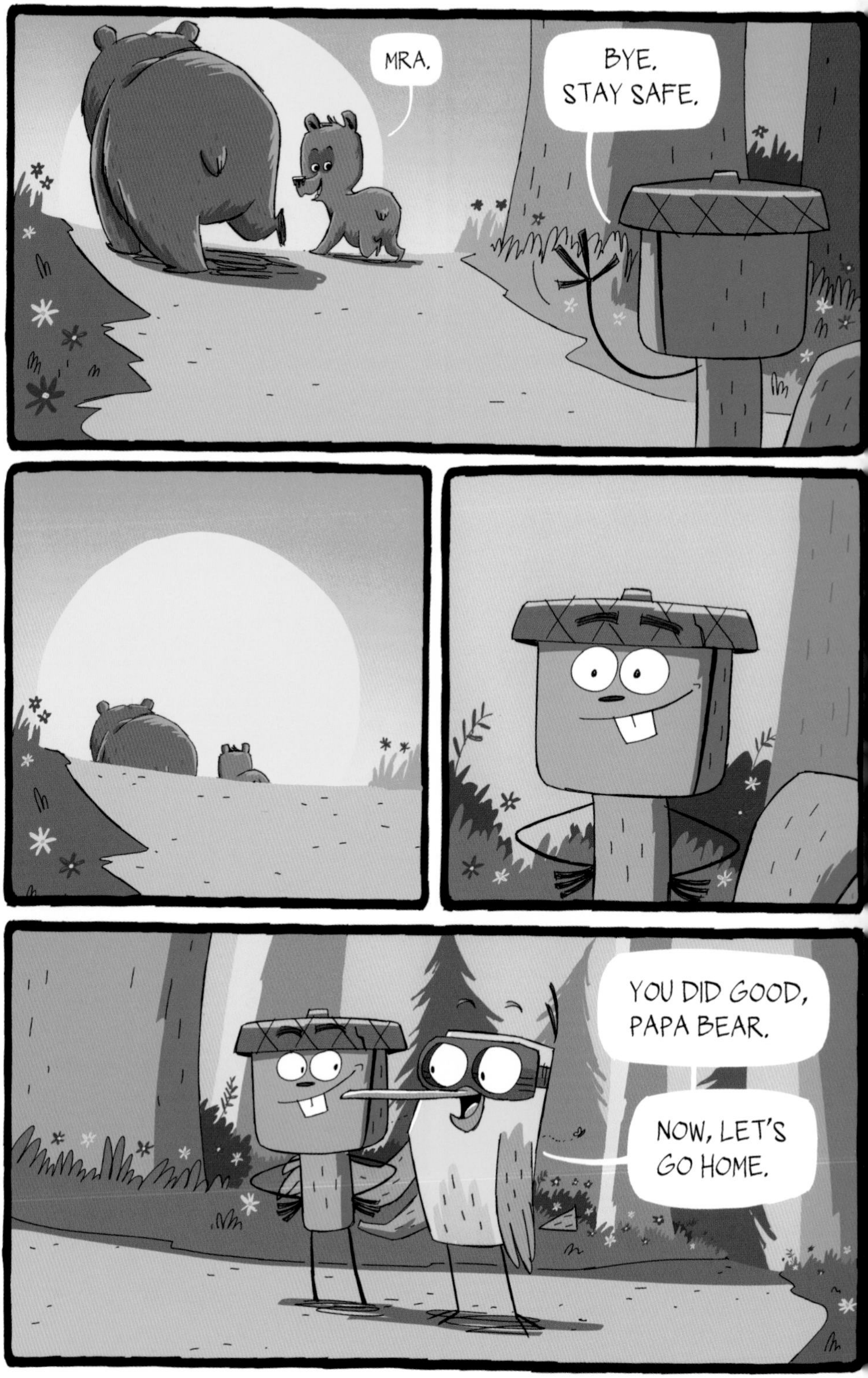
MRA.
BYE. STAY SAFE.
YOU DID GOOD, PAPA BEAR.
NOW, LET'S GO HOME.

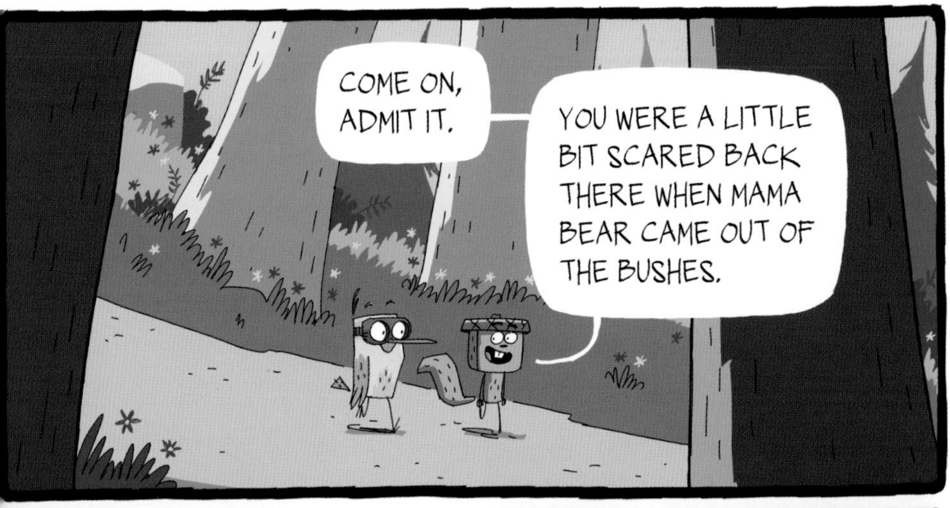
COME ON, ADMIT IT.
YOU WERE A LITTLE BIT SCARED BACK THERE WHEN MAMA BEAR CAME OUT OF THE BUSHES.

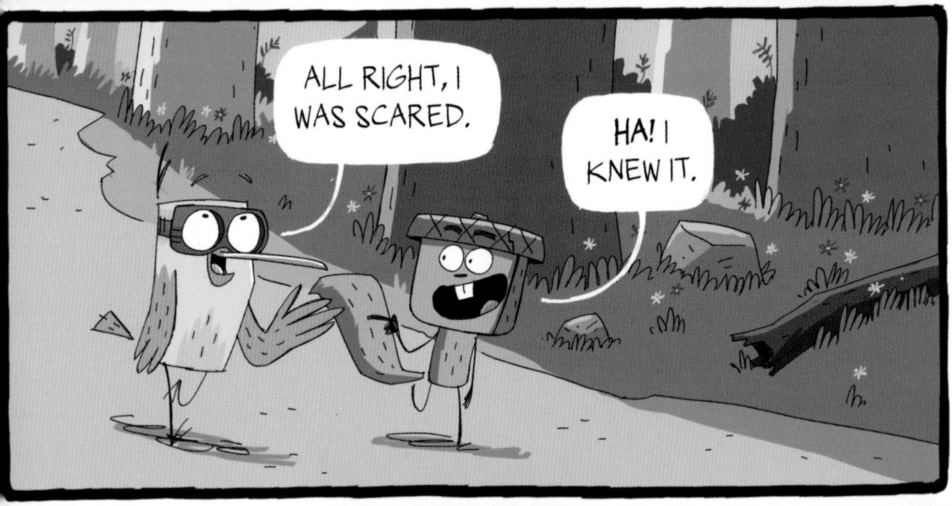
ALL RIGHT, I WAS SCARED.
HA! I KNEW IT.

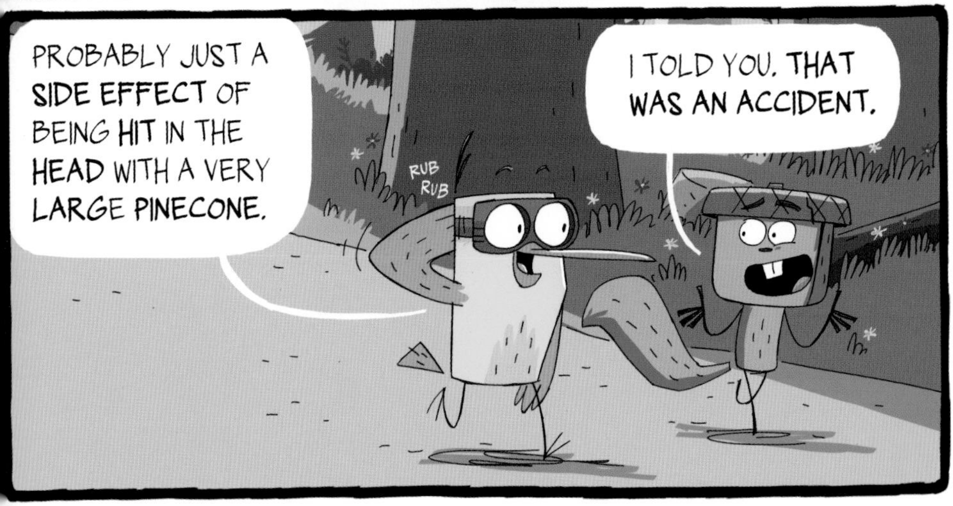
PROBABLY JUST A SIDE EFFECT OF BEING HIT IN THE HEAD WITH A VERY LARGE PINECONE.
RUB RUB
I TOLD YOU. THAT WAS AN ACCIDENT.

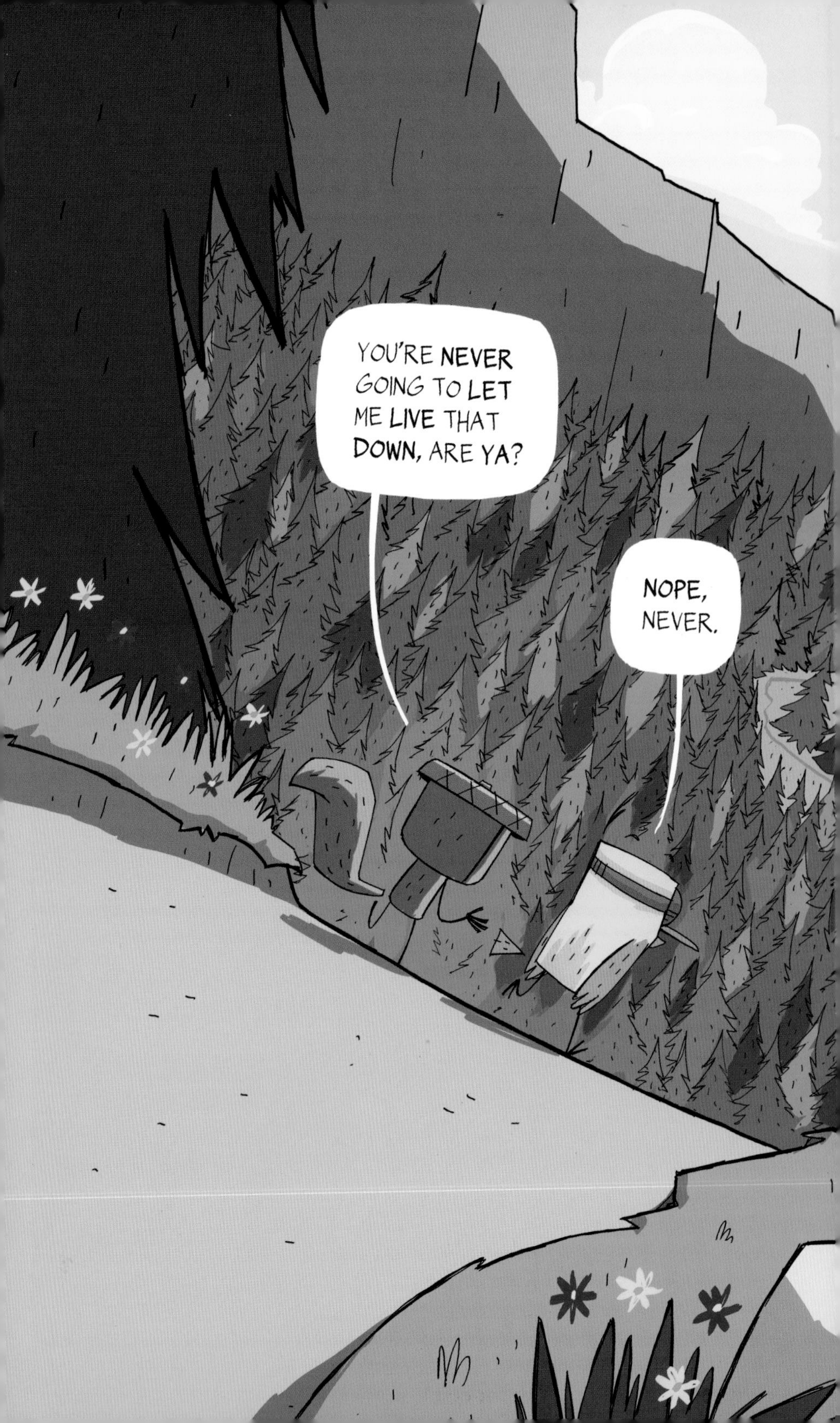
YOU'RE NEVER GOING TO LET ME LIVE THAT DOWN, ARE YA?
NOPE, NEVER.

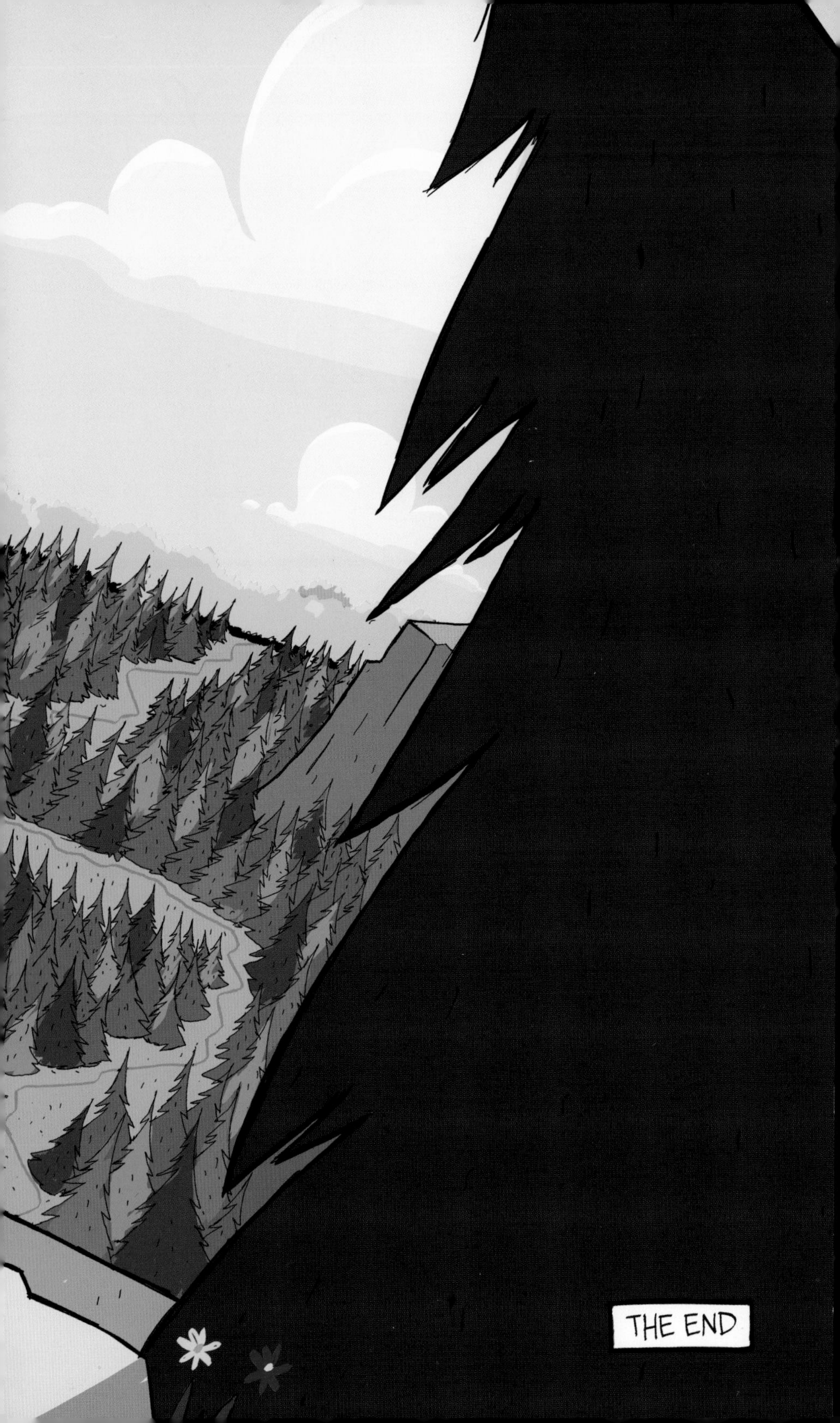
THE END

James Burks was a kid who always dreamed of being a light saber-wielding, truck-driving space pirate with a monkey for a first mate. But his parents refused to buy him a monkey! So he had to choose to be the next best thing when he grew up: a pen-wielding father of two with a lovely wife, two cats, one dog, a hunger for Mexican food, a love of running marathons, and a never-ending need to write stories and draw pictures about anything and everything he could imagine.

Go to www.jamesburks.com to see more art and follow James on Twitter at @jamesburksart.